RAVE REVIEWS FOR *COUGAR'S WOMAN* AND RONDA THOMPSON!

MORE PRAISE FOR
COUGAR'S WOMAN

A TASTE OF PASSION

Clay couldn't believe Melissa's daring. The stew she'd thrown at him, thankfully only warm and not boiling, covered his face and chest. Had she done this to another brave in the camp, the brave would have slit her throat. She needed to be taught a lesson.

He snatched her wrist and hauled her up. His captive stood tall for a woman, but Clay still towered a good four inches over her.

"Unlike those of your kind, the Apaches don't tolerate waste. Clean it off!"

To his satisfaction, she flinched. Her eyes darted nervously around the structure. He knew what she sought and smiled. "With your mouth."

"I won't," she gasped.

"You will. This isn't the place to let rebellion cloud good judgment. Defiance demands a price. This"—he indicated his chest with a nod—"is the only meal you'll get today."

"Do I at least have the right to hate you?" she asked, proving she was still far from docile.

"Only if I give it to you. And I do."

"Thank you," she countered, defiance alive and smoldering in her eyes. His captive took a deep breath, obviously steeling herself for the task ahead. She leaned forward and gently touched her lips to his skin. His body filled with heat—not a result of the fire burning in the grate, but one she started deep inside of him.

COUGAR'S WOMAN

WOMAN

Ronda Thompson

LEISURE BOOKS   NEW YORK CITY

To Rosie, an angel even before she became one.

A LEISURE BOOK®

June 1999

Published by

Dorchester Publishing Co., Inc.
276 Fifth Avenue
New York, NY 10001

ISBN 0-8439-4524-9

COUGAR'S WOMAN

Prologue

Clay Brodie, known as Cougar among the Apaches, watched the fading embers glow inside the tepee. A gust of wind stirred the flap behind him, swirling ashes into a small twister above the grate. Sullenness blanketed the enclosure, as thick as the dryness coating his mouth—the smoke stinging his eyes. Sitting across from him, an old woman shivered. She sighed, as if dreading what she must tell him.

"Your sister is gone, Cougar."

He knew what Laughing Stream meant. He knew and still refused to accept the sorrow in her dark eyes, the added wrinkles of grief etched deep in her skin. The pain on her face was fresh—recently born.

"Where has she gone?" he asked, a flicker of hope still struggling to survive. Maybe his sister had set off for the mountains to find him. Maybe she had been captured by another tribe. There were a dozen possibilities to consider, all of which were preferable to the truth.

"She has gone to the spirit world, Cougar. We must speak her name no more."

9

The emotions he'd battled since returning to the Apaches' somber camp engulfed Clay. True, he'd never paid much attention to his sister, had left her upbringing to Laughing Stream, but deep down, he felt a loss and a tremendous sense of guilt. His sister had never been to blame for the bitterness inside of him, for the scars he carried in his heart, as well as upon his back. But he had blamed her.

"What happened?"

Again, Laughing Stream shivered, clutching a woven blanket tighter around her thin body. "It brings me pain to speak of it. My son and the other warriors have gone to avenge her death. Is that not enough?"

"No!" His feeble control snapped. "If her death needed avenging, I should have been the one. It is my right!"

"Cougar," the woman beseeched him, "they could not wait for you. Those responsible would have slipped through our fingers."

Unable to remain stationary, Clay rose and ran a hand through his hair—hair as dark as Laughing Stream's and nearly as long. His sister was dead, and to speak her name would tear her from the spirit world. The Apaches had called her Silent Wind. Until she was three, her name had been Rachel.

"Who do they make war on?" he demanded. "Who is responsible for this crime against me, against The People?"

Laughing Stream bowed her head. "I think you do not want to know."

He bent, capturing her wrist. "Tell me!"

A withered hand settled upon his arm. Crooked Nose, Laughing Stream's husband of thirty summers, cast him a warning look. Clay released the woman.

"I meant no disrespect," he said to the couple. "You were good to the one we cannot speak of. You took her into your lodge. Raised her as your own. But her blood and mine are the same. I should be with Swift Buck and the others."

"My son was more of a brother to her than you." The Indian woman pulled herself up proudly. "Swift Buck will see that she is avenged. His blood is Apache, and the blood of those who will pay for this crime runs the same as yours. White."

Clay stumbled back a step. At one time, to see a white man in New Mexico Territory was rare. Now the profit to be made in trade goods brought many. With the War Between the States ended, efforts to wipe out those who stood in the way of progress would soon take precedence. The Apaches were an obstacle, and they sensed the coming danger.

"My skin is white, but my heart is Apache."

"Yes, it is your white skin that allows you to roam freely in Mexican and white camps. And it is your Apache heart that allows you to come and go as you choose in ours. Would you take up a bow against the white men responsible for this crime against us?"

It was a question Clay had hoped would never confront him. He felt neither totally white nor wholly Apache, but was a man who could fit into both worlds without rightfully belonging to either.

"The color of a man's skin cannot lessen his crimes. I would have ridden with your son. I would have raised my bow and taken my revenge."

Laughing Stream's dark gaze searched his face. "You would kill your own kind for the one we cannot speak of, but you could not find it in your heart to say a soft word to her? It saddens me that only death stirs the feelings you long denied her. It saddens me, but today I see that you are a man, flesh and blood, and not the cat spirit The People call you."

The guilt Clay battled increased. He resumed his position across the fire. He would hear the whole tale of what had happened to his sister. Hear and steel himself against the pain. He could no longer hold his sister responsible for the actions of a woman who had brought him the worst suffering imaginable. A woman who had loved her blond-haired daughter, even if she despised the dark-haired son who came before her. Their mother.

Chapter One

Five days Clay waited, staring with helpless rage at the distant horizon, willing his brothers to return, wishing he were with them. To avenge Rachel, Silent Wind, Clay could have killed, even if he couldn't find it in his butchered heart to love her.

"Brodie?"

He glanced sideways, watching Martin Hanes dig the heel of his toe into the moist dirt.

"I told you to go," he reminded him.

"Hell, Brodie, I thought if I hung around a few days I might change your mind and either come on back up the mountain with me or head for Santa Fe."

"I can't leave. Not yet."

"I don't know why," Martin blustered. "There's no reason to stay. They've gone off to do the killing for you. What do you want, details?"

"Yes."

Martin swore softly, then spit a stream of tobacco juice. "Look, Brodie, I know you think of these damn Injuns as

12

your kin, but you gotta get out of here. It wouldn't hurt to be seen in Santa Fe before word of a massacre reaches town. As it is, those folks would just as soon string you up as look at you. They're gonna know it was Apaches who attacked the caravan. Don't give them more reasons to kill you than they already have."

"They can't prove I run with the Apaches. Not unless you tell them."

Hanes scowled at the younger man. "I've got to live in these mountains, too. I'd as soon take on twenty white men as one Apache warrior. *I* ain't about to confirm rumors that Clay Brodie's a whitewashed Injun. Every spring it's the same—I dread riding into town to trade our furs. Hell, it wouldn't throw so much kindling on the fire if you didn't dress like one of 'em."

"I dress however I choose."

"Yeah, and you do whatever you damn well please. Brodie . . . Clay," his tone softened. "You can't keep walking the middle. This thing that's happened, it's horrible, but staying here ain't gonna bring her back. If you wanted to do something for her, you should have done it long ago. Hell, she didn't even know she was white."

"She knew," Clay argued, but walked over and patted the older man on the back to soften the sting of his earlier words. "Like me, how could she not have seen the differences between herself and The People? She preferred the Apaches. They raised her."

"You and that no 'count papa of yours should have done better for her," Martin grumbled. "What kind of pa would just give his daughter to the Indians and never look at her again?"

"Ours," Clay answered dryly. "Hiram Brodie had no use for a girl child. She couldn't do his work, and her skin bruised too easily. Giving her to the Apaches after our mother died was the only kind thing he ever did for her."

Martin didn't argue the matter. Clay supposed it was because he'd seen the scars crisscrossing his back. The two of them rarely spoke of Clay's family, but the friendship they had shared over the past five years had given Martin Hanes insight into a past Clay would as soon forget.

"Reckon you're right," the trapper said. "Still, you should have took her to town after Hiram died. She could have learned some manners. Learned about being a proper lady and all."

Clay laughed, a sound without humor. "Those so-called decent folk would have taken one look at her and known where she'd been. The men who killed her didn't care that her skin was white. They saw her as a squaw. They used her like an animal and left her body for the wolves. By the time the search party found her and the two women with her, only bits and pieces lay scattered around the area. Of my sister, nothing remained except a bloody shoe and her berry basket."

The older man crossed himself. "Don't know why you made that old woman tell you all the grim details. At times I think you live on pain."

"You'd be better off if you didn't think so much, Hanes," Clay suggested. "And you should follow my advice and get the hell out of here. The Apaches allow you into their camp because you're my friend, and for no other reason."

"I'm going," Martin assured him. "I'll head up to the mountain for a month and stop back by on my way to Santa Fe. You should be with me when I ride into town."

"Maybe," Clay responded. "I'll see."

"They might bring captives back with them. If they do, you'll be in one hell of an awkward situation. No matter how you feel about these people, you can't stand back and not lift a finger to help your own kind."

"I mind my own business and don't worry over anyone else. You know that. I told you five years ago we could trap together as long as you kept your opinions to yourself and didn't try to change me. You seem to forget that more and more often lately."

"This situation's getting worse every year," Martin pointed out, but lifted his pack. "One of these days, you're gonna have to choose sides." He walked away, then turned around.

"I'm sorry about the girl. Didn't know her too well. How could anyone know a wisp of smoke? But I'm sorry she came to a bad end. I seen her a few times up on the mountain, running with the wolves and sitting by your ma's grave. Maybe it's better—not to go the way she did—but for her to be gone. A wild girl like that, dumb, she didn't have much in this life to look forward to."

"She wasn't dumb."

"What?" Martin asked. "I never heard her say anything. You mean she wasn't mute?"

"The day Hiram put my mother in the ground, my sister's voice died. She never said another word."

As Clay moved off toward a bluff overlooking the campsite, Hanes called, "If she was only three when your ma died, you couldn't have been more than thirteen. Maybe you just don't remember."

"I remember," Clay said softly. "I remember like it was yesterday. Their laughter, their whispers, the songs they sang, the sound of their love."

"I'll look in on your place while I'm up there," Hanes offered.

"Don't look too close. I don't want you snooping around inside."

"I know, I know," Martin grumbled. "Be seeing you, Brodie."

Waving his friend away, Clay turned his attention to more pressing matters. Overhead, a hawk circled. He felt the air of its wings without glancing up. His senses were in tune with nature. Not a leaf stirred he didn't hear. Not a scent floated on the breeze he didn't recognize. In the distance, a spiral of dust increased the pounding of his heart. His brothers were returning.

He called the signal. Excitement immediately stirred the lazy campsite. Female voices rose in pitch. Children squealed. Sons and husbands were returning. The low rumble of hooves penetrated his ears and reawakened his helpless rage. He should have been with them.

Clay had never ridden against those of his supposed race

before, but now he had a reason. No matter that he'd never loved his sister, nor she him, it would have assuaged a degree of his guilt to kill those responsible.

Anger turned to concern when the braves came within eyesight. Gray Wolf sat tall on the lead horse, but many warriors were smeared with blood. Clay searched for his blood brother, Swift Buck, among the group, but couldn't locate him through the dust clouds. He hurried down from the bluff.

Loud whoops of victory accompanied his brothers into camp. With a measure of relief, Clay realized most of the blood staining their bodies wasn't from their own wounds. He spotted Swift Buck, but after a closer look, felt a flash of alarm.

A sheen of sweat stood out clearly on Swift Buck's face, the darkness of his eyes glazed and unseeing. His horse pranced nervously without guidance until Clay snatched the leather strips of his makeshift bridle. Slowly, the brave fell forward.

Sharp as Clay's reflexes were, it was Gray Wolf who caught Swift Buck. Another weight settled in Clay's arms. A woman whose matted hair hung down her back. Her mud-covered face turned upward. Green eyes wide with shock stared back at him.

"Your brother took a Comanche arrow in his shoulder," Gray Wolf said in Apache. "An arrow laced with poison."

"Comanche?"

The leader nodded. "They attacked us two nights ago. They wanted the woman we took from the whites. Your brother fought hard to keep her."

Clay wondered why his blood brother would. Swift Buck was a handsome brave and didn't lack for female attention. And, judging by the woman's appearance, she wasn't worth fighting over. "I hope my brother doesn't die for his bad judgment," he commented lowly.

"If he dies, it will be because I ordered him to protect her. I saw the woman in a vision. Not her face, but the hair. She is the test. Come, we will take Swift Buck to his mother's lodge."

Gray Wolf's order left Clay indecisive regarding what to do with his burden. "The woman. What should I do with her?"

The leader's mouth turned up in a slight smile. "I will have a warrior take her to Swift Buck's lodge and guard her. Later, do what you wish with her. She is yours."

Not until Gray Wolf walked away did his words sink in. Clay's gaze lowered to the scarecrow. Her dirt-caked lips trembled. "Dammit," he swore in English. He unceremoniously dropped her and walked away.

There was no call to worry that she'd try to escape, and already the women were crowding around the captive. A tearing noise sounded above the excited chatter, then a slap echoed off the bluffs. A louder one followed.

"Ouch!" the scarecrow yelped. "H-Hey you!"

Clay kept walking.

"I know you understand me! I heard you swear in English. Don't leave me with these animals!"

Abruptly, Clay turned, retracing his steps. As if the Apache women knew a confrontation would unfold, they parted.

"These *animals* are my friends. Don't give them any trouble. They want your clothes."

Her eyes widened a fraction before he turned away. Renewed ripping noises were the only sound that accompanied his departure. The woman would be naked by the time they finished with her. Not his worry, Clay assured himself. He'd simply tell Gray Wolf he didn't want her. Hell, the leader knew he wouldn't involve himself with captives.

When Clay entered Laughing Stream's tepee, the woman's fate became less of a concern. Swift Buck tossed upon the robes, sweat running in rivulets down his face. He babbled in delirium.

"How bad is it?" he questioned Gray Wolf.

"The wound festers. His body is filled with Comanche poison."

Clay knelt beside Laughing Stream. She turned to him,

worry renewing the ravages of grief on her face.

"My husband has gone for the shaman. He must sing songs over my son to drive away this evil."

Songs wouldn't do Swift Buck any good, Clay thought, but said nothing. Indian superstition was one aspect of Apache life he'd never been able to embrace.

"We need a poultice to draw out the poison."

"I think the evil is too great." Laughing Stream pointed to her son's shoulder. "See the angry red streaks? It has spread too far. I fear the evil spirits will take him away."

"No," Clay argued. "He is strong. Swift Buck will fight the poison and ride with me another day."

"Silent Wind," Swift Buck mumbled.

Laughing Stream gasped, placing a hand over her son's lips. "He speaks of her. He calls her from the spirit world."

The sound of his sister's name sent a shock of pain through Clay. Not speaking of Rachel the past few days had dulled the reality of her death. "The fever," he explained. "It will make him see things. Say things."

"Where is the light?" Swift Buck moaned, tossing restlessly on the hides. "Where is the light in this dark place? What is the heart you keep hidden, my brother?"

Laughing Stream glanced toward Clay. "What does he ask?"

"He speaks of the light," Gray Wolf said, stepping forward. "Of the woman with pale hair and of Cougar's unwillingness to give his heart wholly to the Apaches. He speaks of the test."

"What test?" Clay demanded.

"We will discuss your destiny when the shaman comes to sing his songs," Gray Wolf answered. "I did not understand the vision until I saw her. The sun caught in her hair and turned it to silver. She will decide your true heart."

"I want no woman. I refuse her."

Silence followed Clay's words. Gray Wolf was a powerful man among The People. He led most raids and decided important matters. To defy him meant to go against the wishes of the tribe.

18

"You forget yourself," he warned. "Many times you have ridden by my side in battle against our enemies. More and more whites intrude upon our land. Soon, they will be more in number than The People. When that day comes, will you fight with us, or against us?"

"The day is long off," Clay said, wishing it were true.

"No. The time is short. I have seen this in my visions. What I see is not good for The People. We will need a man among us who knows the white ways. Although you taught Swift Buck and I the tongue well, your skin will get us what we cannot. The time to prove yourself has come, Cougar. This woman is the test."

"She is nothing!"

"Then show me she is unimportant," Gray Wolf insisted. "I give her to you. Treat her as an Apache would treat a captive. Kill her if you want, but you cannot set her free."

Clay tried to control his anger. For years he'd lived by his own rules. Now both worlds threatened his indifference. "I stay only until summer's end. Do you suggest I take her with me when I go?"

Gray Wolf turned thoughtful. "You can sell her to another brave when you go, or give her to a family."

"What about a ransom?"

"No. Not this woman. The test is too easy if Cougar believes she will be returned to her world. If you cannot walk away and ignore her plight at summer's end, then you are not one with us. If you fail this test, it will mean your death. You know our ways too well."

The anger Clay tried to control escaped. "The People insult me! Testing Cougar with a worthless woman. I would have ridden against those who killed my sister. Would have slit their throats and enjoyed their screams. That is a test. This is a farce."

Gray Wolf appeared rightfully enraged by his outburst. "You do not respect my visions, and you should. I saw you become our enemy! I saw you die for her."

Hackles rose on the back of Clay's neck. Visions, he took seriously. He'd had a few himself. "I will do this to prove she is nothing, and at the end of the summer, I will sell her."

"Maybe," Gray Wolf responded. "Take Swift Buck's lodge. I hope soon he can return. If not, he would want you to have his possessions."

"Your generosity would not please my brother. He will need his belongings."

Gray Wolf's gaze traveled to the now unconscious brave. He sighed. "I hope you are right. Also, I hope my vision was wrong."

"Have they ever been?" Clay asked curiously, moving to Swift Buck's side.

"No."

When Clay glanced toward the leader, he was gone. Laughing Stream's husband and the shaman entered. The songs began. Crooked Nose held a bundle of long sticks. Clay placed himself beside the old man and removed a knife from the top of his moccasin. Although he didn't believe in most Indian superstition, he'd help sharpen the ends of the sticks into points.

Later, while the shaman boiled herbs and shook his beads over Swift Buck's still form, Clay slipped outside to place the sticks point-up around the lodge. The tribe believed that if evil approached, it would become trapped on the points and rendered helpless to enter the lodge.

Laughing Stream blocked his path when he thought to reenter. "Go, Cougar. I will come for you if . . ." Her voice trailed. "See to your woman."

"The scarecrow is not my woman."

"Her fate rests in your hands. For too long you place one foot in the white world and one in ours. For too long Cougar cares for no one but himself. It is fitting, this test."

"This is no test," he repeated, his anger on the rise again. "I'll ignore the woman for the summer and either sell her or give her to someone else."

"Living is not always so simple. Go and ignore her then. I want to tend my son."

As Laughing Stream disappeared inside the tepee, an unfamiliar feeling settled over Clay. Helplessness. He hadn't allowed himself time to deal with Rachel's death. Filled with rage and thoughts of revenge, grief hadn't yet stolen inside his butchered heart to demand attention. It came now, wrapped in the fear that he'd lose his closest friend. He steeled himself against the pain, choosing instead to ignore it as he would the white woman given to him.

She'd be frightened, naked and shivering within the tepee. If the woman showed bravery earlier because she thought his blue eyes and English words were her salvation, she'd soon realize her plight. The reality would break her spirit. Clay owed her nothing except to see that she understood her lot in life. That of a captive.

He turned, moving with reluctance toward Swift Buck's lodge. A shape left the shadows. Even in the dark, Clay recognized the man. Wariness alerted his senses. Tall Blade and he were not friends. Since boyhood, they'd disliked each other.

"Does Swift Buck still live?"

"Yes," Clay answered. "And there is no need to pretend concern for my blood brother. I know it for a lie. What do you want?"

A set of white teeth flashed briefly in the dark. "You know me well, Cougar. Yet you are blind. I have come to trade for the woman, Huera."

Tall Blade's reason was the last one Clay would have expected, and it seemed the scarecrow had already been given a name by the Apaches. Huera meant blond, or light hair. "Why would you want her?" he responded with true puzzlement.

"She lifted her hand against me during the raid and must pay for her insult. With me, she will learn the punishment for her crimes. Lifting her hand against a warrior, being white," he added harshly.

With Tall Blade, she probably wouldn't last the night. The brave hated whites with an obsessiveness—all whites, which Clay supposed included a white boy grown to manhood among the Apaches.

"Gray Wolf insists she remain with me until the grass turns yellow. After that time, we will speak of a trade," Clay lied.

21

He wouldn't entrust any breathing thing into Tall Blade's care.

"Do not forget, I offered for her first. If your brother lives, he too might want the woman. Swift Buck has a taste for sun hair and pale skin."

The brave's insinuation hung between them. His sister, Silent Wind, had been blond and blue-eyed. Clay refused to consider the implication seriously. Tall Blade instigated trouble whenever the opportunity presented itself. He'd always done so.

"If Gray Wolf meant the woman to be mine, Swift Buck would not touch her." He purposely misinterpreted the suggestion.

"I do not think your brother touched her while she lay next to him those many nights while we journeyed home. But she has been touched before. The women she traveled with painted their faces and showed their skin."

It was just as well if she were a prostitute, Clay reasoned. She'd be tougher, wiser. He doubted she had any family with her on the caravan, nor any waiting for her in Santa Fe. His guilt, what little he possessed, eased somewhat at the rationalization. The way he saw it, she didn't have much of a life to miss.

And from what he'd seen of her, she couldn't have been too profitable at the one she'd left behind. Feeling less hindered with the burden of her future, he moved with purpose

Chapter Two

The first thing Clay's senses registered after entering the tepee was the unpleasant smell of her. The second, her uneven breathing. The third, whatever whizzed past his head and hit the hide wall behind him, was a heavy object meant to maim or kill.

He moved calmly to the grate, keeping his eyes trained on the corner where he sensed her presence. His gaze never leaving the darker shape of her against the pitch, Clay struck a flint against stone. The tiny spark indicated his position. Something hit him in the head.

"Damn," he swore softly, rubbing his temple.

"Oh, it's you."

The relief in her voice was evident. Clay didn't offer a reply, but struck the flint again. When a spark caught to the kindling, he blew softly on the flame, bringing a soft glow to the tepee's interior.

"Well?"

His gaze lifted. She resembled a raccoon, staring out of a

Ronda Thompson

mud-covered face while she tugged at the blanket tucked snugly beneath her arms.

"Well what?"

"When are we leaving?" she huffed indignantly.

The slight throbbing in his temple that had begun earlier grew worse. "Not tonight," he answered evasively. "I wouldn't throw anything else if I were you."

"I thought you were an Indian come to attack me. You can't imagine how relieved I am to find you among these savages. What is your name?"

In response, he ran a lazy inspection over her. "The 'savages' call me Cougar, and you shouldn't do any name-calling."

Her hand went immediately to her tangled hair, the other retaining a tight grip on the blanket. "My appearance is the least of my concerns at the moment. And I meant your Christian name. If your eyes weren't blue, if you hadn't sworn in English, I might not have recognized you for a white man. You will get me out of this mess, won't you?"

"I didn't get you into it," Clay answered, knowing that wasn't entirely true. "Your caravan sealed their fate when five of your men killed two Apache women and my sister."

She gasped. "That's a lie. We hadn't even seen any Indians until this group attacked our caravan. The men with us were for the most part decent." She shuddered slightly. "Certainly they weren't the kind who would kill women, Indian or otherwise."

Clay laughed at her naïveté, then recalled that, according to Tall Blade, she wasn't an innocent. "A man's a different animal when he's rutting between a woman's legs for the price of a few coins than if he thinks he can take what he wants for free and won't have to answer for his crimes. They didn't leave much of my sister and the other two women, but they left their tracks all over the area."

"You're lying," she accused again, although her voice trembled. "Your *friends* killed innocent men! They forced me to come with them! Tied my hands and dragged me behind their horses! Starved me! Frightened—"

"Did they beat and rape you?" he asked casually.

24

Her hand tightened on the blanket. "No, thank God."

"Then it could have been worse. If Gray Wolf hadn't had a specific reason for capturing you, I doubt you'd be alive to complain about your treatment."

"What reason?"

Under the circumstances, her demanding tone played on his nerves. The woman wasn't nearly as afraid of him as she should be—as her survival among the Apaches would call for. Clay wouldn't tell her he was the reason. That she was a test of his loyalty. A test he had no intention of failing.

"Tribes often take women to replace the ones taken from them. It keeps them from dying out."

She took a courageous step toward him. "I refuse to become a squaw!"

The past few days had taken their toll on Clay. He hadn't slept, had eaten very little, and was in no mood to be ordered around by a woman. The sooner she understood the seriousness of her situation, the better. He rose from his position before the fire and approached her.

"*Squaw* is a white man's insulting term for an Indian woman, and I take offense at the word. Having a strong warrior take you as a wife would be an improvement over your current status. You're a captive. A slave. A possession and nothing more."

She had the sense to back away from him as he drew closer, all the while clutching the blanket wrapped around her as if it were the threads of her sanity. "Are you telling me I'm at the mercy of savages and you intend to do nothing?"

Something in her voice, perhaps the disbelief tinged with a note of vulnerability she hadn't yet displayed, struck a nerve in Clay. Damn Gray Wolf for placing him in this awkward position. "For the time being, you're at my mercy. The Apaches have given you to me."

Hope sprang to life in her eyes. "Then you can rescue me. Take me to Santa Fe—"

"No," he interrupted. "I cannot. What I can do is prepare you for a life among the Apaches. Teach you to survive. Show you—"

Her attack surprised Clay and cut him off in mid-sentence. Teeth bared and fingers curled into claws, the woman came at him. He barely managed to secure her wrists in time to save his face from her nails.

"I will not accept this cruel fate you claim I've been dealt! I cannot! I am a woman of position! A woman on the way to meet my fiancé in Santa Fe. A—"

"A white whore from what I understand. And now an Apache captive. Can your new fate be any worse than your old one?"

Within the mud caking her face, her eyes widened. "How dare you speak to me in that manner? I am a lady. Nellie Jackson told me she intended to open a finishing school in Santa Fe. I had no idea what she and her women were until the caravan was well underway." Her widened gaze narrowed. "Who told you about my traveling companions?"

"That isn't important." Clay loosened his grip on her wrists. "Learning to survive among the Apaches is. Who you were is in the past. Now you must think about who you will become."

A stifled sob was her response. She swallowed loudly. Her eyes filled with tears. "But Robert is waiting for me. By now, he's received my letter. I knew he wouldn't permit me to come. Not with the dangers along the trail. I grew bored waiting for his return and decided—"

"To take matters into your own hands?" He shook his head and stepped away from her, the sight of her tears affecting him more than he cared to admit. "Disobedience will get you into as much trouble in this world as it did in yours. Are you the type who learns from her mistakes, Huera? Or the sort who just keeps repeating them?"

"My type is none of your business. And don't address me by that word. My name is Melissa Sheffield, of the St. Louis Sheffields. If you won't help me escape, I'll do it on my own."

His hand shot out to capture her arm when she flounced past. Clay brought his face within inches of hers. "Here, you are Huera, and I wouldn't try to escape. I'd have to kill you."

To his relief, she showed the first signs of fear he'd seen since her arrival. "You'd kill a defenseless woman?"

Of course he wouldn't, but the scarecrow need not know he had any reservations in that area. She must fear him. Learn obedience in order to survive. Rather than answer, he wrinkled his nose and stepped away from her.

"You need a bath. I'm not sleeping with you until you wash."

Her head snapped in his direction. "You're not sleeping with me, regardless."

The relief he'd felt earlier was short-lived. She'd used that snooty tone with him again. Clay rubbed his pounding forehead. "Unless that mud's hiding a hell of a lot, you haven't got anything to worry over."

A slight tensing of her shoulders indicated she understood his insult. "It wouldn't be decent," she insisted. "That sick Indian made me sleep next to him, but he's a savage and you're a white man. You know better."

"That 'savage' is my *blood brother*," Clay stressed. "And, just so you'll know who you're dealing with, he's more decent than I've ever thought about being."

"You can't frighten me." Her chin lifted, but the tremble in her voice spoiled the effect. "If you were truly one of them, you wouldn't speak English. Don't you think I've heard tales about what Indians do to white women? If you were truly one of them . . ."

If he were truly one of them, Clay would have stormed the tepee, thrown her on her back, humiliated her, hit her a few times for good measure, and made her situation a hell of a lot plainer than he had. The Apaches had respect for their own women, but captives were the enemy, that was different. He'd never raped a woman and didn't see any reason to start now. Especially this woman.

Plain and simple, he felt no motivation. Proving her wrong wasn't uppermost in his mind. Clay reached out and hefted her over his shoulder. A squawk of protest followed. Her fists pelted his back.

"Unless you want an audience while you bathe, I'd settle down and be quiet once we step outside."

All abuse to his back ceased. His captive became very still and very quiet. Clay smiled to himself. Despite her bravery, it wouldn't take him long to tame Melissa Sheffield, formerly of St. Louis.

Wood smoke hung on the breeze, along with the night sounds of creatures, and muffled laughter. Melissa might have found her surroundings pleasant under different circumstances. She bit her lip to keep from releasing the rage trapped in her throat. This couldn't be happening! God wouldn't do this to her.

The attack on the caravan seemed like a dream. Hazy images burned inside her memory. A nightmare she kept waiting to wake from. She'd fought the first Indian who'd attacked her. A response of survival and nothing more. When the now-wounded brave stepped forward, stopping the other, Melissa at first thought he'd been sent to save her. His stare had held a hopeful expression when he'd brushed the hair from her eyes, then pain had crossed his features and he'd released her.

She might have become the other's victim again had the stone-faced leader not ridden up, touched her hair, and obviously ordered she be brought along. For days she'd stumbled behind their horses, pulled by a strip of leather securing her wrist, and choking on dust. Trapped within numb denial, her life had been drastically altered.

A second attack had shattered her shroud of insanity. Odd, that she'd become accustomed to one nightmare and considered another one worse. If she hadn't been treated well, at least she hadn't been molested or beaten. That small comfort sent her scrambling behind her protector in fear when they were attacked by another group of Indians. When the arrow had struck that Indian, she'd felt panic.

Not concern for his safety, but for her own. For whatever reason, he had kept the others away from her, and represented at least a measure of safety. She should never have ventured into this untamed territory.

Robert hadn't intended for her to come, although he'd painted an exciting picture of his journey along the Santa Fe Trail. Once Melissa had made the courageous decision to join him, an obstacle presented itself. Families did not travel the dangerous trail, but only caravans of men loaded down with trade goods. She'd given up on going when a woman who claimed to be a finishing school instructor graciously offered her conveyance. Graciously, for a price.

Melissa had used most of her inheritance to pay Nellie Jackson for passage. Shortly after departure, she'd learned the truth: The women she was traveling with were prostitutes who'd decided the women-starved men of New Mexico needed female companionship. Her impulsive nature had landed her in a fine mess.

The feel of freezing water served to remind her that the situation had only worsened. Melissa gasped before her head dipped below the surface. She came up choking, aware the blanket had not accompanied her into the water.

"Scrub yourself with sand. Use it on your scalp, too. I don't want my brother's lodge infected with bugs."

"Overbearing brute," Melissa mumbled through her teeth. Why did he continue the charade? Cougar, indeed. He obviously wasn't an Apache, not with his blue eyes and educated voice.

In her denial, she chose to believe his treatment represented some sort of lesson. Like Robert, he probably thought decent women didn't long for adventure. She shivered, both with the water's frigid caress and her fiancé's foresight.

"If you want to keep all your fingers and toes, I suggest you hurry."

She glanced toward the bank. He stood, a tall shadow among the aspens. Doubt crowded past denial. Even though the darkness hid his features, he seemed part of the scenery, as if he belonged. If she hadn't known he was there for a fact, she might not have noticed him at all.

Ronda Thompson

"Want me to help you hurry?"

His threat speeded her efforts. Teeth chattering, Melissa bent, scooping up a handful of sand. She scrubbed vigorously and despite the uncomfortable temperature, sighed in bliss as the grime left her body. Her spirits lifted. She felt more like herself, stronger, more confident the nightmare would end and she'd soon be back among the civilized.

"Out."

A snapping sound followed his command. Melissa tensed. "Put the blanket down and turn around."

He laughed in answer. "Get out, or I'll come in and get you."

"I'm not decent."

"You haven't got anything I haven't seen before."

"I won't!"

"All right. I'll take the blanket and go back to camp. I'm sure Tall Blade would like to run across a white woman, naked and alone."

"Tall Blade?"

"He said you lifted a hand against him. I don't think you'd enjoy his company."

The one who'd attacked her, Melissa correctly identified. She shivered again. "At least promise you'll close your eyes."

"I don't make promises to women. I'm not the sort who'd keep them. Get out."

Would he really kill her if she tried to escape? Melissa's gaze darted back and forth in the darkness. She wouldn't last the night. Not naked, half-frozen, and weaponless.

"Go ahead. You'll save me a lot of trouble."

Abruptly, she glanced back at him. How had he known what she was thinking? Melissa doubted he could see her expressions any clearer than she could his. Realizing the choices were nil, she crossed her arms over her breasts and waded toward the bank.

"Very sensible, Huera."

"You're insufferable," she ground out.

"I'm finally getting through to you."

"It didn't take long to prove you were an inconsiderate jackass. That doesn't make you an Indian."

A blanket went around her shoulders, and his hand clutched her long hair. "You almost sound disappointed. Did you expect to be thrown on the ground, taken roughly, and slapped around? Is that what you want?"

Once upon a time, Melissa Sheffield from St. Louis wouldn't have understood his questions. Her education along the trail, disgusting as it had been, had stolen that innocence away from her. "No," she answered quietly.

"I didn't think so." He released her hair. "I can be as savage as you consider these people. Don't assume you know anything about what I will or won't do to you."

A moment later, he swept her up in his arms and moved toward the distant fires. Melissa stumbled as he shoved her inside the tepee, and scrambled on hands and knees toward the farthest corner. The secure hold he maintained on the blanket resulted in her leaving it behind. She squawked in panic, pulling her legs against her chest.

"Don't come any closer," she warned, placing a hand out in front of her.

Cougar rubbed his forehead. "There you go again. Issuing orders. Maybe I haven't made myself clear." He moved toward her with the grace of a cat. "I give the orders. You follow them."

She screamed when he grasped her arms, lifting her from the ground. Melissa's body slammed into his. A shiver raced through her as heated flesh met frigid skin. She lifted her face. His eyes, thickly lashed and too blue to compare with a summer sky, widened. He swore, then shoved her away.

Instinctively, she brought her arms up to cover herself, watching him move to the far side of the tepee. He bent, fumbled through some baskets, and tossed her a brush and a dry blanket.

"If you step foot outside this tepee you become fair game to whoever or whatever's roaming the night."

When he opened the tepee flap as if he intended to leave, Melissa couldn't believe her good fortune. She grabbed the blanket and covered herself, wondering at his strange reaction to seeing her without the dirt coating her face. A reason for his sudden disinterest in her occurred.

"What's the matter? Has the color of my skin pricked your conscience?"

Her question drew him up short. "I don't have a conscience. And all skin's the same color in the dark. I'll return shortly."

His parting words were in no way casual and sounded closer to a threat. Melissa clutched the blanket tighter around her, afraid she couldn't hold her hysteria at bay much longer. She hadn't cried. Not much. She hadn't screamed and pulled insanely at her hair. The thought of killing herself had yet to enter her mind.

Did her behavior suggest she was a strong person? Or simply a stupid one? A glance around the small enclosure brought a sob to her throat, a stinging to her eyes. Crude objects hung from the hide walls. The hoof of some poor animal. Pouches made of buckskin. She shivered despite the cozy fire. She was a captive. Trapped in this godforsaken place not with an Indian, but with a white man.

A strange giggle escaped her lips. Melissa clamped a hand over her mouth, afraid a whole string of them would follow. She slumped to the ground, surprised by the soft feel of buffalo robes beneath her. It found her then. The realization she'd been desperately trying to deny. The truth. The nightmare had not ended. It had only begun.

Chapter Three

Clay breathed deeply of the night air. The sound of the woman's sobs slashed at him. It took every ounce of his willpower not to go to her, offer her comfort, although there was little comfort he could offer her. No hope of escape, or even ransom. He hadn't expected this. So quick a confrontation with a conscience he claimed not to possess. He certainly hadn't expected the jolt that traveled through him the first time she raised her clean face to his.

The scarecrow was no scarecrow, but a beautiful woman. Perhaps the most beautiful woman he'd ever seen. It made no difference, he warned himself. Scarecrow or angel, her fate had been decided. His also. The only way he could save her was to teach her to be a good slave. A valuable one.

After all, hers wasn't a fate worse than death. Clay cared for the Apaches. They were good people unless you were on the wrong side of them. In time, she would come to accept them and be accepted by them.

He caught himself before the lies grew bolder. Melissa Sheffield was young, but not young enough to forget the past. She claimed a man waited for her in Santa Fe. Judging by what he'd just seen, he was surprised only one waited. In the space of an afternoon, she'd altered his life.

She was the test, and beautiful or not, he had his own skin to think about. Gray Wolf didn't make idle threats. If Clay failed in his duty to the Apaches, they would hunt him down and kill him. As the leader said, he knew their ways too well.

Tempted to clamp his hands over his ears to blot out the soft sounds of her weeping, Clay glanced up at the moon. It hung, a big orange ball just cresting the tops of the distant mountains. A wolf howled, then a keening began inside the tepee. A sound that rose the hairs on the back of his neck. Clay hardened his heart.

Melissa Sheffield was not the first woman to cause him grief. Because of the other, he'd all but forsaken his white blood. Because of his mother, he was ashamed it flowed through his veins.

Regardless of his parentage, the Apaches accepted him. He'd run wild through their camps since childhood. For them, he could ignore the woman's plight. For them, he could be cruel. And for Huera, as they called her, being cruel was the kindest thing he could do. She must learn their ways—learn to fear the Apaches in order to respect them. And he would teach her.

With purposeful strides, he marched toward Laughing Stream's lodge. He entered after announcing himself, moving quickly to Swift Buck's mat. The brave's mother merely sighed in acknowledgment of him and kept stirring a kettle of boiling herbs.

"I said I would come for you, Cougar," Laughing Stream said. "The shaman has gone to seek a vision. There is no change."

When Clay placed a hand against Swift Buck's brow, an argument formed in his mind. There was a change. The fever was worse. He didn't handle helplessness well, and that's what Clay felt. "He will live," he said, trying to assure himself more than Laughing Stream.

"I hope even Usen fears the mighty cat enough to do his bidding. Does the woman?"

Her question brought his gaze from Swift Buck. "She should," he answered evasively.

"But she does not. I went to the river for water not long ago. I do not hear the white words and understand them as does my son, but her voice held no respect."

"It will."

"As I said before, some things are not so simple. Does she walk naked among us tomorrow?"

Clay hadn't thought that far ahead. He supposed that to humble her, forcing her to work naked among the Apache women would be suitable. An image of her clean face flashed through his mind, the remembered feel of her breasts pressed against his chest.

"No," he answered. "For many years I have traded you pelts to make my clothes. I brought six skins of white rabbit for . . ." He hesitated. He'd brought them for Rachel, thinking she could fashion herself a warm cape. "I will trade them for women's clothes."

"There is no need to trade," Laughing Stream argued. "Make use of your sister's things. They belong to you."

When he glanced toward a basket against the far corner of the tepee, his chest tightened. "She would want you to keep her possessions. You have been kind to her."

Laughing Stream's eyes shone with tears when she turned them on Clay. "I loved her as a child of my own body. She was like the ice frozen over a river in winter. Beautiful when the sun shone down on her and silent of all that flowed beneath the surface. Soon, the men of my lodge grew to accept her among us. Now, it hurts my heart to see the reminders she leaves behind. Take them, Cougar."

A nod was his answer. Clay pulled the hides up closer around Swift Buck before he stood. His hands shook slightly as he lifted his sister's belongings. The basket felt heavy with the proof he hadn't been able to remain as detached as he'd have wanted.

"Those things, the trinkets, the extra meat you left before

35

winter, they would have meant more if you ever once gave them to her, instead of to me."

"I gave her all I could and allowed your family to give what her own would not," he said softly, then took the basket and disappeared through the flap.

Laughing Stream's soft moans of grief followed him outside. Clay almost envied her the release. Tears were long lost to him. He'd pledged long ago, a woman's weakness would never fill him. He'd kept his vow.

Now, to keep the one Gray Wolf demanded of him. He imagined Melissa Sheffield would have ceased her crying and now be sitting cowering in the tepee. Waiting to be defiled. He'd purposely left the threat hanging between them, hoping to get through to her. He was not a decent white man. He was not her salvation. In all truthfulness, they were enemies.

After entering Swift Buck's lodge, he saw her huddled beneath a mound of buffalo robes. Clay sat the basket down and approached her, debating whether to find his own mat and leave her choking on fear, or to assure her that, for the time being, she could rest easy.

Better to allow her to get some sleep, he decided. She would need her strength in the coming days. Clay placed more wood on the fire, then bent, easing back the hides. Melissa Sheffield, formerly of St. Louis, was not cowering in fear. His captive was asleep.

"I'll be damned."

His voice brought a soft moan from her lips. Lips as full and ripe as summer berries. Dark lashes rested against the paleness of her cheeks. Perfectly arched brows graced her smooth forehead. He lifted a strand of her hair, wondering over the contrast of darker brows and lashes. The half-damp tendril caught the firelight, turned to molten silver, curled with life around his fingers, and felt like corn silk to his touch. Abruptly, he dropped it.

"Robert?"

A dream, Clay realized. Was Robert the name of the man she claimed as her fiancé? Whoever he was, she was lost to him. The lush pink of her lips, the silken texture of her hair, the graceful length of her neck. Creamy skin rested above the blanket she'd wrapped around herself. The covering had inched indecently low. His fingers tingled with the temptation to touch her.

"Robert, please don't be angry with me."

She tossed fitfully, the blanket sliding a hairsbreadth lower. Beads of sweat broke out on Clay's forehead. Her lips parted. They beckoned him—called to the deepest, darkest part of him. Slowly, his face lowered to hers. Her brow puckered, her breathing increased.

"No," she gasped. All signs of softness left her features. Her back arched, thrusting her breasts against his chest. An animal groan squeezed past Clay's clenched teeth. She was obviously fighting a dream demon.

"Cougar?"

His name left her lips with a sigh, and in her voice, the hope of salvation resounded. Serenity erased the furrow in her forehead and relaxed the tense line of her jaw.

Anger brought Clay's hot blood to a boil. Damn her for pricking his conscience, cluttering up his life. "You think I'm here to save you?" he asked under his breath. "I'll show you how safe I am."

In sleep, her mouth yielded, uncaring that his tongue stole inside to taste, caress, and seduce her. When she moaned softly, he deepened the kiss, fighting the natural urge to touch her, to cover her body in a gesture of dominance. The feel of her fingers in his hair made him pull away. Thick lashes fluttered, then lifted, revealing twin turquoise pools. She returned his stare with eyes dazed and unseeing.

Slowly, her lids lowered and her breathing steadied. Clay wondered, in a moment of insanity, how far he could get before reality invaded her dreams. Resentful that she stirred even lust in him, he removed himself from her temptation. Clothes. Huera definitely needed to cover herself. He glanced toward the basket holding his sister's possessions.

Rachel's scent floated up once he removed the lid. Pine, wood smoke, and sunshine. Everyone and everything had a distinctive scent. He knew Rachel's from the many times he'd sat in Laughing Stream's lodge with Swift Buck. He had felt relieved if confused when his blood brother had demanded his own lodge.

It wasn't odd for a brave to stay with his family until he married. Rachel had been sixteen then, and he'd felt her gaze boring into his back while he and Swift Buck talked. He'd felt her hatred, her resentment.

He understood her feelings—*the punishment he demanded of her.* With her birth had come the understanding that his mother wasn't different because she wasn't Apache. A white woman could touch, love, and comfort. It was in his tenth year that Rachel had been born. His tenth year when the truth found him. It was only her son his mother couldn't give her love to—him and Hiram Brodie.

Clay gently removed a buckskin dress from the basket. Rachel hadn't been as tall as his captive. He'd trade one of the younger boys something for a pair of leggings tomorrow. He thought the moccasins would stretch to fit her. Having removed the necessary items, he shoved the basket along the wall next to his own belongings. He retrieved the lid and paused while staring down at his sister's possessions.

A silver-backed brush caught the light when he brought it from the basket's darkness. He studied the bristles. They held no wheat-colored strands to evidence that Rachel had used it. It didn't surprise him that she'd ignored the subtle gifts he'd included over the years with Laughing Stream's trade items, only that she'd kept them.

Rachel had worn no evidence of her true race, except a small gold bracelet that had belonged to their mother. She had refused to either wear or use the gifts he'd given her.

The presents were expensive ones. Trinkets he could well afford. The mountain produced thick pelts worth a great deal to the fur companies in the east. Replacing the lid, Clay slid the basket against the wall. His gaze moved toward the buffalo hides. A strand of silver hair rested against the fur of his captive's protective burrow. He spread his own mat across from hers and allowed the glowing grate to separate them.

Her steady breathing kept him awake longer than it should have. His thoughts kept straying across the fire. His mind conjured the feel of her lips, the firm rise of her breasts. Dammit! How was he supposed to ignore a woman as desirable as that one? And if he couldn't, how would he remain immune to her plight?

Melissa snuggled deeper beneath the covers, wondering where her pillow had gone and why her sheets felt coarse. Safe, familiar memories drifted in and out of her consciousness. She floated on a cloud of peaceful dreams until vague pictures of painted bodies began the nightmare. With a start, she sat up.

A savage squatted next to the fire. His steely stare locked with hers. He smiled, then slowly lowered his gaze. Melissa glanced down and gasped. The blanket around her had slipped indecently low. She quickly jerked it up around her neck.

"Get dressed." He nodded toward a bundle at her feet. "In those."

Clothes, even Indian trappings, were a blessed sight. "Kindly leave," she instructed.

"I'm not kindly," he reminded, stirring a kettle of something that smelled heavenly. "Unless working naked appeals to you, I suggest you do as you're told."

She frowned. "What sort of work?"

"Probably nothing more than gutting a deer. Maybe digging out the gums, lips, and forehead to make glue. Of course, you won't be trusted with a weapon. You'll have to use your fingers."

Melissa tried not to shiver in disgust. She wouldn't give the man who refused to tell her his Christian name the satisfaction. Besides, Cougar, as the Apaches referred to him, hadn't made good on any of his threats. As far as she could tell, once she'd cried herself out and fell into exhausted slumber, she'd slept unmolested the entire night.

"You don't have to continue this farce," she said, impressed by the steadiness of her voice. "I've learned my lesson. I should have stayed home. Robert said this territory was no place for a woman. I should have listened to—"

"Get dressed!"

His angry command made her jump. He looked tired and irritated . . . and maybe worried. Was it her fate that bothered him? Or that of the Indian he claimed as a blood brother? She opened her mouth to ask him.

"If I have to tell you again, I'll do it for you."

Quickly, Melissa closed her mouth. A night of rest had not improved his surliness. She bent, snatched up the clothes, and disappeared beneath the hides. Dressing beneath their bulk took some doing, not to mention the fact that she had to guess how the garments were to be worn. She did the best she could with the dress, but had trouble with the strange trousers. Frustrated, she threw the robes aside and sat up.

"Hurry," he ordered. "I have matters to tend to and so do you. We begin with breakfast."

"It smells good," Melissa admitted. She bunched the trousers up and slipped them over her feet, embarrassed when she caught the man staring at her bare legs. Using the robes to cover her, she managed to pull the trousers to her waist. They were a little big, but would do.

"What are you cooking?" she asked, slipping the soft moccasins on her feet.

He cast her a dark look. "I did not prepare the stew. Swift Buck's mother and father had no appetite this morning and gave it to me when I went to check on him. From now on, it is your duty to prepare the meals."

She frowned. "I don't know how to cook. Constance, my housekeeper, prepared all my meals."

"Do you see this Constance here?"

A burst of heat exploded in her cheeks. He had cruelly reminded her she was not in her world, but caught in a nightmare. "I'm simply stating a fact. I can't very well cook when I haven't been taught."

"I will teach you." He sat back from the fire. "But for now you must learn that the men of a lodge are always served first. Dish up some stew and hand it to me."

The wonderful smell of food made Melissa's stomach growl. "I haven't eaten in a while," she said softly. "I'm starving."

"Then serve me so you can serve yourself."

White man or not, he was no gentleman. His insistence she learn the Apache way of doing things began to grate on her nerves. Melissa had no intention of becoming a slave. She refused to accept this cruel twist of fate, and told herself something would happen. Somehow, she would be miraculously plucked from the Apache camp and returned to her own people.

"I refuse to serve you," she said, lifting her chin.

His gaze had lowered to the kettle, obviously in anticipation of her compliance. He glanced up abruptly. "What did you say?"

It was difficult to keep her cool composure under the intense scrutiny of his eyes. Harder yet not to buckle and do his bidding. She wanted it understood she wasn't the type to easily accept her situation. Melissa took a steadying breath.

"I said no."

"No?" he repeated incredulously. His face, already darkened by the sun, turned even darker. "You do understand that if you do not serve me, you will not eat?"

Her bravery fueled by his lack of aggressive action toward her, Melissa reached forward and snatched up a crude wooden bowl. "Yes, I will," she decided.

Hands trembling, Melissa dished the stew into the bowl, choosing to ignore that the utensil was fashioned from the bone of some animal rather than silver. Since she saw no evidence of other eating utensils, she scooped a heaping bite on the spoon and brought it to her lips. The food never made it inside her mouth. He moved so quickly she didn't have time to react. A strong hand clasped her wrist.

"That was very stupid."

Slowly, she glanced up. His face was mere inches from hers. The expression he wore was frighteningly calm considering the anger in his words.

"You will deny me nothing I ask. Nothing!"

She wanted to burst into tears. Instead, she lifted her chin another notch.

"I am master, you are slave," he ground out. "You must learn your place in order to survive. Now, serve me the stew!"

The wisest course of action was to do as he asked. Melissa knew that, but she couldn't bring herself to be so quickly brought to rein. Serving him stew was an easy enough task. What if the next request he made was not so simple? *Anything?* He said she must not deny him anything.

"Here." She threw the contents of the bowl in his face. "Breakfast is served."

Chapter Four

Clay couldn't believe her daring. The stew, thankfully only
warm and not boiling, covered his face and chest. Had she
done this to another brave in the camp, the brave would have
slit her throat. She needed to be taught a lesson.

He snatched her wrist and hauled her up. His captive
stood tall for a woman, but Clay still towered a good four
inches over her. He used his height to intimidate her.

"Unlike those of your kind, the Apaches don't tolerate
waste. Clean it off!"

To his satisfaction, she flinched. Her eyes darted nervously around the structure. He knew what she sought and
smiled. "With your mouth."

"I won't," she gasped.

"You will." He wrapped a thick lock of her hair around
his hand to keep her from bolting. "This isn't the place to let
rebellion cloud good judgment. Defiance demands a price.
This," he indicated his chest with a nod, "is the only meal
you'll get today."

Her eyes shot daggers at him. She hated him, which Clay

couldn't blame her for—but he still saw no sign of fear, which it was his responsibility to inspire. If she refused, he supposed his duty would include striking her. That meant he couldn't let her refuse.

"Would you prefer I demand something else of you?" He purposely allowed his gaze to slide down her body.

The woman understood his insinuation. She tried to put distance between them, but Clay kept a firm grasp on her hair.

"We can do this the easy way, or the hard way. Those are the only two choices you're allowed here."

"Let go of me," she whispered. "Please," she added, rather reluctantly to his ear. "I will do what you ask."

After casting her a warning glance, Clay released his grip on her hair. She'd put the brush he'd given her to good use the previous evening. Long, wavy tresses of silver hung to her waist. Her beauty hadn't been a trick of the night. He'd tried not to notice her desirability this morning. He had failed.

"Do I at least have the right to hate you?" she asked, proving she was still far from docile.

"Only if I give it to you. And I do."

"Thank you," she countered, defiance alive and smoldering in her eyes. His captive took a deep breath, obviously steeling herself for the task ahead. She leaned forward and gently touched her lips to his skin.

Clay jerked. When her tongue lapped at the stew on his chest, accidentally grazing his nipple, he swallowed loudly. His body filled with heat. Not a result of the fire burning in the grate, but the one she started deep inside of him.

Lower her lips traveled. Clay fought his desire for her, realizing her punishment had now become his own. When she went to her knees, his fingers twisted in her hair. He forced her to look up at him.

The sight of her flushed cheeks, her slightly parted lips, nearly caused him to groan in agony. He propelled her upward, his hands moving to her slender shoulders. Still she stared at him, that same innocent expression on her face. He wanted to kiss her again, take her mouth when dreams did not hold her prisoner.

As if she sensed his struggle for control, she tried to step away. The innocence left her eyes, replaced by wariness. And she should be wary. He could take her if he wanted. It was his right. But he wouldn't exercise that privilege. No man had the right to take an unwilling woman, be it out of lust, revenge, or even duty. Clay released her and searched for a rag to clean himself.

"Think very hard before you act, Huera. You may not like the consequences."

She turned from him, her long blond strands fanning out around her shoulders. "Are threats and humiliation the only way of life here?"

He wanted to touch her hair, gently, not as he'd done earlier. Clay wanted to assure her the Apaches were good people, but he knew her mind had been poisoned. She would have to learn on her own, and he had a feeling that with her, it would be the hard way.

"You cannot earn respect until you learn to give it."

She wheeled around to confront him. "I don't want their respect. I don't want yours. I want to go home!"

His jaw clamped shut. When was she going to get it through her head she couldn't go home? When would she accept her fate and allow his conscience a reprieve?

"Tell me your name," she said quietly. "Your real name. Tell me who taught you to speak such eloquent English. Tell me—"

A shout from outside the tepee cut her off. Fortunate, because Clay had no intention of telling her his white name. He wouldn't tell her of his white mother who spoke the English tongue so differently from his crass father. He wouldn't tell her he'd learned to mimic his mother's speech in hopes it would please her. In a pitiful attempt to win her love. He finished wiping the stew from his face and chest, then threw down the rag.

"Come, they are calling for me. Swift Buck grows worse."

Her emerald eyes widened. She glanced toward the tepee flap. "I can't go out there. What will they do to me?"

"Nothing if you stay close to me. Keep your eyes downcast and walk behind me."

"But if I'm behind you, how will you know if one of them attacks me?"

There wasn't time to offer her assurances, to lead her gently among a people who would not view her in a gentle light. Clay grabbed her arm and pulled her behind him.

Once outside, Melissa fought panic. Would the women storm her again? Tear the clothes from her back? Would they shoot arrows at her? Throw rocks? Poke her with spears? She was at their mercy, at his mercy. Her gaze fastened on the white man's broad back. White man?

His skin had been darkened to bronze by the sun. His dark hair hung well past his shoulders, and he wore Indian trappings. From a distance, he looked like an Indian.

Only when one gazed into the blue of his eyes, noticed the fine-boned structure of his face, the strength of his jawline, or heard the English roll impressively off his tongue, could one see past his disguise. But what was he doing among the Apaches? More importantly, why had he refused to help her escape?

Her gaze glued to his back, Melissa found a reason that made sense. She saw them. Scars. Faded, but proof he had not been treated well in the past. It hit her with force, the reason a white man walked freely among a savage people.

He must have been a captive also. Perhaps taken as a boy. Now she understood his insistence that she learn respect. He knew all too well the price of disobedience.

Despite the fear squeezing at her chest, and the despair threatening to overwhelm her, Melissa's heart softened toward the man who called himself Cougar. Although he walked with his head held high and with a sureness to his step, the scars on his back were proof he had not always commanded his own fate. Were the scars his punishment for trying to escape in the past? Were they the reason he refused to help her now?

The white man paused at a tepee, threw the flap open, and disappeared inside. Melissa held back, uncertain if she was to follow or not. He reached out, grabbed her arm, and resolved the issue. Once inside, the smell of sickness assaulted her. It was a scent Melissa knew well.

Several sets of dark eyes swung in her direction. The old man and woman she dismissed as no immediate threat, feeling a stab of alarm when she recognized the one who'd led the attack on her caravan. His black stare was totally devoid of emotion until he turned his head toward the woman at his side. Only then did the hardness in his eyes soften.

Cougar regained her attention when he spoke, the Apache sounding as natural on his tongue as English. A path opened to him, one that revealed the wounded Indian, tossing in fevered delirium. Melissa fought her natural response to go to him. To place a hand against his forehead and determine the seriousness of his condition. Despite the fact that he'd saved her life by stepping in front of an arrow, he was a savage.

Hackles rose on the back of her neck when the rattle of beads began. She glanced up to confront an old man leaning over the brave. A bony finger pointed in her direction. Whatever information he divulged brought a murmur from those gathered. Melissa didn't like being the center of attention.

For all she knew, the group might be discussing how fine her hair would look on a scalp belt. She glanced toward the tepee flap, wondering if she could escape before they were upon her. A strong hand clasped her arm.

"Don't," Cougar said under his breath, then he addressed the old man. Words flew between them, sounding close to an argument before Cougar turned back to her. "The shaman says you can save him. He had a vision last night. In it, he saw a light spread through Swift Buck's body and remove the poison. The light came from a white woman."

Melissa lowered her gaze. "Th-That sounds crazy."

His grip on her arm tightened. "Look at me."

Slowly, she lifted her face.

"Who are you?"

A lump formed in her throat. That the Indian had associated Melissa with healing unnerved her. How could he have known? She was determined to play dumb. She wouldn't help an Indian. "I told you: Melissa Sheffield from St. Louis, on my way to Santa Fe to marry Robert—"

"Who are you?" he repeated harshly.

His stare reached into her soul. Melissa panicked. "My father was a physician, the best in St. Louis until my mother's death. Then he turned to a bottle for comfort and let me tag along with him on his calls, but I'm not a doctor. I can't help him."

"You can't, or you won't?"

The images of her nightmare took shape. The screaming, the blood. "He rode against our caravan. He killed innocent men—"

Her sentence ended abruptly, silenced by the cold feel of a blade. Cougar had removed the knife so quickly her brain hadn't had time to register his intention. Not until the knife rested against her throat.

"You *will* help him."

When she swallowed, the reflex brought her a small measure of relief. The knife bit into her throat, letting her know he held only the dull edge against her skin. Judging by his skill at removing the blade from his moccasin, she doubted it was a mistake.

Melissa pushed the knife away, moved through the group, and knelt beside the sick Apache. She placed a palm against Swift Buck's forehead, then withdrew it with a gasp. "The fever's out of control."

"Then bring it under control."

Although his voice sounded calm, Melissa detected a note of suppressed rage. Helplessness.

"I'm not sure anything can be done at this point but pray it breaks before the spasms begin."

"I'm not a praying man. Find another way."

She glanced up at him. "Or I suppose these people will kill me. Or will you be given the honor?"

His gaze hardened on her. "There is no honor in killing a woman, but the Apaches take their visions very seriously. If they believe you can save him, and you don't, they'll also believe it's because you didn't want to. The loss of his life will mean the loss of yours."

He may as well have danced on her grave. A chill ran up her spine. Despite the consequences, she said, "I'll trade. His life for my freedom. Promise me you'll take me to Santa Fe if he lives."

"I can't do that," Cougar countered, the words barely making it past his clenched teeth.

"You can't, or you won't?"

"Both. Dammit!" He glanced around and lowered his voice. "If you know something to do for him, do it."

She'd cracked his control. Melissa saw something in his eyes she hadn't seen before. Fear. Did he fear for the Indian he called brother, for her, or for himself? Maybe his supposed love of these people was just that—a pretense. How could a man care for anyone who'd done that to his back? She realized she'd asked too much of him too soon. For now, she would settle for a confession.

"I want your name."

He blinked, as if surprised by her condition. "I told you my name."

"Your Christian name," she persisted.

Swift Buck groaned softly. Cougar's gaze drifted to the brave, then quickly back up to her.

"Do something!" he ordered.

"Tell me your name."

He ran a hand through his hair. "Do you want to die?"

His question didn't sway her determination. Although she didn't want to die, Melissa shrugged. "If I'm not leaving this place, I'd rather be dead."

A spasm contorted Swift Buck's body. The Indian nearly came up off of the mat. Cougar held him down. His blue stare collided with Melissa's.

"Brodie," he bit out. "Clay Brodie."

The resentment in his eyes stole any pleasure Melissa might have received at hearing his name. She had a feeling war had just been declared between them.

"Move him to the river," she instructed.

"Swift Buck shouldn't be moved," he argued.

She met his glare with one of her own. "His body must be completely submerged. It's the only way."

"If he dies . . ."

The sentence went unfinished. Melissa couldn't tell if his warning was another reminder of what the Apaches would do to her if she couldn't heal the Indian, or if he was making a personal threat. Not personal, she decided. Surely Clay Brodie didn't really care what happened to the Apache. How could he when these people had taken him from his home, beaten and abused him?

Melissa rose on trembling legs as he lifted the unconscious brave in his arms. She followed him from the tepee, still trying to puzzle the pieces of Clay Brodie together. He couldn't have been too young when they took him or he wouldn't have remembered his white name or how to speak English. To her, he looked anywhere from five to ten years older than her own nineteen years. He could have been taken in his tenth or eleventh year, she supposed.

That he'd held on to his white past lifted her spirits somewhat. It meant that inside, he still wanted to be civilized. All she need do now was tame the savage in him and find the boy he once was. How difficult a task would it be, and how long would it take her?

With a relieved sigh, Clay removed his hand from Swift Buck's forehead. Holding him beneath the water's frigid surface brought the fever down, as she'd said it would. Now his blood brother lay wrapped in blankets while the woman studied the wound on his shoulder.

"It has to be lanced," she said. "I'll need a knife, heated over the fire, and something to clean the wound. I don't suppose you have any liquor?"

He battled over whether he should divulge that information. Clay didn't want her to know he walked in both worlds. The knowledge would further complicate the mission given to him by the Apaches. Still, if the liquor was needed . . .

"The Mescalero Apaches got their name from mescal. They make their own liquor, but ration it more cautiously than in days past. I could probably get you some."

She frowned. "Whiskey would work better."

After giving the matter a moment's deliberation, he shrugged. "I can get that, too."

Her gaze lifted. "Where would you get whiskey?"

He smiled slightly. "I slit a white man's throat for it."

Other than a telltale tremble in the hand she held over Swift Buck's wound, Clay thought she handled his answer well. Too well. The woman had more courage than was wise for a captive in unfamiliar surroundings.

"Would you get it, please?"

When he rose to return to Swift Buck's lodge, her courage visibly faltered. His gaze roamed the others. "Don't make any sudden moves."

Clay wasn't gone long. His captive appeared the same as he'd left her, still as a rock. The small sigh of relief she expelled when he settled next to her irritated him.

"The knife." She held out her hand.

After removing the knife from his moccasin, Clay placed it over the fire. "If anyone cuts on Swift Buck, it'll be me." He uncorked the whiskey bottle with his teeth, took a long pull, and waited a few moments before retrieving the knife. "You're sure this is necessary?"

She nodded. "The incision should be a straight line across the wound. His injury festers worst there. I'll have to squeeze on him after you've finished. Tell the stone-faced one to help me hold him while you cut."

"Watch what you say," Clay warned softly. "Your tone reeks of authority, of which you have none. They may not understand your words, but they know the sound of disrespect when they hear it."

"You should slice it from her mouth." Gray Wolf's gaze

came even with Clay when he bent, securing a hold on Swift Buck. "Her tongue," he explained in Apache. "There is no fear in her eyes for you, Cougar, only confusion. Her mind has not accepted who you are."

"Her mind is empty," Clay muttered, casting a dark look at his captive. "Where there is no sense, there is no fear."

And Melissa Sheffield should have been very afraid at the moment. By her instruction, he would take a knife to his blood brother. He'd be lucky if the woman didn't end up getting them both killed. His last thought caused a skitter to race up his spine. He remembered Gray Wolf's words. *In my vision, I saw you die for her.* Neither Clay Brodie nor Cougar would die for a woman. Neither had met one worth dying for, or ever would.

"Hold him," he instructed her, then steeled himself for what would follow.

Chapter Five

Melissa grasped Swift Buck's shoulders. The knife flashed. A streak of blood bubbled up. Seconds later, the pain seemed to have found its way to the Apache's brain. An inhuman growl left his throat, and his back arched. Melissa gasped with her efforts, surprised that he maintained the strength to fight so gallantly.

"Do what you have to do," Clay instructed, placing his hands on either side of hers.

"B-But he should have a moment to rest."

"I said do it now. Let's get this over with."

Heart pounding against her chest, she placed her hands against the puffy wound and pressed. The brave's hoarse cry cut into her. It was no different, she told herself, from hearing a dog whimper. Still, she eased the pressure.

"Dammit," the white man swore. "You haven't got the strength to hold him down or I'd do it myself. Don't prolong his agony!"

She bit her lip and squeezed with all her might. Swift Buck fought against the arms holding him prisoner. Finally, pus began to seep from the wound. She pressed until beads of moisture dotted her forehead and the pus turned to blood, then gratefully sat back.

"That will do for now. I need a relatively clean cloth to sponge the wound after we pour whiskey over it, then a drawing poultice should be placed against his shoulder."

"The shaman's already prepared the herbs for a poultice," he said. "I'll get a cloth."

It took all of her willpower not to reach out and grab his arm. She didn't like being left alone with the Apaches. When he rose to leave, Melissa quickly lowered her gaze. Silence prevailed. An old man's grumble brought scurrying sounds.

From beneath her lashes, Melissa watched two women begin the preparation of a meal. She thought the old man's demand for food was rather cruel under the circumstances. One woman was clearly the injured brave's mother. Her worried gaze strayed often to her son. The other, Melissa noted, didn't look much older than herself.

She studied the younger woman's features, surprised by her startling beauty . . . more surprised by the dainty cross she wore around her neck. Suddenly, Melissa realized the woman wasn't Apache. Her ancestry appeared to be Spanish. Melissa's housekeeper had been Spanish. She had picked up the language over the years.

"Hola," she blurted out.

The woman froze in her task. Her gaze lifted abruptly. A tinge of red surfaced beneath her skin.

"¿Comprende?" Melissa tried again.

When the woman turned away from her, it was obvious she meant to ignore Melissa. It was also obvious the woman had understood the Spanish words. She wouldn't be ignored.

"Por—"

A low growl from the stone-faced leader diffused Melissa's third attempt to converse with the woman. The threat in his dark eyes sent a shiver up her spine. She cringed when he stood, expecting to be beaten for her boldness. Instead, the Apache turned his glare on the Spanish woman

54

and left. Although he said nothing to her, she cast an apologetic look at the injured brave's mother and quickly followed the man outside.

Clay Brodie appeared only seconds after her departure. He wore a scowl and clutched a piece of white cloth in his hand.

"What did you do?"

"N-Nothing," Melissa stammered. "I mean, I said *Hola* to her. The woman is Spanish, isn't she?"

He shook his head. "You shouldn't have spoken to her."

"But she's—"

"Half," he interrupted quietly. "She's half-Spanish. Jageitci is also Gray Wolf's woman, and he doesn't like to be reminded of her tainted blood. Don't speak to her again."

A protest formed on Melissa's lips. He couldn't tell her who she could or couldn't speak to. She opened her mouth to tell him so, but the garment he tossed into her lap distracted her. The material had yellowed with age, but felt soft, and carried a particular scent. Not a perfume she could identify. A pleasant, clean, natural smell. The same as the clothes she currently wore. Melissa glanced from the chemise to Clay Brodie.

"I suppose you slit a white woman's throat to get this?"

Her sarcasm received no response. Cougar lifted the whiskey bottle. Melissa waited for him to hand it to her and take a firm hold on the Indian. Instead, he took another drink.

"It surprised me to find it among her things," he mumbled distractedly.

"Whose things?" she asked.

He seemed to realize his mind had wandered. Clay sat up straighter, handed her the bottle, placed his hands on Swift Buck's shoulders, and told her to pour.

It stung the Indian even in unconsciousness. His face contorted with agony. He groaned. As Melissa gently dabbed at the blood, Brodie spoke to the old woman. She appeared beside Melissa with a pot of foul-smelling herbs.

"Have her cut the cloth," Melissa instructed. "A piece to contain the herbs and the rest in strips."

"A slave does not give orders," he reminded her.

"You'll be giving the order," Melissa countered. "I'm tired of this game you insist I play. I'm tired of the one you're playing."

Her outburst brought heat to his eyes. "Later, we'll talk about games." He snatched the chemise from her fingers and tore the fabric into strips, The man who claimed to be her master filled a larger section of fabric with the herbs and pressed it against the brave's wound. Without instruction from her, he secured strips across Swift Buck's shoulder to hold the poultice in place.

"What now?"

Already regretting her loss of temper, Melissa lowered her eyes and tried to appear docile. "His face needs washing, then the woman should force water down his throat in small amounts. Too much will make him sick."

He handed her a bowl of water and a strip of cloth. "Wash him while I explain to her."

Melissa preferred to refrain from any more contact with the Apache. To her, it seemed that washing him was too intimate, and therefore indecent. She also suspected Clay Brodie wouldn't care how she felt about the matter.

A refusal on her part would only prolong the ordeal. She took a deep breath, dipped the cloth in water, and began washing the sick Indian. When she leaned closer to Swift Buck, wetting the dryness of his lips, the Apache's nostrils flared slightly.

"Silent Wind?"

She jerked back, gasping in surprise. Not only had the Apache spoken, but he'd done so in English. The rattle of beads sounded. She'd forgotten the shaman sat in the shadows. His chanting began.

"I smell you, Silent Wind," the brave rasped. "I heard you once. While dreams held you, your voice, beautiful as the nightingale, floated to me. It was my name you whispered. When I come to you, I will not come as a brother, but as a man."

A low-spoken curse lifted Melissa's gaze. Clay Brodie

stared at the Apache, his expression one of disbelief. In the space of seconds, a look of anger replaced the shock. He reached out and encircled the Indian's throat. Gasping sounds filled the small enclosure. A cry of distress broke the spell. Swift Buck's mother, the old man, and the shaman were on the white man immediately, their babbling voices raised.

"*Da!*"

Finally the command penetrated Clay's rage. Slowly, he released his hold on Swift Buck.

"What has happened?" Gray Wolf demanded, moving into the tepee's interior. "Why do you lift a hand against your brother?"

"He is no longer my brother," Clay said, rising. "The day he stopped being a brother to the one we cannot speak of, he stopped being mine."

"I do not understand," Gray Wolf said, puzzled.

"There was no wrong in it, Cougar," Laughing Stream intervened. "It is *your* blood that ran the same in her, not his."

"There is no difference," he spat harshly. "I expected—"

"You demanded my son be what you would not be," Laughing Stream accused. "You thought we could take the place of those lost to her. She hid when her father came to camp, but she loved her mother and remembered you were her clan. She did not forget, Cougar."

Clay nodded toward Swift Buck. "How soon did he forget that the blood we mingled made him her brother, too? How old was she before he crept to her mat? Thirteen, fourteen?"

Laughing Stream struck his face. "You dishonor my son. He felt wrong in wanting her, although there was no wrong in his heart. He left my lodge to hide his shame."

"He cannot hide from me!"

"Do not lift your hand against Swift Buck again," Gray Wolf warned. "He committed no crime in wanting a woman not of his own bloodline. The vengeance you seek is empty. He is weak."

"His weakness is soon to pass. Huera will see to that." Clay took his captive's arm and hauled her up.

Ronda Thompson

"Your woman may tend my son, but you are no longer welcome in my lodge," Laughing Stream said softly. Her head lifted, her dark eyes filled with tears. "I told you, life is not always simple."

The fire had lost its morning warmth. Coals glowed in the grate and cast a hellish hue against the hide walls. Lucifer paced before her. Melissa's gaze followed him across the tepee, waiting for an explosion. Anger seeped from his pores. The blue of his eyes glittered in the darkness.

Clay Brodie had tried to kill the very Indian that he'd ordered her to save. What had the Apache said? In her shock at hearing him speak English, she hadn't paid much attention to his words. He had whispered a name when she leaned close to him. Unconsciously, her gaze lowered. The doeskin dress held the same scent as the chemise.

"Who is Silent Wind?"

"She is not your concern. Keep quiet."

Melissa would not obey him. The woman had obviously caused a rift between Clay and the Apache he claimed as a blood brother. She hadn't figured out if the development would work to her advantage.

"Is she your wife?"

He didn't answer, just kept pacing, clenching and unclenching his fists. Melissa tried to recall the Apache's words again. What had he said to so infuriate Clay Brodie? He'd said, *When I come to you, I will not come as a brother, but as a man.*

"His sister?" she said, frowning over the implications. She felt her eyes widen. "Your sister."

Although the white man didn't confirm her suspicions, the glare he cast in her direction indicated she'd hit upon the truth. When he made the ridiculous accusations against the men of her caravan, he'd said his sister had been murdered.

"Was she a captive, too?"

"What?" he stopped pacing long enough to growl.

"I asked if your sister was a captive. Was she white?"

"And I told you, she is none of your concern."

58

Despite his anger, Melissa felt her own temper rising. "If she's the reason I'm here, I believe she is my business. They took a white captive to replace a white captive, didn't they?" She paused, realizing a flaw in her reasoning. "Then why give me to you? If she belonged to Swift Buck—"

"She belonged to no one!" He squatted before her. "She was not a captive. *I* am not a captive! Understand?"

No. Melissa did not understand. What other explanation could there be for two white people living among the Apaches? She needed Clay Brodie to have been taken captive. How could he be sympathetic to her plight if he hadn't suffered the same one?

"I've seen the scars on your back," she said.

He laughed. "They're hard to miss."

"How can you care about anyone who did that to you? The Apaches—"

"Didn't cause the scars," he interrupted. "My father did. My *white* father."

His explanation was like a slap in the face. Melissa instinctively drew back from him, but his hands on her shoulders kept her from retreating.

"My sister wasn't taken captive. She was given to the Apaches after our mother died. Our father didn't want her."

What kind of father gave his children away? What kind would beat them? And what kind of man would emerge from a boy with scars on his back? Although the explanation of his abuse was not the one she'd expected, was not the one she'd hoped for, Melissa couldn't find it in her heart to feel disappointment. Instead, she felt sorrow for his pain.

"I'm sorry," she whispered, gently touching his face.

The man jerked away from her. He seemed surprised, taken off guard. Deeply he stared into her eyes, until a hard expression replaced his confused one. He rose to resume his pacing.

"Don't feel sorry for me. I have no use for your pity. All I want is for you to learn your place here and heal Swift Buck."

"So you can kill him?"

The fact that he didn't answer immediately made her think he was weighing his options. A few moments later, she realized he had no intention of sharing his plans with her.

"Why not let him die if you plan to kill him?"

"He must pay for his mistakes."

"The way you've paid?"

The heat in his eyes flared when he stopped to look at her. His approach had her scrambling away. He pinned her beneath him, his face an angry mask hovering above hers.

"You talk too much for a slave. Gray Wolf thinks I should cut your tongue from your mouth."

She refrained from commenting, sensing he was waiting for her to make that mistake. The silence between them became a punishment in itself. His body, pressed intimately against hers, only served to remind her of his superiority. Clay Brodie stood well over six feet tall. His body was lean and well-muscled. If he'd wanted, she imagined he could have snapped her like a twig.

"Have you run out of questions, Huera?"

When she didn't answer, his features relaxed.

"Fear is a good teacher."

His taunt caused her to stiffen beneath him. If she cowered now, he'd believe she could be controlled by the threat of violence.

"Judging by the number of scars on your back, learning to be afraid was a hard lesson for you."

The slight smile he wore melted from his mouth. Something out of place shone in his eyes for the briefest moment. Something akin to respect. He ran his fingers down the side of her face.

"I don't think your soft skin would hold up well under the whip."

Melissa fought the impulse to mimic his earlier reaction and jerk away from him. His touch was gentle, a silken caress that wasn't unpleasant the way it should have been. Nor should she have stared into the face of Satan and found him as beautiful as David.

Confused by her thoughts, she said, "I also have a fondness for my tongue."

"I have a fondness for it, too," he countered, his lips closing the distance between their mouths.

For an instant, she was too shocked to react. His mouth wasn't rough or forceful against hers, but gentle and coaxing. She should have struggled, pushed him away, slapped his arrogant face. Melissa did none of those things. If she'd fought him, he would have found a weapon to use against her—a way to bring her to rein when verbal threats fell short of their mark. She meant to show him Melissa Sheffield wasn't a woman to be cowed. Not a woman who would willingly accept the fate he claimed belonged to her.

She lay beneath him, passive to the feel of his powerful body on top of hers, to the pounding of his heart and the rapid beat of her own. Even when his tongue stole inside her mouth, she didn't gasp at his boldness. Oddly enough, she felt as if they had been here once before. As if she had already experienced the feel and taste of him—and the traitorous emotions both evoked.

Robert had kissed her, but her fiancé was a gentleman. His mouth had never taken total possession of hers. His kiss could not reach deep inside and compromise her soul. Despite her vow to show no fear, Melissa was afraid. An unfamiliar tingle began to dance beneath her skin.

She couldn't breathe—couldn't think beyond sensation. When he gently sucked her tongue into his mouth, her passiveness fled. She splayed her hands against his broad chest and pushed him away.

The sound of their labored breathing echoed off the walls. The heat in his gaze scorched her. That she was at his mercy, and her strength would be no match for his, scampered across her mind like a frightened animal.

"Are you afraid of me, Huera?"

If she said yes, he would have won. Melissa wasn't certain she feared him as much as she feared herself. She feared the way his invasion of her mouth had stormed her senses.

"No," she answered.

"I can take you."

Melissa hoped he didn't feel the sudden lurch of her heart. Prayed he couldn't smell the panic his casual words brought. She shrugged. "You're stronger. To fight you would be useless."

He lifted a dark brow. "Then you are willing?"

"Weaker and willing are not the same thing. I can't stop you, but I won't surrender to the fear you think to instill in me by using force. You will have won nothing."

His gaze slid to her breasts. "I don't think that this man who you claim waits for you in Santa Fe would consider what I would take as nothing."

She met his questioning stare with one of sureness. "Robert won't judge me about matters I cannot control."

To her surprise, he laughed, and moved from his position on top of her. "You don't even know the world you came from."

Freedom brought her courage to life. "And what do you know of my world? I don't understand why a white man would walk willingly among Apaches. Who are you?"

Her release was short-lived. In an instant he was in her face.

"I will tell you who I am so the question no longer plagues you. So you will not ask it again. I am *Tchindees*. A monster. I am your enemy."

Chapter Six

For a week Swift Buck hadn't opened his eyes. Now Melissa found herself the study of his cold regard. She tried to ignore the Apache and concentrate on dressing his shoulder. The skin looked raw and puckered, but she felt certain he would mend to massacre again.

When the old woman realized her son had regained consciousness, Melissa was shoved aside. The woman babbled excitely in her guttural language.

Swift Buck answered his mother weakly. His deep voice was as low as Clay Brodie's. Melissa steered her thoughts from the white man. The enemy. He'd said little since the night he'd tried to strangle his blood brother and frighten her into submission. Mostly, he gave orders, taught her how to build a fire, how to make corn cakes, things important to her position of servitude.

Resentment festered inside of her. If Brodie wouldn't help her escape, she'd do it on her own. Somehow, some way, Melissa Sheffield would find her way back to civilization.

A name she understood brought an end to her plotting.

Clay had taught her the Indian pronunciation of his own name. She supposed she could count herself fortunate in a way. How many captives had translators?

She couldn't understand the words being exchanged between son and mother, but the expressions crossing their features were easier to comprehend. Whatever Laughing Stream explained to her son paled his already waxen skin. He countered. She shook her head in refusal.

"Bring him to me," he ground through his teeth.

Her gaze snapped to the Apache. "W-What?" Melissa stammered.

"Find Cougar and bring him here."

His English was good. She wondered if Clay had taught him. She also thought that, for a man barely recovered from his deathbed, the Apache was annoyingly arrogant.

"I'm his slave, not yours."

Swift Buck's eyes widened. He smiled, not a genuine one, but a sarcastic twist of his mouth.

"I see Cougar has not broken your spirit. That is good. Speak with disrespect to him, it is time a woman who could, did, but to me, and in my mother's lodge, your sharp tongue will be silenced, with a knife if necessary. Go now."

He didn't have to tell her twice. Melissa scrambled up and past the flap into the sunshine before she came to an abrupt halt. She still wasn't comfortable venturing outside of the two tepees where she'd spent most of her week. Heart pounding, she surveyed her surroundings.

Children squealed at play, darting in and around women poised at one task or another. Of the men, Melissa saw nothing. Not at first. As her gaze scanned the area, movement just beyond a cluster of tepees drew her attention.

Clay wasn't difficult to find in a crowd. If his bronzed skin and long hair easily disguised him among the Apaches, his height commanded attention. Unwilling to leave her place outside the tepee, Melissa studied him.

It took only a moment to surmise that while the women worked, the men played. They involved themselves in a game of sorts. The objective appeared to be who could shoot an arrow the farthest.

Although their skill with a bow was impressive, Melissa couldn't give them her respect. She shivered in the afternoon warmth, all too clearly remembering the sight of arrows whizzing past her. The soft thud they made upon entering flesh. Death unannounced.

Clay stepped forward. Muscles rippled along his arms as he stretched a string made invisible from her vantage point. When he released it, the arrow shot into the distance with rapid speed and lodged in the center of a tree. The stone-faced leader stepped forward and slapped Clay on the back. Shouts of good humor followed from the other men gathered there. They all seemed to embrace him as one of their own. All but one.

Another chill raced up her spine when she spotted the Apache. The first night of her captivity, Clay had referred to him as Tall Blade. He attacked her during the raid on the caravan. She had no doubt then, or now, that his intention had been to kill her. He hung back from the others, and if none saw the way he stared at the white man among them, Melissa did. There was certainly no brotherly love shining in his heated gaze.

As if sensing he had been discovered, the Apache glanced in her direction. Melissa wasn't certain she could as easily disguise her fear when confronting this man. His gaze swept her in a lewd manner. A way that made her feel like he'd stripped away her clothes and now looked upon her naked flesh. He smiled. It was a chilling expression that didn't reach his strange eyes.

She remembered staring up into them while he'd pinned her to the ground. At the time, all she'd thought about was the need to fight, to get away before he slit her throat. Now she had time to reflect on what she'd found odd about his eyes besides the glow of bloodlust. They weren't dark brown like Swift Buck's, or even a lighter hue like the wounded brave's mother. They were gold.

Rattled by the memories, Melissa glanced away from the

Apache. She didn't find solace. Tall Blade wasn't the only one who had noticed her standing outside the tepee. Several dark sets of eyes were leveled at her. She couldn't find the will to make her legs move, to courageously entrench herself among a hostile people. Clay wasn't too far away to hear her screams were she attacked. That small relief made her realize he could also hear her, and she called out to him.

"Brodie!" she shouted.

His head turned. Even from the distance, she detected the slight tensing of his jaw muscle. He turned back to the men, ignoring her.

"Cougar!" Melissa tried again. She shouted the name in Apache, aware that it sounded awkward. She waved her arms in the air to get his attention.

For some reason, the Apache men who stood with Clay found her antics amusing. They began to laugh and poke him in the ribs. The boy sent to retrieve his arrow returned, puffing and grinning. Clay snatched the arrow and placed it in a small pouch strapped to his back. He walked away. Not toward Melissa, as she expected, but in the opposite direction.

Stunned that he had chosen to disregard her, she followed his movements toward a crudely built corral. He bounded over the fence and disappeared, materializing at the gate with a horse. Not just any horse, but the most beautiful animal she'd ever seen.

The paint's head and chest were black. A ring of snowy white encompassed the area behind the front legs and spread to the flanks, where ebony began again. A perfect circle of white stood out clearly on the left hindquarter. When Clay turned the animal, in order to close the gate, Melissa saw that a matching circle graced the horse's right hindquarter.

Sunlight glinted off the stallion's coat. He tossed his pearly mane as the white man slipped a bridle over his head. Clay gathered the reins and gracefully swung atop the stallion. The horse tried to bite his rider's leg.

A gentle slap to the nose was his punishment. A squeal of protest from the horse followed. Powerful front legs lifted off the ground and pawed at the air. Melissa sucked in her breath, certain the stallion would unseat the rider on his back. As hooves met with dirt, Clay loosened the reins and pressed his knees to the beast's sides. The result sent her heart pounding against her chest. Mount and rider came charging toward camp in a full run.

In an unconscious reflex, Melissa quickly surveyed the area, concerned for the children who might have stood in harm's way. None did. The Apache women had gathered their chicks and stood lining a path—an open trail that led straight to her.

Her heart rose in her throat. If she hadn't known better, she'd have thought he meant to run her down. With a jolt, Melissa acknowledged that she didn't know better. He was the enemy. She wasn't certain what he would or wouldn't do. That thought uppermost in her mind, she ran. She'd almost made it to the tepee she and Clay shared when the thundering in her ears merged with the quaking beneath her feet.

A strong hand grasped her arm. She felt herself being lifted. As her stomach made hard contact with the horse's broad back, the air left her lungs in an unfeminine grunt.

Excited whoops of approval followed Melissa's scream of terror. Dust closed her throat. While she choked, her fingers searched for anything solid to grasp. She heard Clay swear when her nails dug into his thigh.

Frantic for something to hold on to, she grabbed the front of his leggings in search of his waist. The horse came to an abrupt halt. Had he not twisted a hand in her hair, she suspected she would have been flying through the air.

"Let go of me," Melissa gasped, struggling to free herself.

"You let go first," he said between clenched teeth.

She glanced up at him, noted his tense expression, lowered her gaze, and realized she held him in a place far from the waist of his leggings. She quickly released her hold. He let go of her hair and she slid off the horse, landing with a thud.

She scrambled up as soon as he'd dismounted. "What do you think you're doing? You could have killed me!"

"Don't ever do that again," he warned, his face within inches of hers.

"Do what?" she demanded.

"Don't ever screech at me like a bothersome wife. If you need me, come quickly and quietly, eyes lowered, and stand there until I acknowledge your presence."

Disbelieving, she took a step backward. "You tried to kill me because I embarrassed you in front of the other men?"

He stepped closer. "If I'd been trying to kill you, you'd be dead. Your lack of judgment doesn't call for a punishment that severe."

Clay slapped the reins he held against his palm, and Melissa couldn't help but jump. Her gaze lowered.

"You're not going to hit me with those," she informed him.

His brow lifted. "And you're not going to tell me what I will or will not do. I am your master, dammit!"

Again she flinched, not from the sound of leather slapping skin, but because of the anger in his voice. She wanted to cower, wanted to go to her knees and beg him not to beat her. Pride wouldn't let her. She turned away from him, untied the straps of her dress, and bared her back.

"You've probably been waiting for this a long time. Go ahead. Get even with your father."

Her words stung like rubbing salt in an open wound. Clay stumbled back a step. He glanced at the reins he held, noting the tremor in his hands. Slowly, he let the reins slide from his fingers. He moved her long hair over her shoulder. She tensed, obviously waiting for the slap of leather. He traced his finger down her back, marveling at the smooth whiteness of her skin. With a gasp, she wheeled around.

The green color of her eyes reminded him of the trees dotting the distant mountains. Her shoulders were as smooth and white as her back. He wondered how her skin would feel beneath his mouth, how it would taste. Maybe she had the sight, the same as Jageitci, Gray Wolf's woman, because she seemed to know what he was thinking.

She tried to step back, but Two Moons blocked her exit.

He was surprised the horse didn't swing his head around and take a bite of her. Clay wouldn't have blamed the animal. Melissa Sheffield, formerly of St. Louis, was a juicy morsel.

"Scream," he said.

The wariness in her gaze turned to confusion. "What?"

For emphasis, he retrieved the reins and slapped his palm again. "I said scream. Scream like you're getting the hell beat out of you."

"Why?"

He nodded toward camp. "They don't think I brought you out here to pick wildflowers. I'm supposed to be teaching you a lesson."

"For calling your name?"

"For being disrespectful."

Anger flashed in her eyes. "Would you turn around so I can get dressed?"

"Be quick. We've been too quiet."

Staring at a distant mountain peak, the place he called home, Clay wished he could ride away at that very moment. Leave Melissa Sheffield and the Apaches' test of loyalty behind him. He'd go to Santa Fe, get good and drunk, find himself a willing woman, and get good and—

A stinging pain cut into his thoughts. The reins had been ripped from his grasp. He turned, but not fast enough. The woman was already on Two Moons's back. Clay scrambled from her path, relatively sure she'd have no qualms about trampling him. He didn't run after her. He merely waited. Two Moons let her ride longer than he expected. She made it a short distance away before the horse pitched her off.

Placing his hands on his hips, Clay waited for her return. Two Moons trotted up, received an affectionate pat for his surly nature, then made a break for camp. Clay let him go, more concerned that his captive hadn't moved. He relaxed a moment later, when she rose and glanced around. His gaze narrowed on her. Surely she wasn't stupid enough . . .

"Damn," he swore, taking off after her. The woman had more speed than he'd anticipated, but she was no match for him. A boy whose father had a fondness for the whip knew how to run. Clay quickly closed the distance between them, making a lunge that sent them both to the ground. They rolled, stirring up the dust and adorning their clothing with thistles. Clay ended up on top.

"That was foolish! Even if you'd managed to get away, you wouldn't have made it through the night. There are all kinds of things just waiting for a sweet piece of meat like you to stumble into their path."

"I could have made it if not for that crazy horse of yours!" she shouted up at him.

"You wouldn't have made it with or without him. You're stuck where you are! Accept it."

"No!" She tried to pound her fists on his chest.

Clay captured her wrists and held them above her head. That's when the screaming started. She didn't scream in pain. She screamed in outrage, in denial of what he'd said to her. Clay let her. He figured she'd been bottling it up for the past week, and besides, they lay in the dirt, him on top, the woman screaming her head off. The Apaches would believe he'd just decided on a different form of punishment.

His ears were ringing by the time she wore herself out. Her hands went limp. She started to cry. Clay released her wrists and thought to rise when her arms encircled his neck. She clung to him, sobbing. His heart constricted inside of his chest.

Clay had never held a woman this way. Always, there had been a motive other than this to even lay with one. He brushed her tangled hair from her face and let her cry, wondering, once again, how her punishment had become his own.

Later, she sat across from him in the tepee they shared. Her hair was tangled, her face scratched, her eyes red and puffy. When they returned to camp, he doubted if anyone questioned what they had been doing in the brush. By the looks of his captive, he imagined they thought she'd been thoroughly molested.

He squatted next to her with a bowl of water and a cloth. She said nothing when he began washing the bloody scratches on her face. Her dazed expression worried him more than her refusal to accept slavery.

"What did you want to tell me earlier?"

She blinked, wet her lips, and seemed to escape her stupor. "Swift Buck sent me to fetch you. He wanted to talk to you."

"Is he well?"

"Not well enough to derive much satisfaction from killing him."

"When he is, tell him I'll talk to him."

"Besides the fact that he's an Apache, what's wrong with Swift Buck's feelings for your sister?"

"I will not discuss it with you. It's—"

"I know, none of my business." She took the cloth from him and dabbed at his temple. "I thought you considered him your brother."

"I considered him hers, too."

"Oh," she said quietly. "You look upon it as a sin."

"I look upon it as a betrayal of his trust," he corrected, rising. "Come, we will wash in the river."

Her startled gaze flew up to his face. "Together?"

He took her hand and helped her up. "I won't look if you won't."

Chapter Seven

Melissa fought herself not to look in his direction. The river felt cold but refreshing. To Clay's obvious amusement, she'd worn her dress and leggings into the water. She figured they needed washing anyway. The sun had almost set, so she felt comfortable enough to strip once the water reached her shoulders. Her gaze darted toward Clay. He washed a short distance away. She knew for a fact that he was as naked as a newborn babe.

After she'd waded into the water, she turned to him on the bank, surprised to find he'd already undressed. He hadn't acted at all shy, and from what she'd seen of him, he had nothing to be embarrassed about. The coming dark had cast him mostly in shadows, teasing her with flashes of smooth male flesh, only to distort areas she had no business seeing or wanting to see. But the shadows could not hide the obvious. He was all male. And he was her enemy.

A strange mix, Clay Brodie, Cougar to the Apaches. A man who threatened to beat her one moment and let her weep in his arms the next. A man who insisted she learn to serve him, then gently washed her scratched face. A man whose kiss . . . well, she wouldn't think about that.

"Hurry. The darker the day grows, the colder the water becomes."

She ducked her head beneath the surface, scooping sand into her hands to scrub her scalp. Once she had completed the task, she turned toward the bank. Her clothes lay in the shallows where she'd thrown them after stripping. She glanced at Clay from the corner of her eye. He still washed, the muscles in his back shimmering with droplets of water as he scrubbed. Since he faced the opposite direction, she hurried for the bank.

Once she made the shallows, Melissa snatched up her wet clothing and scurried into the trees. Her teeth were already chattering and she had trouble handling the water-soaked clothing. Irritably, she began wringing out the dress. That's when she felt it. The prickly sensation of eyes boring into her. She became very still, listening, her gaze searching the trees.

"Brodie?" she whispered.

Splashing noises from the river assured her it wasn't Clay who watched her, but she felt certain that someone or something did. A rustling sound made her jerk to the left. A deer raced past. Melissa laughed and put a hand against her pounding heart. She fumbled with her dress, struggling to get the wet buckskin over her head and hips. She'd barely accomplished the feat when she saw something move directly in front of her. A figure stepped from the trees.

Frozen in place, she stared straight ahead. The shadows hid his face, but there was no mistaking the fact that the figure was that of a man. Not a woman, not a child, but an Apache warrior. Melissa had a feeling she knew who he was, and that he hadn't been hiding in the trees for any purpose save to watch her.

When he took a step toward her, she felt more than defiled, she was terrified. She snatched up her leggings and ran toward the river. Glancing over her shoulder as she ran, she collided with a tree. Or it felt like a tree. Only this tree had arms.

"Don't go off without telling me," Clay said.

"Someone was watching me," she gasped.

He laughed. "The night has many eyes."

"No," she insisted. "I saw him. It was a man. He started to chase me."

Clay pulled her behind him and walked into the trees. He stopped in the same clearing where she had paused to dress.

"Whoever it was, he's gone." He turned to her. "And now you see why it isn't safe to sneak off by yourself."

"But I needed to dress," she argued.

His hand impatiently pushed his long hair behind his shoulders. "You were standing here naked?"

"Of course I was naked," she shot back. "I told you, I went into the trees to dress."

He glanced around the clearing again, more thoroughly this time. "Now I have to wonder which Apache brave will come stealing in the night to slit my throat for a chance to climb between those long legs of yours."

Heat exploded in her cheeks. Her embarrassment over his crude comment quickly became concern. "I thought these people were your friends."

"I thought so, too," he muttered distractedly, still searching the trees. He ceased his search and took her hand, leading her back toward the river. "Don't worry, Huera. I'm a light sleeper."

Surprisingly, she didn't have a doubt that Clay Brodie could protect her should the need arise. What bothered her was the way she walked so close to him. What bothered her was that she had already begun to think of him as her protector. Who, she wondered, would protect her from him if the need arose?

She deliberated these developments on the way back to camp. They were nearing the tepees when another form materialized from the shadows. It was the stone-faced leader. The man Clay called Gray Wolf. Melissa wondered for a moment if he had been the Apache watching her. She quickly dismissed the possibility. The leader hardly glanced in her direction. He seemed more interested in speaking to Clay.

"Stay here," he said to her, then followed the leader a short distance away.

Teeth chattering, her hair a wet, tangled mess, Melissa did as he instructed. She glanced longingly toward the tepee they shared and wondered why Clay hadn't instructed her to go on without him. He seemed reluctant to allow her to spend time there alone. Recalling what had happened at the river, she had to assume it was for her own protection.

The men's voices recaptured her attention. In the dark, the Apache rolling off his tongue so effortlessly, she could easily forget that the man the Apaches called Cougar was white. Although he'd told her not to dwell on the questions rolling around in her head, she couldn't dismiss them. What was he doing here? How had he come to be among the Apaches, to learn their language and their ways so well? Whether he wanted her to know the answers or not, Melissa intended to find out.

"Soon the days will grow longer," Gray Wolf said.

"They will," Clay agreed, wondering whether the leader had stopped him merely to chitchat. It wasn't Gray Wolf's way to waste time.

"And the nights warmer," Gray Wolf said, rubbing his arms briskly.

Due to his wet hair, Clay was also aware of the chill. He could hear Huera's teeth chattering from the distance that separated them. He didn't need a sick woman on his hands.

"Gray Wolf did not call me aside to talk about the coming summer," he said bluntly.

The leader smiled. "Cougar has always been a smart man. Too smart, sometimes," he added without a smile. The leader glanced up. "It is a good night. We hunt."

Clay eyed him coldly. "Now?"

"Why not now?" the leader asked.

When Gray Wolf's gaze strayed in Huera's direction, it was difficult for Clay to keep his from doing the same. He understood the leader's intent. This was another test.

"Do I bring the woman?"

75

One of the Apache's dark brows lifted. "Have you not had enough of her this day?"

"I do not trust her to stay alone," he explained.

The leader scratched his chin as if deliberating. "If she tries to escape, she will be captured and punished."

"She is mine. The right to punish her belongs to me."

"True," he agreed. "If she belonged to a family, it would be the right of any member. I have already found a place for her while we hunt. She will stay in Crooked Nose's lodge."

"With Laughing Stream," Clay commented.

"And your brother, Swift Buck."

He felt the twitch in his jaw begin. Clay tried to control it. "She has been in their lodge many times."

"She should sleep well there."

His jaw muscle jumped. "Yes."

"Then we go. Tell her quickly, before the night is too far gone."

"When will we return?"

Gray Wolf shrugged. "When I say."

Under normal circumstances, Gray Wolf would not insist he hunt with him. The leader would have asked, and Clay would have either said yes or no without his decision being questioned. Since Huera had entered his life, his come-and-go-as-he-chose existence with the Apaches had ended.

How could one woman bring such disruption? And why should the thought of leaving her alone cause him even the slightest discomfort? He shouldn't care what happened to her. His ability to remain indifferent to her plight was part of the test.

With resolve, Clay walked to where she stood shivering in the evening air. "Gray Wolf and I will hunt. Stay with Laughing Stream while I'm gone."

Even in the coming dark, he saw her eyes widen. "Gone?" she whispered. "You're leaving me here? Alone?"

Although he had the oddest desire to reach out and pull her close, to assure her she would come to no harm in Crooked Nose's lodge, Clay did not. He had trouble viewing her as he should, as the Apaches expected him to, and in order to pass their test of loyalty, he must harden himself against her. She was the enemy.

"Go," he said, pointing toward Cooked Nose's tepee. "They're expecting you. Learn from Laughing Stream while I'm away."

"But when will you return?" she asked, her tone bordering on panic.

He shrugged. "When I want."

For a moment, he thought she might burst into tears. Or worse, throw a tantrum in front of Gray Wolf. She seemed to be fighting herself to do neither. In the end, she straightened her spine and lifted her chin. She walked away without a backward glance. Her show of strength affected him more than tears or tantrums. Damn the woman, he had to admire her courage.

"Bring your bow and I will get the horses," Gray Wolf called.

His steps were leaden as Clay moved toward the tepee to retrieve his weapons. Once inside the dark enclosure, he closed his eyes and breathed deeply. Huera's subtle scent lingered on the air. He tried to ignore the pleasure the sweet smell of her brought him. Too much about his captive pleased him. Maybe a hunt was just what he needed. A chance to put distance between them. A chance to remember all the reasons he must allow her into his life, but not into his heart.

Moving to his belongings, Clay took up the weapons he kept hidden from her. His bow, and other belongings. When he returned, he would store them elsewhere. He removed a small black journal from a pouch, wondering if he shouldn't take it with him. Clay replaced the book. Huera would be staying in another lodge during his absence. He need not worry she would go through his personal items.

After snatching up his bow, he grabbed a water skin and left the tepee. Gray Wolf waited for him. Clay swung onto Two Moons's back, and silently rode from camp. He cursed Huera under his breath. Without thinking, he had turned to look back.

* * *

Loud snores kept Melissa awake. She stared up at the stars through the opening above the fire and cursed Clay Brodie. Two days! Where was he? Although she hadn't been beaten or molested during his absence, Melissa couldn't say she'd been treated well.

Earlier that evening, a young girl had approached her while she was helping Laughing Stream fill water skins. Having decided children weren't responsible for being born to uncivilized parents, Melissa had smiled at her. The girl had pulled a knife, lopped off a piece of Melissa's hair, and run giggling to her friends with the prize.

Her fingers strayed to the missing lock. She was in desperate need of a brush. And desired privacy above even that. She glanced across at Laughing Stream and her snoring husband, then turned on her side to stare at the fire. Two months ago, she would never have imagined herself in this predicament. Two months ago she'd been an innocent girl who longed for adventure.

The thought of cursing Robert Towbridge crossed her mind. In a way, her troubles could be blamed on him. He shouldn't have left her in St. Louis. Without him, society doors had once again slammed shut in her face. Due to her father's drinking, which had led eventually to his death, she was considered an outcast. A girl of good breeding but scandalous background. Robert had changed people's attitudes toward her, or so she believed until his departure for Santa Fe.

It was a sad lesson, to realize people only pretended to accept her because of Robert's wealth and influence in the community. When his letters began arriving, she'd lost herself in his adventures. She'd imagined building a new life together away from the scandal that plagued her. That's when the idea took shape. Her plan to join Robert in an untamed territory.

Her journey had gone terribly awry. The shame of traveling with prostitutes, the attack on the caravan, and her capture by Indians. She felt tears of self-pity rising to the surface. Melissa blinked them back. She would not cry. Not tonight, and never again in front of Clay Brodie. She doubted tears touched a man like him.

Not a man who could walk away and leave her alone and defenseless against a savage people. He would think her weak. Her father had been a weak man. He had died a slow death over the loss of her mother. Melissa would be nothing like him.

She started to close her eyes, when movement across the tepee drew her gaze. Swift Buck moaned softly and kicked the robes from his body. He'd been looking well for the past two days. She thought the Apache had made a remarkable recovery, considering the seriousness of his injury. Maybe he wasn't well. Perhaps the fever had returned.

Warring emotions kept her snuggled beneath the buffalo hides. Was it her duty to help those she considered the enemy? Would she be judged by God for her willingness to heal a heathen? Or for her unwillingness? She could not know the answer, just as she couldn't smother that within her that was called to tend the sick.

Silently, she crept to Swift Buck's bed. A thin sheen of sweat coated his body. He muttered soft words in Apache, words she could not understand, but which nevertheless tugged at her for the passion with which they were spoken. Melissa reached out and touched his forehead. He felt warm to the touch, but not overly so. Suddenly, a vice-like grip closed around her wrists. The Apache yanked her down on top of him, quickly reversing their positions so that she lay trapped beneath him.

Chapter Eight

A scream rose in her throat. The Apache stared down at her with the glittering eyes of a night creature. Melissa realized that to scream would be pointless. Who would save her?

"Please," she rasped. "Let me go."

His grip on her wrists slackened. "Why do you sneak into my robes, white woman?"

"I only meant to help you. I thought your fever had returned."

He stared at her for a moment longer before rolling away. Swift Buck sat up and ran a hand through his hair, a gesture much like that of his blood brother.

"You cannot squelch this fire in me, Huera. It burns for another. She came to me in a dream."

"Silent Wind?" she asked.

"Say her name no more," he warned. "You will call her from the spirit world. Now she is the one whose name we cannot speak."

Melissa was curious about the white girl given to the

Apaches, Clay's sister. To know more about her meant knowing more about her brother.

"Who were her parents? How did—"

He placed a finger against her lips. "It is not for me to tell you. Or for you to ask."

"She's the reason I'm a captive, isn't she?" Melissa persisted.

In the glow of the firelight, she saw him frown. "Do you not fear me?"

Should she tell the truth? Or pretend bravery despite her shaking knees? "Yes."

"And still you ask." He sighed. "Cougar has not taught you your place." His expression turned to one of curiosity. "I do not understand why. He knows our ways."

Regardless of the fact that the Indian probably didn't expect an explanation from her, Melissa said, "He's white. Maybe he does not always agree with your ways."

To her surprise, the Apache smiled. "You know nothing of this man."

She wasn't sure if a defense of Clay Brodie sprang to her lips because she truly thought he deserved one, or because she wanted to believe in him. "I know he wasn't with you when you attacked the caravan. I know—"

"He would have been," Swift Buck interrupted. "Had Cougar not been gone when we left to make war on the caravan, he would have ridden with us. Many times he has fought by our side against our enemies. His skin is white, but inside, he is Apache. These things you have let yourself believe about him, they are false, Huera. What little heart he has belongs to us."

His words drove her away. Melissa scrambled back to her mat and pulled the buffalo robes over her head. She hoped she would wake in the morning to find her conversation with Swift Buck had been a dream. Better, she wished she'd wake to discover her capture had been one. Clay Brodie couldn't be an Apache.

Apaches didn't have white names, white sisters, or white parents. Not unless they were taken captive as children.

Swift Buck suggested she had been lulled into a false sense of security. If so, why? And when would Clay Brodie show his true colors?

Her eyelashes fluttered downward. Despite the uncertainty of her future, exhaustion staked a claim on her. The past two days, she had worked by Laughing Stream's side from sunup until sundown. It was a hard life these women endured, a life far from the one she'd known, a life far from the one she had planned. She felt she must escape, and although Melissa fooled herself at times into believing she could do so on her own, deep down she knew that in order to survive the wilderness, she would need help.

His face came to her unbidden, on the wings of sleep. A face she had seen sketched in anger, and also in tenderness. His hair was dark as a raven's wing, his skin the color of rich maple syrup . . . but his eyes were blue. She'd barely escaped into her dreams when a nudge to the shoulder roused her.

"Come, Huera."

For a moment, she thought sleep still held her. Even in a dream, it bothered her to have conjured up Clay Brodie. She should be thinking of Robert. Of the life they would share once she escaped.

"Huera," he whispered again.

She liked the sound of his voice, if not the name he called her. Since it was only a dream, she said, "Call me by my name. I want to hear you say it."

"You are no longer her."

"I will always be Melissa Sheffield," she argued. "If you won't say it, go away. Let me sleep."

"Maybe the woman prefers my mother's lodge. And she is right. You should go away. You are not welcome here, Cougar."

Melissa sat up abruptly. She nearly bumped heads with Clay. It took the sound of Swift Buck's voice to shock her awake.

"I came to get what belongs to me," he said, nodding toward her.

His reference to her, as if she were a possession, made her

wonder why she'd cursed him for leaving. Her gaze swung to Swift Buck. The brave had risen from his mat.

"Take her and go."

"It is good to see you up, *brother*. Soon you'll be well enough to . . . talk."

"I have known you for many years, *brother*. The only words you wish to speak to me will be said with your fists."

"Do you have a problem with that?" Clay taunted.

Swift Buck smiled. "No. My fists wish to speak with you also. They will talk for one who could not."

"So will mine."

They stared at one another, locked in battle with their eyes. Melissa hurried to slip on her moccasins before a war broke out between them. She didn't want to be caught in the middle. Her soft tug on Clay's arm broke the spell between them. He stormed from the tepee, leaving her as always to follow behind. She glanced at Swift Buck before slipping through the exit. His legs were shaking, possibly with anger, more probably with the strain of standing so long.

"Rest," she instructed him quietly.

The Indian cast her a dark look, but lowered himself to his sleeping mat. "Huera," he called. "You believe the one we cannot speak of is the reason you are here. She is not. Cougar is the reason."

Melissa waited for him to explain. Swift Buck said nothing more, and if he had, she wouldn't have heard him. A hand came through the flap, took her arm, and pulled her from the tepee. She stumbled along behind Clay in the dark. What had Swift Buck meant? Why would the man she followed be responsible for her captivity? Since she hadn't gotten an explanation from the Apache, she would demand one from the white man.

Once inside the tepee she shared with Clay, Melissa wasn't afforded an opportunity to demand anything. He issued the orders.

"Build a fire and tend the meat on the spit. I have a deer to skin before I return."

"Nice to see you, too," she muttered sarcastically.

He turned, a towering black shape in front of her. "Are you glad to see me? I thought by your reluctance to part company with Swift Buck you had developed an attachment to him."

"Don't be ridiculous," she responded. "He may speak English almost as well as you do, but the man's a savage."

In the dark, he gently traced a finger down the side of her face. "So am I."

Before she could step away, he was gone. Melissa absently touched her cheek. "A savage with a tender touch," she said, then she shook her head. There was work to do, and for once, she welcomed the distraction. If she kept herself busy, she wouldn't have to think about the strange lurch of her heart when she'd realized Clay had returned. Or the one that followed the feel of his fingers on her face a moment ago.

Using the skills Clay had taught her, Melissa quickly started a fire. She drew back in disgust at the sight of the skinned rabbit on the spit. Once, she'd never thought about what the food she placed in her mouth looked like before Constance prepared a meal. However, she knew her grumbling stomach wouldn't allow her to refuse the meat.

She needed the strength it would give her. By the time it cooked through, morning would have arrived. Another day of gathering firewood, filling water pouches, grinding corn into flour, and countless other chores. Another day of fighting with her hair.

She pushed the tangled mass from her face and thought that if she had a knife, she'd cut it off. Another solution came to mind. Her gaze strayed toward Clay's belongings. Surely the brush he'd allowed her to use was among them. She crept to the buckskin pouches, slid her hand inside, and felt the bristle she sought. Melissa stared at the brush thoughtfully, glanced toward the tepee flap, and dumped the contents of the pouch.

A small gold ring caught the firelight. As she lifted the object, she realized it was tied to a thin scarlet ribbon and attached to a book. A Bible. What was Clay Brodie doing living among savages and carrying the word of God with him? She quickly stuffed the Bible back into the pouch and began gathering the other objects littering the ground. Melissa lifted another book, the leather worn and the pages crackled with age. Curious, she opened the journal in the middle.

A date was missing, but the name stood out clearly against the top of the page. Anna Wingate . . . Brodie. The last seemingly added as an afterthought. Her gaze scanned the entry.

> *The child stirs. Soon, life will rip its way through my body and deliver me deeper into punishment. Hiram anticipates the arrival as much as I fear the inevitability. Maybe the babe will die, or better still, perhaps I will. If God refuses me mercy, I pray the child is not a son and bears no resemblance to his father, for my heart could not suffer the torture, not with the plans Hiram makes for his future. He says the boy's name will be Clay, after my father, and the middle name will be, fittingly, Morgan. God, don't let me deliver a son into this hell. A daughter might stand a chance.*

Melissa's eyes stung from reading Anna's faded script, and her chest felt tight. How could a mother dread the birth of her child? The babe to be born was obviously Clay. Who were these people who brought him into the world? And where were they now? A thud outside had her quickly stuffing the journal back into the pouch. The brush followed. She hadn't had time to run it through her hair, and Clay would question how it came into her possession.

When he entered, she sat by the fire turning the spit. If she managed to keep her expression calm, her mind whirled with unanswered questions. He brought with him a large mound wrapped in buckskin. From the smell, she assumed it was the deer he'd skinned.

"Must you bring that in here?" she asked, wrinkling her nose.

"If I leave it outside, the scent of blood will encourage predators to roam into the camp."

"And what will keep them out of the tepee?"

"Me."

Clay settled across from her. His silence and the feel of his eyes had Melissa glancing up.

"Did you forget what I look like?" she asked.

A slight smile formed on his lips. "I don't remember your hair looking that way."

Unconsciously, she tried to run her fingers through the thick, tangled mass. "I didn't have your brush, and when I tried to use pinecones as I saw Laughing Stream do in the evenings, they broke off in my hair. If you'll give me your knife, I'll cut if off. It's too thick."

"You won't cut your hair," he said, rising. "The Apaches believe a woman's hair is her treasure."

"Her treasure or theirs?" she asked dryly.

He walked to a basket against the wall, one he'd told her to leave alone. "Unlike the whites and the Mexicans, the Apaches don't take scalps for decoration. The Indians believe that to take an enemy's hair is to take their power. Then the power becomes their own."

"So the more scalps a warrior takes, the more power he has?"

"Yes," he answered, digging around inside the basket.

The sizzling rabbit on the spit regained her attention. "Have you ever taken one? A scalp?"

There was no sound to evidence his return until he sat beside her. "Yes."

Her head turned in his direction. She felt bile rise in her throat. "White scalps?"

His lashes lowered. She noticed how incredibly long they were.

"No. Here." He held out his hand.

She was afraid to take the small bundle wrapped in old parchment. What if it contained scalps?

"Take it," he said. "Take it before I withdraw the offer."

With trembling hands, she obeyed. If she opened the package and some dried-up bloody scalp rested inside, she had no doubt she'd become ill. Nothing foul lay in wait for her. Melissa gasped. She held up the silver-backed brush so that it caught the fire's glow. It was slightly tarnished, but she felt certain she could buff it back to gleaming with a cloth made of buckskin.

"It's beautiful," she whispered, then abruptly glanced up at him. "Where did you get it?"

"It belonged to my sister."

"Where did *she* get it?"

He reached forward and turned the spit. "Not everything you see in an Apache camp from the white world has been stolen or taken from a raid. Different clans trade goods. The items change hands often, and no one knows the origin of most of them."

"But I know this one's origin." She held the brush out to him. "I must refuse your offer. If the brush belonged to your sister, you should keep it."

Clay took the brush, but rather than returning it to the basket, he began running the bristles through her hair. "She never used the brush. It meant nothing to her. Why be foolish and not use something for its purpose?"

She flinched when he met with a stubborn tangle, and she reclaimed her prize. "Thank you," she said softly, going for the tangles herself.

While she worked on her hair, Clay turned the spit and watched her. He'd thought the hunt had done him good. Gray Wolf was clever. He had spoken often about their childhood antics together. Boyish pranks that included Swift Buck. Clay knew what the leader was trying to accomplish. He wanted to remind him that along with the scars Hiram Brodie had put on his back, there had also been good times in his youth. The ones spent with his Apache friends.

The leader also thought to distract him from his slave, give him time to remember his loyalty belonged to The People, and not to the blond woman yanking half of her hair out. Clay had felt as if he'd had his priorities back in place, until he'd returned home. He'd meant to cook the meat himself and fetch Huera tomorrow. Tomorrow hadn't come fast enough. His gaze had kept straying to Crooked Nose's lodge. He had kept imagining Huera there, tempting in her sleep. Maybe too tempting for his blood brother to resist.

For once, Tall Blade hadn't been just trying to cause trouble when he'd said Swift Buck had a weakness for sun hair and pale skin. That his blood brother had kept his feelings hidden from him meant his intentions toward Silent Wind were not honorable. He would pay for taking advantage of his sister.

"Why don't you braid your hair?" he asked, once she had brushed the tangles out.

Her face darkened a tinge. "I don't know how. My mother did it for me in my childhood, and after her passing, Constance dressed my hair. Braiding was never my strong suit."

"I'll show you." Clay stood up and pulled his buckskin shirt from his leggings. He saw her blush deepen. "The blood," he explained. "Skinning's a messy job."

He felt her eyes on him as he pulled the shirt over his head and threw it aside. Clay bent before her. He reached out and pulled an equal amount of hair over each shoulder. She moistened her lips, calling his attention to them. He tried not to think about the sweetness he'd tasted there. Or the innocence. He supposed the man who waited for her in Santa Fe was a gentleman. Clay knew if she were his woman, her lips would not go neglected.

"Swift Buck told me your sister is not the reason I'm here. He said you were."

The statement took him by surprise. He quickly hoped to hide the fact. He shrugged. "Swift Buck is sick. He doesn't know what he's saying."

"He seemed lucid at the time. And he seemed so while the two of you argued. I understand why you're angry with him, but I don't understand why he's angry with you."

He pulled her closer, to begin braiding her hair. "His reasons are of no concern to you. And you can't trust anything he says. He's a liar."

"Did he lie to you about her?"

"He didn't tell me the truth. It's the same thing."

"But—"

In order to stop her ceaseless questions, he pulled her closer. "I forgot how silent the night can be."

She became still and quiet. The latter did not last long.

"I'm making conversation. You and Swift Buck are the only ones who understand a word I say."

"You ask too many questions."

"Then ask me some," she suggested. "They don't bother me the way they seem to bother you."

He wondered if their closeness made her prattle. She seemed nervous. Her eyes would settle on his face, lower to his bare chest, and quickly dart away.

"What happened here?" he asked, lifting a much shorter piece of hair.

"One of the Apache girls cut it from me. She seemed to think she'd won herself a great prize."

"It's called a *coup*. Stay away from the children. An Apache warrior is deadly, but not as fierce as an Apache woman protecting her children."

Silence stretched between them again. Clay figured if he didn't start talking, she'd start asking questions again.

"You said your mother was gone."

"When I was six," she responded. "My father is gone, too. He died last year."

"Then you're alone?"

"No. I have Robert."

Clay purposely furrowed his brow, as if he hadn't heard the name.

"My fiancé."

"No longer," he said.

She managed to look him in the eye. "That is not true. Robert will wait for me." Her gaze suddenly widened. "But of course, why didn't I think of it before? He's probably mounted a search. He'll be coming for me."

"I wouldn't count on it," Clay said honestly. "This is a big territory, and not many men are foolish enough to ride into Indian country. Not even for a beautiful woman."

By her expression, Clay imagined she wouldn't be dissuaded from her beliefs.

"You put the Apaches in danger by keeping me here."

"If this man is foolish enough to attempt a rescue, he's the one who will be in danger."

Her pretty jade eyes widened. "Promise me you won't hurt him."

The urge to laugh overtook him. Clay stifled it. If the man was foolish enough to try to rescue her, he'd be tempted to take his first white scalp. His last thought sobered him in truth. The sudden stab of jealousy was unfamiliar to him.

He hadn't felt the emotion in years. Not since he'd seen his mother cradle his baby sister close and whisper sweet words to her. And this didn't feel the same. This felt dangerous. Dangerous not to her, or to the man she claimed would rescue her, but to himself.

"I can promise I won't hurt him, because I can promise he won't come."

She stiffened. "You'd like me to believe that, wouldn't you? If I have nothing and no one to return to, you're conscience can take a rest. Robert will find me. Wait and see."

"It is you who will be waiting, Huera. Waiting for him as you've already done. I don't think he's too smart, or he wouldn't have left you behind in the first place. If you're looking for someone to blame, blame him. Is he worth what he's cost you?"

Her chin lifted, affording him access to her ripe mouth. "Of course he is. I love Robert."

Clay took both her braids between his hands. "Do you?"

She swallowed, but other than that, matched him glare for glare. "Robert is kind and gentle. He's a man of wealth and importance. He makes me feel secure and—"

"But does he make you feel alive?" His mouth nearly touched hers. "Does he steal that little sound from your throat when he kisses you?"

She tried to pull away, but Clay held tight to her braids. "You didn't answer me."

"I don't know what noise you're talking about."

"Let me show you."

Chapter Nine

Melissa splayed her hands across his chest to push him away. The feel of his hot skin sent shocks of pleasure racing through her fingertips. He slanted his mouth across hers and the protest she would have issued died in her throat. His tongue stole inside her mouth, tenderly exploring before boldly caressing.

In response, her fingers slid over the muscled rise of his chest, past the throbbing pulse at the base of his neck and twisted in his thick hair. His hands moved down her back before he pulled her up and closer.

They faced each other, knee-to-knee, thigh-to-thigh, mouth-to-mouth. The steady strokes of his tongue ignited a dormant spark within Melissa. She felt cast into the flames, surrounded by heat, helpless to resist. A soft moan escaped her lips when he mimicked the rhythm of his tongue with the suggestive grinding of his hips against hers.

"That was the sound," he broke from her to whisper. "The same one I stole from your lips the first night you slept in this tepee. Does the man you supposedly love know you're in the habit of kissing other men?"

She pulled away from him, shame and embarrassment over her actions quickly replacing the heat of desire. "I didn't give you permission to kiss me then or now," she said shakily. "Nothing you steal from me will change my feelings for Robert. You disgust me."

"Do I?" Clay recaptured the braids hanging down her shoulders. "Your lips are sweet and inexperienced, but they were hungry beneath mine. Should I kiss you again? Make you hungry for my touch, for the heat of my skin pressed against yours, for all the man you claim to love has not made you feel?"

More frightening than his threat was the sudden leap of Melissa's pulse. She didn't understand what dark power Clay Brodie held over her, but the simple lowering of his gaze to her mouth set her blood on fire. When the pressure on her braids tightened, when he pulled her closer, she knew she must resist. Stop him before there was no turning back, before he made a mockery of her feelings for Robert.

"I could never love you," she said.

The passion in his eyes flickered, died, and went out. He released her. "Love has nothing to do with that little sound I stole from your throat. What you felt was lust. It's only natural."

"Natural if I were an animal," she shot back.

He smiled. "We are all animals, Huera. The strongest dominate, and the weak either die or use their minds to outsmart their enemies. If you want to survive in the company of animals, you must learn to become one."

"Never," she whispered, scrambling away from him.

"*Never* is a word used often, and proven wrong more than right. Remove the rabbit from the spit to cool. I will bathe before I eat."

There was no sound to tell her he'd gone, but Melissa's senses, sharper than they once were, knew the moment he'd left. Her gaze traveled the tepee's hide walls, the strange utensils hanging on pegs, the basket holding another woman's possessions, and landed on Clay's belongings. He'd shown her a side of herself she hadn't known existed. A side she must suppress. She wasn't an animal, nor would she become one in this strange world, so different from her own.

While Clay bathed, she would read more of his mother's journal. Somewhere in the man he had become was the boy he'd once been. The white boy. She meant to find out when and why the transformation took place. And how to civilize the savage within him. If she couldn't, there was no hope of escape, or of being reunited with Robert.

Robert. Clay cursed the name as he made his way to the river. The name incited anger in him, anger and something he did not want to acknowledge. Jealousy. A sense of ownership. He'd vowed not to become Melissa Sheffield's owner. Vowed to teach her the ways of a good slave and ignore the desire she stirred in him. Yet here he was, angrily striding toward the river to cool his temper as well as his lust.

"Robert will wait for me," he mimicked. "Robert will search for me. Promise me you won't hurt him. Like hell I won't." Clay caught himself before he continued. He stopped and took deep, even breaths. Damn her. She had him acting like an idiot. Babbling to himself. He glanced around, worried someone might have witnessed his behavior.

The trees were silent. Too quiet. Preoccupied with thoughts of Huera, he had failed to register the presence of another. He saw a shadow to his left. Clay called a greeting in Apache. The man stepped into the moonlight. Rather than relax, Clay's senses went on the alert.

"It is good the others do not see Cougar roaming the night, speaking to himself like an old woman," Tall Blade said. "They might think the white woman has cast a spell on you. They might believe she is a witch."

That could work to his captive's advantage. The Indians were superstitious. They might trade her after he left to get her out of their camp. On the other hand, they might just kill her.

"She is nothing," he said flatly.

Tall Blade grinned. "I see the way you look at her. I be-

93

lieve you like the paleness of her skin. The lightness of her hair. I believe she is more than a slave to Cougar."

The Apache's taunts were not the easy banter exchanged between friends. A note of challenge hung between them. That and something more. The unmistakable dislike that grew stronger each time they met.

It hadn't always been this way between them, although Clay couldn't say they'd been friends, even in boyhood. Tall Blade's animosity toward him had started shortly after the death of the brave's father and the disappearance of his mother—about the time Clay turned twelve. Tall Blade was two years younger. For some reason, he seemed to blame him for the tragic turn of his life. But then, maybe he blamed everyone.

"Huera is none of your concern," he said shortly. "And neither am I." He took a step, but the Apache blocked his progress toward the river.

"When an enemy walks among us, it is my concern."

Did he refer to the white woman, to him, or to the both of them? Clay didn't really care. Tall Blade added to his earlier aggravation. The Indian unsettled him, made the back of his neck itch.

"I need to bathe before the water becomes colder." He stepped around Tall Blade, suddenly wondering if it was wise to present his back to him.

"You do not bring her with you this time?"

Clay stopped dead in his tracks. He and Huera had only shared a bath on one previous occasion—the time she'd thought someone was stalking her. He turned around.

"Is that what you are doing out here? Waiting for a chance to spy on her again?"

Tall Blade shrugged. "I am here to protect our camp. The river is its most shallow there." He pointed to the spot. "It is the place an enemy might sneak across."

His explanation was lost on Clay. The movement of Tall Blade's hand made something around his wrist glitter gold in the coming dark. Without thought, he stormed the Indian, shoving him up against the rough bark of a tree. Clay lifted the Apache's wrist. His heart lurched. Tall Blade wore his sister's gold bracelet.

"Where did you get this?" he asked, his voice raw with emotion.

The Apache glanced at the bracelet, back at Clay, and smiled. "I found it."

"Where?" Clay demanded.

The leer never leaving Tall Blade's face, he shrugged. "I found it on the ground close to where the women were killed."

Seeing his sister's possession cut into Clay. Sharp. He grappled with the pain and loosened his hold on Tall Blade's wrist. "You should have given it to Laughing Stream or to me. You know it belonged to my sister."

"Did it?" the Apache asked innocently.

Clay had the distinct impression that Tall Blade enjoyed his suffering. His eyes gleamed with excitement, his lips still turned up in a hint of a smile. Clay ripped the bracelet from his wrist and turned away. In his mind, he could clearly see the hand of his sister's attacker grabbing at her ankle as she tried to scramble away, dislodging both her shoe and the bracelet.

Grief and guilt warred for equal attention inside of him. He hadn't made it far when he realized Tall Blade hadn't explained how he knew of the time he and Huera had bathed together. He turned back.

"Stay away from her."

For a moment, Tall Blade's smug expression faded. His guard lowered, Clay saw the hatred staring back at him. Hatred and something more. A moment of alarm and confusion. As if he didn't know to which *her* Clay referred.

An insect found the moisture on Melissa's forehead of interest. She swiped the pest away and stretched. Tall stalks of ripened maize offered her a measure of privacy. A moment to be alone without someone watching her. Longingly, she surveyed the surrounding mountains.

"You wouldn't last the night."

She chose to ignore Clay's prediction, as she'd tried to disregard him in general for the past two days. When he'd returned from his bath, she'd feigned sleep, watching curiously as he opened the basket holding his sister's possessions before dropping something inside. Earlier that night, she'd read as much as she dared of Anna Brodie's journal, starting at the beginning. She hadn't learned much.

Anna's life was much like any other girl's. She'd written of parties and dresses and of a young man who'd caught her eye. Anna had also been a motherless girl, but at least her father ran a prospering fur trade and hadn't found more solace in a bottle than he had in her.

"Aren't you curious about what they're doing?"

Despite her mental oath to converse with him only when necessary, Melissa said, "I assume a ceremony of sorts is underway."

"They honor Mesa. She walks the path of womanhood."

His explanation turned her gaze toward the festivities. The young girl who'd cut a chunk of Melissa's hair stood proudly in the middle of a circle. One by one the women stepped forward to sprinkle pollen over her head and shoulders.

"That child can't be more than twelve or thirteen," Melissa muttered. "Mesa's far from being a woman. I certainly hope this isn't a wedding celebration."

"No," Clay assured her. "Mesa probably won't marry for another two or three years. This is her *naies*. The Apache pay homage to their children's passage to young adulthood. Both the boys and the girls. Mesa's merely begun her cycle."

Heat engulfed Melissa's face. She hurried back into the stalks. Clay's low laughter followed her.

"These women find no shame in a natural occurrence. Mesa has been given a gift in their eyes."

A trickle of perspiration weaved a path between Melissa's breasts. The afternoon heat was bad enough, without discussing so personal a subject with a man.

"Don't you want to watch?" Clay asked.

"No," Melissa snapped, wheeling around to find him too close. She stumbled back. The smile he wore widened.

"Are you afraid of me? Or of yourself?"

"Neither," she said. It occurred to her that if he insisted on pestering her while she worked, she might as well try to get useful information from him. "You asked me about my parents. You said your mother was gone. What about your father?"

"Gone also."

"Did they live in Santa Fe?"

"No."

Impatient, she threw an ear of maize in her basket and turned to him. "What binds you to these people?"

"A long friendship. Respect for their ways and their beliefs."

"But how did you come to be among them?" she demanded. "If you weren't taken captive and your parents didn't live close—"

"Why can't you accept that I choose to live among them? That I prefer their company to that of your kind?"

"Because I can make no sense of your decision!"

"Lower your voice," he said softly. "Maybe in time it will make sense to you. I must participate in the ceremony. Come, stand with Laughing Stream."

"At least tell me where you were born."

He ran a hand through his long hair. A sign he too grew impatient with the conversation. "There." He pointed to the distant mountains. "That is where I was born."

As he walked away, Melissa continued to stare at the place he'd indicated. The mountains? Why would two white people decide to settle in an isolated place like that?

"Huera," he called over his shoulder, and the irritation in his voice had her hurrying after him.

While she watched the ceremony, she would try to come up with sensible answers. Melissa took her place next to Laughing Stream. The woman almost smiled at her. Although Swift Buck's mother couldn't converse with her, Melissa felt comfortable in the woman's presence. She might be uncivilized, but she had gentle eyes, and a gentle spirit. She followed the direction of the woman's stare. The ceremony recaptured Melissa's attention.

She found the scene curious. Several objects were littered across the ground. A handful of Apache braves had mounted their horses, Clay among them. He sat taller than the others on his magnificent stallion. The sun gleamed off his bronze skin and the wind played with long wisps of his hair.

He was handsome, she could admit as much without feeling guilt. She was also not the only female present who noticed how fine a figure he cut upon his mount's back. Several dark eyes were focused on the man she currently shared her misplaced life with. She wondered why Clay had not taken an Apache bride.

It was another question she would ask him, one of many to help her fit the pieces of Clay Brodie together. When an opportunity arose, which wasn't often, she would read more of his mother's journal.

A loud war whoop startled her. A rider broke from the group and raced toward them. Melissa's hand went to her throat. She gasped when the brave slid sideways on his horse and plucked an object from the ground. As loud cheers broke out from the Apaches around her, the brave presented the girl being honored with a transparent rock that caught the light and reflected the joy on her face.

With sudden dawning, Melissa realized the objects scattered on the ground were gifts, presents that might be counted worthy in a young Apache girl's opinion. Another rider came thundering toward them.

His ride was no less spectacular, even more so, Melissa decided, since his gift wasn't as easily retrieved. From the rider, Mesa accepted a pouch made of fine doeskin tanned until it gleamed white.

It seemed as if the process of elimination determined who rode next. Clearly whoever ended up last faced the most difficult task. The items readily grasped while riding at full speed were the first to go. The event continued until Melissa found herself caught in the excitement. Never had she seen horsemanship put so dangerously to the test. Her enthusiasm ebbed somewhat when only one rider remained.

Clay's stallion pranced nervously. Melissa's gaze scanned the ground and found only one item left: a small white feather. A chant began. A single word.

"They ask to see his gift."

Swift Buck spoke. He stood beside her, pale but obviously much improved.

"I don't understand," she said.

"It is why they call him the cat spirit," the Apache explained. "Cougar has *Gakehondi*. Running power."

By the time she glanced toward Clay and back again, Swift Buck had left. He moved off toward the trees. A loud roar filled her ears. Melissa wheeled around to confront a frightening scene. Clay was racing toward them. The stallion's speed exceeded that of any horse she'd seen to present. Black hooves sent clots of dirt flying in his wake. One moment Clay sat on his back, the next he was on the ground, running beside the beast.

She blinked in rejection of what her eyes saw. No man could match the speed of a horse. Certainly no man could reach down, scoop up the feather, place it between his teeth, grasp the stallion's mane, and heft himself onto the animal's back, all without breaking stride. But he did.

Dazed, she watched Clay halt his horse before Mesa. The Apaches whooped as he bent down and placed a white feather in her hair. Melissa couldn't help herself, she began to whoop right along with them. Clay Brodie wasn't Apache; at the moment, she wasn't sure he was even human. When he turned back to his appreciative audience, his gaze locked with hers.

A current passed between them. In that brief instant, Melissa forgot who she was, who he was, even who Robert Towbridge was. Clay's chest gleamed with sweat. The male scent of him found her, heating her blood. Traitorous emotions rushed to the surface. A need, primitive and unfamiliar, tightened her nipples and quickened her breathing. A single thought entered her mind. Frightening in its conception, and forbidden in its sinfulness. *I belong to him.*

Denial immediately chased the thought away. Afraid Clay might sense her short flight into madness, Melissa turned from his gaze and walked toward the maize field. A movement in the trees drew her eyes.

Swift Buck stumbled from the brush. His dark eyes scanned the campsite. When they settled on Melissa, he motioned frantically. Concerned that the Indian had exhausted himself, she hurried forward. Halfway there, she realized no one was trying to stop her. The others were still caught up in the ceremonies. It would have been a perfect opportunity to escape.

"Hurry," Swift Buck panted. "This way."

"W-Wait." His retreat confused her. "I thought you were ill!"

"Come, Huera!" he shouted impatiently. "Jageitci asks for you. She is hurt."

Without hesitation, Melissa followed. As she picked her way through low hanging branches, it occurred to her to question the rashness of her actions. How easily she'd been lured from camp and Clay's watchful eyes. Soft moans drifted from the clearing ahead. Melissa almost stumbled over the leader's half-Spanish wife. She bent beside Swift Buck.

"What happened?"

He shook his dark head. "She would not tell me where the pain is, only to find you."

The woman's dazed eyes stared up at Melissa. They closed tightly as a groan left her lips and she clutched her stomach.

"Ask her if it hurts here?" Melissa placed her hands over Jageitci's abdomen. She felt a bulge she hadn't noticed beneath the woman's loose-fitting clothes. "She's with child?"

"Yes," Swift Buck answered.

"Ask her how many months," Melissa instructed.

The brave quickly related her question.

"*Cuatro*," the woman answered.

The use of Spanish surprised Melissa as much as the woman's calculation. She would have guessed her to be further along. "Are you sure?" she questioned in the woman's native language.

"There are two. I have seen them." Jageitci gasped, then brought the pain under control. "In my visions, they were strong, healthy. They cannot come. It is too soon."

"What happened?" Melissa asked.

"I went to bathe while the others busied themselves with the ceremony. In my haste to return, I tripped. The Apaches will see this as a sign my children are not destined to survive. You are from another world and have knowledge of medicine. Can you save them?"

Searching her memory, Melissa recalled an incident she'd overheard her father once relate to another physician. "Liquor," she whispered. "Swift Buck, find Cougar and tell him to get the whiskey." When the brave did not hasten to do her bidding, she asked, "Do you understand?"

"I will search his belongings and find it myself," he answered stiffly.

Anger coursed through her. "Your petty war has no place here. It will take you longer to search for the bottle than for him to get it. Besides, he's in better condition to bring it back. Go!"

Swift Buck bristled at her authoritative tone, but a moan from Jageitci sent him to his feet. "Remember who you are," he warned before disappearing through the trees.

"Now." Melissa sighed with relief. "I need to look at you."

While the opportunity presented itself, she methodically examined her patient. She judged the contractions to be of some strength—but hopefully not beyond discouragement. A sheen of perspiration dotted Jageitci's forehead. Her lips formed a tight line.

What seemed like hours later, though likely only ten minutes at most had passed, she heard the sound of running feet. Clay crashed into the clearing, a bottle of amber liquid clutched to his side.

"Thank God," she breathed. "I need the whiskey."

He eyed her outstretched hand. "First tell me what you plan to do with it."

"I don't have time to properly cower and beg!" Melissa lost her temper. "Give me the bottle."

To her astonishment, he obeyed. "I hope to hell you know what you're doing. Otherwise, a certain young chieftain will lift your scalp."

"I'm going to pour it down her throat and hope the pains stop."

"She's losing the child?"

Melissa uncorked the bottle with her teeth and glanced up at him. "Didn't Swift Buck tell you?"

The question brought a slight flush to his features—a face, Melissa noted, that wore a purple bruise along the jawline.

"He didn't tell me exactly what the problem was. Do it before—"

"Da!"

Bottle poised, Melissa jumped, spilling a few drops of the precious liquid. She glanced up to confront an unwelcome sight. The leader.

"Let me assure her husband you mean Jageitci no harm," he suggested.

"Talk fast," she instructed quietly.

Clay launched into an explanation. The leader's dark gaze settled on his wife, a grimace of regret crossing his features before he spoke.

"Remove the bottle," Clay said. "It's not their way to cheat destiny."

"She tripped. The pains have nothing to do with fate!"

"Gray Wolf has made his decision."

"What about hers? Doesn't she have a say—"

"Careful," he warned.

"Give me the liquor." The command came in Spanish. Jageitci stared defiantly at her husband.

With trembling fingers, Melissa obeyed. A shadow crossed her face. She glanced up. The leader drew back to strike her. A strong hand snatched a descending fist. Dark eyes locked with blue and waged a silent war above her.

Chapter Ten

"You challenge my authority," Gray Wolf growled. "A punishment became yours when you raised a hand against Swift Buck after I forbid it. Will you suffer the snake of fire for a slave's disobedience as well?"

Clay's stare never wavered. The line had veered from the middle this time. He wouldn't allow Melissa Sheffield to be beaten. "Yes."

The leader wrestled his wrist from the other's hold. "I gave you a choice. It cannot be taken back. You disgrace yourself over a white woman."

"And you shame all men this day. Huera is ignorant of our ways. Will you teach your sons and daughters with your fists?"

"*Yodascin*, those born outside, are not taught the same as our own!" Gray Wolf snarled. "She is the enemy who creeps across the mountains to steal our children's future!"

"*Cika*," his wife beseeched. "My pains are less now. Because of her, you might yet hold your sons and hear their cries of life."

"She brings only trouble," Gray Wolf argued. The hard lines around his mouth softened when he met his wife's sleepy gaze. "You have not spoken the language of your past since we joined. Does she remind you of what is lost? Do you regret—"

"*Da*," Jageitci whispered. "You gave me my freedom. I stayed and accepted all you are. Now you must do the same. Our beliefs walk a different path this time. My sight sees no enemy when I look at Huera. The healing gift shines within her. A light for a dark place." Jageitci's gaze slid to Cougar before her lids closed.

Gray Wolf bent quickly. When he turned toward Melissa, his stare held accusation and renewed threat.

"T-Tell him the whiskey's made her sleep," she stammered, looking up at Clay.

"Will she keep the child?" he asked.

"I can't say for sure. It didn't take much whiskey to stop her labor. I consider that a good sign. She should be moved to her lodge and watched for a couple of days. Complete rest is mandatory."

Clay relayed the information in a stiff tone. The leader's response filled him with helpless rage.

"He says you'll stay with Jageitci . . . and do her work, as well as your own."

"In his lodge?"

Her obvious fear cut into him like a knife. "Yes."

"B-But I belong to you. He can't demand this without your permission, can he?"

Her indignant tone brought a tense smile to his lips. "Gray Wolf doesn't need my consent. You answer to me, and I answer to him . . . while I'm here," he added under his breath.

She rose, and Clay imagined her knees were shaking. "You've warned me that disobedience here demands a price. Is the additional work my punishment for going against his wishes?"

"Yes," he lied.

Gray Wolf gently swept the sleeping Jageitci into his arms and glanced toward Clay. "The words between us were angry. I cannot change what has been decided, but the punishment will be private. Your first crime was against Swift Buck. The snake of fire becomes his to wield. I will wait until tomorrow."

"Gray Wolf is generous," Clay countered, with sarcasm. "How many lashes?"

"Four, until your tongue grew so wise. Five."

The feel of a hand curling around his arm halted Clay's rebuff.

"Thank you for protecting me," Melissa said after Gray Wolf retreated. "It was very—"

"White?" he supplied with a lifted brow.

"Noble," she decided.

The softness in her eyes took Clay unprepared. As had the sweetness of her lips when first he tasted them, as had the desire flooding his senses after he kissed her the second time, as did everything about her confuse him.

"Assume only one thing about me. I am not noble. Watch your tongue in Gray Wolf's lodge. If you anger him again, I won't be around to protect you."

His instruction drained the smile from her lips. As they approached the cluster of tepees, fear clouded her eyes. "He won't consider me his while I attend Jageitci, will he? I mean, he—"

"Gray Wolf has no interest in you as a woman." Halting before the leader's lodge, Clay pulled her around to face him. "He can demand your presence, but by Apache law, your body belongs to me."

Melissa hated the sudden heat his claim brought to her lower regions. Flustered by her reaction to him, she quickly entered the tepee. Once inside, panic threatened to seize her. Nothing looked familiar. She glanced nervously toward the flap.

"Cougar will not follow."

Her head swung from side to side. Only Gray Wolf, who added wood to a low fire burning in the grate, and his wife occupied the tepee.

"See to my woman."

"Y-You speak English?"

Gray Wolf's expression darkened as the kindling caught. "I speak the white words so Huera understands her fate. If the medicine you made today brings Jageitci's death, you die with her."

She fully understood his message, and now understood that he had been privy to many a disrespectful conversation between her and Clay.

"She won't die," Melissa said, hoping to assure him . . . and herself. "But she may still lose the child."

"To know my sons are gone would bring me great sorrow, but there are others inside us. Jageitci cannot be replaced in my heart. See that she does not seek the spirit trail, or your walk from this world will be a painful one."

Although his eyes reflected the cold promise of death, they also revealed a gentle emotion. Love, deep and encompassing, glistened in the ominous depths of his stare. He glanced away from her, but he failed to undo the damage. Gray Wolf became only a man to her in that instant. His threats stemmed from fear—his anger from helplessness. Human weakness.

"I'll need fresh water and clean cloths," Melissa instructed, bending over the sleeping woman.

"Huera does not command Gray Wolf," the leader warned. "Ask for all you need and I will tell you where to find it. My words to a slave are few. Long ago, Cougar, Swift Buck, and I traded our language in a game. Now the white tongue becomes a weapon. Its power is greater when hidden."

His stone-faced countenance returned. Gray Wolf may have achieved human status in Melissa's eyes, but he remained dangerous. She wisely nodded consent to his terms.

Later, after she'd sponged Jageitci and prepared a stew for the evening meal, Melissa dished up what remained of dinner. "I must feed Cougar," she reminded.

"Go quickly and return the same," Gray Wolf said. "My wife sleeps long. I want you here if she wakes . . . or if she does not."

Melissa suspected his wife's deep slumber had nothing to

do with the whiskey. A normal workday for an Apache woman proved grueling enough, without the burden of being with child.

The scent of pine and wood smoke greeted her outside. Melissa breathed deeply, but for the first time since her capture, she did not gaze toward the mountains and crave the civilization beyond. Her thoughts were with Clay. He'd stood up for her against Gray Wolf.

The leader had said Clay taught him English when they were boys. That meant he'd been among the Apaches for many years. Was Hiram Brodie responsible for his son's infiltration? And if so, why? She'd confront Clay with her questions while serving his supper, and she wouldn't be sidetracked this time.

With purposeful strides, Melissa entered the tepee. Her gaze sought the tepee's occupant. She found him sitting by the fire. He wasn't alone.

"I'm tellin' you, the whole place was up in arms about that attack . . ." The grizzled man's voice trailed away. "Who the hell—"

"Put down the bowl and leave," Clay interrupted.

Melissa supposed her mouth was hanging wide open. "But—"

"I said go!"

She wouldn't be ordered around by him. Certainly not this time. The stranger with him was a white man. "Help me," she pleaded. "You must—"

Before the words formed again, Clay rushed forward. Melissa struggled as he pulled her from the tepee.

"No!" she shouted. "He's white! He can help me if you won't!"

Clay clamped a hand over her mouth. "Hanes can't help you. You should have remained hidden from him. The only reason the guard let him pass was because the whole camp knows you've been temporarily moved to Gray Wolf's lodge. Go back before someone realizes he's seen you!"

Melissa wrenched his hand from her mouth. "Who is he? Why is he here?"

107

"Not now," Clay warned. "For once, do as you're told."

"He looks like a mountain man. . . . " She felt her gaze widen. "He's a trapper, isn't he? And you're very skilled at skinning yourself. You said you were born in the mountains." She recalled that Anna Brodie's father dealt in furs. "Your father was a trapper, and you're one, too, aren't you?"

"Not now," Clay bit out. "You put his life in danger by being here. Go back to Gray Wolf's lodge and say nothing about seeing a white man to anyone. Not unless you want his death on your conscience."

All hope of rescue flickered and went out. Clay's concern for the man's safety seemed genuine. She wanted to be rescued, but not if it put another's life in danger. Biting back a sob of frustration, she turned and started toward Gray Wolf's lodge.

"The bowl," Clay reminded. "Leave it, or Gray Wolf might become suspicious."

"I'm sure he'd simply question me about the matter." She wheeled back to him. "Why didn't you tell me he spoke English? Why won't you tell me anything?"

"I told you to return to him. Telling you doesn't get results."

"I'm going," Melissa clipped. "Here's your supper."

He read her thoughts even before she realized her intentions. Clay received a faceful of stew. He swore, wiping mush from his eyes. He cursed the day Melissa Sheffield stumbled into his life. Martin Hanes was certainly a problem he could do without. With a sigh, he turned toward the tepee housing another unwanted guest. He wouldn't think about tomorrow. About the punishment he would receive in his captive's stead. His back ignored his wishes and stung with faded remembrance.

An odd noise made Melissa cease her chores. She shifted the firewood in her arms and listened. Minutes later, a loud explosion echoed off the surrounding mountains. The sky appeared hazy but cloudless. Thunder wasn't the cause. She scanned the area, noting the somber expressions of those around her. Was it her imagination, or had two women returned her stare with hateful glares? A week ago it would not have seemed odd, but now the women mostly ignored her.

Nervously, she clutched her bundle and walked back to Gray Wolf's lodge. The leader had thankfully been absent when she rose to prepare breakfast. Jageitci slept peacefully through the night, if Melissa tossed and turned, fearful the woman's husband might seek distraction on her side of the tepee. Only the eventual sound of his steady breathing allowed her to rest.

Her lips tightened as she drew closer. Jageitci sat outside the tepee even though Melissa had given her strict orders to spend the day inside. As she looked closer at the woman, her irritation turned to alarm. Gray Wolf's wife was pale and her eyes were squeezed shut.

"Are you in pain?" Melissa asked. She cursed her inadequacy with the language when her inquiry received no answer. She tried again.

"*Sí,*" Jageitci whispered. "The snake of fire has bitten me as it bites him. Cougar pays the price of our rebellion."

Melissa followed Spanish better than she spoke it; however, she still couldn't grasp the woman's meaning. "I do not understand. What price?"

"Punishment for disobeying my husband. Cougar's skin takes the lashes yours would receive."

A knot began to form in Melissa's stomach. Moisture beaded her forehead. The sound registered in her subconscious—a whip's snap over sluggish oxen along the trail. "No," she gasped. "How do I find them?"

"To see his suffering would bring him shame."

"Where is he?" Melissa shouted.

"The sound travels over rocks that cross the stream and comes from the meadow beyond. But you must not—"

"Go inside and lie down. I must stop this."

"*Da,*" Jageitci called as Melissa darted away. "Huera! Come back. You are not free to come and go as you wish!"

Melissa wasn't listening. Her heart raced with her legs. Clay had lied to her. She should have known his interference yesterday wouldn't go without consequence. A tear slid down her cheek as she ran, blond braids bouncing in the sunlight. Another shout issued. Melissa ignored the warning, unaware that a bow lifted, a thin line of sinew stretched, and an arrow aimed itself at her back.

Clay clenched his jaw muscle. Sweat trickled into his eyes as he waited for the whip's whistle—a whirling noise that preceded rawhide. Swift Buck's hand lacked enthusiasm. He obviously thought the punishment unjust for nothing more than a silver-dollar shiner. Using their fists might have been avoided altogether had either of them taken the time to listen. All Clay remembered seeing after Huera slipped into the woods with Swift Buck was red.

He'd been headed in their direction when the brave came crashing from the trees, running toward the tepee he once called his own. The discovery of Swift Buck frantically going through his belongings further angered him. Clay demanded to know where Huera was—Swift Buck demanded the location of his whiskey. Neither were of a mind to answer the other's question.

Fighting came as naturally as breathing to Clay. After Swift Buck lost his patience and dealt a blow, he'd responded in kind. It might have continued had Gray Wolf not entered the tepee and put a stop to it. Only then did Swift Buck's urgent demands make sense. Knowing he was the faster of the two, Clay had quickly found the whiskey and run ahead.

Swift Buck had evidently been ordered to stay behind, no doubt soothed by the compensation Gray Wolf promised him. Hell, the brave had him at a disadvantage. Why wasn't he making the most of the situation?

"Get it over with," he ordered hoarsely. "Waiting's the worst."

The sound came. Clay took a deep breath and tightened his grasp on the ropes. Gray Wolf respected him enough not to order that he be tied. Strips wrapped around two trees were used for leverage. A crack, a pause, then the pain. His body lurched, the sting burned all the way to bone. A groan rose in his throat. His knees grew weak.

How many was that? Four? He must concentrate on something else—remove himself from the screaming flesh on his back. His mind fastened on last night's confrontation with Martin Hanes. The enticement of liquor and women had changed the mountain man's plan to go home. Instead, he'd ridden to Santa Fe.

The poster Hanes had withdrawn from his saddle pack had taken Clay unprepared. Whoever the sketch artist had been, he'd captured Melissa Sheffield's likeness well.

Robert Towbridge, the pitied bridegroom, had plastered the reward for her return on every shop window in town. Clay had almost laughed after scanning the poster. No man in his right mind would risk hide and hair to rescue a captive for the measly bounty promised.

Towbridge was either sadly ignorant or very smart. Maybe he no longer wanted for a wife a woman who'd been living with Indians. Clay's response to Hanes's demand that he return the poor girl to her intended now echoed in his ears. *She belongs to me now!*

Why had he said that? Poor girl, his ass. She wasn't the one on the bad side of a whip, hoping like hell she wouldn't cry out. He felt guilty about his abruptness with Martin, as well. Hanes was the only white friend he had, and the only reason he didn't judge a whole race by the actions of two. He'd sent his trapping partner away, fuming about Clay's lack of conscience over the woman's welfare.

It was his damn conscience that had gotten him into this predicament. Women seemed destined to be his downfall. Early in life he'd realized his attempts to win his mother's approval were useless.

After that, Clay had gone the opposite direction and concentrated on being everything she hated most—his father. He'd vowed never to suffer for a woman's sake again. The whip's whistle sounded once more, proving otherwise. In the silence before lash met skin, he thought he heard Huera's voice. He blotted out the sound, knowing she wouldn't venture here, knowing he must escape his body to stand the pain.

"Stop!" On shaky legs Melissa rushed forward to snatch Swift Buck's wrist. The sight she'd stumbled upon made her feel sick, made her head spin. "How can you do this to him?" she shouted at the Apache.

"I have no choice," Swift Buck answered through clenched teeth. "I am ordered to give his punishment. Go quickly. He would not want—"

"Me to see his shame? Or he wouldn't want me to see the savagery of the people he values above his own?" Her angry gaze sought Gray Wolf and pinned the leader with an accusing glare. "Is this the way you show gratitude for saving your child?"

"Huera," Swift Buck warned softly, "go before you—"

"Receive the beating he took for me?" she finished, dangerously outraged. With an expression insulting in its lack of fear, she placed herself at Clay's torn and bloody back. "You'll have to go through me to get to him."

She waited for the whip's answer, and when it did not come, walked around Clay. Sweat ran in rivulets down his chest. His eyes didn't focus or register her presence. Melissa looked closer. He seemed in a daze.

"Clay?"

He blinked at the sound of his name. A loud gasp followed when his body absorbed the pain. "What the hell are you doing here?" he demanded in a raw voice.

Melissa pulled herself up to meet his hard gaze. "I've come to save you."

The muscle in his jaw jumped. "You can't save me. You have no business here. Return to camp." His gaze lowered. "You're bleeding."

She glanced down. A bright red stain had soaked through the side of her dress. She remembered the sharp sting she'd felt earlier and suddenly felt dizzy. It wasn't the sight of Clay's blood that brought the darkness, but the loss of her own.

"What happened?" Melissa asked a while later.

"Lie still," Clay ordered. "You've been grazed by an

112

arrow. Tall Blade insists he thought you were trying to escape. Since his actions were acceptable under the circumstances, there's little I can do about it. Jageitci's offered to stitch you up."

"She should be resting."

Her soft scolding brought a tense smile to his lips. He fought his own dizziness and contemplated Melissa Sheffield's complexity. She called these people savages, yet mothered those under her care. Why had she risked her life to search for him?

Why had she tried to save him? She was truly an extraordinary woman. His vision grew blurry, his thoughts vague; then he journeyed to a place beyond thought or pain, a land of muted voices and blackness, blessed oblivion.

Chapter Eleven

Although the water she added to a mixture of dried venison and piñon nuts flowed from a container made of buffalo entrails, Melissa handled the flask as easily she would a sturdy crock pitcher. Without her usual shudder of repulsion, she dipped a spoon fashioned from the hoof of an animal into the broth and stirred.

A low groan from across the fire sounded as she rose to stretch. Her side ached with the strain. The tightly stitched skin pulled taut, a reminder that action without thought extracted a serious price. Not only had she paid for her rashness, but Clay Brodie had paid for his, as well.

For three days she'd drifted in and out of consciousness within Gray Wolf's lodge and under Jageitci's care. When she regained her faculties, the first thing she noticed was Clay sitting quietly in the shadows and the unnatural glow in his eyes. Because he'd refused treatment, his cuts had become infected. She must tend to him.

"Swift Buck, I'll need your help."

Melissa knew that the brave sat outside, that he'd taken up

a post since she'd humbly asked permission to move Clay yesterday. She hadn't pardoned Swift Buck for his part in the whipping, but what lay ahead couldn't be handled with only her own strength. The Apache entered.

"I must use what's left of the whiskey on his back," Melissa said. "He's not going to lie still for it. Since you like to see him suffer, you can help hold him down."

Her gaze lifted in time to see a red flush spread over Swift Buck's face.

"I did not enjoy using the snake of fire on Cougar," he protested. "I thought our fists would speak to each other first, then the words would come. When the lash struck him, I felt the sting, and knew that what is in my heart for Cougar has not died. The anger between us must end if we are to be brothers once more."

She lifted a blond brow. "From what I've learned about his past, you've proven yourself the sort of man he could call family. Do you think he'll just forgive and forget what you've done to him?"

The Indian shook his head. "Cougar does not forget. He knows I must follow our leader's orders, but did not see how his pain sickened my spirit. Forgiveness is not within him. He remembers the lessons of his childhood too well."

Stiffly, Melissa fetched what remained of the whiskey. After uncorking the bottle with her teeth, she nodded toward Clay's covered form. "He's been unconscious most of the day. This should wake him up. Hold his shoulders. I'll do my best to keep him still from the hips down."

So instructing, she maneuvered herself into position, straddling Clay before settling her weight on the firm muscles of his buttocks. Indecent as the pose appeared, she doubted Swift Buck gave the matter a thought, and concentrated on the task at hand.

She eyed the bottle's meager portion with a frown. The devil's brew had served her well. When she poured the whiskey over Clay's raw back, he responded within seconds. He groaned, swore, then bucked. Realizing that her strength combined with Swift Buck's wouldn't be sufficient, Melissa scrambled from her position.

"Let him go!"

Her warning sounded too late, as the Apache fell victim to Clay's flailing fists. The blow knocked him backward. Before he recovered, Clay was on him.

"You won't ever hit me again!" he shouted.

Momentarily dazed by his words, Melissa stood frozen in place. When Clay lifted his fist to strike a blow, she roused herself.

"No!" She ran to Clay and grabbed his hand. His gaze gleamed with fevered brightness when he looked down at her.

"You," he accused, shoving Swift Buck away. "Why can't you admit you want me to kill him? Because it's not civilized? It's not Christian? Grab up that Bible you read aloud every time I'm within hearing distance—read to me of love, sacrifice, and forgiveness while that red-haired bastard teaches me about hate, greed, and vengeance!"

Delirious. Clay was obviously caught in a nightmare. A result of his fever. She backed away from him, fearful that the anger in his voice might easily erupt into violence. Men in a delirious state were dangerous. A man filled with an obvious need to settle a past score, doubly.

"I'm Melissa, Huera, remember?"

Her question achieved no result. Clay kept stalking her.

"Don't pretend you don't know what he does to me. Do you think I'm just clumsy? Why won't you tell him to stop! Why, Mother?"

If the rage in his voice hadn't cracked, if Clay's thunderous expression hadn't turned to hurt, Melissa wouldn't have subtly shook her head to instruct Swift Buck to cease his careful approach. Clay's hands were overly warm as they encircled her neck. She met his confused gaze with wary curiosity.

Would he try to kill her? Could a son actually murder his own mother? The pressure around her throat tightened for a moment before Clay released her. He went to his knees. When he glanced up, a man no longer knelt before her, but a boy.

"What have I done to make you despise me? I thought it might be because I'm part of him, but then Rachel came and you held her close and sang songs to her. Why can't you touch me? Why can't you love me?"

That plea, delivered in the husky voice of a man and laced with childish vulnerability, brought a knife-sharp stab to Melissa's heart. She'd thought she wanted to find the boy in him, but she had no idea the monstrosities that had been committed against him. Why had Anna treated him as badly as his father? She reached forward to touch his hair.

"Your parents are gone. They won't hurt you anymore."

"You are wrong," Swift Buck said quietly. "Those who scarred him, turned him against his own kind, hold him still. I do not forgive Cougar for punishing the one I cannot speak of, but now the reason is more clear to me. It was with her coming that Cougar realized the truth about his mother. He would not speak of her in our childhood. He was ashamed, but he thought the wrongness came from himself and not from those guilty."

"Why would a mother be so cruel to her child?" Melissa whispered hoarsely, never glancing away from Clay's mesmerizing stare. Her touch seemed to place him in a trance. "How could she not love him?"

"The answer is gone. It died on the mountain."

Perhaps not, Melissa mused. The journal might still unravel the mystery. But now, she must tend to Clay's physical wounds. "Leave," she instructed Swift Buck.

"Do you not fear Cougar while the fever controls him?"

Glancing down into his dazed eyes, she answered, "No. He won't hurt me."

Swift Buck eyed her with skepticism before moving toward the tepee exit. Clay suddenly jerked from her touch and crawled to his mat. Coating his back with healing roots would have to wait. When he slept, she'd finish her administrations. Tired to the teeth, Melissa mentally tallied her list of tasks to be completed as day approached dusk.

More water must be fetched, a bundle of wood for morning, not to mention a load for Jageitci's lodge. Because she'd been unable to fulfill her obligation to handle the woman's chores, Melissa felt honor-bound to do what she could now. The sinew caused her skin to itch, but at least Jageitci had sewn nice straight stitches.

After removing the broth from the fire, Melissa searched for the water skins to be filled. They lay next to Clay's pouches. She glanced nervously toward where he'd crawled beneath his robes.

If her curiosity had been piqued before, Clay's delirium and what it had revealed to her made the journal impossible to ignore. Melissa fumbled inside the pouch and removed it. She nervously scanned the entry before her.

> *Hiram has his revenge. I watched Clay today from the safety of my bedroom window. Although I can scarce stand to look at him without remembering, without the pain, I forced myself and hated the truth my heart has tried to deny. Today I saw the promise Hiram gave me nine years ago when the nightmare first began. My son is a savage.*

A low groan caused her to jump and clumsily drop the journal. Quickly, Melissa replaced the diary. The last line of Anna's entry echoed in her head. Her gaze traveled to the lump beneath Clay's buffalo covering. He claimed to be a savage. His own mother thought he was one, and yet, he'd taken a beating that should have been Melissa's. He had not been violent with his slave, had not done the many unspeakable things he might have done.

He hadn't helped her escape, though, reason argued. He'd challenged the love she felt for Robert and made her pledge weak with his lips. Clay Brodie was no gentleman. He rode a horse and shot a bow with the same skill she'd seen the Apaches display. And still, something beyond his rugged beauty attracted Melissa, seduced her into caring that his back was torn and bloody, that his parents had mistreated him, that he seemed neither fully white nor totally Apache, but to her, a man misplaced.

Realizing she was wasting precious time, Melissa grabbed up the water skins and left the tepee. Swift Buck fell into step beside her.

"Stay within sight of the women," he instructed. "Cougar's eyes cannot watch you, and so the others will. If you—" His face darkened. "—if you must leave, let the others know."

With a nod, Melissa left the brave and ventured out among the women. She'd gathered two piles of firewood before her need to be excused could no longer be ignored. She stood still until one of the women glanced in her direction, then used her hands to explain her departure. The woman said something to the others and they snickered. Melissa assumed her request had been granted when they returned to their tasks.

Firewood strapped to her back, and water skins slung over one shoulder, Melissa made her way toward the trees skirting the stream. She quickly attended to her needs, spurred by the sounds of children nearby and the lull of conversation in the not-too-distant clearing. Having emerged from her hiding place, Melissa glanced toward the stream. Filling the water skins was next on her list of chores.

She chewed her bottom lip. Not more than a few minutes had passed since she'd walked into the trees. Perhaps she should fill the skins before returning. The thought of the time to be saved propelled her toward the stream. She pulled the skins from around her neck and dunked them in the fast-moving water.

Once she'd settled the last skin around her neck, rising proved difficult. She had firewood strapped to her back as well as the weight of the full water skins to contend with. After a couple of attempts, she managed to gain her feet. She started back toward camp, but from the trees, a dark shape emerged to block her path.

Her heart slammed against her chest. She knew the Indian. Tall Blade. The Apache who'd tried to kill her once, the man who she suspected had spied on her while she dressed. A man whose strange golden eyes glared down at her—and the message she read in his gaze was not one of peace.

Ronda Thompson

He grinned at her, more of a sneer than a smile. She took a step back, but the sound of the rushing river limited her ability to retreat. When the Apache's strange eyes raked her body in a suggestive manner, she decided drowning would be preferable to an attack by the man. Before she could turn and run, however, he grabbed one of the braids hanging over her shoulders and pulled her closer.

His scent sickened her. He didn't smell of wood smoke and sunshine, but of filth. Hoping the Apache understood English the same as Swift Buck and Gray Wolf, she said, "Let go of me."

Her words had no effect on him. He didn't release her. The man boldly splayed a dirty hand over her breast. She recoiled from his touch. Melissa tried to pull away, but the Apache dragged her toward the trees. Fear engulfed her. She wanted to scream for help . . . but would the Apaches come to her aid, or simply stand by and witness the attack?

Feeling a rough shove, Melissa tumbled to the ground. With the firewood strapped to her back, scrambling up became impossible. Tall Blade wasted no time. He was on her in seconds, his touch painful and determined. When he shoved his hands beneath her dress, fumbling with the ties to her leggings, she swiped at his face. Her broken nails left jagged, bloody scratches down one side of his face.

Tall Blade's eyes widened. He brought a hand to his cheek, pulled it away, and stared at the blood on his fingers. With a growl of outrage, he pulled a knife and held the sharp blade against her throat. Melissa had no doubt he would kill her. She almost welcomed death. At least she would die without suffering defilement.

"*Da!*"

Swift Buck's angry features appeared above them. Still, the knife remained at her throat. Words were exchanged between the two Apaches. A heated exchange, a battle of wills. Finally the pressure against her throat vanished. Tall Blade rose, glared at her, and stomped away.

"Now you see the danger of wandering away from the

120

others and not quickly returning," Swift Buck scolded. "In your world, are there not men who only follow the darkness of their hearts?"

"Yes," she managed to whisper. Melissa brought a hand to her throat in an unconscious gesture. When the Apache made no attempt to help her up, she rolled to the side and struggled into a sitting position.

"I wanted to fill the water skins before returning to camp."

"If I had not noticed you had been gone too long, you would not be returning. Wise women travel together. In our world, a lone animal, one that is weaker, becomes a meal for the strongest. Remember this lesson, Huera."

On shaking legs, she managed to rise. Melissa adjusted her dress and the water skins around her neck. "Thank you," she said softly. "If you hadn't come looking for me . . ." Her voice trailed away.

"Yes, Tall Blade has much hatred in his heart for the whites. He might have killed you. We are even in the lives we trade. Go to Cougar. He needs your medicine."

She didn't balk at his orders. Melissa was all too anxious to return to the tepee that had oddly become her haven. Today she had learned a lesson. Not only would she never venture off alone again, but she realized how different her life here might be without Clay. What would happen to her if he died? The answers were too horrible to contemplate. She hurried toward camp, and once among the women, moved slowly, with her gaze lowered submissively.

After depositing a bundle of firewood in front of Gray Wolf's lodge, Melissa went to her own, where she promptly collapsed. She began to tremble violently, the shock of the attack just beginning to register. Should she tell Clay what had almost happened? Her gaze strayed toward his sleeping mat. He lay huddled beneath the buffalo robes.

She found that odd, since the morning chill had disappeared hours ago. Stranger yet was the way the hides quivered. In the silence, she noticed the sound of his teeth clicking together. Melissa hurried to his side. She threw back the heavy robes and gasped. Although Clay's hair and skin were damp with sweat, his body jerked, wracked with chills that resulted from fever.

"So cold," he whispered hoarsely.

Fumbling to remove the water skins from around her neck, she pitched more wood on the fire and placed a hand against his forehead. He felt hot to the touch, but his fever hadn't yet reached the point where she would consider submersing him in the stream as she had done with Swift Buck.

The best thing to do at this point was to wait and see if it broke. She sat beside him for a few minutes, and when she could no longer stand the sight of his shivering, lifted the robes and climbed into his bed.

He needed the heat of her body, and from a medical standpoint, Melissa saw nothing wrong with slipping from her dress to allow him full access to her warmth. She drew him to her like a fire beckoned a man just come in from the cold. Clay covered her, his head nestled against the rise of her breasts.

Melissa tried to ignore the sensations having his bare flesh pressed against her nakedness brought. She tried to view him as a patient rather than a man, and tried not to notice that he was hard everywhere she was soft.

Her hands crept to his hair, brushing the damp locks away from his face. She traced the strong line of his jaw, then lowered her fingers to his broad shoulders. She supposed she should reach for the mixture of herbs she'd concocted and doctor the angry cuts on his back.

Duty did not immediately call her to do so, and instead, Melissa held him to her for a while longer. While the savage in him slept, her defenses lowered. She admitted she found Clay Brodie attractive. In face and form, she'd never seen a man to rival him.

The boy he'd become when delirium claimed him spoke to the deepest part of her soul, a soul that had also suffered the pain of losing a mother, the resentment of watching a father slip slowly away, lost to the numbing comfort of a bottle. Were she to be totally honest with herself, she might admit that she had accepted Robert's proposal, not because she loved him, but because she was afraid of being alone. Afraid of being an outcast. Afraid of everything.

Fear drove people to desperation. Was it now driving her into the arms of the enemy? Her fingers returned to Clay's long hair. She wasn't afraid of him. Her fear stemmed from the way he made her feel. The shame. He was right.

Robert was safe and secure, but he couldn't penetrate the walls she'd built around her heart. Everyone she loved left her. The secret was simply not to open herself to the possibility of pain. She'd closed off her feelings, and the man on top of her had managed to slip past the gate.

Exhaustion must have claimed her. When Melissa resurfaced from a sea of dreams, her skin slick with sweat, the tepee was dark except for a few glowing embers. She glanced up into the glittering eyes of her patient. The cat had awakened.

"Tell me what you're doing half-naked beneath me, Huera. Otherwise, I might jump to the wrong conclusion."

Chapter Twelve

He sounded wonderfully lucid. Melissa sighed with relief. "You were wracked with chills. Judging by the dampness of my skin, your fever has broken."

"I don't think it's gone. It's only moved to another place."

Since he lay on top of her, his body flush against hers, Melissa knew exactly where the fire in him burned. Rather than feeling frightened by his arousal, she felt an answering spark of desire in her lower regions. An undeniable attraction to the forbidden.

"Don't you want to run away?"

The correct response would not form on her lips. She'd been running away most of her life. Melissa needed to test her feelings for Robert. She also wanted Clay to erase the ugly attack by Tall Blade from her mind. When she said nothing, made no move to slide from beneath him, the flame in his eyes grew brighter.

"A man can mistake silence for willingness," he warned her.

She didn't speak. Not until his lips fastened on hers, not

until his tongue stole inside her mouth and forced that little sound from her throat. Her defenses lowered, Melissa let sensation rule her. She hungered for Clay. Burned for his touch. Longed to give in to the passion only he stirred within her.

As if he sensed her surrender, he deepened his claim on her mouth. His touch was neither gentle nor cruel when he cupped her aching breasts, his thumbs brushing her nipples. She moaned, her body arching slightly in response. Clay trailed hot kisses down her neck, his mouth fastening greedily upon one passion-filled bud.

When the breath left her lungs in short gasps and she could stand the torture no longer, she twisted her fingers in his hair and brought him back to her lips. Their tongues touched, their bodies melted together, the flame of desire engulfed them. She might have been totally consumed by passion had her nails not accidentally raked his back. The sharp intake of his breath brought her crashing back to reality.

"Oh, my God," she broke from him to whisper, shocked by her brazenness. "We can't do this!"

"It's nothing," he said against her lips. "Trust me, I'm more than capable of continuing."

"I don't trust you." Melissa shoved against his chest. "You've taken advantage of me!"

His head snapped up. "You started this."

Yes, she mentally admitted. And she had achieved her objective. She knew a man could give pleasure as well as pain, and as for Robert, he hadn't crossed her mind while Clay was kissing her. In fact, she had trouble recalling what he looked like. Her weakness for Clay angered her.

"And now I'm telling you to stop," she snapped.

The flame in his eyes continued to burn as he stared down at her. "Some men won't stop once a woman gives them permission to begin."

"Then the woman must make her wishes understood." Without applying much pressure, Melissa lightly raked her nails over his back again.

Clay jerked away from her, cursing in English, then proving himself equally adept at cursing in Apache. She took advantage of the distraction to scramble from beneath him. When he rolled onto his stomach, rested his head against his forearms, and grappled with the pain, she hurriedly slipped her dress over her head.

"I said some men. I didn't mean me."

"Oh." She frowned. "Then you should have said so." Melissa took a hesitant step toward him. "Are you all right?"

Clay didn't glance up. "Hell no," he ground through clenched teeth. "But then, that was the point, wasn't it?"

"I'm sorry I hurt you."

He looked up. "Don't be sorry about defending yourself. Follow your instincts."

She followed her instincts all right. If she wasn't careful, Melissa would follow them straight to the devil.

"I want you to know I wasn't thinking clearly a moment ago."

A dark brow lifted. "When you started it, or when you ended it?"

Heat exploded in her cheeks. "When I didn't stop you right away. Something happened to throw me off balance."

"What happened?"

Should she tell him about the attack? Clay was in no condition to defend her honor, and he might be crazy enough to confront Tall Blade.

"Never mind. Forget I mentioned it . . . and could we forget what just happened between us?"

He laughed and lowered his head to his forearms again. "You're trying to drive me insane, aren't you?"

"I'm trying to help you," she countered.

"How? By torturing me? Thanks but no thanks," he muttered. "If you want to help me, stay the hell away from me."

His suggestion was one she fully intended to take. She'd almost ventured too close to the flame. So what if she'd proven her feelings for Robert were not those a wife should feel for a husband? It didn't mean Clay Brodie should replace him. It didn't mean she had accepted her fate and would live contentedly inside this tepee with him for the rest of her living days. Fate had brought her to New Mexico for a reason. Clay Brodie wasn't it.

"I will gladly stay the hell away from you," she said. Her gaze landed on the herbs she intended to smear across his cuts. "As soon as I doctor your back."

In response, he groaned and lowered his head to his forearms again.

"You shouldn't go out," Melissa huffed. "If you break open those scabs, I swear I won't patch you up!"

"So now you've taken to swearing, along with day-to-day torture!" Clay bellowed. "I'm walking out of this tepee and no salve-smearing, bandage-packing slave woman is going to stop me!"

"Then go!" Melissa pointed toward the flap. "Go amuse yourself and get your back infected again. I'll let you die next time."

He snorted softly. "I don't think you're that crazy. You'd be cast to the wolves before my body grew cold."

To his satisfaction, the anger drained from her face. She seemed to mentally shake herself.

"I'm not so sure that wouldn't be better," she decided. "Jageitci and I have become good friends. Although I still don't particularly care for Gray Wolf, he isn't nearly so fearsome when his pretty wife turns her doe eyes on him. Laughing Stream has a gentle nature despite her Apache heritage, and Swift Buck . . . well, as far as savages go, he isn't too difficult to look at."

Clay snapped his sagging jaw into place. What had she been doing for the past two weeks besides driving him slowly insane? "Don't grow too comfortable, or too careless in your surroundings," he said. "You haven't earned a place among the Apaches."

"I don't want a place," she countered stiffly. "I only want to return to—"

"Robert?" he interrupted. "What if you could see him tomorrow? Would you tell him you find Swift Buck handsome? Would you tell him you've felt another man's touch, his mouth—"

"Stop!" Melissa placed her hands over her ears.

"No, you wouldn't." Clay stormed to her side and forced her to listen. "But if he's like most of his narrow-minded kind, you won't have to. By now, he's lain awake many a night, wondering how many Indians have had you. By now, he's hoping you're dead, because if you did happen to stumble back into his life, he wouldn't want you."

"That's a lie!" Melissa growled. "Robert would never forsake me due to circumstances I have no control over! He's decent, caring, and—"

"And won't act any differently toward you than the decent, caring society you believe is waiting to welcome you back with open arms! Truth is, the good citizens of Santa Fe might still be shaking their heads and talking about what a shame it is that a white woman was taken from the caravan, but inside, they've all forsaken you. The only way they'd pity your waiting bridegroom more than they do is if you were to actually show up."

She slapped him. Clay didn't blame her. The truth was ugly, but he thought it best she hear it. She should know what to expect, so when, or if, she was reunited with this saintly man she intended to marry, the shock wouldn't snap her mind. Worse than the stinging in his cheek were the tears that gathered in her eyes. When she turned away, he wanted to touch her. Instead, he marched to the tepee flap and escaped his confinement.

He drew in deep gulps of fresh air. Clay wanted to warn her of what to expect were she to be rescued, but deep down, he knew he'd been trying to turn her from him, too. Something had changed between them the day he took a beating for her, and she took an arrow for him. For two weeks he'd been her captive. She was getting to him. Breaking down his defenses. He felt jealousy over a man he didn't even know, and he took too much pleasure in just watching her.

The coldness he'd cloaked himself within had begun to thaw. Clay couldn't allow the feelings threatening to seep through the cracks of his armor their freedom. He'd be damned if he did.

"You are not dead?"

He glanced to his left. Swift Buck stood suspiciously close to the tepee, his arms folded across his chest.

"Were you waiting to pounce on her the minute I drew my last breath?"

His blood brother smiled. "If I wanted her, it might not be too difficult to take Huera from Cougar."

"And not worth the pain trying would cost you," Clay countered.

Swift Buck nodded. "Then it is good I do not want her. Our fight is over another. When do we face that battle, brother?"

"I am ready," Clay decided. "Name your choice. Fists? Knives?"

"Tongues," Swift Buck answered dryly. "We both use our fists too often and say too little. It is time we talk."

"Words from a man I cannot trust mean nothing to me."

The Indian sighed. "You are still as stubborn as the skinny boy your father could not break. The one whose name we cannot speak, she was the same."

"Then I hope she did not make betraying my trust too easy," Clay said stiffly. "She, at least, should have seen the wrong in allowing a man raised as her brother beneath the mats with her." So saying, he walked away.

Smiles of relief over his return to the living followed his progress through camp. Clay hardly noticed. He felt weaker than his show of temper suggested, and wanted solitude.

"She had no trouble seeing the wrong in everything," Swift Buck said, falling into step beside him. "You and her were the same in that way. I told myself she was forbidden. My heart would not listen."

"I doubt it was your heart you were hearing."

A strong hand grasped Clay's arm, halting his steps.

"Because you do not understand the difference between wanting a woman for a night and wanting one for a lifetime, you know nothing about what I felt for her. Like you, she believed that to care is only to suffer. I did not share her mat. I did not tell you I could see her as a sister no longer, because the one whose name we cannot speak felt only fear in her heart for me. The love inside her was frozen, like the words that died in her many years ago."

Discussing Rachel brought a dull throb to Clay's chest. He felt curious eyes trained on them, and snatched his arm free, once again seeking privacy. The rushing noise of the river drew him. His skin itched with the need to bathe. A few women were filling water skins as he approached. Clay shrugged from his buckskin shirt, then bent to remove his moccasins. Swift Buck's shadow fell across him.

"I feel the need to say more."

Clay threw his moccasins on the ground and reached for the ties on his leggings. "And I feel the need to bathe."

"There are women present," the brave pointed out.

Unconcerned, Clay pushed his buckskins to his ankles, stepped out of them, and waded into the water. He sucked in his breath sharply as the cold water seeped through his bandages. Glancing up, he noticed Swift Buck's reproachful glare at the women. They rose and moved toward camp.

"Some of them will not be thinking of their husbands beneath the robes this night," Swift Buck predicted. "Why does a man with no shame so easily condemn others?"

"Your mother taught you better," Clay answered. "Mine did not."

"When the fever had you, she came." Swift Buck worried a rock with the toe of his foot. "You thought Huera was the pale woman from the mountain, and put your hands around her throat."

In the process of scooping sand into his palms, Clay froze. "Did I hurt her?"

"No," his blood brother quickly assured him. "You . . . wept."

"I what?" Clay demanded.

A slight smile crossed Swift Buck's lips. "Like a small child," he explained unkindly. "I do not forgive you for treating the one whose name we cannot speak as you did over the

130

years, but I understand why you sought vengeance. She first taught you about love, and then you knew you did not have that from your mother."

Clay kept his eyes downcast, angrily scrubbing his body with sand and wondering what else he'd done or said. "I have not asked for your forgiveness, nor your company."

"My words are not finished," Swift Buck persisted. "I once believed that if the one whose name we cannot speak opened her heart to me, you would be pleased to have me as a brother in truth."

His presumption lifted Clay's gaze. He cocked a brow sarcastically. "And if you had a sister, I feel certain you would be equally anxious for me to take an interest in her."

The Indian frowned. "No. I know you too well, Cougar."

Low laughter danced upon the stream's bubbly surface. Clay shook his head. "When Little Bird's husband was killed in our fifteenth year, it was you she sneaked into her tepee to give her comfort. If I remember correctly, she did not cry long."

Red crept up Swift Buck's neck. "I did not want to shame her by refusing. It is accepted among us that when a woman has had a man, her needs do not die with the husband who once slept beside her. The same is not so for a maiden. That is the difference between us, Cougar. You do not respect innocence. You do not understand that when a man gives his heart, he wants more than only the pleasure a woman's body can give him."

"You should have told me how you felt about her." Clay rose from the water and approached the bank. "I wanted—dammit," Clay switched to English. He ran a hand through his wet hair and grabbed up his leggings. "I wanted her to have a family."

"She had a family." The Indian's dark eyes were hard as coals as he met Clay's stare. "She had a father who gave her away and a brother who tried to buy her forgiveness with gifts. The blond child was never ours. My mother loved her, my father accepted her, and I resented having a sister thrust on me whose blood was not the same as mine. I say this

131

about her, and it hurts me inside to tell the truth; she was not Apache. Not of my father's lodge. She was Brodie."

His accusation ripped through Clay. *Brodie:* Full of hate. Eaten up by anger. He'd hoped she'd escaped the legacy.

"You tell me you cared for her one minute, then insult her the next." Clay slipped in to his buckskins. "Since your words no longer make sense, they are finished." He made it a few feet before Swift Buck's response reached him.

"Does that not speak the real truth? She gave us only the labor of her days. The silence of her pain, and yet, she received the greatest gift. Love she did not deserve. Sometimes we cannot control the wishes of our hearts. Even if our minds do not agree."

He turned to look at Swift Buck. The brave lowered his gaze. The confession obviously embarrassed his blood brother. Clay related with Swift Buck. He'd also carried the shame of loving a woman who couldn't love him back.

"Then I can no longer feel anger toward you. Instead, I will pity you."

"As I do you," Swift Buck returned. "I saw you with the fever. If you do not understand your heart, you have felt the sting of giving it unwisely. We will not do so again."

Clay nodded. "In a few days, when I'm stronger, will you hunt with me?"

His blood brother smiled. "If you feel it is wise to leave the trouble in my tepee alone. Tall Blade has taught her a lesson about wandering away from the others, still—"

"Tall Blade," Clay interrupted, his voice dripping with anger. "I cannot confront him about shooting the arrow, but—"

"The arrow?" Swift Buck appeared confused then shook his head. "I did not mean that lesson. I meant the one he taught her at the river while you were too weak to protect her."

The hairs on the back of Clay's neck bristled. "What are you talking about?"

Swift Buck sighed. "Did she not tell you Tall Blade attacked her? That he forced her to the ground? Put his hands on her?"

132

Clay didn't bother to answer. He set out with purposeful strides toward the tepee that he'd wanted to escape a short time earlier. He almost made it to his destination when he spotted Tall Blade standing with a group of braves. Thoughts of the man putting his hands on Melissa drove him beyond control. Without a word, he walked up and pulled his knife.

Tall Blade immediately went for his own weapon. Swift Buck's hand closed around Clay's wrist.

"Cougar, you are not strong enough to fight him. It is wrong to defend a slave against a brother!"

"He's no brother of mine," Clay growled.

At his declaration, the brave smiled, taunting him with the flash of his blade in the sunlight. Clay tried to shake off Swift Buck's hold.

"Get out of the way."

"No!" His blood-brother's grip tightened around his wrist. "What honor do you bring Huera by dying this day?" he whispered. "He will kill you and take what I stopped him from taking at the river."

As much as Clay wanted to ignore Swift Buck, his words penetrated the red haze clouding good judgment. Clay's legs were shaking, mostly with anger, but more probably with the strain he'd placed upon himself. Swift Buck was right. If he tried to fight Tall Blade in his condition, he wouldn't win.

Backing down was not in Clay's nature, but he must consider Melissa's welfare, trade his pride for her future safety. Slowly, he lowered his knife. Tall Blade's smile faded, replaced by a look of disappointment.

"Another time," Clay promised the brave.

"As you wish," Tall Blade countered. "I would take no pleasure in killing a man too weak to fight."

By the fading glow of anticipation in the Apache's eyes, Clay doubted his honorable statement. He couldn't confront the man who had attacked his captive under present circumstances, but he could damn sure confront Melissa. Why hadn't she told him?

Chapter Thirteen

Melissa's gaze darted from the pot of rabbit stew she'd placed over the grate to boil to Clay's belongings, then toward the tepee flap. Clay's recuperation had left her little privacy. The journal beckoned. Keeping her eyes trained on the flap, she scurried to the pouches.

Her hands trembled as she removed the diary. She knew that to understand Anna's strange entry concerning the birth of her son and the reference to him being a savage, she must start at the beginning. What she'd already read of Anna's girlhood was hurriedly skimmed over. A few pages were blank, then Melissa found the next entry.

> *Has the spring grass smelled so sweet before today? Have the birds ever sung more beautifully? The skies are bluer, the sun warmer. A more perfect man surely exists nowhere else on this earth. He is handsome, and tall, and when he looks at me from across a room, I forget what is being said to me, or what I am about to say.*

I see no one but him, hear no words except his. I am to-tally, helplessly, irreversibly, in love.

Guilt tugged at Melissa. Her heart swelled with joy for Anna, then constricted with sorrow. She'd never felt that way about Robert. How had Anna's feelings for her husband changed so much? When had he gone from this perfect man to one who would scar his child's back? Hungry for answers, she carefully turned the page.

"What are you doing?"

Anna's diary fell from her fingers. Melissa's clumsy attempt to retrieve the journal only resulted in dropping it again. When she reached for the diary a second time, a hand closed around her wrist. She glanced up into Clay's angry eyes.

"I asked you a question."

"I-I was just—"

"Snooping through my things?"

"No—yes," Melissa quickly corrected when his gaze narrowed on her. "I-I'm curious," she admitted.

"What did you want to know?"

His lips were so close that Melissa felt the warmth of his breath. A lump formed in her throat. She swallowed loudly. "I wanted to know about you."

"And what have you learned?"

Although his voice was low, husky, and not in the least threatening, a dangerous current swirled around them.

"Nothing," she lied. "I only read a little about the woman's girlhood. Anna Brodie was your mother, wasn't she?"

He didn't say a word for a moment, his blue stare boring into her. Melissa wanted to squirm uncomfortably, but fought the impulse.

"Yes," Clay finally answered. "And the journal is my private possession. I forbid you to touch it."

The command stiffened her spine.

"I don't see the harm in entertaining myself with your mother's journal. My days are filled with endless tasks, my evenings, with boredom."

Clay captured her chin and lifted her face to his. "If you're bored, I can think of a better way to pass the time. Then you can learn all you need to know about me, and the both of us will be entertained."

A stronger current ran between them, more dangerous than Melissa's alarm when he caught her tampering with his possessions. She made a pretense of returning the journal to his pouch. He snatched the diary from her grasp.

"Take up sewing, or basket-weaving, otherwise I'll be tempted to teach you the difference between one man's cruel attempt at force, and another's skill at seduction. Why didn't you tell me about Tall Blade?"

Melissa glanced up abruptly. "It happened before your delirium. He didn't . . . I mean, he would have, but Swift Buck stopped him."

"I know that. If he'd raped you, he'd be dead."

His declaration stirred conflicting emotions in Melissa. Part of her felt pleased over his protectiveness, the other part, the rational side, hated his casual reference to death.

"And given your weakened state, you might be the one whose name we cannot speak."

He appeared momentarily surprised. "You almost sound as if you care what happens to me."

For all his intelligence, the man was an idiot. Had he not thought to question why she'd risked an arrow to the back to stop his beating that day in the clearing? Didn't he wonder why she'd nursed him? Melissa didn't want to examine the answer. She told herself she did these things because they were in her nature.

"Your well-being concerns me. Since we haven't discussed what my fate would be if you were to die, maybe you should tell me what to expect. Then I'll know how much effort to devote to seeing to it you stay alive."

Although he couldn't fault her logic, Clay couldn't ignore the pang of disappointment he felt that her reasons were rational. What he felt for her wasn't at all sane. He wasn't certain what befell a captive not owned by a family in the event of the owner's death.

"I guess they would auction you to the highest bidder."

It was obviously not an answer to her liking. Her face suffused with red. "The same as a piece of used furniture? As if I were nothing more than a possession?"

"To the Apaches, that's exactly what you are," he pointed out.

"And to you?" she asked softly.

The trembling in her lower lip belied the courage in her eyes. Clay fought the urge to bend forward and crush her mouth beneath his, thus ending her questions. What she had become to him wasn't a subject he cared to deliberate. What she should be to him made more sense.

"Besides a pain in the backside, I consider you mine," he answered.

"Mine!" Melissa fumed, ripping the husk from an ear of maize violently. "Never," she ground out, uncaring that the remarks received curious looks from the women around her. Jageitci lifted a brow. Melissa clamped her lips together and attacked another ear. The pretty woman wouldn't converse with her in Spanish while the others were within hearing distance.

After Clay had answered her question, he'd replaced the diary, given her a stern glare of warning, and gone to his mat. Melissa had sat watching him, stunned. She'd said nothing as he removed the wet bandages from his back. In fact, she hadn't spoken a word to him since. That was two days ago.

Her gaze lifted, settling too easily on the tall figure standing not far from the corral. "Conceited bastard," she mumbled, but couldn't seem to look away from the muscles rippling along his back when he threw a knife, which hit dead-center a natural circle eaten into a tree.

Although she knew he kept the knife in his moccasin, Melissa wondered where the rest of his weapons were stored. Surely he had a rifle. He'd gone into Gray Wolf's lodge once and come out with his bow, she suddenly remembered. He stashed his weapons somewhere else so she couldn't gain access to them. Her stare hardened on his healing back.

"Coward!"

As if sensing a hostile force, Clay's head turned in her direction. His eyes narrowed dangerously. In a gesture of alarm, she brought a hand to her chest. After a moment, she realized he wasn't glaring at her, but at something behind her. Glancing over her shoulder, she found the object of his disdain. Tall Blade sat his horse with a group of braves. A small hunting party was preparing to leave camp.

The two men remained locked in a silent battle of wills until slowly Tall Blade's gaze lowered, settling on Melissa. A shiver raced up her spine. She felt his cruel hands on her again, smelled the rancid odor of him. Afraid he'd see the fear in her eyes, she turned around, her focus on Clay. Without speaking a word, he delivered a message to Tall Blade. If death had a face, if it could assume a human form, it would have been known at that moment as Clay Brodie.

Only the sound of horses thundering away relaxed his stance. The world shifted, returned to what she now considered normal. Flies buzzed, children screamed at play, women spoke softly among themselves, and the frightening mask Clay wore melted, revealing features equally disturbing. He was beautiful.

Melissa's hands shook when she resumed husking. She shouldn't find him handsome. It was this place, these people. She felt trapped in a spell, felt herself slipping away at the end of each passing day. If she wasn't careful, she would become one with them, become one with . . .

"Come, Huera."

Clay sat mounted before her. When he stretched a hand toward her, Melissa's heart gave a sudden lurch. "W-Where are we going?" she asked breathlessly.

An expression she might have likened to sympathy crossed his rugged features. "Not far," he answered. "I hunger for something sweet."

When his eyes fastened on her lips, Melissa felt the pounding of her heart increase. Did she dare take the hand he offered? Did she dare refuse in front of the women?

"Don't make me climb down from this horse," he warned. "You wanted a distraction, remember?"

She longed for a break from her endless tasks, but recalled his husky promise to teach her the difference between force and seduction. Clay's annoyed sigh indicated his patience had worn thin. When he started to throw a long leg over the horse's back and dismount, Melissa dropped the ear of maize she held.

"I'll go with you," she decided.

Hesitantly, she reached out. Clay grasped her elbow and hefted her up in front of him. The heat of his bare chest crept through the back of her dress. Melissa shifted, uneasy about riding a horse without a saddle.

"Grip Two Moons with your thighs, like you would a lover," he said softly.

The vulgar comparison embarrassed her. She knew nothing of lovers, but did as he instructed. Their pace was unhurried as they rode from camp. Melissa closed her eyes, wondering how it would feel to ride away for good. She imagined the luxury of rising from a bed in the morning instead of a pile of buffalo robes.

However, she had trouble envisioning a big room to herself, or the absence of Clay's scent, the sound of his breathing as he lay across from her each night.

"In the fall, the leaves turn from green to gold, and then to red. That's when the mountains are the most beautiful."

Captivity had hampered Melissa's ability to view her surroundings with any amount of appreciation. She glanced around, rightfully awed by the tall aspens and majestic pines flanking both sides of their path. The air was cool beneath a canopy of limbs overhead.

Dappled sunlight filtered through the gaps. Pine needles crunched under Two Moons's hooves. The forest was alive with sound. Birds, scurrying noises, the ever-present gurgling of the river.

"It is magnificent," she admitted.

"And deadly," Clay reminded. "Nature embraces those who live in harmony with her, and destroys those unmindful of her power. To survive here, you must become as cunning as the fox, as determined as the wolf, as strong as the bear."

Either his words or the air made her shiver. "The Indians are the worst menace. Why can't they just let the caravans pass in peace?"

"The wagons carry their enemies. The Indians were here first. They fight for their children's future. People must eat. Game is killed along the trail, and soon the whites will start spreading out, staking claims, cutting down the trees. Civilization is a hungry animal. One that feeds even when it's full, one that rapes the land without thought to the barrenness left behind."

"They can't stop progress," Melissa argued.

"No," he agreed. "But they can slow it down."

"With violence," she said bitterly. "I don't understand why they won't try to live peacefully among the whites. If only they would adapt, learn our ways, accept our God—"

"Become the white man's slave?" he interrupted harshly. "Many years ago, the Spanish came here. The People welcomed them. In return, they were enslaved, slaughtered, beaten, shackled, and sent into the mines to work. All of these cruelties were performed in the name of God, your God."

Despite the horror of his revelation, Melissa felt impassioned to defend her faith. "Satan often does his best work under the guise of goodness." She took a deep breath. "If you don't believe in God, why do you carry a Bible in your pouch?"

He tensed, his arms tightening around her for a brief moment. Gradually, the pressure abated. "It belonged to my mother," he answered. "I've kept it and the journal all these years, planning to give them to my sister. I thought she might want something of hers. I waited too long."

Mention of his sister stirred conflicting emotions within Melissa. Although she felt sorrow over Clay's loss, she also resented the girl whose death had so drastically altered her own life. "Would she have been able to read them?"

Once again, a slight rigidness in his body followed her

question. He didn't answer, but guided Two Moons through the lush vegetation, headed toward a break in the trees ahead.

"Could she read?" Melissa persisted.

"No," he clipped. "And you ask too many questions."

Undaunted, she reasoned aloud. "But you planned to tell her about the journal, about your mother's girlhood in Boston, about her father being a wealthy fur merchant and a very important man in the community?"

"Boston?" he repeated, as if testing the name. "I wondered where she came from. She spoke differently from Hiram Brodie."

"So do you, I imagine," she mused.

On occasion, Melissa had found herself sharing unwanted space in one of St. Louis's many shops when a gruff fur trader ventured inside. For the most part, the men were dirty and unkempt, and conversed with the shopkeepers in a crude, uneducated manner. "Your mother taught you well."

Anna Brodie had been responsible for many lessons in Clay's life, none of which included a purposeful intent to see to it he didn't butcher the English language as his father had. He wouldn't tell his prying captive he'd learned to speak like his mother in an attempt to please her. Or that it had done him little good in his efforts to win her affection.

"You seemed surprised that your mother came from Boston. Had you just forgotten?"

He frowned down at her. The part in her hair was crooked, one braid much thicker than the other. She'd refused to allow him to help her with the tangled mass after the last lesson. Huera was smarter than he sometimes gave her credit for being. He should have known she'd mull over his ignorance concerning Anna Brodie's past and find it curious.

"I know very little about my mother," he admitted.

"But the journal." She turned her head to the side. "Even if you can't remember her telling you, she wrote it all down."

"She didn't tell me, and I haven't read her journal," Clay ground through his teeth. "Now, stop asking me questions about things that are none of your business."

Melissa ignored his command. "Why haven't you? Surely you're curious about—"

"I can't read! There, will that shut you up?"

Melissa almost unseated herself in an effort to look at him. "Why not?" Her brow furrowed. "Didn't your mother teach you?"

Clay felt his face grow hot. "She never offered, and I never asked, and that's the end of this conversation, understand?" When her lips parted, Clay further warned, "Leave it alone or I'll give your mouth something to do besides meddle."

Her teeth clicked together with force. She faced forward, sitting straighter in an obvious attempt to keep from touching him. Clay thought her prudishness a little ridiculous considering the liberties she'd already allowed him. She couldn't fool him. She was as aware of him as a man as he was of her as a woman.

Without conceit, he knew she liked the way he looked. When Hiram had decided it was time he learned what he considered the only good thing about women, Clay discovered that whatever his mother found so disgusting about him wasn't on the outside. He'd halfway expected the whore who owned a thriving establishment in Santa Fe to refuse Hiram's generous bribe to practice a trade she'd long retired from.

"He needs an experienced woman," Hiram had insisted. "I know you own the place and don't have to make a living on your back no more. You got all these nice young girls to earn your keep, but I ain't paying good money for the boy to spend himself in five minutes and be finished. I figure you've got more patience. You'll see to it he has a good time so's he'll hurry back at the end of trapping season. How about it, Sally? I'll pay double what you charge regular for a poke at one of your gals."

Clay had stood with his gaze lowered, hoping the woman would laugh in Hiram's face. She looked old enough to be his mother. Her hair was a brash, bright yellow. Her cheeks and her full lips were both berry red. He'd never seen a woman expose so much bosom or have so much to expose. Plain and simple, Clay wasn't interested. Unfortunately, Sally was.

"Any other time, I'd tell you where to shove your money, Hiram Brodie," Sally had said crudely. The blonde walked a slow circle around Clay. "This boy makes me wish I was young again. All I can say is, he must take after his ma. Tell you what, Hiram, I'll do him for the regular price, and if he's near as good as he looks, I'll give you your money back."

Hiram nodded; then winked at Clay. "Even though she ain't around to hear tell of this, you make your ma proud tonight."

Amidst loud catcalls and shrill whistles, Clay had been led upstairs. When Sally asked what he wanted first, he bluntly told her he didn't want anything. She laughed at his honesty, then suggested they at least lie on the bed and make some noise. He stayed with her that night because Sally said she thought old Hiram would be jealous if his boy got what she'd never given his crude old man. A whole night and his money back to boot.

The next time Hiram took him into Santa Fe, a pretty Mexican girl working for Sally caught his eye and invited him upstairs. Clay decided he was ready to be with a woman. He'd been ready ever since.

"I could read the diary to you."

The offer brought him from the past. He snorted softly. "I remember enough about her."

Clay cursed the resentment in his voice. How many times had he held the journal and wished he knew how to read? Clay felt certain whatever hideous thing about him a mother couldn't love was in there somewhere, and he didn't want the woman sitting in front of him to learn the truth.

Let her despise him for not being her savior, for not having the conscience to see her fate altered and believe those were the worst of his flaws. He could stand her blind judgment, he could stand a lot, but having come to know her, he feared she might pity him for being born to a mother who hated him, and that he could never tolerate.

"This is what I wanted to show you," Clay said, sensing

another argument gathering on her lips. "Well, what do you think of it?"

The rebuttal Melissa had been preparing died in her throat. They moved from the shelter of the trees into a small meadow. The grass stood tall, waving in the breeze. A multitude of colors dotted the countryside. Wildflowers. Hundreds of them.

"Oh my," she breathed.

He laughed, slid from the horse's back, and helped her dismount. Melissa walked around Two Moons to better survey her surroundings. A lovelier spot she doubted existed in the world. Sunlight shimmered off the stream a short distance away. The drone of insects drifted on the perfumed air. It was a peaceful place, one where Melissa felt no eyes boring into her back, one where she might forget her tragic circumstances for the moment and simply be.

"Now, to satisfy my craving for something sweet."

Alarm quickly replaced the tranquil feeling spreading through Melissa. Clay stood before her, grasping a braid in each hand. She'd been awestruck by her surroundings and forgotten he might have had ulterior motives for bringing her to this secluded glen. It became more obvious as he untied her braids, separating the strands with his fingers.

"I like your hair wild around your shoulders."

"W-What are you planning to do?" Melissa took a step backward.

His gaze lowered to her mouth again. "Steal some honey."

"It won't be easy," she assured him, retreating another step.

"No, I don't imagine so," he agreed, then turned and walked away.

Dumbfounded, she watched him leave. He only made it a few feet when she called out, "Where are you going?"

Clay glanced over his shoulder. "I told you. To find honey."

Confusion slowed her response. He'd almost reached a clump of trees bordering the meadow to her right when she shouted, "But what should I do while you're gone?"

Displaying his annoyance by turning and placing his hands on his hips, Clay shouted, "Whatever the hell you want!" He gestured toward the meadow. "Pick flowers, find berries, you're free to amuse yourself in whatever way you choose."

Her sluggish mind had trouble understanding. "Free?" she whispered. "Whatever I choose?" It seemed a lifetime ago when Melissa could move about unrestricted. Always, dark eyes followed her through her tasks. Only when she went in the trees to attend to private matters did she truly feel alone, and then she hurried to return, lest someone come looking for her.

Dazed by his offer, Melissa took a hesitant step. Two Moons passed her, seemingly anxious to dine on the meadow's tall grass. She eyed the stallion appraisingly.

"I wouldn't try it!" Clay warned loudly. "Remember what happened last time? He hardly tolerates me on his back. Don't bother him, and he won't bother you."

For a fleeting instant, she was tempted to try the horse again.

"I'm serious!" he shouted. "You'll end up getting hurt again, only this time, he might even stomp on you a little!"

"All right!" she shouted, her tone as irked as his. "I won't go near him. Now, if you don't mind, I'd like to do whatever the hell I please!"

He smiled at her slip in etiquette. Melissa smiled back. Clay turned, resuming his quest without a backward glance. For a while, she merely drank in the beauty of the meadow. Her sharpened senses absorbed sights and sounds she would have once taken for granted. Freedom now had a smell, a taste, a feel, and Melissa vowed to treasure it from that moment forward.

Although she couldn't recall the conscious act of placing one foot in front of the other, the brush of blades tickling her palms verified the fact that she had indeed ventured from a stationary position. Melissa moved at a leisurely pace, careful to avoid the grazing Two Moons.

Halfway into the meadow, she began to run, then to twirl

in wild abandon. Around and around she went, her hair flying out in all directions, her sight blurred, and her head spinning. She giggled with the gleeful innocence of a child at play, then halted abruptly, tried to walk, and fell to earth. Thick grass cushioned her fall.

Laughter echoed across the still meadow. Melissa marveled over the simple pleasure of expressing joy, of being able to feel lighthearted, even if her freedom would last only until Clay's return. Suddenly panicked it would end all too soon, she tried to decide what to do next. Lying on her back, staring up at the sky, she decided to play a game her mother had taught her.

Several fluffy clouds drifted overhead. She found in their hazy forms the shape of a bowl, a dragon, and a creature with two heads. Odd that she remembered so vividly the sound of her mother's laughter as she'd pointed out various objects the clouds resembled. Melissa couldn't have been more than five that summer. That wonderful year before her mother became ill.

In an effort to dispel her dreary thoughts, Melissa rolled over and plucked a red bloom from its stem. Within the imagination of a young girl, the flower was not a flower at all, but a woman draped in a beautiful ball gown. Not too many years ago, she'd envisioned herself in such refinement, dancing upon the arm of a gentleman. Her skirts of satin would billow out as she twirled, and the man who held her would say she resembled a lovely bloom, a wildflower.

She giggled at the absurdity that a grown man would say such a thing to a woman, then sobered as she recalled another aspect of the fantasy. Her partner hadn't resembled Robert. He hadn't been of medium build, nor did he have blond hair. Always, he had been tall, dark, and handsome.

"That doesn't mean anything," she scoffed aloud, rising. She picked a few more flowers and placed them in her hair, then glanced around in search of berries. A bush of blackberries stood a short distance away. She shoved several in her mouth before she even removed the firewood sling from around her neck. The long pouch was half-full when Two Moons's nervous snort drew her attention.

Melissa scanned the area in search of what might have distressed the horse. She spotted nothing unusual within the meadow, and focused on the spot where Clay had earlier disappeared. She heard a noise. The crunching sounds of something beyond the trees. Something big. Something moving at an alarmingly fast pace.

Instinctively, she began to back away. A shape stumbled from the trees. A beast to be sure. Clay Brodie. Melissa sighed with relief, then had the presence of mind to wonder why he hadn't slowed down.

"Run!" he shouted. "Get to the stream and hide under the water! Now!"

Chapter Fourteen

"My feet hurt," Melissa complained. "Is the knot on my forehead any bigger?"

Clay stepped on a sharp rock and swore softly. He turned to study her face. "The mud seems to have helped. It's not as huge." His gaze scanned the trees skirting the stream. He whistled. "Where is that damn horse?"

"Probably back at camp by now," she muttered. "He's smart enough not to get a hive of bees mad at him. Why can't we just walk the same path you took to the meadow? My toes are numb."

"Keeping to the stream is faster. There's a fairly strong current in the middle. When we get tired, we'll wade out and let it carry us back."

"Oh, no." Melissa shook her head. "You've already almost drowned me once today."

"At least I didn't kick you in the . . . don't ever do that to a man unless you find yourself in a dangerous situation."

She glanced sideways from the corner of her eye. "I wasn't aiming, I just wanted you to let go of me. I'm not half

148

fish like you obviously are, and I consider not being able to breathe a dangerous situation."

"So is an attack by angry bees. You're damn lucky you only got stung once."

"I want to know why I did and you didn't? You were the one they were after, not me."

Her cross tone brought a smile to his lips. Long strands of damp hair hung over her shoulders. Her dress was soaked and clung to her body. He'd smeared mud on her forehead to soothe the sting.

"Maybe they thought you were a wildflower. In the meadow, I saw you dancing in the breeze and thought you looked like a pretty yellow flower."

"You spied on me?" Melissa turned an accusing glare on him despite the flush of pleasure spreading up her neck.

He shrugged. "I wanted to make certain you didn't try to steal my horse and get yourself trampled in the process. What do you call the dance?"

"The dance?" Her brow creased. "It wasn't a dance. It was a childhood game. You know, you spin around until you get dizzy and then fall down?"

It was Clay's turn to be puzzled. "Why?"

She rolled her gaze upward. "Because it's fun, silly. Surely you did the same as a child?"

"I had little time for foolish games," he answered. "And I'm not silly." Clay cast a dark glance her direction. "Ignorant maybe," he muttered, lowering his gaze. "But not silly."

His inability to read bothered him, Melissa suddenly realized. That was the reason his tone had been so defensive earlier. And well he should be angry. A mother should pass all that is important on to her children.

"I could teach you to read." The thought left her lips before Melissa had an opportunity to examine why his feelings of inadequacy mattered to her.

He eyed her mistrustfully. "Not that I care whether I can read or not, but why would you bother? What would you demand in return?"

Must the man always appear suspicious of every act of

kindness? Did he believe nothing in life could be given without extracting a price? Perhaps not, Melissa answered her own question. Even a brief encounter with freedom had gotten her a bee sting, along with a long walk back to camp.

"If you're interested, I'll think of something I want from you. We can make a trade."

"It can't be anything of great value," he specified. "As I said, learning to read isn't all that important to me."

The bland expression he wore belied a slight note of excitement in his voice. Melissa suspected he wanted very much to learn. Maybe not so desperately that she could trade for more than another trip to the meadow, but teaching him would give her one small victory. Clay Brodie would take a step toward his white heritage, whether he was aware of doing so or not.

"I'll think about what I'd consider a worthy trade," she mused. "Teaching letters is a grueling task, I wouldn't want to feel cheated."

"You said you found the evening hours after dusk boring," he reminded. "Maybe another distraction should be trade enough."

He worried she'd demand a price too high. "You mentioned basket-weaving. I've watched a few women at the chore, and it looks rather enjoyable. You could teach me."

When Clay said nothing, Melissa knew she'd outwitted her clever captor. They hobbled along a few more paces, both grimacing over the sharp rocks beneath their wet moccasins. Clay snatched her arm. "Come on, my toes are numb, too."

Soon, their feet were covered in mud. The dark ground beneath the shelter of trees stuck to their soles. Melissa shivered as the cool breeze caressed her wet hair and clothes. Seeking a diversion from the discomfort, she removed her sling, reached into the pouch, retrieved a berry, and almost had it in her mouth when Clay's hand grasped hers.

"If you want one, try asking," she scolded.

"I need to make sure it's not poisonous."

"Oh." Melissa uncurled her fingers. "I thought they were blackberries."

"They are," he confirmed. "You should be careful, though. Some in the area are dangerous to eat. Mostly, the red or orange colors. It would be wise to let me inspect any you pick from now on."

She nodded, then popped the dark berry into her mouth. A few berries later, a disturbing realization occurred to Melissa. She trusted Clay Brodie with her life. Over the past weeks, he'd become more than her captor, he'd become her protector. Every day, she grew more dependent on him. The admission panicked her somewhat. She choked on the berry in her mouth.

Clay thumped her on the back, correcting the blockage without breaking stride. Beneath the cover of her lashes, Melissa regarded him thoughtfully. He was always quick to question her about any act that included kindness or concern over his well-being. What were *his* motives?

"Why did you start trouble with Tall Blade today?"

"The trouble between us began when we were children, although I can't say why. For as long as I can remember, he's never liked me, and I've never liked him."

"He's . . . different from the others," Melissa said. "Somehow odd even among those I consider strange. More savage, if that makes sense."

He nodded. "He is different. I don't remember him always being so. His father killed himself, and shortly afterward, his mother disappeared. He wasn't but ten. I think he's been like a tightly strung bow ever since. Waiting to snap."

Melissa shuddered in remembrance of the man's attack—of the strange glow in his eyes. Insanity. "It would be best if you just ignored him," she decided. "Your back hasn't healed enough to risk reopening the welts. Swift Buck said Tall Blade has a bad heart. I don't believe he'd fight fairly."

Clay glanced at her and lifted a brow. "Don't you think I'm capable of protecting you?"

Recalling his fierce transformation earlier, Melissa shuddered slightly again. "I'm sure you can be every bit as savage as him when the mood strikes you." She gathered her courage. "What I'm most confused about is why you continue to court danger for my sake?"

When she leveled a questioning stare at her captor, he glanced away. Melissa persisted.

"You didn't have to take a beating intended for me. You said if Tall Blade had accomplished his dark intentions by the stream that day, he'd be dead. Why do you care?"

"I'll give you an answer, but you won't like it," he said. "Don't believe for a moment I see you as anything but a slave to the Apaches. The simple truth is, you wouldn't have survived the beating. My skin is tougher. A dead slave is a worthless slave. As for Tall Blade, if I don't make it plain right now no man can consider you a pleasant diversion to pass the time, you won't get any work done. You'll be on your backside all day."

Angry heat spread through her veins. "I suppose those are logical reasons," she ground out.

"As rational as yours were."

Melissa halted a berry's progress halfway to her lips, ready to defend her claim that she'd only tended Clay because she feared her fate were he to die. He nodded toward the berry between her fingers.

"Don't eat too many or you'll be seeing them again later tonight. And they won't be as pretty."

Rebelliously, she placed the juicy treat in her mouth. He sighed. They continued in silence, Melissa consuming over half the sling's contents. She intended to keep the fruit of her labor to herself, but after a while, she began to feel guilty. Clay had taken her on the outing because she complained of boredom. If she thanked him, she felt certain he'd provide her with a rational excuse for his thoughtfulness.

"Would you care for one?" She held the pouch toward him.

A slight smile crossed Clay's lips. "No. But thank you for the kind offer."

"I'd hoped you might have a strange reaction to them. You know, break out in huge ugly bumps?"

His smile stretched. "I just don't want to walk into camp looking like you do. Your mouth is purple."

"It is?" Melissa glanced at her fingers. They were stained as well. "Let me go to the stream and wash before we arrive."

Clay shook his head. "We've already wasted too much time. If both Two Moons and the hunting party have returned, I'll probably have hell to pay."

"Aren't you free to come and go as you choose?"

"Yes, but you're not. My horse thundering into camp without us might cause an uproar. They'll think I've run into trouble."

"Well, we did," she pointed out.

"A swarm of bees is nothing compared to a gang of Mexican bandits. They hunt this area."

"Mexicans?" Melissa tried to sound nonchalant.

"Bandits," he stressed. "And what they hunt is Indians. Scalps are a profitable business. So are white women. That blond hair would fetch a high price from a brothel owner in Mexico."

She wondered if he was telling the truth, or only meant to frighten her. "Robert has money. He'd be willing to pay a good deal to get me back."

An argument was expected. Clay simply lifted a brow and continued forward, his strides longer so Melissa had to hurry to keep up.

"He would," she insisted.

"I didn't say otherwise."

"No. But you were thinking it!"

He stopped abruptly. "I think you're the one with doubts."

The anger in his tone confused her. Why did the mention of her fiancé always upset him? Not him, Melissa mentally corrected, his conscience, the one he fought to ignore. Clay Brodie wanted her to forget Robert, to forsake all dreams of reclaiming the life stolen from her. Then he wouldn't be tempted to do what he surely knew in his heart was decent.

153

"At least I understand the difference between good and evil, right and wrong. I know who I am, and what I believe in. Can you say the same?"

His blue eyes met hers. "No," he surprised her by admitting. "But neither can you. You understand what is familiar, and believe what you've been told to believe. In a world of grays, you see black and white. Who or what we truly are cannot be taught, but only learned by circumstance. The leaves above us don't remain green forever, Melissa. They must change with the seasons."

"Which is to say you are also capable of . . ." Her voice trailed. "You called me Melissa," she whispered.

A flood of color rose in his cheeks. "You're mistaken," he said gruffly.

Stunned, she watched him walk away. Her heart began to pound. Warmth touched a tiny bud of hope still struggling to survive inside her and opened the bloom. He could deny calling her by her Christian name all he wanted, but it wouldn't change what she'd heard. His voice echoed in her ears. And never in her life had her name sounded so beautiful.

Clay silently cursed his slip while Melissa cleaned the bowls from supper. He hadn't said a word to her since, or to anyone, for that matter. As he suspected, Two Moons's return caused an uproar. Although the hunting party had not returned, a group of braves were mounted, Swift Buck among them, preparing to ride out in search.

He'd figured the fact that he was obviously alive and hadn't misplaced the woman who walked beside him should be explanation enough for them. Having heard the hunting party ride in a few moments ago, Clay wondered how long his reprieve would last.

"I have more berries if you'd care for some now."

Her gracious mood brought a frown to his lips. She had a smug look about her. So what if he'd accidently called her Melissa? It meant nothing, changed nothing.

"No," Clay muttered, refusing to thank her for asking.

"And you shouldn't have any, either." He reached inside his shirt to remove a bundle wrapped in buckskin. "I'll share the spoils of today's war, since you were wounded in battle."

"Spoils?" Melissa stacked their bowls by the grate and joined him on the other side of the fire. Curious, she sat beside him, watching as he unwrapped the bundle. "Honeycomb?"

He smiled at her surprised tone. "You don't think I would have braved an angry hive of bees and come away with nothing to show for it, do you?"

A small pink tongue wet her lips before she shook her head. "I should have known you'd demand something for your troubles. I suffered the injury, I deserve the first bite."

"It seems only fair." Clay removed a knife from the top of his moccasin and cut off a small piece of honeycomb. "Open up," he instructed.

Without hesitation, she obeyed. A groan of pure bliss left her throat when she bit down and honey oozed from the comb. "Mmmmnn," she drew out. "I've died and gone to Heaven."

"There's only one thing sweeter than honey, and it's a far cry closer to being in the hereafter." He cut a chunk for himself.

"I can't imagine what," she said, eyeing the remaining treat with longing.

"Oh, I believe you could. If you let yourself."

Melissa wrenched her gaze from the honeycomb to glance up. A fat glob of honey rested on his chin. Distracted by the amused gleam in his eyes, she unconsciously reached out and removed the sticky nectar. He captured her wrist. Slowly, he brought her hand to his lips. She jumped when his tongue ran the length of one finger, then gasped when he took it inside his mouth and sucked softly.

"That's disgusting." Her voice was husky, breathless. She rescued her finger from the moist heat sending shocks of pleasure up her arm.

"Is it?" he questioned, tightening his hold on her wrist to

155

pull her closer. "I'd like to smear honey all over you and lick it off. Can you imagine anything more repulsive?"

Visions flooded her mind. Hot, sticky, forbidden scenes flashed in Melissa's head. Now she understood what he'd meant by "if you let yourself." But she wouldn't envision her naked body coated in honey, couldn't picture his handsome face poised above hers, didn't dare conjure the feel of his tongue sliding down her neck or the sensations his hungry mouth against her breasts evoked. She couldn't, shouldn't, wouldn't give him the satisfaction.

"No, I can't imagine anything I'd find less appealing," she lied. "Now, please release me. I-I don't feel well, for a fact."

Tension-filled seconds ticked past before he complied with her wishes. She had barely scrambled from his reach when a shout sounded outside the tepee. Judging from Clay's expression when Gray Wolf entered the lodge, she could only assume this was no social call. Heated words were exchanged.

If Melissa couldn't understand them, Gray Wolf's glare in her direction proved enlightening. Clay had taken her to the meadow—he later admitted that she wasn't allowed that far from camp. Once again, he'd brought vengeance down on himself because of her.

The confrontation didn't last long. Gray Wolf stormed out. The growing knot of discomfort in Melissa's stomach intensified. She felt nervous in Clay's brooding company and wished he and Gray Wolf had conversed in English. Of course they wouldn't. The language barrier gave them the edge and left her an outsider. Suddenly, a solution came to her.

"Why don't we start your lessons."

Her suggestion lifted Clay's gaze. "Tonight?"

"Might as well."

"What about the trade?"

"I've decided what I would consider a worthy exchange."

"And that would be?"

She ignored both his suspicious stare and the grumbling noise of her stomach. Melissa took a deep breath. "Teach me Apache."

He laughed as if she were making a joke, then sobered.

"Their language is difficult. It's more than words. As you've seen, they also use their hands to speak."

"I don't want to speak it so much as understand their conversations. I feel intimidated when they talk about me and I can't understand what they're saying. I feel so isolated, so alone."

"You're a captive. That's the way you should feel, the way they want you to feel. Most of them know Spanish. They know it so they can't be placed in the same situation you're in. As time passes, a captive will learn words, come to understand, but that can't be helped. The language isn't taught to their enemies, understand? They'd consider it the same as if I gave you a weapon to use against them."

"Then it will be our secret," Melissa persisted. "I won't try to speak with them, won't act as if I understand what they say." The stubborn set to his jaw made her all the more determined. "You may not always be around to protect me. Give me this weapon, not to use against them, but to protect myself."

Her plea had an obvious effect on him. Clay glanced away and ran his fingers through his hair. Melissa could tell she'd at least presented an argument he counted valid. Then she had the presence of mind to wonder why. Hadn't his lessons been those of survival from the beginning? Hadn't he been teaching her to master the role of submissive slave in order to ensure her safety? But to what end?—So she wouldn't need him anymore.

The answer startled her. Perspiration popped out on her brow. Her insides twisted. Had he been preparing her to live without him? Because if so, his efforts would be in vain. She couldn't, not here.

I'm being presumptuous, Melissa told herself. Still, she felt weak with worry. Bile rose in her throat. Her stomach heaved. Panicked, she scrambled to the large pot sitting beside the grate, and retched. The smell of berries wafted up from the pot. She unburdened her stomach again. To her embarrassment, Clay squatted beside her. He pulled her braids back and, with a sigh, said something in Apache.

Ronda Thompson

"What did that mean?" she asked weakly, testing him to see if she'd won this battle.

He didn't answer for a moment, then sighed again. "This is your first lesson. It means, 'I told you so.'"

Chapter Fifteen

By the end of two weeks, Melissa knew the Apache word for most items in the tepee. Clay would point to an object, give her the word, and make her repeat it several times. The next night, he would ask for the objects in Apache, and Melissa would fetch them for him. His patience with her came as a surprise, and his lack of it with himself was even more astounding. He'd proven to be a horrible pupil.

She'd decided that as long as he had a mind to learn to read, he might as well learn to write as well. He taught her at night after evening meal, and her lessons began in the morning, before breakfast.

"Try again," she instructed, pounding a corn cake into a flat ball between her palms. "You've made the letter upside down. That isn't a *b*, it's a *p*."

"What is a *p*?"

"A ways down the road," she answered sternly. "We're working on *a* through *e*. Gradually, we'll get to *p*."

"Give me a word it starts with."

"Persistent," Melissa grumbled. "Now, write the *b*." She smiled wryly. "As in, bee sting."

The grin he returned was blatantly seductive. Idiot, Melissa mentally chastised. Bee, as in honey. Honey, as in 'I'd like to rub it all over you and lick it off.' She'd discovered over the past two weeks that she did for a fact possess the ability to imagine. And quite often, too.

"Or, as in berry?" he tried.

Despite the immediate roll of her stomach, the smile that had died on her lips returned. "That's very good. I don't care to ever hear that word again, but you're beginning to associate the letter with the sound it makes."

"I am?" he asked skeptically.

"You just did. Learning to read and write is difficult for anyone. You're doing remarkably well given the short amount of time we've been working together."

His face darkened. "It seems stupid that I can say the words but don't know how they look."

"You're not stupid!" She felt a blush rise in her cheeks over her defensive tone. "Ah, that is to say, none of us are born with the ability to decipher words. We must learn to speak first, otherwise, none of this would make sense. Write the *b* and we'll find more words that begin with the letter."

Obediently, he used the thin stick in his hand to wipe smooth the ashes inside the grate. He sat for a few moments, concentrating, then reached forward and drew a straight line. The half circle at the bottom, facing the correct direction, came slower. After he finished, he glanced up expectantly.

Melissa was struck dumb by the contrast of his eyes against dark lashes, and by the innocence of his expression. At that moment, she saw the child in him: hungry for approval, desperate to please.

"Perfect," she whispered, admiring the rugged handsomeness of his face.

"Persistent, perfect."

Join the Historical Romance Book Club — and GET 4 FREE* BOOKS NOW!

A $23.96 Value!

Yes! I want to subscribe to the Historical Romance Book Club.

Please send me my **4 FREE* BOOKS.** I have enclosed $2.00 for shipping/handling. Each month I'll receive the four newest Historical Romance selections to preview for 10 days. If I decide to keep them, I will pay the Special Members Only discounted price of just $4.24 each, a total of $16.96, plus $2.00 shipping/handling ($23.55 US in Canada). This is a **SAVINGS OF AT LEAST $5.00** off the bookstore price. There is no minimum number of books I must buy, and I may cancel the program at any time. In any case, the **4 FREE* BOOKS** are mine to keep.

*In Canada, add $5.00 shipping/handling per order
for the first shipment. For all future shipments to
Canada, the cost of membership is $23.55 US,
which includes shipping and handling.
(All payments must be made in US dollars.)

NAME: _____

ADDRESS: _____

CITY: _____ **STATE:** _____

COUNTRY: _____ **ZIP:** _____

TELEPHONE: _____

E-MAIL: _____

SIGNATURE: _____

If under 18, Parent or Guardian must sign. Terms, prices, and conditions subject to change. Subscription subject
to acceptance. Dorchester Publishing reserves the right to reject any order or cancel any subscription.

"Yes." She rolled her gaze heavenward. "But we're working on the *b*." Melissa glanced around the tepee and pointed. "Basket."

Clay repeated the word, placing emphasis on the beginning sound.

"Blue." She pointed to his eyes.

Again, he mimicked her.

"Buckskin." She fingered her dress, then lifted her braids. "Braids. Now it's your turn."

Her pupil obviously hadn't gotten past buckskin, since he still stared thoughtfully at the front of her dress. He traveled a slow path up to meet her eyes.

"Breasts."

A muscle twitched in the corner of his mouth. His stare held a mischievous glint. Melissa refused to allow him to fluster her. She pinched her lips together the same way the prim Mrs. Talley, who once taught in St. Louis, had with naughty students. "That will be all this morning. I need to light a fire and get breakfast started."

"Just one more thing," he said, all traces of humor gone. "Write my name."

His request touched her. The years had stolen the wonder of seeing her own name written for the first time. She recalled asking her mother to do it for her, and the feeling of somehow being more than she was upon viewing the letters drawn in Emily Sheffield's lovely script. Melissa took the slim stick from his fingers and wiped the ashes smooth again. With a great deal of care, she scratched out his name, hoping he might experience the same feeling of awe she'd once felt.

"Clay Brodie." She pointed. "Well, what do you think?"

When he didn't answer, she glanced up. He sat very still, his gaze riveted on the letters etched in ash. Finally, he looked away. Without a word, he rose and left the tepee. Melissa stared after him, confused by his lack of response. She took the stick and began erasing the letters when the enormity of what he must have felt occurred to her. Clay

Brodie. A white man's name. His name. Her gaze strayed to the tepee flap he'd disappeared through.

She sighed. "You are white. And getting whiter every day. . . . Either that, or I'm turning Injun."

Later that afternoon, Melissa bathed with the women and children. Modesty had long been forsaken in light of necessity. The baths were too few to suit her, but she wasn't certain Clay could be trusted to stand guard over a private attempt. At times, she envied his disrespect for decency. Nakedness was a natural state to him. He thought nothing of standing before her in no more than a loincloth.

Melissa slept fully clothed, and alternated between the dresses that once belonged to Clay's sister. The leggings and moccasins were the only things she dared remove to sleep. She wondered how the fuzzy buffalo hides might feel against her bare skin. How Clay Brodie's flesh stretched out beside her would feel.

Her indecent thoughts were quickly brought to rein, lest she allow herself the sin of imagining again. Melissa picked up a knotted bundle of clothes. Laughing Stream sat to her left, scrubbing her own household laundry, and Jageitci to her right.

She felt relaxed in both women's company. Swift Buck's mother was a gentle creature, and Melissa suspected Laughing Stream very much missed another blond head who once worked beside her.

Jageitci, on the other hand, emitted the strength and courage it must have taken her to move from the position of captive to leader's wife. Although small-framed and fine-boned, she walked with a confidence that made her seem twice her size.

Melissa wished their words in Spanish to each other were not always hurried and few. She wanted to know how the young woman had come to be among the Apaches. How she had captured the heart of the handsome if hard-edged Gray Wolf.

Unconsciously, her gaze strayed to Jageitci's middle. Her

condition had become more noticeable in a very short time. Perhaps she did have the sight; the rapid weight gain might suggest she carried twins. Sons, she had said.

And what beautiful children they would be, considering Jageitci's loveliness, and Gray Wolf's savage appeal.

Clay Brodie would likely produce strong sons. All devilishly handsome like their father.

What matter was it to her what type of children Clay Brodie might spawn in the future? Melissa tried to block the vision. The one that forced its way into her consciousness: her belly round with child, his child. She stopped pounding the dress in her hand against a rock and glanced around. What kind of life would this be for the babies she hoped to have one day?

In the distance, the innocent screams of children at play floated to her on the breeze. They sounded the same as the children she'd heard outside the lonely house she lived in through her father's withdrawal, and after his death. Even in a world fraught with danger, they could laugh, pretend, be happy with their fates, because they knew nothing else.

"Huera, come."

Startled, she turned at Swift Buck's command. Alarm gripped her at his worried expression. "Is it Cougar?" she whispered, dropping the wet bundle to rise. "What's happened?" she asked upon reaching the brave. He averted his gaze and walked away.

"Has something happened to Cougar?" she persisted, falling into step beside Swift Buck.

"I saw him a moment ago with the children," he answered solemnly. "He has gone bad in the head."

"Bad in the head?" she repeated, confused. "You mean, crazy?"

Swift Buck's brow furrowed. "Crazy, yes, that is the word."

Seeing his name written in the ashes had affected Clay strangely that morning, but Melissa couldn't believe such a trifling thing would make him snap. She followed Swift

Buck to where she'd heard the children playing. Something struck her as odd and raised the fine blond hairs on her arms. Silence.

The giggles and screams had stopped shortly before Swift Buck appeared. The brave held out a hand to halt her before they left the cover of trees. Ahead, Clay stood encircled by a group of wide-eyed children. He spoke softly, lifted his arms, and began to twirl around. Melissa clamped a hand over her mouth. Swift Buck misinterpreted her actions. He nodded sadly.

"See, his head has gone bad."

She tried to bring her humor under control. "No, he's not crazy. He's teaching them a game. You twirl around until you become dizzy, and then fall down."

Swift Buck regarded her skeptically. "Why?"

A sigh escaped her lips. "Did you not do this as a child?"

"No. Our children learn about life in their games. The boys pretend war, and the girls play at work and mothering. I see no purpose to this game."

"There isn't any," Melissa agreed. "The only reason is to laugh."

"They think Cougar has gone bad in the head, too," Swift Buck pointed out. "By tonight, their mothers and fathers will believe the same."

"Then it will be my fault. I told him about the game yesterday. He thought it odd, the same as you. Did Cougar play war games as a child?"

"Yes, and it was hard to be his friend. Always, he had to run faster, shoot farther, be the most cunning warrior. And always he was. When I remember those days, I see now that Cougar was the best because it pleased the red-haired man."

"His father," Melissa mused to herself. "Was Hiram Brodie accepted among you the same as his son?"

Swift Buck snorted softly. "Cougar earned his right to be here. The red-haired man bought our fathers with firewater and trinkets. He lusted for our mothers, stayed long after his welcome, and was not missed when he came no more. The People grew to respect Cougar for his bravery, for his Apache heart. The red-haired man showed no pride in his son unless he proved himself skilled at war, a necessary game to us, but one that teaches hate. Among The People, Cougar learned acceptance. We do not judge him by his skin, or by his father's blood. He is simply one of us."

As the sight of his name had hit Clay with force earlier, Melissa felt staggered by Swift Buck's revelation. "The ties that bind," she whispered weakly. How would she ever sever them? With the alphabet? Hardly. She could think of only one force more powerful than acceptance. Love. Melissa dared not contemplate the remote possibility of stealing Clay Brodie's heart from the Apaches. She dared not consider it, because if she managed the feat, her own heart might become compromised.

Watching his attempt to mimic her actions of yesterday, she felt an unmistakable tug in the vicinity of her chest. Robert Towbridge seemed like a distant dream, vague and unimportant. Clay was reality. And not as frightening as once she'd thought. Not nearly so unappealing to her as he should be.

A chuckle from Swift Buck recaptured her attention. Three of the children were humoring Clay in his obvious insistence they attempt the game. They were awkward and slow at first, then speeded their efforts. Two stopped abruptly, tried to walk, fell down, and dissolved into fits of giggles. The third joined them shortly. Curious, the other children began to participate.

To her surprise, Swift Buck left her side and joined Clay in the clearing. When he began to twirl as well, she laughed out loud. Although she doubted Clay heard her over the noise, he must have sensed her presence. He glanced toward the trees, his gaze scanning the area until he found her.

His face darkened for a moment, then he returned the smile she aimed in his direction. She couldn't say when harmless amusement gave way to something more. Their eyes locked and sent messages past the limits of innocence, beyond the boundaries of mere suggestiveness. He looked away first, much to Melissa's embarrassment. But not before she saw the same wariness mirrored in his eyes. Whatever was happening between them, it was dangerous.

Shouting penetrated the noisy clearing. The laughter died away. Melissa squinted up at a distant bluff where she knew a guard stood posted. The man cupped his hands around his mouth, then jerked forward. Horrified, she watched him plummet to the ground, an arrow protruding from his back.

The scene unfolding was too familiar. Like the nightmares still haunting her dreams. Frozen in fear, she heard Clay's harsh command to the children, saw them scurry into the trees, and couldn't seem to move her feet.

"Go with them, Huera! They know where to hide!"

Dumbly, she stared back at him. It wasn't that Melissa didn't want to follow Clay's order; it was simply a matter of being unable. Fear rooted her to the spot. The heathens would appear out of thin air, the same as before. Her eyes frantically searched the distance, waiting to catch a glimpse of hell. When the demons struck, they did so in a suicidal fashion, considering there weren't but a handful of them.

A group of about five charged over the bluff. Two quickly met with arrows and fell from their horses. Loud cries sounded to her left, then to her right, and finally from behind. With a feeling of dread, Melissa realized they were cut off.

The blood racing through her veins roused her from shock. It was too late to catch up with the children and find their hiding place. The tepee, Melissa decided, would at least offer a measure of protection. She turned to run, then halted, glancing over her shoulder at Clay. The knife he kept in his moccasin caught the sun's glint. Other braves had come from camp, loaded down with spears and bows.

Clay placed the knife between his teeth and bent to quickly strap on a pouch of arrows, then take up a bow. She saw no fear etched in the lines of his face. He'd become Apache, and in all honesty, Melissa could only thank God he possessed a savage nature.

The fact that she made it to camp without being struck by the arrows whizzing around her, Melissa counted as a small miracle. She'd almost reached the tepee when she heard a scream. Mesa, the girl who'd cut Melissa's hair and been honored with a ceremony, suddenly appeared from behind a tepee. A painted savage came thundering behind her.

He grabbed Mesa by the braids and tried to pull her onto his horse. Without thought to her own safety, Melissa retrieved a sturdy stick littering the ground and rushed toward the scuffle.

Her shaking hands threw her aim off, and instead of hitting the Indian, she delivered a solid blow to his horse's rump. Melissa snatched Mesa's arm while the brave fought to keep his horse under control. They'd only gotten two steps when she felt a cruel tug against her scalp. Her eyes watering with the pain, she twisted around to confront another Indian. This one had his hand twisted in her hair.

"Run, Mesa!" she shouted, releasing the girl. "Run!"

Although she hadn't spoken in Apache, Mesa needed no prompting. The girl ran toward the cover of trees bordering the stream. A horse raced past Melissa, the same animal she'd smacked on the rear. Mesa's speed was no match for the mounted Indian who came alongside her and swept her up. With a cry of victory, the brave continued toward the trees.

Melissa raised the stick against her attacker. He easily wrested the weapon away, then tried to jerk her up in front of him. She fought back, clawing frantically at the hand clasped around her arm. One minute the Indian sat his horse, the next he tumbled to the ground, Clay Brodie attached to his middle. No, it wasn't Clay. It was Cougar who quickly straddled the Indian and drew his knife across the brave's throat. Cougar who rose without batting a lash, having just killed a man, and turned angry eyes on Melissa.

"You should have gone when I told you to! Get inside the tepee, beneath the mats." He wiped the bloody knife against his buckskins, then motioned toward the lodge. "Go!"

167

On trembling legs, Melissa hurried to do his bidding. At the flap, his voice drew her up short.

"If they take you, I will come for you. Know as surely as the sun will rise, if I'm alive, I'll find you."

Chapter Sixteen

"If I'm alive" echoed through her head as she lay trembling beneath the mats. Melissa had clamped her hands over her ears to block out the sounds of trampling hooves and war cries. It seemed as if hours passed before the hides were thrown back. She gasped, terrified by the sight of a bloody Indian looming over her.

"It's over. Your help is needed."

"Clay," she whispered in relief, then scrambled up to get a closer look at him. His body was coated with blood. "I can't tell where you're hurt. I'll get a cloth and wash you off."

"No need," he said. "Very little of the blood is mine. Killing is dirty work, about the same as skinning. I've never cared for either, but out of necessity, I've learned to do them both well."

It wasn't a day to examine his morals, or to judge him by too strict a code of ethics. Survival of the fittest reigned, and Melissa could only find it in herself to be thankful Clay Brodie was among the fit.

"How bad is it?" She glanced toward the closed tepee flap.

"Only three tribe members dead, a handful seriously injured, and many with minor cuts and scrapes. The women and children are safe."

"Mesa?"

"Taken."

The news threatened to crumple Melissa to the mats. She swayed. "What will they do to the girl?"

Clay clasped her arm in a supportive gesture. "I don't know. It depends on whether the Comanche took her as a slave for his family or to be his wife."

"Wife? She's not old enough to marry!"

"Mesa is of childbearing age now. To some, that's old enough."

Outraged, Melissa pulled away from him, her strength fueled by anger. "They should go after her this very minute. The longer they wait, the farther away the Comanches can take her."

"Those in any condition to follow are exhausted. Injuries must be seen to, the damage surmised. A council meeting will be held later tonight to decide what should be done about Mesa."

"Tonight?" she repeated incredulously. "Who knows what they might do to her between now and the time a plan of action is decided upon? Don't her parents care what may be happening to their daughter?"

Even though his face was streaked with blood and dirt, weariness shone in the natural lines etched at the corners of Clay's eyes. Regardless, he mustered the ability to become aggravated.

"They're sick with worry, but understand the tribe does not consist only of Mesa. The Comanches trampled the crops, scattered horses, stole jerky drying on the racks meant to help feed The People through winter. Sometimes the good of one must be sacrificed for the good of all. A plan not well thought out is most often a failure. Mesa must wait until other matters of importance are attended to. The shaman needs your help. Come on, we're wasting precious time."

To argue further seemed futile, and he was right, they were compromising the lives of others. Melissa quickly

170

gathered what items she thought would prove useful in tending the wounded, and followed Clay outside.

By nightfall, death had claimed another brave, one who left two wives and five children behind. Melissa had done what she could, or what the injured would allow, and now sat in the dirt with her head between her hands, exhausted. The council had assembled.

Cougar was not among the group of men she saw file into a lodge Clay told her had been constructed for meetings. Her gaze searched the darkening distance. He was out there somewhere, moving the Comanche dead to the outer perimeters of camp, to be collected by their own later, or consumed by predators, whichever found them first.

She'd shuddered when he'd told her his remaining tasks for the day. Melissa had seen enough of death and destruction since coming to this untamed territory to last a lifetime. How did these women bear it, the beauty of one sunrise, and the horror of the next? The crops were all but lost.

Learning they'd been purposely trampled by the hooves of Comanche ponies infuriated her. She'd helped tend the maize field, picked the ripened ears so the women could cut the kernels and make cornmeal, and now there were few stocks left standing. They'd rationed out a portion of corn to each family, and stored the rest. A safeguard, Clay said, against the coming winter. Now the stores were gone.

Male voices carried to her. Melissa straightened, recognizing one deep-pitched tone in particular. His taller frame stood out clearly among the group of braves approaching camp. Melissa couldn't ignore the sudden leap in her pulse, the relief in seeing him again, alive, whole. A boy hurried up to the group and said something to Clay. He turned toward the council lodge, then noticed her sitting in the dirt.

"Go inside. All that's needed for tonight has been done."

"I'm waiting for you," she admitted. "I wasn't sure when to prepare the meal. I'll fix your supper now."

"I'm not hungry," he countered softly. "What I did today

171

was necessary. I imagine killing works up an appetite in some, but I won't be able to eat for a couple of days. Find your mat. Go to sleep. Gray Wolf has requested my presence."

"I can't sleep," she argued just as quietly. "Not until I know what they've decided about Mesa. I'll fix you something regardless of whether you eat it or not. It will keep me occupied until you return."

He sighed. "You're the stubbornest woman I know."

"Do you know many?"

The question startled her as much as it obviously did Clay. Melissa wanted to snatch the words back. They hinted at jealousy. She rarely saw him converse with the Apache women, but had noticed more than one interested set of dark eyes follow his movements around camp.

A slight smile fought its way through the grime on his face. "I know a few as well as I want to know them." He turned toward the council lodge. "More than a few," he corrected, still walking. "A few too many, anyone decent would say. A few—"

"White women, like me," Melissa specified, noting the anger in her voice.

He turned. "No. I've never known any like you."

It was happening again, whatever force had held their eyes locked in the clearing before the attack. Melissa made certain she looked away first this time.

"You're not only stubborn, you haven't got the sense to run when you're told," he muttered irritably. "You could have gotten yourself killed today. Or you could have been taken by the Comanches with that foolish attempt to rescue Mesa . . ." His voice trailed off as he continued toward the council lodge. "You're either dim-witted, or the most courageous woman I've ever had the misfortune to get tangled up with. No, Melissa Sheffield, formerly of St. Louis. I don't know any like you."

Despite the afternoon's tragic events, she found the strength to smile as he made his grumbling retreat. Although he sounded annoyed, respect flavored his insults. If he wasn't careful, he might forget she was only his slave, a possession and nothing more. The smile faded from her lips. And if she wasn't careful, she would forget who she was as well.

"What you ask is not fair!" Clay glared at Gray Wolf, then tried to bring his temper under control. "The day has been long," he said, explaining his short fuse. "Huera belongs to me. You have no right to make this decision without my permission."

Gray Wolf lifted a dark brow. "I am leader of this tribe. I have every right. Have you forgotten our rules? The good of The People comes first. Huera is not Apache, but she will get one of our own back among us. The council has spoken; we trade Huera to the Comanches for Mesa."

"No!" Clay took a deep breath and let it out slowly. "Huera has brought good medicine to the Apaches. Did she not heal Swift Buck? Save the sons still growing inside your wife? Today, was she not at the shaman's side helping those injured? And you did not see her, but she ignored her own safety to help Mesa before the girl was taken. Huera does not deserve for her fate to be altered again. She would never survive among the Comanches!"

"Yet she has managed well among the Apaches," Gray Wolf spat. "If she dies in their camp, it is your fault, Cougar. Mesa being taken is your fault! You should have been defending *her*, not a slave with white skin!"

Blue eyes clashed with black. The gathered older men shifted nervously. Clay knew he should lower his gaze in acknowledgment that the leader was right, but he did not. He'd felt no concern for Mesa at the time, only a gut-clawing fear Melissa would be taken from him.

"If it is my fault Mesa is gone, let me get her back. Give me three days."

The leader snorted. "Three days? And you will go alone? You have gone bad in the head, just as The People are saying."

"It will take longer to find them and make a parley," Clay pointed out. "You cannot be certain they will agree to the exchange. Three days, that is all I ask."

"No."

"Maybe I have forgotten the rules. Is this not a matter for the council to decide?"

Red crept into Gray Wolf's cheeks. "It is," he admitted. "I am against your request. Who will say otherwise?"

Slowly, Clay's gaze traveled the lined faces surrounding him. He tried to appear calm, but a trickle of sweat traced a path down the side of his face.

"I will," Crooked Nose spoke up. "The slave did save my son. I say Cougar should be given the three days."

"And I," another said. "It is not so much to ask."

Only one other remained. Mesa's grandfather. He stared thoughtfully at Clay. "I remember the days of your youth, Cougar. You could slip among us and walk our camp for days before any knew you had come. It became a game, and I do not recall you losing." His gaze landed on Gray Wolf. "I want my granddaughter returned. Cougar, I believe, can do this for me. The council has spoken."

A curt nod from Gray Wolf dismissed the meeting. Out of respect, the older men were allowed to leave first. After the last one filed out, Clay rose. Gray Wolf lumbered to his feet. Clay stood taller, but the other emitted a strength equal to his.

"Three days," Gray Wolf reminded stiffly. "If you have not returned with Mesa, we will take Huera and seek a parley."

Clay said nothing as Gray Wolf moved toward the exit. But before the leader slipped outside, Clay asked, "Why do you want me to fail at this?"

His stance remained rigid, then his shoulders relaxed and Gray Wolf turned to face him. "I would rather you fail this time. When you fail next, it will cost your life. Gentle words are hard for me to find, but you and I have been friends for many years. There is a place inside me that holds the special times we have shared together. Tonight, I tried to cheat destiny. I wanted the woman gone from us. My wife sees good in her, but I see only my vision. How can I find anything but hate in my heart for her?"

Gooseflesh rose on Clay's arms. He felt as if someone had just walked over his grave. "Visions have been known to

174

be false," he said in a casual tone. "You worry too much, you always have."

Gray Wolf didn't return his smile. The flap was thrown open. Once outside, the leader strolled toward his own lodge. He turned back. "I did not think it would be so easy for her to tame the great cat, but my eyes have witnessed the looks that pass between you. Fight her, or she will be the death of you, Cougar. That is, unless the Comanches send you to the spirit plane first. Walk softly, brother."

His advice was heeded as Clay entered the lodge he shared with Melissa. Despite her promise to fix him a meal, he expected exhaustion would have gotten the best of her. Not so.

"What was the decision?"

"I leave at first light," he answered, joining her by the grate, where supper simmered over the fire.

"Do you have to go?"

"Yes." He shrugged from his bloody shirt.

Melissa quickly fetched him a water skin and a cloth to wash. He noticed the tremble in her lower lip.

"How long will you be gone?"

"Three days, I suspect. Stay with Laughing Stream until I return. Don't wander off by yourself."

Her lips trembled all the more with his warning. "Why can't you stay here? Didn't you do enough killing for them today?"

Clay sighed. He ran a hand through his hair, not up to a confrontation. She had a strange, desperate look in her eyes. "You should go to your mat. It's been an eventful day, for both of us."

"I'm sure I'll get a peaceful night's rest," she countered. "What do you suppose I'll dream about? Beautiful meadows? Children twirling at play? Passage ceremonies? Or will it be berries? Honeycomb, perhaps? Blood. Screaming. Killing. Destru—"

"Huera." He took a firm hold of her shoulders. "Hysterics won't make it all go away. Try to forget it tonight. I promise, it will still be there in the morning."

175

"Forget?" She laughed. "You'd like me to forget. Forget everything! I'm not Huera! I hate that name!" Melissa began to pummel his chest with her fists. "I hate this place! I hate you!"

She'd clearly slipped over the edge. Clay wasn't certain what to do. He supposed he could slap her and shock her into calming down. But no, he discarded the option. He could kill a man, but he couldn't hit a woman. For lack of a better alternative, he grabbed her flailing fists and pulled her against him.

His captive struggled for a moment, then burst into sobs. He eased her down on the buffalo robes and held her until her tears were spent and her ragged breaths steadied, then gently caressed the wetness of her cheek.

Poised at the abyss of exhausted sleep, she snuggled her face into his palm and whispered, "I hate you, Clay Brodie. I really do."

Chapter Seventeen

It took Melissa a day and a half to make the realization. The male faces she'd come to recognize over the past two months were all present and accounted for, all except five. Four had been buried not far from the camp. And one had slipped away before the hour of dawn the morning after the raid, leaving her to wonder how long she'd lain sleeping in his arms, and why a man of few morals hadn't taken advantage of her vulnerability that night.

Clay Brodie was a constant contradiction. He could slit an enemy's throat and comfort a woman in the space of a few hours, teach children a game one moment and take up a bow and arrow to fight the next. He was ever-changing, like the trampled ground beneath her hands, the stream gurgling in the distance, the green grass slowly turning to yellow; he was life itself.

"You miss Cougar, no?"

Melissa glanced up from picking through the trampled ears of maize, surprised that Jageitci had spoken to her. A quick survey of the area told her why. They were as close to

177

Ronda Thompson

being alone as possible among a tribe of many. Jageitci kept digging through the broken stalks, her head bowed so that from a distance, no one would be able to discern the two were conversing.

"No," Melissa quickly assured her. "I was just curious about who went with him to rescue Mesa. I'm having trouble figuring out what braves are gone."

Jageitci scowled at a ruined ear of maize and threw it in the pile to be fed to the horses. "None," she said softly. "Cougar went alone."

The motion of Melissa's hands ceased. "Alone?" she whispered. "But that would be suicide. Why didn't your husband and those capable go with him? I don't understand!"

"Quiet," Jageitci warned. "Your voice grows loud with worry. The council had decided to trade you for Mesa. Cougar asked them for three days to bring her back."

"They would have given me to the Comanches?"

"It made sense," the woman defended. "You are a slave. A white slave. Mesa is one of our own. Cougar knows the wisdom of such a trade, but these days, his thinking is not straight. His head is too full of a woman with blond hair and green eyes."

Within her growing fear for Clay's safety, and the horror of envisioning herself handed over to a tribe she considered more menacing than the Apaches, a small tide of pleasure rose inside Melissa.

"His head is obviously empty," she argued under her breath. "Why would he make such a foolish offer?"

Gray Wolf's wife rolled her gaze skyward. "For you, Huera. I did not believe Cougar's heart could be trapped, but many women would pay a man much to look at them the way he looks at you. For his captive, the lion might sheathe his claws and lie down with the lamb. My husband is certain that will be a sad day, but I know every dark place needs light. His visions are not as strong as my gift."

"How do you stand this life?" Melissa bit out. "The constant danger, the warring, the death, the fear that every time

178

Gray Wolf rides out, he will not come back? How do any of these women stand it?"

"For those not born outside, it is simpler. This life is all they have known. You and I must be stronger, for we knew a different world before we came to this one. I bear it because I love a man who is of The People. I must trust in Gray Wolf and in our God to protect us both."

The woman's earlier biblical reference hadn't escaped Melissa. "Are you Catholic?"

"Once, I was Catholic. Now, I am Apache. I believe there is only one God, but that he is known by many names."

"Maybe," Melissa agreed. "What happens if Cougar does not return in three days?"

Long lashes lowered over Jageitci's dark eyes. "They will take you and try to parley with the Comanches."

A knot formed in Melissa's stomach. "This sight you have, can you use it to see if Cougar will succeed?"

"No." She sighed. "It is not a thing I can control. Sometimes it comes when I am looking at a person, or a place. The sight visits me less often as I grow older, but once, when Gray Wolf first brought me here, I saw Cougar as a boy in my vision. It was horrible. I am afraid to look at him now, afraid of what I might see, of what I might hear, of what I might feel."

She'd paled under her dark complexion. Melissa shivered slightly in the warm afternoon breeze. "What did you see?"

Jageitci shook her head. "I will not tell you. It is wrong to speak of other's sorrows when they do not know I have seen their past. Pain is a very private emotion for some. Cougar hides the scars inside him well, if he cannot hide the ones on the outside."

"I want to understand him."

"Why?" Gray Wolf's wife transfixed her with an intense stare. "So you can use the knowledge against him? Or because you care for Cougar?"

The truth wasn't simple. "I'm not sure," Melissa answered. "I've seen the boy in him, too. It touched me deeply, but the man should know keeping me a prisoner is wrong. He isn't a savage, but he's far from civilized. I don't know who he is."

A smile shaped the Spanish woman's lips. "You and Cougar are both captives. Is it not clear to you that he does not know, either? Maybe you were sent to help him find the answers." Jageitci rose and dusted her skirts, then picked up a basket of ruined maize and walked toward the corral.

To call out a denial would be to expose the fact she and Jageitci had been conversing in Spanish. Melissa continued her search for undamaged maize. Sent to help him find the answers, indeed. She hadn't been up for ten minutes the morning he'd left before her thoughts had turned to the journal.

After only a second's deliberation concerning his stern warning to leave the diary alone, she'd scurried in search of his pouches. They were gone. He'd taken them with him or placed them elsewhere. If she found him a puzzle, Clay obviously knew her too well.

Her gaze scanned the distance, willing him to appear. What if he never returned? Her eyes began to sting. She sniffed loudly. "Foolish man," Melissa grumbled. "You'll get yourself killed and then where will I be? Traded to the Comanches. Probably dead within a week. Why do you take these risks, Clay Brodie? Why can't you just remain the devil and be done with it?"

"Some are saying Huera is as crazy in the head as Cougar. Talking to yourself only strengthens their beliefs."

There was no need for Melissa to look up and verify who spoke to her. Only one man besides Clay conversed with her in English—conversed with her at all for that matter.

"You should have gone with him," she said between tight lips. "How can he possibly rescue Mesa from thirty or more Comanche braves?"

"I did not know he was going," Swift Buck answered. "The band that attacked us were not all from the same tribe. They will split up and go their separate ways. He will wait until this happens, and only have maybe ten or fifteen to deal with."

"Oh, that's better," she replied sarcastically. "Ten or fifteen shouldn't be any trouble for the great Cougar."

He smiled over her cross tone. "You do not show much faith in his abilities as a warrior. There is more to fighting than killing. Cougar knows when he is outnumbered. He must be cunning, must be smarter than his enemies."

"The man isn't too smart or he wouldn't have gone alone," she argued. "How can you make light of this? Aren't you worried about him?"

Swift Buck shrugged. "Cougar will return, or he will not. Worry changes nothing."

"No, but it helps pass the time," she snapped. "If you won't humor me, go bother someone else."

She didn't glance up to verify his departure. Her ears heard the soft rustle of cornstalks. "Swift Buck, wait!" She lifted her head. "Do you have faith in him? I mean, do you believe—"

"Yes," he interrupted. "He will return, Huera."

"How can you be certain?"

The brave lifted his chin and sniffed the air. "I smell him."

Heat from the warm afternoon sun suddenly seemed hotter against Melissa's skin. "You smell him on me," she explained.

His dark brows lifted. "Yes, but I also smell him in the wind. Close your eyes, do you not catch his scent?"

Melissa tried. "No," she answered with a sigh. "I only smell his fading scent on my dress."

"To tell the truth, I did not catch his scent on the wind, either. But I know he will come."

She sighed again. "Because you have faith?"

A smile tugged at the corners of his lips. "No, because I see him, skirting his way through the trees. He knows where the guards are posted. Cougar has always liked to come and go as he chooses, to make his Apache brothers ashamed they were unaware of his arrival."

Her heart lurched inside her chest. Melissa squinted in the direction Swift Buck gazed. She didn't see anything, not at first. The moment her eyes found him, the sentry on the bluff let out a whoop. The cry was taken up by others. Women dropped their baskets of scavenged crops, their bundles of firewood, and raced toward the trees.

Had her knees not been trembling so badly, Melissa would have risen from her crouched position. Instead, relief settled her in the dirt on her bottom. She waved away the hand Swift Buck offered her.

"No, go on ahead and welcome him with the others. I'll just stay here."

"You cannot fight him forever, Huera," he said softly. "These feelings you have for Cougar, they will escape, no matter how you try to keep them inside. I know this to be true."

"He's the wrong man for me," she claimed, tilting her head defiantly.

"And *she* was the wrong woman, but our hearts do not always listen to the wisdom of our words."

As he walked away, a scream of joy echoed off the bluffs. Tears gathered in Melissa's eyes when Mesa slid off Two Moons's back and ran ahead, flinging herself into her mother's arms. The girl was surrounded in seconds, shouts of happiness resounding off the trees. For Cougar, the Apaches displayed only reverence as he picked his way through the woods.

Dark whiskers shadowed his cheeks, the redness in his eyes spoke of nights without sleep, and still, Melissa thought he must be the most perfect man ever created. Her stomach fluttered when his gaze traveled the faces lining his path. An older Indian wearing an expression of gratitude stepped forward. The Apache clasped Clay's hand and spoke to him.

In answer, the hero of the day merely nodded, his gaze ever searching the area. She had no idea what to expect when he spotted her among the maize husks. Certainly not the instant heat that flooded her veins, the tension that stretched between them and filled her with longing. Desire for what she couldn't identify in her innocence.

Unconsciously, she moistened her dry lips. He shifted uncomfortably on Two Moons's back, then nudged him forward. Their eyes held until he stood before her. Clay lifted one leg and slid off his mount's back. The silence between them became uncomfortable.

"I'm surprised to see you," Melissa said to fill the void. "I figured you for a dead man."

The smoldering embers within his eyes flared. "You figured wrong. Are you disappointed?"

"That I won't be traded?" Her laugh sounded nervous. "Hardly. Like I said, I find it amazing you managed to rescue Mesa from fifteen Comanches and come out of it in one piece."

"There were only twelve, and sound sleepers—most of them, anyway."

"Twelve?" she repeated, as if his feat were no great accomplishment. "Well, even so, you must be tired and hungry."

"I am hungry." He ran his heated gaze over her from head to toe.

"And exhausted," she insisted, praying to God he'd leave her so she wouldn't do something foolish. She had the strongest urge to throw her arms around his neck and kiss him.

"Maybe you should follow me to the lodge and see that I'm sated and settled in."

"I have chores to complete," she blurted. "There's skins to fill, wood to gather, clothes to wash—"

His finger pressed against her lips halted her excuses. "It was a simple yes or no question. Considering that I've just returned from a dangerous mission few could have accomplished without being killed or captured, no one would object if you were to abandon your tasks. They'd probably find it insulting if you didn't."

Although his innuendos were sometimes puzzling, Melissa had no trouble understanding what he'd just said. "Oh, I see. I'm to show my gratitude. Humbly follow you to the lodge and gladly give you whatever you ask in exchange for what you've done for me? Now I'm no longer confused about why you'd stoop to anything so heroic. You expected a different trade to take place."

His face turned red. "If I wanted a woman that badly, I wouldn't have to look hard or travel far to get one!"

"Then why did you risk your life to keep me from being traded to the Comanches?"

He seemed at a loss for words, but only for a moment. "Because Mesa's grandfather asked me to. He didn't want to wait for a parley. I went for him, not you."

"Oh." The bluster left her voice. Melissa suspected she was blushing to the roots of her hair. "Well, that makes sense."

"Yes," he agreed.

Another awkward silence followed, thankfully broken by Mesa's appearance. She spoke softly to Clay. Other than a bruise along one cheek, the girl looked no worse for wear from her ordeal. When Mesa turned dark eyes on her, Melissa tamped down the odd disappointment she felt having learned the true reason behind Clay's courageous rescue, and smiled.

She was genuinely happy to see Mesa back where she belonged. The girl did not return her smile, but said something to Clay. After a second of deliberation, he removed a knife from his moccasin and handed it to Mesa.

Alarm skittered up Melissa's spine. The maiden faced her. In a slow, deliberate manner, Mesa cut off a lock of long, dark hair. She held out the glossy strands.

"Take it," Clay instructed. "She offers you her friendship and does so at the risk of censure from her people. You've won yourself a coup, Huera."

With hands still unsteady from the day's excitement, Melissa took the offering. Only then did Mesa smile at her. Tears misted Melissa's eyes as the girl handed Clay his knife and turned to join her less than enthusiastic family.

Stunned she'd actually made a friend among the Apaches, one with the courage to openly acknowledge that friendship, Melissa watched the retreating figure of Mesa. The girl's family remained stolid until she reached them. After a stern glance from her parents, their joy resurfaced with a show of hugs and laughter.

"I can't believe she . . ." Melissa's voice trailed off. Clay no longer stood before her, but led Two Moons toward the corral. She chewed her bottom lip indecisively, then went after him.

"I suppose I owe you an apology for my earlier accusations." She stared at her feet rather than looking at him while he slipped the bridle from Two Moons's head. "I'm sometimes too quick to jump to conclusions. If you're truly hungry, I'll fix you a meal."

After giving the stallion a light slap on the rear that sent him trotting into the corral, Clay hung the bridle on a peg and turned to her. He lifted her chin.

"You didn't misunderstand me. It wasn't food I felt a craving for, but the sweetness of your lips, the softness of your skin, the sound you make in your throat when I kiss you. What I honestly want is to feast on the pleasure we can give one another. But I shouldn't desire you, because you've been nothing but trouble for me, and trouble is the last thing I need. Return to your chores, I'm going to bed."

Without a backward glance, he left her slack-jawed, and dry-mouthed, reeling from the onslaught of his husky admissions. Melissa leaned against the slats of the corral fence for support. She felt weak, breathless, ashamed of the heat in her lower regions, of the rapid beat of her heart. She must escape this place before it was too late. Swift Buck's words came back to haunt her in that moment.

You cannot fight him forever, Huera.

Forever seemed to be slipping away like dirt swirling in a dust devil. Her every thought seemed to be connected to Clay. Her very existence. She rallied her strength and pushed away from the corral. The sight of Tall Blade standing a short distance away drew her up short. He held a squirming rabbit in one hand and a knife in the other. The poor animal had not yet made the transition from winter white to brown. In horror, she watched him pull his blade across the rabbit's snowy neck. As its blood spilled, her stomach recoiled.

She knew that with the Indians' way of life, and with her own for that matter, animals must be sacrificed in order to survive. Still, Tall Blade seemed to take perverse pleasure in

185

slitting the rabbit's throat. He watched the animal struggle, then smiled as the life drained from its butchered body. When he glanced up, she expected him to look at her. Maybe to indicate he wished that she and the rabbit could trade places.

But it wasn't Melissa his strange eyes sought, but the retreating figure of a man these people considered one of their own. She suspected in that instant that the Apache more than disliked Clay Brodie. He didn't want him to walk among them—deeply resented the fact that he did. Why was the mere sight of Clay a thorn in the Apache's side?

Was it the color of his flesh beneath the sun's camouflage, or did Tall Blade's hatred go deeper than skin? Beyond red or white? She had no way of knowing. She knew only one thing. Clay should watch his back around the man, or perhaps more fittingly, his neck.

Chapter Eighteen

In sleep, the chiseled lines of his face softened and Clay Brodie looked almost innocent. The buffalo hides spread across him had slipped indecently low. Melissa tried to keep her gaze focused above his neck, but failed miserably to do so.

His broad chest rose and fell with steady breaths, smooth as polished marble, with the exception of a few coarse strands around his copper nipples, and a thin line of dark hair that ran the length of his muscled stomach. Her eyes traveled the line until they met with the furry nap of a buffalo hide.

She wondered if he was totally bare or wearing a loin-cloth. Naked, she suspected. Indecent and obliviously unaware a woman studied him. Lest she became too tempted to touch him, she busied herself with preparing a stew.

Clay slept through the night, and by all indications, meant to pass his day in the same manner. She would leave him something to eat, even if by his confession yesterday, it might not completely satisfy his appetite. When she'd first seen Clay among the trees, the emotion that gripped her was stronger than mere desire.

187

When she feared he wouldn't return, the thought of never seeing him again seemed far worse than worry for her own fate.

Her feelings for Robert were shallow in comparison. If she didn't marry him, didn't have the secure, prosperous life she intended, would it be so horrible?

That question alone deeply disturbed Melissa. She tore her gaze from the sleeping man and hurriedly finished the meal preparations, wanting out, away from him, away from this place where Robert and an existence among civilized society drifted further from reality. Clay's overwhelming maleness too easily lured her from her objective: to be free.

Once outside, Melissa walked briskly toward the women making use of the damaged crops. Husks were being laid out to dry, and trampled maize cut up for horse feed. She kept her head lowered, her eyes downcast. The arms she stretched out before her were no longer white, but sunkissed. Her hands were red with the amount of work she did daily, and she couldn't recall what actual cotton felt like against her skin. How quickly she'd adjusted, how soon she'd forgotten.

A basket of corn was shoved in her direction. An old woman nodded toward the corral. Melissa lifted the heavy basket and carried it to the fence. Swift Buck took the feed. He and two other braves were doling out rations to the horses.

"Where is Cougar?"

"Sleeping."

"What is wrong, Huera?"

His perception unnerved her somewhat. A people so in tune with each other made having even a private dilemma difficult. "Nothing. He's fine, just tired."

"I know Cougar is well. I saw that he had no wounds. I meant with you. What brings that look into your eyes?"

Swift Buck's inquiry surprised Melissa. But then again, they had become relaxed in each other's company. She found that odder yet. What next, would she be inviting savages over for supper?

Although joining a quilting bee was out of the question, she supposed she'd be tanning hides in the future, if they ever trusted her enough to allow a sharp instrument into her possession. Her sarcastic thoughts sped the hysteria fast rising inside her.

"Fear," she whispered.

"Has Cougar hurt you?"

His handsome features reflected true concern. As she gazed up at him, Melissa recalled a time when she regarded him as less than human. But he was human, a man, one who wasn't afraid to care, one who might help her when another one wouldn't.

"I must speak with you," she said softly, glancing around. "Alone."

The dark eyes staring down on her turned wary. "It will cause talk if we go off together."

"Then meet me in that thicket of trees." She nodded toward the spot. "I'll tell the women I need a moment of privacy." When he appeared hesitant, she stooped to begging. "Please."

"Huera," he said her name with a sigh. "Whatever trouble you are having with Cougar, I cannot interfere. You know that."

"This isn't about him. It's a personal problem. I need your advice." She hated to lie to Swift Buck, but desperation drove her.

"We must return soon or someone will come looking for you."

"Yes," she agreed. "It won't take long."

After an uncomfortable amount of deliberation, he agreed. Melissa returned to the women, wondering how she could possibly convince him to help her. What would she say? That she was afraid she'd give in to the feelings she had for Cougar and ruin her life? That she was afraid he'd become her life? That she could not give him her passion, without giving him her heart?

189

No, she couldn't confess that she might be falling in love with the wrong man and hope Swift Buck would take pity on her. Robert. She would use the man who once meant something to her, if she couldn't honestly say he still did.

No one seemed suspicious when she excused herself in sign language. Melissa thought they might hear the loud beating of her heart and know she was lying. Her steps were hurried, but not unnaturally so. The spot she'd chosen didn't take long to reach, but she saw no sign of Swift Buck. In the process of craning her neck in search, she ran smack into his arms. Her fingernails dug into the corded muscles of his biceps.

"Help me escape," Melissa blurted. "I can't stay here anymore!" When Swift Buck tried to step away, Melissa dug her nails in deeper. "I know you understand what it is like to love someone and not be with them. There's a man waiting for me in Santa Fe. A man I promised to marry, join with," she clarified. "He's suffering right now because he believes I'm lost to him, the same way you're suffering. You have the power to restore my destiny, to steer my fate to the right path. Help me, Swift Buck."

"Do not speak to me of escape," he warned, his gaze darting back and forth. "You are a fool, Huera. Cougar is my brother and you go behind his back and ask me to help you deceive him, deceive my own people! I should slit your throat for plotting against us."

"Then do it," she ordered passionately. "I can't live without the man I love. If this is to be my fate, have mercy and kill me!"

"The Apaches show their enemies no mercy." Swift Buck tried to pull away again.

"I'm not your enemy." Melissa held fast, frantic to soften him. She knew of only one weakness he'd openly admitted. "Was Silent Wind your enemy?"

A hand clamped over her lips. "You will call her from the spirit world!"

Melissa shook her head, freeing her mouth in the process.

"And if she were alive and had been taken from you, wouldn't you go to any lengths to get her back?"

He lowered his gaze. "Yes. But she is gone, and you are not her." To demonstrate her weaker strength, he escaped, leaving bloody marks on his arms from her fingernails. "You must forget the man waiting for you. And I do not believe your heart belongs to him. Cougar has stolen it."

Despair swept over her as he walked away. If Swift Buck so easily saw through her facade, how long before Clay realized she'd become his for the taking? Her life would be altered forever were she to give herself to him. There could be no going back, no marriage to Robert. Melissa wasn't a woman to deceive a man in that way.

Force was one thing, or even manipulation. Hadn't she asked Swift Buck if he'd do anything to be reunited with the woman he loved? *But you don't love Robert*, the voice of guilt sounded in her head. Perhaps she could once Clay's overwhelming male presence was removed from her life. But then, an ordinary man would fade beside his magnificence. Suddenly, Melissa wondered if what she felt for Clay wasn't what any woman would feel given her circumstances.

Transference, wasn't that what they called it? Maybe she did love Robert, but had transferred that love to the most dominant force in her life. Her state of mind had been unstable at best since being captured. Surely she didn't maintain the clarity of mind to know whom or what she wanted anymore. Freedom, that was the only answer. She needed to make these decisions in her natural habitat.

"You should return," Swift Buck said from a short distance away, where he'd stopped.

Freedom. The word seduced her. Shouldn't she be willing to exchange whatever was necessary to gain her objective? She recalled the way Swift Buck's gaze often lingered on her hair. He missed Silent Wind. Could she use his weakness for a white woman to her advantage?

"You're wrong about what I feel for Cougar." She walked toward him, her knees trembling. "My desire for Robert tempts me to be weak with another. I want so badly to see him, to touch him." Although she trembled with fear, Melissa traced the strong line of Swift Buck's jaw. "To close my eyes and pretend his fingers are brushing my skin, igniting my passion."

His hand closed over her wrist.

"Is my skin not the same color as hers?" she whispered. "My hair the same color? If you closed your eyes, couldn't I become the woman you want me to be?"

The pressure on her wrist increased. His chest rose and fell with quickened breaths. Melissa honestly didn't know if she could continue with a seduction. Not even for freedom. But his hesitation spurred her on. She leaned forward and pressed her lips to his. They were firm and well-shaped, but sparked nothing inside of her. Likewise, he did not respond. She glanced up from beneath her lashes. His eyes were open.

"What is it you are doing?" he asked against her mouth.

Horrified she'd stooped to these measures, Melissa ended the contact. "I-I was kissing you," she stammered.

"Kissing?" He seemed puzzled. "The People do not put their mouths together. We consider it disgusting."

"Oh." Judging by the heat in her cheeks, her face was bright red. "Cougar does this. He does it well . . ." Her voice trailed thoughtfully. "Where did he learn it, if not here?"

Swift Buck shrugged. "Maybe with the women he visits in Santa Fe."

A ringing noise started in her ears. "He goes to Santa Fe?"

"Where else would he trade his furs?" Swift Buck provided, then clamped his lips tightly together.

It was too late to undo the damage. "Of course he does," she whispered, shocked it hadn't occurred to her before.

"You have been gone too long. Return, and do not ask me or anyone to help you escape again. You are not good at deception, Huera."

"I should ask Cougar to give me lessons," she countered, too furious to worry over her fate at the moment. "He's Apache when he feels like being an Indian, and white when the need calls for it. He could take me back, he just doesn't want to!"

"No," Swift Buck argued. "Gray Wolf forbids him to let you go. More and more whites are coming to our land. We must know that Cougar will not use his knowledge of our ways to help them fight us."

"And you believe if he can ignore my plight, he can ignore the plight of all his kind?"

"He must choose. Cougar will either be with us in battle—or against us."

"And where does that leave me?" she fumed. "Caught in the crossfire," she answered bitterly. "I didn't kill his sister. This isn't my war."

"When you came here to settle with a white man, it made this your war. Now, return to the women before they send someone to look for you. I do not want to explain why we are here together."

Her eyes filled with tears of frustration. Melissa stormed past him. She'd only gotten a few steps when he spoke again.

"While you belong to Cougar, I cannot interfere. Maybe when he leaves, I will ask for you, and then something can be done."

She wheeled around abruptly. "When he leaves?"

Color crept up his bronzed neck and darkened his high cheekbones. "I thought he would have told you. He stays with us only until the grass is yellow, then he returns to the mountain."

"He's leaving?" she repeated with disbelief. Now she understood what he'd been preparing her for, why he insisted she learn the ways of a good slave, although he personally seemed lax with her. "That coward!" The insult left her lips in a hoarse cry.

Swift Buck looked uncomfortable. "Go, Huera. When you reach the women, hold your stomach and wipe your mouth as if you were sick. That will explain your long absence. I have said too much today. It was not my place to tell you."

"No, it wasn't," she ground through her teeth. "He should have told me the truth from the beginning."

"Maybe Cougar is waiting until he believes you are strong enough to hear the truth."

"The wait is over," she countered calmly, despite the outrage churning her blood. "As soon as I finish my chores, I'll show him just how capable I've become!"

Chapter Nineteen

He must be dreaming. Clay guessed he'd fallen back to sleep after rousing himself to dress, ladling up a bowl of stew, then stretching out to let it cool. Her hands were gentle as they glided down his chest, her touch feather-light against his skin. A smile settled over his lips. Could he control the dream? If so, she would grow bolder.

In compliance with his wishes, her fingers traced the trail of hair leading to his leggings. When she hesitated, Clay willed her to continue. Too many nights he had lain awake, listening to the sound of her breathing, battling the temptation to steal across the invisible boundary she'd constructed and seduce her.

Wrapped within the hazy world of sleep, he allowed his desire full rein. Here, there were no tests, no differences to stand between them, no conscience that demanded he tell Melissa he must soon leave. He groaned in agony over what he must do, and in ecstasy over the feel of her hands sliding down his thighs.

If he could truly control the dream, she would have removed his clothing, but instead, she continued down the length of his legs. His feet seemed to be her destination. She wanted him naked, he reasoned. That goal couldn't be achieved without first removing his knee-high moccasins.

The dream became confusing. Her hands weren't intent on stripping, but searching him. He struggled up from exhaustion, his senses suddenly in tune to danger. Too late, he shook off the cobwebs of sleep. He opened his eyes and she was indeed there, her body stretched out on top of his, her gaze bright with passion. The blade pressed against his throat, however, assured Clay that her only desire at the moment was to kill him.

His stare locked with hers. She smiled. Clay fought his natural instinct to reverse their positions. He knew her reflexes were no match for his, knew with little effort he could snatch her wrist, roll on top of her, and end the threat she posed. Instead, he waited, curious as to what his captive thought to prove.

"How helpless am I?" she growled down at him. "How weak? Too feebleminded to figure out you're nothing more than a lying, hypocritical coward? Too stupid not to ask myself how the son of a trapper, a man who's confessed to that profession himself, makes his living in these mountains? You don't claim to be an Apache when you're walking the streets of Santa Fe, do you? No," she answered for him. "You just put on your white face and take their money for your furs, then probably spend it on whores, on women who don't find touching mouths disgusting!"

"How do you know the Apaches consider kissing unclean? I never told you that."

Her face exploded with pink. Clay wasn't certain if she considered his calm inquiry insulting, or embarrassing. Neither, he decided. She looked guilty. The pressure against his throat intensified. A mistake, since she used the dull edge.

She'd obviously learned the trick the day he'd held this same blade against her throat. He'd assumed she would be too frightened to notice. Another mistake, his that time.

Melissa Sheffield, formerly of St. Louis, wasn't a woman to be underestimated.

"You're not in any position to ask questions," she pointed out. "It's my turn. When you decide you're tired of playing Indian, will you just sneak away like the coward you are, or did your interest in learning to read and write stem from a desire to leave me a note?"

Clay sighed. In one swift movement, he reversed the situation. His attacker ended up on her back, her arms stretched overhead. He squeezed her wrist until she gasped and released the knife. With a growl of outrage, the woman brought her knee up, in all likelihood with the intent of compromising his ability to produce future generations. He pressed down, using his powerful thighs to part her legs.

The sudden widening of her eyes expressed a shock he imagined resulted more from the ridiculous fact he was still uncomfortably aroused, rather than surprise that he'd foiled her attempt. Clay tried to will the problem away. It wouldn't go.

"Who," he began, then paused to clear the gravelly sound from his throat. "Who told you I'd be leaving?"

When she squirmed in an obvious effort to put distance between them, Clay swallowed the groan of agony rising inside him. "You're only adding to the problem," he informed her tensely. "Lie still and answer my question."

"First let me up!"

Melissa was furious that she no longer held the advantage, and equally disturbed by the thoughts racing through her mind. She should be concerned with his explanation, not questioning how she could survive an intimate encounter with him.

"Not until I get an answer."

She should have killed him when she had the opportunity. Angry as she'd been, Melissa never truly intended violence. Stealing his knife and scaring the hell out of him was her objective.

"I already told you. I'm smart enough to have figured it out on my own."

A lift of his brow suggested doubt. "How you know isn't as important as the fact that you do know. So now you understand I have one foot in your world and one foot in this one. I'm white when necessary, and Apache by choice. But whatever I am, you're still a captive. If you won't be mine much longer, you'll belong to someone else. What difference does it make if I'd told you from the beginning, or if I just got on my horse when the time came and didn't look back? It wouldn't change anything."

Her eyes stung with unshed tears. It would have made a difference. Had she known from the start he was really as heartless as he pretended, she wouldn't have given him hers.

"Can you walk away that easily? Don't you care what happens to me, even a little?" She hated the tremble in her voice, despised the feel of wet drops sliding from the sides of her eyes to disappear into her hairline.

An expression she likened to pain twisted his features. He cursed under his breath and glanced away. Melissa noted a twitch in his jaw, sensed a war taking place within him. When he focused on her again, his eyes glittered with emotion.

"Yes, damn you! I care! Is that what you wanted to hear? Will knowing that I'm being torn apart as I leave make you hate me any less?"

To say yes seemed ludicrous. Nor should his impassioned admission have been able to speed the beat of her heart. But it did, and it sickened Melissa to respond to a man without the courage to sacrifice for her sake something as trifling as his affiliation with a tribe of savages. The day had proven too enlightening. If Clay hadn't told her of his impending departure because he didn't believe her capable of handling the truth, he had been correct. Today she'd brazenly offered her body in trade to one man, then threatened another with a knife.

These were not sins she would once have committed. She wasn't Melissa Sheffield any longer. Desperation had driven her past decency, and it seemed as if acceptance remained the only option left.

"No," she finally whispered, her spirit broken. "You are right. I don't hate you any less."

Clay rolled away from her and gained his stance. He retrieved his knife, replaced the weapon, and stormed toward the tepee exit. "I'd try to explain why I can't help you, but you wouldn't understand. I'm not sure I do anymore."

Even his last muttered remark didn't improve her listlessness. "Clay?" She stopped him. "When it's time, will I have a say in whose property I become next?"

"Under normal circumstances, no. Do you have a preference?"

"Swift Buck."

The muscles in his back tensed, rippling the red scars from his beating. He nodded. "A wise choice. He speaks English, is a fierce warrior, a good hunter, and has a weakness for white women."

Despite his praise, Melissa sensed she'd hit a nerve. "W-When, I mean, how soon until . . ."

"Not long," he clipped. "I usually stay until the last big hunt of the summer. Since most of the crops have been destroyed, they'll go earlier than normal. Possibly next week. I'll return with them and take a portion of the meat to help see me through the winter, then . . ."

Then he'd be gone from her life, Melissa mentally completed. She wondered why the thought devastated her. Swift Buck wasn't cruel. He implied there might be something he could do for her once Clay left. Things could be far worse, but Melissa's natural optimism refused to surface.

"Who knows, maybe by next year I'll be a proper squaw. I might even have a papoose strapped to my back and another baby on the way. What more could a girl hope for?"

Slowly, he turned to face her. The thunderous rage reflected in his stare started her sluggish blood pumping.

"I told you once before, *squaw* is a white man's word, and an insulting one. Don't refer to yourself in that manner again."

Her spirits plummeted with his going. It was the word *squaw* he'd reacted to and not an insane jealousy over the picture she'd planted in his head. He desired her, even admitted walking away would cost him a few nights' sleep. It changed nothing. Freedom lay far off on the horizon, no closer than on the day of her capture. Clay Brodie wouldn't help her—not then, not now, and not in the future.

His conscience might suffer on her behalf, but he knew nothing of sacrifice, nothing about loving a person more than loving himself. Melissa hadn't truly understood that emotion before either—not until she'd been thrust into unfamiliar territory and lured to listen with her heart, awakened to the sensuous pleasures of a man's touch, forced to judge a race of people by their actions because she couldn't understand their language.

She'd always assumed loving Robert had been the best choice for her. Secretly, she'd craved acceptance, and for a girl shamed by her father's failures, Robert Towbridge seemed the only man willing to overlook her less than perfect pedigree.

She glanced about at the crude dishes and odd utensils. Clay Brodie had taught her something of true worth: Melissa Sheffield couldn't survive this world without him, but Huera could, although neither woman much wanted to do so.

Camp bustled below. Clay sat atop the bluff. His duty provided him with a good excuse as to why his gaze strayed often to his captive. Guards posted around the encampment paid heed not only to what went on outside the camp perimeters, but to all that went on inside as well.

She hadn't spoken to him except when necessary since their confrontation. He'd never thought of himself as a coward, but he'd had trouble looking her in the eyes for three days. Guilt ate at him. When had she crawled beneath his skin and attached herself like a tick? How had she managed to get to him, make him care? Dammit, he wasn't sure what the test was about anymore. Wasn't positive who he was.

As if the majestic aspens and lush mountains would give him an answer, Clay scanned the area. This was his home, this valley and these mountains. They were the only home he'd ever known. Santa Fe had taught him early that the whites and Spanish might tolerate his presence, but decent society would never accept him.

They thought his long hair and Indian trappings made him a savage, untrustworthy, dangerous. Hiram Brodie had made certain he introduced his son to the pleasure of that world, but saw to it he could never fit in.

Of white men, only Martin Hanes accepted him, was a man he trusted, even if they didn't always see eye to eye.

The Apaches accepted him, white blood and all, but now he understood that Gray Wolf's test proved he didn't entirely fit into their world, either.

Now, watching Melissa Sheffield as she gathered drying husks, he realized it wouldn't have mattered had her hair not caught the sun and framed her face with light, had her eyes not been as vibrant as turquoise. It wouldn't have mattered that just looking at her made his blood hot. She could have been any woman, and he'd still be staring down at the same dilemma.

"The hunt is moved up. We go four days from today."

With the quickness of the great mountain cat, Cougar turned. He hadn't heard Gray Wolf's approach; he was losing his edge, for the leader had had to climb the bluff to reach him.

"It is not wise to allow a man with a woman who steals his thoughts to protect us," Gray Wolf said quietly. "I've been watching you watch her. Have your eyes been too full of a slave to notice that the grass is changing?"

"I have noticed," Clay answered. "After the hunt, I will return to the mountains."

"What is to be done with Huera?"

He shrugged. "Swift Buck might offer for her."

"Your blood brother has no need for a slave. You should sell her to a family, or to me."

"To you?" Clay lifted a brow. "Why does a lodge with only two need a slave?"

"Jageitci grows rounder with each rising sun. If her sight

201

Ronda Thompson

truly saw more than one son, her days and nights will be busy."

"And she will not have time to tend to your needs." The accusation in his voice sounded damning even to Clay's ears. He tamped down his jealousy. "You have spoiled Jageitci by taking only one wife. A woman between you might cause more trouble than it is worth."

"Even Jageitci, who leaves no room inside me for others, is more trouble than she is worth," the leader countered dryly. "You have been wise to take the pleasure a woman can give and keep your heart guarded. I hope you will remain as smart."

"My wisdom is a result of ignorance. I know too much about pleasuring a woman, and too little about loving one. A lack of curiosity about the difference is what keeps me out of trouble."

The slow smile spreading over Gray Wolf's lips didn't reach his eyes. "Your mind is as fast as your feet, Cougar. The council wishes to reward you for your courage in returning Mesa to her family. At the hunt ceremony, you will be the Giver of Life."

The decision stunned Clay. "I am honored."

Gray Wolf inclined his head in acknowledgement of his sincerity. "Huera will stay with my wife while we are on the hunt. When we return, I will ask Jageitci if she wishes her to remain in our lodge."

"The choice is mine to make," Clay said forcefully. "You said I could sell her to whomever I wanted at summer's end."

"True," Gray Wolf admitted. "But I did not know of her healing powers. My wife may need Huera when her time comes. As leader, I lay claim to the slave after you go."

"Huera belongs to me! It is my right to place her."

Once again, the two locked eyes in battle. Clay cursed his hot head. Now his refusal seemed suspicious. Dammit, why had the woman made herself valuable? If Gray Wolf took possession, he wouldn't want to part with her for Jageitci's sake, and ransom would be out of the question.

"I think maybe she no longer belongs to you, but that you

belong to her. The hunt will help you regain the wisdom of your days before she came among us. The days when you thought my visions were foolish and a test of loyalty over a woman insulting. Remember back, Cougar. We taught you to laugh, taught you pride, gave you more than your own flesh and blood. What we ask in return is not so much, not worth dying for."

Clay remained silent as the leader walked away. After Gray Wolf scrambled down the bluff, Clay closed his eyes and rubbed his forehead. He felt pulled in opposite directions. Gray Wolf was right. If not for these people, he would have only seen life through the eyes of a battered, embittered boy. What little he knew of love, he'd learned from them. The values of right and wrong warring inside of him he'd also learned from them.

What had Melissa Sheffield given him? Nothing but trouble and new scars. For her, he'd lied to those he considered his friends, deceived them, rebelled against them. And for what?

A woman who said she hated him, despised him and loved another man. He laughed out loud at the absurdity of his situation. Suddenly, he longed for the upcoming hunt. Maybe he did need to get away from her to see things clearly again. Maybe she was a witch who'd cast a spell over him. It made more sense than being in love with her. Clay Brodie didn't know for sure what that word meant. A discreet cough swung his gaze to the left.

Another brave had arrived without his notice. Judging by the look on Too Many Rivers's face, he thought Cougar was suffering the strong effects of the sun. Clay stretched, smiled at his replacement, and muttered a parting in English.

"You're right, Too Many Rivers. I'm crazy as hell."

Chapter Twenty

Melissa tried to pretend she had no interest in the hunt ceremony, quietly informing her master she had no wish to attend, and adding that she imagined she'd see many a heathen social before her life ended. Despite her resolve to ignore Clay, she found his preparations distracting.

She hadn't seen his hair braided before tonight. The neat plaits made him appear all the more savage. He wore nothing but moccasins and a loincloth, and the sight of too much exposed flesh made it impossible to remain unmoved. Rather than dwell on the corded muscles in his long thighs, or contemplate the smoothness of his flanks, she shifted her attention to his chest and followed the jagged stripes of red running from his shoulders down his stomach.

The painted design resembled the slash marks of an animal. A cougar, she assumed. His face also bore the painted scratches, but white paint had been applied beneath. Although Melissa doubted he realized the irony of his creativity, to her it looked as if a red man were clawing his way out of a white one. And Melissa supposed he was, for she saw no sign of Clay Brodie in him, only Cougar, the Apache warrior.

"Are you sure you don't want to attend? You might find it an amusing distraction."

"I find very little amusing these days," she countered softly. "I'm tired, I'll just go to bed."

"The drums will start shortly. You won't be able sleep anyway."

"Oh," She lifted a brow in mock surprise. "You didn't tell me there'd be music. I do so love to kick up my heels to the tune of a jaunty reel." At his puzzled expression, she muttered, "I guess it's safe to assume there won't be any dancing."

"We dance," he argued. "It is part of the ceremony."

Curious as she found the thought of Clay Brodie gliding around a dance floor, she schooled her features into a mask of boredom. "Well, I'm sure their definition of dancing and mine vastly differ. I said I'm not interested."

"I shouldn't leave you here alone tonight. These ceremonies have been known to impassion The People."

"Impassion?"

"Get their blood up," he explained. "I'd feel better if I could keep an eye on you. With the drums, if you screamed, I couldn't hear you."

Suddenly nervous, she glanced toward the tepee flap. Melissa smothered her fear. It was time she faced her fate without him. "You won't hear me once you're gone, either. What difference does it make if something happens to me tonight, next week, next month, next—"

"Nothing will happen to you!" He rose, glaring down at her before a tired sigh left his lips. "Where's the stubborn spirit you came here with?"

Guilt flooded her. She lowered her gaze. "Should I still have faith? Should I refuse to accept that you would go and leave me in a world in which I don't belong?"

"I wonder sometimes if belonging is as important as we believe."

That wasn't an answer, in Melissa's opinion. She lifted

her head as he walked to the exit. "Who should I place my faith in? Cougar, or Clay Brodie?"

He paused. "Neither. Or both, Huera. Beneath the skin, they're the same man. You can't trust one without trusting the other."

She thought the loud beating in her ears was her heart, but then she realized the drums had started. He'd already gone by the time the questions rolling around her head formed into words. Had he just insinuated something she'd misunderstood? *Have faith in neither, or both.* That wasn't much of an assurance.

But he did suggest she should trust him. Melissa fought the temptation to read more into his statement than was there. "I won't get my hopes up," she cautioned herself. Clay Brodie was a most confusing man. One she still didn't feel she knew well enough to judge.

Unconsciously, her gaze strayed to his belongings. Had he replaced the journal? What she did know about the man was that he would have anticipated her snooping again after being told to leave his personal things alone. By now, he would assume she'd looked, found them missing, and given up. Melissa crawled to his possessions. She glanced inside the basket of his sister's belongings to make certain he hadn't hidden the journal there. A gold bracelet she hadn't seen before rested on top.

Curious, Melissa held it up. It looked old and well-worn, but it was obviously expensive. How long had it been since anything from her world adorned her body? After glancing nervously toward the flap, Melissa put the bracelet around her wrist.

It was too big, but she wore it as she searched Clay's pouches. She didn't understand why Anna Brodie's journal called to her, but she felt compelled to learn all she could about Clay. A smile came over her lips when she found the diary.

Melissa settled beside the grate, where a low fire burned. Gently, she turned the yellowed pages. They crackled with age and came to life with Anna's refined script. Since her time was limited, she didn't know where to begin. After Clay's birth, she decided, flipping past the first pages, which she knew depicted Anna's early life as a girl in Boston. Her eyes scanned an entry she found of interest.

Rachel is one month old today. As I watch her nurse, her beautiful blond head nestled against my breasts. I wonder how anything so beautiful could result from something so ugly. Hiram barely glances at the outcome of his violent lust. He wanted another son to steal from me.

Of my first child, I see little. Clay keeps himself outside. Away from the sight he witnessed last week. I did not realize he stood at my door as I smiled down at Rachel, a soft lullaby on my lips. Glancing up, my eyes met his and the beat of my heart slowed nearly to a stop. I saw hurt, accusation, hate. Instinctively, I pulled Rachel closer, frightened of a boy born of my own flesh and blood.

It was only after he stormed away that I cursed my actions. Clay wouldn't hurt Rachel, and he wouldn't hurt me, no matter what I've done to him. Had he not tried to stop Hiram that night ten months prior, when he came in, too far gone with drink, and attacked me? I screamed more over Hiram's fists smashing into Clay's smaller body than from fear for my own safety. I noticed the bruises on my son, the welts on his back when he washed.

These past years, I've ignored them, told myself he was a clumsy boy, but I couldn't deceive myself any longer. That is the worst sin I've committed against my son: looking the other way. Regardless of what Hiram threatened when he learned of my deception, I should have put a stop to the abuse, should have killed the bastard when he lay in one of his drunken stupors. But I fear God too much to deliver myself from this hell. Perhaps in His wisdom, He linked Clay's life with the Indians.

For the first time, I can't resent the Apaches for turning my son into a heathen. Hiram is the savage, not Clay. Those people, no matter how different, have given a boy crucified by fate, scarred by the injustices of love, pride in himself. Somehow, despite the poor example Hiram and I have provided him, Clay knew the wrongness of using force against a woman. I think God might have mercy on me after all, might deliver my son from the legacy of evil Hiram has so purposely laid for him.

I pray for the years to pass quickly. When Clay is old enough to defend himself against the devil, I will tell him the truth. He must understand that the cruelties he's suffered were not due to a fault within him, but to an obsession, to my weaknesses, to the sins of his mother, and to the sins of his grandfather. My darkest fear is that something might happen to me and he will never know, never understand he is not evil, not unworthy of the love Hiram allows me to give his sister.

How can the gentle nature that runs in his blood battle the hatred so instilled? How can he ever give his heart, unless someone else first offers theirs? Who will teach him that caring is not always painful? Who will show him that true love demands no conditions; that it is sacrifice, unthinking and ungoverned by rules? Who will rescue him from his dark world and set him free? Who, if not the woman too skilled at hiding her feelings for him, one whose neglect and disinterest in him are nothing but lies?

"Huera?"

Melissa jumped. Her guilty haste to conceal the journal proved unnecessary. It was only Mesa, who'd entered while she remained enthralled by Anna Brodie's confessions, her worries. The girl smiled shyly and motioned toward the exit.

"No. I stay here." She patted the robes.

Mesa's bright expression faded. She spoke, again pointing at the flap. Since friends in a hostile camp were hard to come by, Melissa sighed, crawled to the pouches, and replaced the journal.

Reluctantly, she rose, dying to read more and to try to unravel Anna's cruel treatment of her son, but next time someone caught her unawares, it might be Clay. She understood why he didn't want her to read the diary. He was ashamed.

Why had Anna refused to nurture him the way every child deserved? And Hiram, she shivered, running her hands up and down her bare arms, what sort of monster was he? Melissa fought any softening of feeling the entry inspired toward her captor. She couldn't admit what she felt for him, not until Clay proved himself . . . worthy.

The thought startled her. She'd placed a condition on her heart. Demanded he conform to her rules, become what she expected of him. Before she could further examine the right or wrong of her logic, Mesa snatched her hand and pulled her from the tepee.

A huge moon hung overhead, lighting the campsite, as if the bonfire they approached didn't do the task well enough. The drums pounded in Melissa's head. Her eyes began to sting from the smoke. Painted warriors circled the fire, orange flames casting shadows on their near-naked bodies. She tried to find Clay among the dancers, but saw no sign of him. Although she'd claimed disinterest in the ceremony earlier, curiosity now got the best of her.

She couldn't have been more correct in her presumption that the Indians' form of dance and hers were different. Never had she seen men move in this fashion, and yet, she couldn't say they weren't graceful. In fact, as she spotted Swift Buck, painted in bold blue circles, she smiled at his agile abilities. She tried to picture the men dressed in gentlemanly splendor, waltzing around a dance floor, and she giggled softly. Mesa's puzzled expression sobered her.

Suddenly, the drums ceased. The gathering quieted. Anticipation laced the air as the braves crept into the darkness. Melissa strained to see through the smoke and over heads taller than hers. He appeared seemingly from nowhere. A specter painted red and white, muscular flesh gleaming in the fire's glow, a buffalo headdress perched atop his braids. The drums started and Clay began the dance.

Even without the headdress, she would have thought him majestic. His movements were purely male, subtly seductive. Around and around the circle he danced, the flames leaping higher one minute and settling the next. Melissa twisted this way and that to keep him within her eyesight, mesmerized by his grace, captivated by his savage beauty. She hardly noticed when the other braves sneaked back into the firelight, their spears raised. She saw only Clay, heard only the quickened sounds of her own breathing, felt only the beat of her heart, matching the drum's rhythm.

Something stirred inside her and fanned the flames of a primitive need. Her gaze worshiped the shadowed planes of his sleek perfection, feasted on tantalizing glimpses of bare buttock beneath his loincloth. She suffered no shame for desiring him. This was not her world, it was his, but tonight, Huera tempted her to accept the truth in her heart. She could not want Clay Brodie without wanting Cougar. As he'd said earlier, they were the same man.

The drums intensified, and the dance grew frenzied as braves surrounded Clay, their spears jabbing at him in a mock play depicting the hunt. When they backed away, he went to his knees, head bowed, chest heaving, the mighty buffalo felled. The tide of excitement building within her ebbed. Melissa felt disappointed that the dance had ended.

In a slow, hypnotic beat, the drums resumed; women now formed a circle around Clay. Mesa tugged at Melissa's hand, urging her to join in. She shook her head, sensing a slave's participation would be frowned upon by the Apaches.

Spurred forward by a gentle nudge from Melissa, the girl walked toward the women. Melissa had already noticed that no girl under the age of twelve or thirteen claimed the honor, and suspected Mesa's recent journey into womanhood gave her the right to dance for the first time in a tribal ceremony.

"The kill is only the first part of a great hunt. After the men perform their tasks, the women must do theirs."

Jageitci's whispered explanation sent Melissa's gaze nervously scanning the faces surrounding them.

"They will not notice," the Spanish woman assured her. "The ceremony demands their attention. The buffalo is life itself to The People. Since women prepare the hides and meat, they are honored in this portion of the ceremony. The Giver of Life will choose one among them, mingle his breath with hers, and insure the continuance of our race, and the future of our children."

"He's going to kiss one of them?" she demanded in a whisper. "I thought the Apaches considered touching mouths unclean?"

A smile crossed Jageitci's lips. "To The People, the Breath of Life is not an intimate act. The contact is symbolic and nothing more." She glanced down and frowned. The leader's wife bent, retrieving the bracelet that had slipped from Melissa's wrist.

"I-I forgot I wore the bracelet," Melissa gasped. "I found it—"

"It belonged to Cougar's sister," Jageitci said quietly. "This is strange."

"What?"

The woman handed her the piece. "It is warm to the touch. Not cold, as I expected of an object from one passed from this world into the next."

Melissa studied the woman's puzzled expression. "With your sight, can you see the men who killed Cougar's sister? I still don't believe those from my caravan were responsible."

Jageitci stared at the bracelet, then sighed. "As I said, my sight fades with my age and my condition. I see only blackness." Her attention shifted back to the ceremony. "Watch, it is time for the Giver of Life to mingle his breath with ours."

"Maybe to The People it's only a symbolic gesture," Melissa muttered. "But Cougar does not share their repulsion over joining mouths. He might enjoy his duty too much."

"You sound like a jealous wife," Jageitci teased. "Maybe if we move up where he can see you among the crowd, the glare of your eyes will caution him against performing his part with greater enthusiasm than necessary."

"I am having trouble seeing over everyone's head."

"A good excuse," Jageitci replied, still smiling. "Here, take this bowl of paint and follow me. Because in my state, I represent all women, all givers of life, I must mark the forehead of each dancer as she leaves the circle. You will act as my slave in the task."

"How appropriate," Melissa mumbled. She took the bowl of yellow paint and followed her temporary master through the throng. Once they reached their destination, heat from the large bonfire warmed her less than Clay's nearness.

The stirring began again as Melissa watched the women dance around him, their bodies undulating in sensuous rhythm. She supposed Clay sensed her regard; he looked directly at her. Their eyes clashed, held, were separated by the dancing form of a woman, then freed to refocus on one another. Gradually, the drums faded inside her head.

She became aware only of Clay, conscious of nothing but the beat of her heart, the heat spreading like wildfire through her veins. It was as if she'd become someone else. Yet she was the same. Huera had lived in her all this time. A woman she hadn't known. A woman stronger than Melissa Sheffield. One who listened with her heart, followed her instincts, took what she wanted today, because tomorrow it might be gone.

Huera placed no stipulations on her feelings for Cougar. She accepted all the good and bad about him and understood that deep down, his differences were what drew her to him. Huera could fulfill his mother's wishes. But did she dare shuck the skin of Melissa to become Huera?

"Lower your gaze," Jageitci whispered. "You have more than prevented Cougar from enjoying his duty. You make him forget all but the flame of passion I see burning between you."

Abruptly, Melissa obeyed. Beneath the cover of her lashes, she watched Clay's attention return to his duty. The young woman he chose was pretty enough to cause her a moment of uncontrolled jealousy, but the brief contact between them didn't for a moment appear intimate. When the Giver of Life released the woman, whoops of approval ended the ceremonial dance. Recalling her own duty, Melissa extended her bowl of yellow paint.

As each woman left, Jageitci dipped her finger in the mixture and marked the dancer's forehead. After the last had rejoined her relatives, Melissa glanced toward Clay. He remained before the fire, the headdress clutched in one hand, and his gaze bright. She assumed the ceremony was responsible for the fevered look of him, just as she tried to tell herself it had affected her own behavior.

It was the drums, the dancing, the savage moon overhead that seduced her, made her long for a man's touch, not any man, but the one gazing boldly at her while wearing hardly a stitch of clothing. Appreciatively, she eyed his tall frame from the top of his head to the toes of his moccasins. When she finally glanced up, Melissa noted the tight set of his jaw.

"Cougar is not a man to tease," Jageitci warned softly. "Your eyes cannot keep telling him one thing, and your lips another. You are a grown woman, and he, a mighty warrior. The evening will be long from the tales told of his skill with a bow. If you want him to return to your tepee before the darkest hours of night, you must give him a reason. A sign that you are ready to walk into the flame."

"But how do I know if I am ready?"

Jageitci shrugged. "It is not for me to say, Huera, but I believe the truth can be lost by asking too many questions. The world you come from makes even the simplest of matters complicated. This is not that world. I must go now. Although the drums will beat again, and the stories told around the fire are amusing, my sons tire me. I hope the morning finds you less confused."

Desperation overtook Melissa as Jageitci disappeared into the crowd. She felt conspicuous, rightfully out of place, torn between two cultures, and at war with her heart. Would dawn still find her a prisoner of the feelings she suppressed?

Ronda Thompson

Could she free herself from the shackles of a past slowly slipping like sand through her fingers, and simply be who she truly was—a woman in love with the wrong man?

"In a crowd of dark heads, you're easy to see."

Startled, Melissa glanced away from watching Jageitci's departure and confronted a broad, bare chest. "I saw you seeing me," she blurted, then felt her face grow hot. "I-I mean—"

"I know what you mean." Clay still stared at her in a way that made breathing difficult. "What did you think of the dancing?"

She moistened her dry lips and moved the hand still holding his sister's bracelet behind her back. "The ceremony turned out to be an interesting distraction after all."

"It was that," he mumbled. "Did your mother never tell you not to make a man promises with your eyes if you're not willing to keep them?"

A lump formed in Melissa's throat. Had her desire for him been so obvious? "No. I was young when she died."

"Then I'm telling you in her place. I said the ceremony had a strange effect on the Apaches. I can now assume it doesn't fire only Indian blood. Go back to the tepee. Because I'm being honored, I must tell the first stories of hunts gone by. The drums will start again, but I'll be close enough to watch the lodge. Good night."

Clay had dismissed her. His assumptions infuriated her. How dare he believe she could become impassioned by so little, when she'd been battling her desire for him days and nights on end. Angrily, she wheeled away, intent on returning to the lodge without another word.

Melissa only made it a few steps when Jageitci's instruction that she give him a sign resurfaced. She guessed the messages Clay had received weren't adequate. Thoughtfully, she studied the bowl of paint in her hands. Maybe he wasn't to blame for refusing to take her seriously.

Hadn't she allowed him to kiss her, to touch her, then quickly conjured an excuse for her actions? Melissa slipped the bracelet into the side of her moccasin. With bravery be-

214

lied by a sudden weakness in her knees, she turned. He stood waiting for her to reach the safety of the tepee.

Slowly, deliberately, she dipped her fingers in the paint and ran them down the front of her face. When his gaze searched hers, she didn't look away. He took a step toward her, then was whirled away in a cloud of men headed toward the council lodge. As they dragged him along, his head turned back to look at her. She smiled seductively at him, an unmistakable invitation.

Chapter Twenty-one

Clay cursed his eventful past with the Apaches. He told only a few stories, all of them brief, and still he couldn't break away from the council lodge. Gray Wolf would recall an interesting incident, then Swift Buck took up where the other left off, reminding those gathered of yet another skillful encounter involving their honored brother. Clay had attempted to keep his attention focused on the stories, but his gaze kept straying past the open flap of the council lodge toward the one he shared with a blond-haired vixen.

At last he'd managed to free himself. Now he stood outside that very lodge, half-wary to step inside, half-afraid to believe the bold overture she'd made before departing the ceremony. He knew if he entered and found her asleep, or worse, busy at some task as if nothing had transpired between them earlier, he would feel both disappointment and a rational dose of relief.

Although he hungered for her, which wasn't an emotion unfamiliar to him, Clay knew what he felt for Melissa Sheffield went beyond desire. He'd tried to seduce his captive, tried to make her admit she was no different on the inside than those she called savage, and deep down, her resistance pleased a sense of decency he hadn't known existed within him.

She'd forced him to look past the beauty of her face, the ripeness of her body and, to his confusion, to discover a need suppressed over the years—a desire to share more than lust with a woman. The wrong woman.

Before he could convince himself to walk away, to stay out all night so he wouldn't be forced into a confrontation with right and wrong, Clay lifted the flap and stepped inside. His captive wasn't asleep, nor had she occupied herself with some mundane task. Melissa Sheffield sat barefoot and bare-legged on a pile of buffalo robes, for all the world looking as though she were patiently awaiting his arrival.

The paint on her face disturbed him, as well as her long hair unbound and wild around her shoulders. Surely if she'd had second thoughts, the paint would be missing and Melissa Sheffield, formerly of St. Louis, would have crawled beneath the hides, sending another message, not the one her eyes were still relaying.

"I've been waiting for you," she verified.

"That was a mistake." Clay avoided glancing at her long, slender legs. "The effects of the ceremony obviously haven't worn off yet. I suggest you crawl beneath your mats and go to sleep."

"And if I refuse?"

Once again, her boldness took him by surprise. She seemed determined to test the limits of his newfound decency. He sighed. "This is a dangerous game. You don't understand the rules well enough to play without getting burned."

The courage faded from her eyes. "Must everything be a game? A lesson? A trade? Can't you ever just once take what's offered without questioning the motives behind it?"

His brow lifted. He turned from the tempting sight of her, and with sudden insight said, "Your sacrifice isn't necessary. You think seducing me might make me feel more compelled to rescue you?" When she said nothing, he assumed he'd correctly uncovered her purpose.

"You've learned the rules better than I thought. Find your enemy's weakness and use it against him. I am your enemy, and you are my weakness. But there is no need to make this sacrifice. I don't know how, or when exactly, but I'll see to it you get to Santa Fe. Whether you want to or not, you'll have to trust me."

Slowly, Clay turned. The relief he expected to see mirrored on her face wasn't there. In its stead, her gaze reflected shock.

"You think I'd trade my body for freedom?" she whispered, then felt her cheeks suffuse with heat. Hadn't she attempted to bribe Swift Buck with that very offer? Regardless of the fact that the brave had seen through her degrading attempt, Melissa would forever carry the shame of that immoral compromise. Now, when she truly wanted Clay, for no reason other than the right one, it seemed fitting he would use her sins against her.

"What else should I believe?" he demanded softly. "What other reason would you have?"

Somehow, she thought she might avoid a full confession. Actions spoke louder than words, or so the saying went, but to truly free the woman inside her, Melissa resigned herself to telling him the truth.

"There are only two reasons I can think of at the moment. One of them is because I want to feel your touch, your mouth on me without fighting the pleasure of being in your arms. The other is the stronger. Whether you rescue me or not, no matter if you're Clay Brodie, or Cougar, regardless of everything that's happened between us . . ." She paused to take a deep breath. "I love you."

Her admission visibly affected him. Clay stumbled back a step. The strangest expression crossed his rugged features. It seemed as if he couldn't fathom what she'd said to him.

"I've declared my love for you." Melissa tilted her head up to show she felt no shame in her admission. "Is that a good enough reason?"

"Why?" he demanded in a raw voice. "I'm not safe, not decent, not any of those things you claimed to love about—"

"Robert," she supplied, rising from the mats to approach him. "And that doesn't seem to matter. I couldn't have loved him, or I wouldn't be standing here begging another man to make me a woman."

He held up a hand to ward her off. "I think you're confused. Maybe you should sleep on this tonight and look at it again in the morning with clearer eyes."

Melissa refused to be detained. She kept walking until she stood before him. "I know exactly what I want. I thought you wanted the same. Have you been teasing me? Pretending to desire me? Have your lips been lying to me, your hands—"

A low animal growl interrupted her, a sound from deep in Clay's throat, as he pulled her against his heated flesh. "Say it again," he instructed. "Tell me again."

"I love you," she whispered, then realized what the look on his face earlier had implied. "No one has said those words to you until tonight, have they?"

Before his mouth descended upon hers, he paused. "No. And I never thought they meant much until I heard them from your sweet lips. I don't understand why you'd entrust your heart to me, but I know this, if you don't stop me now, I might not be able to let you go, not ever. Understand?"

Her answer was to close the space that separated their lips. He plundered the moist recesses of her mouth and infused Melissa with his urgency. Her fingernails dug into his shoulders, their tongues clashed, caught in a dance as primitive as the one she'd witnessed outside the tepee. Free at last to explore sensations she'd tried desperately to suppress, Melissa reveled in the feel, scent, and taste of him.

The heat of his body engulfed her, the slow thrust of his tongue ignited a flame deep within the hidden recesses of her sensuality. His hand moved past her hips, sliding smoothly down the buckskin dress to cup the roundness of her bottom, then around to the front, where she felt him gather the dress higher on her leg. The brush of his fingers sent fire racing up her thigh, but when he lightly caressed her in a place no man had dared to touch, she gasped with shock.

"Dammit," Clay tore his lips from hers to swear. "I don't know how to be with you." He kissed one corner of her already swollen mouth. "I want you to feel pleasure you didn't know existed, a hunger beyond control. I want you to want me more than you've ever wanted anything, even freedom."

The promise in his eyes chased away her shock, her shyness, and without protest, Melissa allowed him to lift her in his arms. He moved to the soft buffalo robes of his mat, then eased her down onto the hides.

"When I touch you, close your eyes and think of nothing but what you feel. When I kiss you, know the taste of you is sweeter than honey to my lips. Tonight, ignore your fears, your conscience, and listen to the needs of your body. Trust me."

Without hesitation, Melissa closed her eyes. He kissed her, slow and deep. Outside, drums still pounded and the voices of those celebrating faded to the furthest corners of her mind. The world revolved around the sound of their uneven breaths, the fusion of their lips, the expectancy building within Melissa.

A hot trail of kisses along the length of her neck found her moaning his name. When he untied the straps of her dress, she wiggled impatiently. His hands were unhurried as they gently eased the fabric off her shoulders and then down further, past the fullness of her breasts.

"You're beautiful," he said huskily. "When I look at you, I see all things natural. A sunrise, a sunset, the glistening of dew on green grass, the brilliance of a wildflower."

He touched her then, tracing the circles surrounding her nipples. Melissa bit back a groan and willed his mouth to continue the torturous ecstasy his fingertips had started. As if he understood her deepest desires, Clay fastened greedily upon one hard crest.

Her hands immediately tugged at the leather thongs securing his braids. She loved the silky texture of his hair, loved the feel of his mouth on her breasts, licking, sucking, spreading an ache to her lower regions.

Melissa wanted the heat of his skin against hers, wanted more than her innocence could identify, but instinct was as old as time, and when she arched her back and dug her nails into his scalp, he seemed to understand her needs.

"Not yet, Huera," he said softly. "It's time to close your eyes and do nothing but feel. Now I'll give you pleasure, because afterward, I must give you pain."

In the process of obeying his request, Melissa's lashes lifted abruptly. "Pain?"

His finger outlined the shape of her lower lip. "I suspect you know as much about it as I do. I've never been with a virgin, but men talk, white and Apache. They say for a moment, a woman feels pain her first time. You'll have to trust me again."

She wished he had warned her, had just continued the skillful assault on her senses and kept his unsettling knowledge a secret. Melissa knew little about intimacy. Only that two bodies joined, and she was relatively certain where, but she hadn't had a mother to explain. When her cycle began, her father had barely found time away from his bottle to tell her she wasn't dying. Still, her body burned for Clay's touch, and he said the suffering would be brief, so she closed her eyes to convey her willingness to brave pain for the pleasure he offered.

"Every part of you is beautiful," he said softly, "every inch of your skin tastes sweet beneath my tongue."

With that assurance, he straddled her. Then all thoughts dissolved as his tongue flicked across her nipple, dipped between the valley of her breasts, and began a slow descent down her stomach. The lazy circle he drew around her navel speeded her already erratic heartbeat.

As Clay moved lower, he took the buckskin dress with him. Cool air caressed her fevered flesh. His mouth on her thigh brought a distressing realization. When she'd removed her leggings earlier, it was the same as removing her underdrawers. The feel of fabric sliding to her knees meant she was totally exposed, that he could see—

"You have nothing to be ashamed of. To me, you are beautiful everywhere."

Melissa fought her inhibitions and willed herself to relax when he kissed the spray of curls between her legs. Shame was comprised of many emotions, one of which was a fear he might find her flawed in some way, but the husky timbre of his voice, the labored sound of his breathing, erased all doubt about whether he found her anything but desirable.

His reaction thickened her blood with excitement. Rather than shrinking from him, Melissa felt herself unfolding, escaping the bonds of restrictions placed upon her by a society long lost to her.

After he'd sampled the length of her leg, the dress disappeared, along with Melissa's previous battle with decency. Her concentration centered on sensation, Clay's hands, his mouth, the low comments he made, sometimes in Apache, and although she couldn't understand him, the hunger in his voice increased the insistent throb pulsing at the core of her womanhood.

He kissed the sole of her foot, nipped gently at her calf, and forged a hot trail up her thigh. When his tongue sought the source of her aching need, shock crowded past sensation. Her knees clamped together, only to find the completion of her action impossible. Clay's sensuous journey up her leg held more intent than merely pleasuring her; he'd wedged himself between her thighs in the process.

The next instinct registered, but too late. Already he'd imprisoned her wrists with his hands. "Don't," she whispered, squirming in an effort to escape. "It's wrong. It's . . ."

Her protest ebbed at Clay's persistence to prove otherwise. She ceased her struggle, and the shame flooding her body with embarrassed heat turned to molten need. Once moans of surrender fought their way past her clenched teeth, he released her hands. Her fingers craved the feel of his hair, her nails against his scalp urged him to end the suffering.

A tremble began in her thighs, a maddening pressure built

with each bold stroke of his tongue, and as if he sensed she couldn't stand another second of torturous ecstasy, he took the sensitive bud holding her passion into his mouth and sent her plummeting over the edge of madness.

As the pressure squeezed at her insides, Melissa's back arched and a tumble of jumbled words escaped her throat. She felt an explosion rip through her, a burst of pleasure so intense she cried out. When she floated back to earth, Clay's face hovered above her.

His paint was badly smeared and, too dazed to be embarrassed, she imagined most of it now graced her breasts, stomach, and thighs. She smiled tiredly at him, but the fire glowing in his eyes was his only answer.

As her senses began to clear, she noticed the warmth of his body. Noticed also that his moccasins and the skimpy loincloth he'd worn earlier were missing. Lastly, but most noticeably, she registered the hard length of him pressed against her.

Gazing down into a pair of glazed, jade eyes, Clay battled his indecision. He fought against the overwhelming needs of his body, and a desire to rekindle the flame in Melissa's eyes before taking her innocence. She fired his blood like no other woman, and hadn't yet caressed the part of him that pulsed with desire for her, but the words she'd said to him earlier, an offer of unconditional love, had reached inside Clay and tugged at the strings of his own calloused heart.

Although it might have been kinder to enter her then, while she still lay sated and languid in his arms, he hungered for more than the pleasure her body could give him. She moaned softly as he claimed her lips, then with greater strength when he nuzzled her neck and ventured lower. Her breasts fit perfectly into his hands, the small rose-colored nipples already stiff with anticipation.

While his mouth teased her straining peaks, one hand stretched to stroke the curls between her legs. His fingers found her moist and hot, and he groaned deep in his throat, wanting to bury himself there, in the sweetness he'd tasted only moments before. With the pressure of his thumb, he gently coaxed her into wakefulness.

A few strokes more, and she began to stir, to move against his hand. Her nails bit into his shoulders and control be damned, Clay couldn't wait any longer. He positioned himself above her. He nudged her knees apart and entered her slowly. An animalistic growl clawed its way past his clenched teeth.

It took great effort not to plunge into the glorious, dewy warmth of her, but the soft gasps of discomfort she emitted warned him to move slowly. A little deeper he delved, stretching, demanding she accept him, and then deeper, even though her eyes were round as saucers. His progress was suddenly halted.

Although Clay hadn't been with an innocent before, he wasn't slow to figure out that getting past the barrier would cause the wide-eyed woman beneath him pain. His body felt no conscience, only mindless need, only her velvety warmth squeezing him, urging him on. One powerful thrust led him past the gates of Heaven, and also delivered him into hell. A loud gasp of shock echoed around the tepee. She whimpered, and the sound embedded itself in his heart.

"I'm sorry." Clay kissed the tears from her eyes. "I didn't want to hurt you."

She sniffed softly. "Is it over?"

The hopeful tone of her voice brought a smile to his lips. "The painful part is over." He moved deeper, filled her completely. "But you and I have a ways to go before we're finished."

Chapter Twenty-two

"Are you finished?"

"That should be all I need," Clay answered wearily. He glanced down at the objects spread out before him. He'd gathered his arrows, his bow, a water skin, and a pouch of jerky and corn cakes. "If I get down the road and realize I've left my head behind, it'll be your fault."

She smiled with lips still tender from last night's fiery passion, a night when desire raged well into the early morning hours. As he bent to retrieve his arrow pouch, Melissa's gaze traveled the length of his long legs and fondly caressed his backside. Warmth spread through her chilled body.

Her fingers tingled at the remembered feel of his firm flesh, the muscles of his buttocks bunching with each controlled stoke he delivered.

Once Melissa had understood that the sharp jarring pain would not reoccur, she'd been able to concentrate on other matters. Such as Clay, and what he was doing to her. He'd filled her to bursting, and despite a certain discomfort she assumed resulted from his largeness compared to her small-ness, the sensations he'd stirred were far from unpleasant.

Gradually, she learned the rhythm of his body, answered the call deep within to seek the glorious release he'd given her earlier. As the drums pounded outside, she'd danced to the tune of his mouth, his thrusts, his husky groans and the shocking but stimulating things he whispered in her ear.

They'd been slick with sweat when she'd felt the first spasm grip her, propel her beyond the stars, where she'd ex-ploded into a thousand pieces, but through her own gasps, she'd heard the sounds of his approaching surrender. With an animalistic growl, Clay had driven deeper into her trem-bling flesh.

Again he'd thrust, harder, faster, reawakening Melissa's fading shudders until she thought she might die of intense pleasure. His face had been beautiful, gleaming with his ef-forts, then she'd felt him pulsating, spilling his seed, and he'd called her name. Not her Indian name, she was certain, because he'd said it over and over again. *Melissa*.

"If you keep looking at me like that, I might forget there's twenty mounted Apaches waiting for me outside and take care of a problem your hot glances have given me."

In the tight buckskins he wore, his problem was more than evident. Melissa could only marvel at his ability. "Aren't you . . . I mean, after having that problem three or four times last night, aren't you—"

"Sated?" he asked, dropping the bow he'd just retrieved from the ground. Clay walked toward her, a wicked twist to his lips indicating that he wasn't.

"Sated wasn't exactly what I meant." She shifted uncom-fortably on her mat.

He squatted beside Melissa, his gaze softening as he touched her cheek. "I planned to leave you alone after we bathed at the stream, but I consider a woman grinding her bare bottom against me in the night an invitation. The third time I didn't need an excuse, and the fourth, well, you asked."

Melissa felt herself blushing. Now that she'd bravely

walked into the flame with Clay Brodie, she wondered if she'd ever find her way out. Although her body ached with soreness, she also ached with desire. "Will the discomfort go away?"

"Probably not as long as you're within arm's reach." He lifted her chin and kissed her tenderly. "Luckily, you'll have a few days reprieve . . . maybe longer."

"Longer?"

Clay rose and ran his fingers through his hair. "Gray Wolf may pull something. He might tell me to go back to the mountain before we return. We're riding in that direction. It would make sense for me to take my share of meat and leave then."

"But what about me?"

"If Gray Wolf calls my hand, I'll try to talk him into giving you to Swift Buck. I have a suspicion my blood brother would wait a month or so, then tell The People he's decided to ransom you. Gray Wolf may not agree. He thinks Jageitci needs your healing skills and the extra help with her workload after their child is born."

"Children," Melissa said dully. "She said there were two, and I'm inclined to agree with her. What happens if Gray Wolf won't allow a ransom? What happens if he claims me?"

"There will be hell to pay."

Although his statement sounded casual, she sensed a struggle taking place beneath his cool exterior. He retraced his steps to the necessities spread out on the ground.

"If you rescue me, what happens between you and the Apaches?"

Her question received no answer. He seemed distracted with draping his bow across his broad shoulders.

"Clay, what will happen?" she persisted.

In the process of tying the corners of the pouch holding the jerky and corn cakes, he shrugged. "They won't consider me a brother anymore. I won't be welcome in their camps."

For the first time, Melissa felt a tug at her own conscience. "I know these people are like family to you. More than family," she added softly. "Are you sure you can sacrifice what you have with them for me?"

Abruptly, he glanced up from adjusting his bow. "I'm certain I can't walk away. Maybe it won't come down to choices."

"But it might."

"And if it does, you'll have to trust me. You were willing last night. Didn't I keep all my promises?"

Heat wound a lazy path through her body. "Yes," she whispered. "I want you more than anything, even freedom."

Rather than appearing pleased by her admission, he glanced away. "But you couldn't truly be happy living this life, with or without me, could you?"

She felt grateful he wasn't staring at her. Melissa knew she'd fallen in love with Clay Brodie, and if she were forced to remain with the Apaches, she wanted him with her, but given the choice of living in the white world or struggling to survive in this one . . .

"No answer at all is usually answer enough."

"I don't know," she whispered. Melissa scrambled up from her mat and went to him. "Maybe if I were free to come and go, the way you are. How can you expect me to find happiness living my life as your slave?"

"You've never truly been my slave," he answered quietly, still pretending a preoccupation with gathering his gear. "I've only taught you how to survive, explained what I thought you needed to understand. Have I ever forced myself on you? Beaten you? All I've done I did to help you, not hurt you."

"But you are hurting me," she said, a quaver in her voice. "I told you I loved you last night, and you haven't told me, you haven't said—"

"Don't ask me to," Clay interrupted. As if realizing he sounded harsh, he sighed, turning to face her. "I won't lie and say I haven't been with many women. I have, but none ever made me feel the things I felt with you last night. I can't say the words you need to hear, not until I know exactly what they mean."

Melissa blinked back tears. She wheeled away from him, cursing her expectations. The touch of his hands on her shoulders caused her to jump. He shoved her thick hair over one shoulder and softly kissed her neck.

"Whatever I feel for you, it goes far beyond lust. I'll try to sort through my emotions while I'm gone. I want you to examine your own carefully." He walked around to look into her eyes. "But remember this."

His mouth crushed hers with hot urgency. Melissa tried to resist, but her knees went weak and her senses stirred, recalling steamy memories of a night spent loving the wrong man. Before he finished with her, she clung to him, gasping for breath, ready to surrender regardless of the fact that he hadn't spoken the words that would set her free, even if she remained his slave.

"If I don't go now, they'll storm in here and drag me out," he said against her lips. With a throaty groan, he broke from her. "Stay close to Jageitci, and away from the men left behind to protect the women and children." He picked up the water skin and the pouch of food, moving toward the tepee flap, where he stopped. "As soon as we ride away, gather what you'll need and go to Gray Wolf's lodge. It isn't safe to be in here alone."

A dazed nod acknowledged his instructions, as Melissa walked to the flap. Suddenly, a feeling of dark foreboding swept over her. He must have seen her insecurity reflected in her expression. He lifted her chin, his startling blue eyes searching.

"I promised not to walk away. Trust me . . . Melissa."

One minute he stood before her, the next he was gone. The sound of her name lingered in the silence. Her heart swelled. Quickly, she stumbled from the lodge and drew up short. His teasing remark that twenty mounted Apaches waited for him outside the tepee wasn't a joke.

As Clay approached the mounted men, he kept his expression blank, although he suspected a tinge of red darkened his face. Gray Wolf sat glaring at him and, positioned behind the leader, Swift Buck held Two Moons. His blood brother lifted a curious brow, then turned his attention to keeping Clay's high-spirited stallion from taking a bite out of him.

"For a man who sleeps long into the morning and delays the hunt, you do not look rested, Cougar."

Gray Wolf's dry remark received no response from Clay. Features set, he brushed past the leader and took the reins of his horse from Swift Buck. Twisting a clump of mane between his fingers, Clay hefted himself onto the stallion's bare back.

When a grunt of discomfort squeezed past his teeth, he felt his face grow hotter. Melissa wasn't the only one suffering from a night of passion this morning. The thought of having a rough-gaited horse between his legs for a week or more wasn't in the least appealing.

Nor could he summon the excitement for the hunt he'd felt in previous years. The future weighed heavy on his mind. If his plans for Melissa's ransom didn't pan out, he wouldn't hunt with his Apache brothers again, he'd become the hunted. He felt her gaze on him, caught her scent in the air. Clay fought himself not to turn and look at her, afraid his expression would say too much.

He imagined Gray Wolf would be suspicious of his decision to give his slave to Swift Buck as it was. The assurances he wanted to send Melissa with his parting gaze might alert the perceptive leader that Cougar had turned traitor, over a woman.

Guilt gnawed at his insides. Clay wanted his life back, the one he'd had before she'd turned his world upside down, before she'd invited herself into his bed and penetrated his heart. The dark plane he'd drifted upon before she'd filled his life with light, that empty place where he could have existed without her, and never known what he'd missed.

"Cougar, ride with me," Gray Wolf said. "Maybe you will tell me what it is about your blood brother's lodge that made you hurry from the ceremony last night, and if it is the same thing that kept us waiting this morning."

A few snickers followed the leader's subtle scolding. Clay scowled at the back of Gray Wolf's head and nudged Two Moons beside the warrior. He refused to be intimidated by a man no older than himself. "I do not ask what goes on in your lodge, Gray Wolf. Whatever I find of interest inside the tepee that my blood brother graciously allows me to borrow is none of your concern."

Dark eyes fused with his. "I am concerned. For the future of my people, and for Cougar's future as well. If you cannot ride away today without looking at her, maybe you should not return after the hunt. You seem different to me this morning. Whiter. Maybe her skin is rubbing off on you."

In response, Clay kneed Two Moons into action. The pounding of hooves told him the others followed. He rode straight past Melissa, his eyes trained ahead, his features noncommittal. Damn Gray Wolf! The wily warrior had forced him to leave without relaying a message of assurance to Melissa. A dark thought occurred to him. What if he never saw her again? The morning's cool air suddenly chilled him to the bone. Clay shivered slightly, trying to dismiss the feeling of doom hovering overhead.

It persisted, grew stronger with each hoof mark Two Moons left in the dirt behind him. He wanted to pull back on the reins, wanted to turn around, see her standing beside the tepee, her hair still loose and her eyes aglow with the passion between them. He wanted to send her a message—wanted to tell her to have faith in him. When Gray Wolf caught up with him, loping his mount alongside Clay's, he did neither.

Chapter Twenty-three

The feeling of unrest preceding Clay's departure stayed with Melissa well into the fourth day after he'd gone. She supposed the fact that he hadn't glanced at her before riding away had added to her agitation. Doubts crowded her mind each night as she lay across from Jageitci. Would he ever love her the same way she loved him? Would he really see to it she was rescued? Or had his promise been one of convenience? A clever ploy to pacify her and save himself the bother of saying goodbye?

She sighed, bending to retrieve a hefty piece of firewood, then slid the wood into her sling. She wouldn't know the answer to these questions until he returned, if he returned. He'd said Gray Wolf might call his hand and force him to go back to the mountain.

How could she be certain that wasn't a lie? And a cruel one. How long would she wait, her senses alert for the sound of his footsteps, her heart ever hopeful he'd come creeping in the night to steal her away?

"He wouldn't lie to me," she muttered irritably. "He said to trust him, and I do."

"It is good Huera and I are alone," Jageitci said in Spanish. "Whether or not we understand English, a woman who talks to herself is still considered crazy, in any language."

Melissa smiled wryly, then frowned. "I told you to sit beneath a tree and rest. One pair of hands can gather enough firewood for us tonight. I will fill the water skins as well. A mother-to-be should not heft heavy objects."

"You spoil me, Huera." The Spanish woman rubbed her lower back. "My husband wants to buy you from Cougar to help me after our sons are born. I worry when I grow big and clumsy, he might look too long at your pretty face, think too much about your slim shape." She settled under the branches of a tall aspen, leaning her head against the trunk, then grinned. "Maybe I could control my jealousy for the pleasure of lying around all day."

The smile on Melissa's lips faded.

"I only tease you, Huera," Jageitci assured her. "Gray Wolf belongs to me, and I will not share him. Besides, I do not think Cougar will sell you to another. He has an option his mind has not yet accepted. When the time comes, which is very near, he will make the right decision."

Goose bumps rose on Melissa's arms. "The right decision?"

"You are his test of loyalty—but he does not have to give up one love to have the other. It is simple. If Cougar becomes all Apache, lives with us, fights with us, abandons the white world, he can prove himself to my husband, and keep you as his woman."

"His slave, you mean," Melissa muttered. She didn't want to spend her life as Clay's prisoner, couldn't bear the thought of him touching her with hands he'd raised against his own kind. Jageitci's option was not one she would consider.

She came close to telling Gray Wolf's wife that Clay would rescue her, take her from this world and hopefully share his life with her in a society she understood. Instead,

Melissa returned to her tasks, worried Clay might consider Jageitci's plan.

"Close your eyes and rest," she instructed. "The others will intrude on our privacy soon. You take risks wandering so far from them so we can talk to one another, away from where you know the men watching camp are stationed. I learn more Apache every day. Before long, we can speak freely among them."

"Maybe," Jageitci agreed, closing her eyes. "In time, you will become accepted here, but I know from my own experience, gaining The People's trust is not simple. It took two years before they allowed me to roam from their eyesight. The life of a slave is hard, but ask yourself this: Is Cougar not worth the suffering? Would you not do anything to be with the man who owns your heart?"

Anything? Melissa wasn't sure she could honestly say yes. She loved Clay, wanted to be with him, but on equal ground, in a place where they weren't torn in opposite directions.

"I can't answer that question. Not yet." Melissa shielded her eyes, searching for a vegetated spot to seek a moment of privacy. She saw a clump of thick bushes behind Jageitci. "Rest until I return. I need to attend to a personal matter."

A sleepy nod dismissed her. Melissa suspected the pretty Spanish woman would be dozing by the time she walked to the bushes and back again. Removing her heavy wood sling, she parted the branches and crawled inside. Her experiences with the Apaches had taught her to be quick in all tasks. A few moments later, she fought to readjust her clothing in the cramped confines of the bushes.

A noise caught her attention. The snap of a tree branch. She waited, annoyed that someone was looking for them already. Another sound reached her ears. A thud, a soft moan, and then another thud.

Curious, Melissa scrambled from the brush, scooping up her wood sling in the process. She glanced toward the tree where Jageitci sat. Her heart slammed hard against her chest. The woman lay sprawled on the ground, a bright streak of crimson flowing down the side of her face.

"Jageitci!"

Her legs nearly gave way before she reached her friend. Melissa bent quickly, trying to survey the damage. It appeared as if someone had bashed the sleeping woman over the head with a heavy object. A thick branch, perhaps. Even as she arrived at her conclusions, the scent of danger made her nostrils flare. Her heart's erratic beat increased. She began to turn. Pain exploded behind her eyes.

Buzzards circled overhead. Clay wiped his skinning knife against the buckskin of his leggings. Unlike the white men who killed buffalo only for their hides, or the delicacy of their tongues, the Apaches left the birds little to scavenge. Four days into the hunt, they'd found the herd. Now, with his skills and those of his brothers, along with the aid of a handful of seasoned women, winter didn't look as bleak.

Litters were being loaded with hides, meat, entrails, any and all parts of a buffalo The People used. Had the herd not been previously scouted and reported to be moving toward Santa Fe instead of in the opposite direction, the entire camp would have packed up and come along.

Civilization meant danger to the women and children of Gray Wolf's band. Twenty mounted riders and a handful of women could escape an attack more easily than the tribe as a whole. Gray Wolf served his tribe well as leader. His strategies were usually carefully thought out, ever conscious of preserving the Apaches' future generations. He was smart. Too damn smart.

The uneasy feelings that had plagued Clay upon departure remained. Two days into the hunt Tall Blade had fallen from his horse and injured his leg. His return to camp only added to Clay's unrest. He didn't like the thought of Melissa being unprotected while the brave wandered camp.

"Your bow shot straight today, Cougar." The leader walked toward him. "How many buffalo did you take down? Ten? Eleven?"

Clay shrugged. "As many as I could. I only need the meat

of four to see me through winter. As always, the rest belongs to The People."

"You are not a man of greed. Although we do not ask, I know you would use the gold received for your furs to feed us if we were starving, to bring us clothes if we were freezing."

"This band is very capable. You have not asked, and so far, there has been no need."

Gray Wolf inclined his head in a gesture of agreement. "It may not always be the way of things. The buffalo grow scarcer as the caravans pass through our land. They hunt our game, trample our ground. What the whites and Mexicans do not destroy, the Comanches try to take. My worries would be greater if Cougar were not one of us. I have no reason to ask on this day, but I may be forced to on another. For the future of my people, I must demand that you return to the mountain now. Go, and the test that stands between us is over."

Despite his suspicions that Gray Wolf would resort to these tactics, Clay had hoped his worst fear would not materialize. "I have matters left unattended to at camp. Personal items to collect. Property to be settled."

"Anything of importance Cougar has left behind can be brought to you on the mountain. You know I will see to this as soon as I return. The 'property' you speak of can be settled here. I will trade two of my best horses for Huera."

"I have a good horse," Clay countered. "And I plan to give Huera to Swift Buck. That is what she wants."

Dark color suffused Gray Wolf's face. "A slave has no right to ask anything of her owner. Your blood brother does not need a worker, when he could easily have a wife. But then, you know this already. I think that you believe if he does not need her, he might sell her back to her people."

A thin bead of sweat traced a path down the side of Clay's temple. "What he does with her is not my concern."

"No, Cougar. Her fate affects you, affects us all. She can point a finger at you when you ride into the white world and call you Apache. Then the soldiers will demand you help them hunt us. There can be no ransom!"

The leader's voice rumbled like distant thunder. His black

eyes flashed with anger. Clay felt a pain in his chest. There was only one option left to him, and when he made the choice, he would no longer run wild with his childhood friends, but run and hope they didn't catch him. He could think of nothing to say, no lies would formulate in his throat, no mask would disguise the agony he felt.

Shouts of distress broke the stare-down between them. Glancing up, Clay noted puffs of smoke floating in the distance. He tensed, reading the alarm signal painted against the sky. The uneasiness that had ridden by his side since leaving camp intensified. The tribe called them back, and to do so on a hunt meant something terrible had happened.

Gray Wolf immediately set to issuing orders. He chose ten braves to ride with him, and instructed the others to bring the litters. Clay stood, clenching and unclenching his fists, unsure if he'd be allowed to join Gray Wolf. Invited or otherwise, he must return to make certain Melissa was safe.

"Come, Cougar; you will whether I ask or not."

They rode night and day. Clay said little. A feeling of dread churned his insides. He recalled the overwhelming desire to turn back the morning they left, remembered the dark thought that had crossed his mind: *What if I never see her again?*

The raw ache in his heart proved the strength of love, and the consequences of surrendering to an emotion he had vowed to forsake after his mother's death. It seemed one couldn't control one's own destiny, could not reason with fate.

Two Moons's ears pricked and his gait increased. Weary as the man on his back, the stallion obviously sensed an end to their journey. Clay's hands tightened on the reins. His knees gripped the animal's sides and they raced ahead of the others. Only a warning whistle from Swift Buck kept Clay from charging into camp, for the first time unconcerned with his own safety. He forced Two Moons to stop.

After the group spotted a sentry who waved permission for them to continue, Clay allowed Gray Wolf to take the lead, as was his right. The plodding of their horses' hooves made an ominous sound as they entered the campsite. There were no joyous shouts of welcome, no laughter, only silence. The People were gathered and cleared a path to the corral, their expressions solemn. Clay scanned the crowd, searching for a familiar blond head.

"She is gone!" Tall Blade stepped forward to shout up at Clay. "The white witch has killed our leader's wife to make her escape!"

Shock nearly tumbled him from Two Moons's back. It wasn't Clay who grabbed the brave's shoulders and demanded details, it was Gray Wolf.

"Tell me I did not hear the words you spoke!" the leader commanded. "Tell me you are lying and I will not slit your throat for causing me this pain!"

"Gray Wolf." Laughing Stream gently touched the tribe's young chieftain. "Your wife is not dead." The woman cast a furious look in Tall Blade's direction. "But until she roused herself from darkness a short while ago, she came very close to walking the spirit trail."

"Where is she?" Gray Wolf croaked, releasing Tall Blade.

"In your lodge," Laughing Stream answered. "The shaman is with her."

"Huera hit her over the head with a heavy stick," Tall Blade interrupted passionately. "She lured her from the other women and committed this crime against us so she could escape!"

"You lie." Clay's voice was low, deadly. He slid from his stallion and pushed Gray Wolf aside. "Huera could not take a life. She does not have the heart of a killer!"

The strange lights dancing in Tall Blade's gold eyes flared. "I believe she does. Because she is clever, cunning as the fox, merciless as the badger, she has stolen your heart. She has made a fool of you."

"No!" The strangled growl escaped Clay's lips. He pounced. His fists connected firmly with Tall Blade's jaw. The brave stumbled back a step, then he pulled a knife. A gasp issued in the silence. As Clay reached for his own weapon, Laughing Stream scrambled from harm's way.

"Stop!" Gray Wolf ordered. "There is no time for this

nonsense between you. I must see Jageitci, then the council will meet and we will hear the evidence against Huera."

"Is she among us?" Tall Blade asked. "Is that not proof enough?"

"What the eyes see is not always the truth," Clay argued. "How long have you been back?"

"Cougar," Gray Wolf warned, "you are too quick to place blame on another. Do not disgrace yourself." The leader turned to Tall Blade. "When did you return?"

Tall Blade appeared insulted by the question. "I arrived the night after this crime was committed. Three days from when I left you."

"With your injury, it would take that long." Gray Wolf nodded toward the bloody bandage wrapped around Tall Blade's thigh. "Did you notice signs of Huera's passage while you rode to camp?"

"If I had noticed, she would be here to face punishment. The white woman should die!"

Hatred flavored Tall Blade's declaration. Anger and something more. Frustration, barely controlled rage. Why, Clay wondered. Tall Blade cared nothing for Jageitci.

"If Huera roams the wilderness alone, she is already dead, or soon will be," Gray Wolf said quietly. "See to your horses and wait for me in the council lodge. All are invited to tell what they know."

Clay's gaze remained fixed on Tall Blade. Reluctantly, the brave replaced his knife, then turned toward the council lodge. Dazed, full of denial, and sick at his stomach, Clay snatched Two Moons's reins. He walked to the corral, opened the gate, unbridled his horse, then sent him trotting inside the fence. Once he stepped into the tepee he'd shared the past three months with Melissa, her scent enveloped him. Clay went to his knees.

"Where are you?" he whispered hoarsely. Only silence answered. The tepee's coolness made him shiver. His gaze searched the dimness, lowering to the buffalo hides where he and Melissa had made love. If he closed his eyes, he might feel her softness beneath his fingers, hear the sound of his name on her lips, see the beauty of her face when she cried out in release.

He refused to believe her capable of attempting to kill Jageitci in order to escape. Hadn't he promised to rescue her, one way or another? Hadn't she said she trusted him? Hadn't she confessed to loving him?

What they shared together wasn't a lie. She couldn't have so completely blinded him to her true nature. Melissa was innocent, and he didn't know what had happened, or where she'd gone, but he would find her. He just hoped it wouldn't be too late.

The whole tribe gathered for the meeting. The lodge wasn't large enough to hold them all, and many were standing outside. Finally their leader arrived, carrying a pale but breathing Jageitci in his arms. Clay sat inside the lodge, a solemn Swift Buck at his side.

Gently, Gray Wolf lowered Jageitci to a soft hide, then settled beside her. A bloodstained bandage graced his wife's forehead, a reminder that the accusations made against Melissa were very serious. Clay stared straight into the Spanish woman's eyes, his gaze penetrating, demanding she deny Melissa's guilt.

"I do not want to believe it of her, either," Jageitci said quietly. "But what else can I think, Cougar? She told me to sit beneath a tree and rest. Huera told me to close my eyes, and I did. Those who found me said her wood sling lay at my feet, a heavy stick covered in blood beside it. Tell me how I can believe she is innocent?"

"You cannot!" Tall Blade thundered. "We cannot. Huera committed a crime against The People. She made too many trust her bad heart."

When a grumble of agreement followed, Clay ground his teeth in frustration. "Huera saved the life of your sons, she saved the life of my blood brother, and she probably saved mine. Have you used your gift to look at what happened that day?"

Jageitci shook her head, then winced, bringing a hand to

her forehead. "As my sons grow stronger, so does my sight become weaker. It is gone from me at this time, but once I saw no wrongness in her. We spoke of you that day, Cougar. I told her you might consider forsaking the white world to have both us and your woman. She said the life of a slave was not for her, and I asked if you were not worth the suffering? I said, 'Would you not do anything to be with the man you love?'"

Clay felt a tightening in his chest. "And what was her answer?"

"Huera said she could not say."

"This deceit speaks for her," Tall Blade piped up.

"Silence." Gray Wolf held up a hand to warn the brave against interrupting further. "Is that all the words that must be said concerning the slave, Huera?"

An awkward pause filled the lodge. Finally, a voice spoke. "I will speak," Swift Buck said.

Surprised, Clay turned toward his blood brother. Swift Buck avoided his eyes. The unconscious action of fidgeting with the ties of his moccasins unsettled Clay. He'd known the brave since boyhood. It meant he was nervous.

"The white woman came to me not long ago and offered herself if I would help her escape."

A gasp left Jageitci's lips. Gray Wolf's gaze widened slightly and Clay thought he surely had misunderstood his blood brother.

"Why did you not tell me of this?" the leader demanded.

Swift Buck ceased his fidgeting and met Gray Wolf's angry glare. "I did not believe she knew her mind. She begged me to take her to the man waiting in Santa Fe, but I thought it was her love for Cougar she wanted to escape." His gaze shifted to Clay. "I am sorry, brother."

For a moment, Clay felt nothing. He held his numbness close, knowing it would soon fade. Stares were leveled at him, that much he comprehended. Slowly he gained his feet and, without a word, walked from the council lodge. A path cleared for his retreat. Even after reentering his tepee, he couldn't grasp all he'd heard.

First, Jageitci's revelations floated through his consciousness. *Would you not do anything to be with the man you love?* Then Swift Buck's damning admission, *The white woman offered herself to me if I would help her escape. She begged me to take her to the man waiting in Santa Fe.*

His body started to tremble. Huera would do anything to be with the man she loved. She would kill, bargain her flesh, seduce and manipulate, all for . . . Robert. Agony so intense it wrenched a groan from Clay's throat ripped through him. He began to make sense of her confusing actions.

From the beginning, she meant to seduce him, win his heart, ensure her return to Santa Fe, and when Jageitci innocently provided an option his captive hadn't foreseen, she feared her plans of being rescued would not materialize. In short, Melissa had taken matters into her own capable hands.

"Damn you!" he growled with fury, transforming the pain, as he'd learned many years ago, into anger in an effort to reduce the ache. The sheet of ice the woman had so recently thawed around his heart began once again to harden. Her love for him had been a lie. Melissa was no different from the whores, who traded their bodies for gain. Every act of kindness she'd administered was only an effort to further deceive him and The People.

"Damn her," he swore again, but his voice shook slightly.

"Cougar?" Gray Wolf called from outside. "May I enter?"

Clay took a calming breath, determined not to show the devastation Melissa had delivered to his feeble hopes for a future of love instead of hate, of peace instead of war, of all he'd been denied in his misplaced life. No sign of weakness flavored his tone when he gave Gray Wolf permission to join him.

"The People find Huera guilty of trying to kill Jageitci. Her punishment is death."

Their sentence didn't surprise Clay. "When will the search begin?"

Gray Wolf lowered his gaze. "There will be no search. By my wife's request, and to honor the friendship that has long been between us, we leave Huera to the wolves, the bears, the Comanches, all the evil she must face in the wilderness.

242

If she is not dead already, she will be soon. It takes many years to learn to survive this land. Bury her in your memory, Cougar. She is gone."

A reprieve was the last thing Clay expected from the Apaches. He presumed the decision hadn't been reached for Melissa's sake, but for his. Had his feelings for her been so obvious? Clay wished he found leaving Melissa to her own deserved fate easy, but he didn't. "Whether she is dead or alive, I will find her."

"And if you do, and she still lives, you must return her. She must answer for her crimes."

Clay swallowed hard, then nodded. "I understand."

Chapter Twenty-four

Melissa couldn't remember going to sleep, but she awoke to a nightmare. How she'd come to be in her current circumstances also eluded her. She'd somehow become the hostage of ten rough-looking Mexicans, and although she pretended not to understand their language, she knew too well what they intended.

Clay hadn't been trying to frighten her when he'd said that bandits dealt in scalps and female flesh. They were headed for Mexico, and she was likely to fetch a high price. So far, they hadn't touched her, but the hot glances she received daily promised the situation might change at any moment.

After her shock had worn away, it occurred to her that they might be willing to take her to Santa Fe if she tempted them with a reward. Then she'd heard one man say he'd seen her picture on a poster, and when he quoted the trivial price offered for her return, the others laughed. Melissa kept her mouth closed. She told herself that Robert had forgotten he was dealing in pesos, but deep down, she feared that was not the case.

The men discussed her freely, assuming she couldn't understand them, and through their conversations, she'd been able to piece together a confusing picture. Her first terrible conclusion was that the men had attacked the campsite. Melissa worried over the fates of Jageitci, Laughing Stream, Mesa, and the innocent children.

Soon, she discovered they'd found her alone and unconscious. Melissa couldn't recall what had happened after she saw Jageitci slumped over and bleeding. She had vague images of someone's rough hands on her. Someone shaking her. There had been a knot on the side of her head. She could only assume whoever had dealt Jageitci a blow had knocked her unconscious as well. Was her friend all right? Had they been attacked by Comanches?

It seemed unlikely that she'd been taken and then accidentally dropped from the back of some brave's horse, lost in the shuffle. But if not that, what? There was only one thing she knew for certain, Clay would save her, just as he'd promised to rescue her from the Apaches. Melissa had no idea when he'd come, or how he'd find her, but he would. She had faith in him.

"Mexico is a long ways. I am thinking she would not be too used up if we took turns with her. One man a night."

In the process of stretching her legs, Melissa froze. She quickly schooled her features into a mask of indifference, but couldn't control the loud pounding of her heart. The man who'd made the lewd suggestion had stained, crooked teeth, a large mole on the end of his nose, and a belly that strained the buttons of his dirty shirt. His companions were no less unappealing. She couldn't stand the thought of these men touching her, forcing intimacy on her after the tender lovemaking she and Clay had shared.

From beneath her lashes, Melissa studied the man she assumed led the scraggly group, since he barked orders and the suggestion had been aimed in his direction.

"The brothel I want to sell her to pays the highest prices. It pays more for any woman brought in who is innocent."

"She has been with the Indians. Apaches or Comanches,

maybe both," a third man joined the discussion. "Even a savage can appreciate a beautiful woman. I suspect many braves have taken their pleasure between her long legs."

"Maybe." The leader scratched his whiskered face. "But I am thinking we will get a dress, make her look white again, and say we took her from a caravan. The brothel owner does not need to know otherwise."

"If we are going to fool him anyway, why not enjoy the woman before selling her?" the first man persisted.

"Because I forbid it! She will not fetch much if she has the pox! Just this morning you said the last woman you were with gave you more than pleasure. At least the Indians do not carry our filthy diseases."

A grumble ran through the group, silenced by the leader's stern expression. "Any man who touches her will have his hands cut off."

Melissa hoped the relief on her face wasn't evident. Sunset fast approached, and now she could sleep without fear of being attacked. She hadn't been able to rest since she awoke in the company of these outlaws. In the long hours of darkness, she thought of Clay, softly wept for him, longed for his scent, his touch, his strength. Where was he? When would he come? Pressure on her shoulder made her jump and spin around. The leader grinned lewdly.

"Any man . . . but me."

Fear snaked up her spine. His beady gaze roamed her body with obvious appreciation. Understanding what he'd said was unnecessary; Melissa easily fathomed the lust in his eyes. She stumbled back a step. Her stomach began to churn, and she recalled Swift Buck's suggestion of pretending sickness the day she'd stayed too long in his company. With a gasp, she doubled over, clutching her middle. When she clamped a hand over her mouth, the leader grimaced, hastily stepping away.

"Louis, take her into the trees. I do not want her fouling our campsite for the night."

Reluctantly, a man broke from the others. With a scowl etched across his face, he nodded in the direction he meant her to go. Melissa quickly staggered from the scene, wondering what to do next. She couldn't wait for Clay, couldn't risk the leader forcing himself on her. Spotting an area where the trees were thick and overgrown with vegetation, she fell to her knees and crawled into the brush.

The sounds of retching she mimicked kept the man at a distance, as she'd hoped. Her gaze darted back and forth, and although Melissa knew she probably couldn't survive the wilderness alone, the horrors that might lie in wait for her out there were no worse than the nightmarish future these men planned for her. She continued to moan softly while crawling deeper into the overgrown vegetation.

The pitch of her voice varied in an attempt to disguise her location, then the brush began to thin, and she was up and running. She hadn't gotten far when she heard a shout of alarm. Her blood quickened, panic urging her legs to move faster. Melissa kept to the trees.

The men couldn't follow on horses, not with the brush so thick in some places and sparser in others. Her captivity had strengthened the muscles in her arms and legs, the days of endless hefting and squatting aiding her ability to scramble over brush and squeeze between trees grown too close together.

Most of the bandits were overweight, but a few were small and wiry. Those were the ones she was worried about. The ones who threatened the short lead that separated her from freedom and the unthinkable. Had she been fleeing the Apaches, Melissa knew there would be no escape.

In that moment, she called on Huera's instincts, the invaluable skills of survival Clay had taught her, and in her mind, she became one with the wilderness. Although fear spurred her onward, Melissa listened to the forest.

She studied her surroundings, and realized too late that a clearing loomed ahead. A place without shelter to hide or tangled brush to slow those in pursuit. She halted, her breath coming in loud gasps. Sounds of men crashing through the brush behind her increased the pounding of her heart.

Frantically, Melissa scanned the area, searching for cover.

Already the trees around her had thinned, and she realized she must go back. She spotted a clump of thick brush not too far away, took a step in that direction, and drew up short. The bushes quivered, then a man scrambled up, training a pistol on her. Another Mexican followed. And then another.

All three men were huffing from their exertions. Sweat beaded their brows and Melissa suspected she could outrun them, but the gun steadied on her held a greater advantage. Had she continued into the clearing, she would have made an easy target.

The victorious grins spreading across their faces sickened her. Melissa stared defiantly back at them, refusing to let the gun humble her. She wouldn't return willingly. They would have to drag her back kicking and screaming.

"She does not look scared of your little pistol, Louis," one man teased. "I am thinking she has seen larger guns than that."

Louis, her squeamish guard earlier, cast him an insulted glance. "Then she is in for a disappointment, aye? Our selfish leader has a big belly, but what rests beneath is very small."

All three laughed loudly. Louis motioned her forward. Melissa stood her ground. The Mexican sighed, then tucked the pistol in the front of his pants.

"I am afraid the pretty gringo forces us to disobey orders. If she will not come without a fight, we must put our hands on her."

"All over her," one agreed, his grin stretching.

"It is necessary, no?" the other added with a chuckle.

"No."

The smiles on their faces froze. Melissa's knees nearly buckled. Although he spoke Spanish, she knew who the voice belonged to. Slowly, she turned. Clay leaned casually against the trunk of a tall tree. Fading light gleamed off the knife he used to clean his fingernails. He didn't glance up, but appeared deceptively interested in his manicure.

"Brodie," Louis croaked.

"The devil," another said.

"Mother of God, help us," the last breathed.

"Clay!" Melissa took a step toward him, still unable to believe he stood before her. He hadn't been there a moment ago. Her eyes drank in the sight of him: his long lashes resting against his cheeks, the dark stubble along his jawline, the rich blackness of his shoulder-length hair. Never had he been more beautiful to her, never would she want another man with the passion she wanted this one.

Melissa knew then, he was her fate, her destiny, and she would follow him to the ends of the earth, or live with him among the Apaches. Which world they shared no longer mattered. She was Cougar's woman, and someday he would belong to her as well.

"Touching my woman is unnecessary." Clay's tone remained undisturbed. "She will not return with you."

"Our captain ordered us to find her," Louis explained nervously. "Her blond hair is worth many pesos in Mexico."

Clay's gaze lifted. His knife ceased its digging. "I will trade your lives for hers. I have friends with me. Red men who would feel honored to place your scalps on their lances. Tell your captain to mount up and ride for Mexico. If he is as smart as he is round, he will not look back."

"I see no Indians with you," Louis pointed out.

"No man sees an Apache until it is too late," Clay countered.

Quickly, Louis pulled the pistol from his pants. He aimed it at Melissa. "The woman will die if you do not call off your savage friends and go."

Clay shrugged. "She is better off dead than making a living on a flea-infested mattress in Mexico, dying of disease. Go ahead and shoot. Not only will you be doing her a favor, but then nothing will stand between you, me, and my friends."

Although the pistol in Louis's hand trembled slightly, Melissa wasn't consoled by his fear. What was Clay doing? Goading the man into killing her? He acted as if he didn't really care one way or the other.

But he did care, she assured herself. Clay wouldn't be

standing not three feet away if she didn't mean anything to him. With a show of courage, Melissa stared straight down the barrel of the gun into Louis's panicked eyes.

He held the weapon one second, then screamed in agony the next. The pistol fell from his hand, the handle of a knife protruding from his wrist. Clay threw too fast to register the knife's journey, but Melissa still heard the sound of it whizzing past her.

As blood bubbled up from Louis's injured hand, the other two men beat a hasty retreat. Clay's broad back appeared before Melissa's dazed eyesight, and she realized he'd walked past her to approach a whimpering Louis. He'd walked past her and not even touched her.

"I like this knife," Clay explained before removing it from Louis's wrist with a sharp tug. The Mexican went to his knees and Clay kicked the man's gun from his reach. "I could have easily hit you square in the heart, but some things are not worth killing for. If I see you in my territory again, hunting for women and scalps, I will kill you. All of you, understand?"

Louis nodded his head frantically, holding his wrist and groaning in pain. His watery gaze lifted, searching the area.

"Better go," Clay warned. "The sight of blood always gets them stirred up."

With a parting whimper, Louis crawled back into the brush. The crunch of his boots running sounded shortly afterward. Melissa began to tremble, the shock of all she'd recently been through hitting her all at once. Clay finally turned to look at her, and she couldn't stop herself from running into his arms, sobbing her relief and joy at seeing him again.

She held tightly to him, promising to never let him go, when a strange realization seeped past her joy. His arms did not encircle her, he hadn't touched her, whispered words of reassurance, or spoken of his own relief at finding her alive.

Confused, she pulled away and glanced up. His eyes were

red-rimmed, clearly tired from nights without sleep, but they didn't belong to the man she loved. They were hard, accusing, unmerciful. Instinctively, she took a step backward, then scolded herself for this reaction. Clay wouldn't hurt her. When his stare didn't soften, she knew more was wrong than the ordeal they'd just been through.

"Clay?" she whispered shakily.

"Shh." He placed a finger on her lips. "Not now. We don't have time. I lied to the Mexicans. I'm alone. We have to get away before they regain their courage."

Rather than take her arm and gently guide her from the trees, he headed for the clearing. Melissa stared after him for a moment, her senses warning her that a stranger had arrived in Clay's place. She fought her feelings, rationalizing that now was not the time for Clay to express his emotions.

They were still in danger, and he was too levelheaded to sweep her into his arms, cover her face with warm kisses, and make love to her in the pine needles. Later, she promised. Later, Clay would give her all she deserved for trusting in him, refusing to give up hope that he would rescue her.

A coyote sang his lonely song in the night. Melissa rubbed her arms briskly, wishing for warmth. The overhang they camped beneath protected them from the wind, but Clay said even a small fire was too dangerous. That had been about the only remark he'd made since they stopped to camp.

A huge bright ball hung in the sky and lit the surrounding countryside. She watched him tend his horse, fetch his saddle packs, and turn to join her. Suddenly, she felt odd in his company. Nervous for reasons she couldn't explain.

"Hungry?" He tossed the saddle pack toward her. "In the left one there's some jerky."

And in the right, Melissa suspected she'd find his mother's journal. He took his pack everywhere with him. Melissa no longer needed to read Anna Brodie's story. She loved Clay whether he was white or Apache or both.

251

"Would you care for some?"

When he didn't answer, she looked up from her scrounging. His eyes glittered in the moonlight. Slowly, he lowered his gaze to her breasts, then to her hips, then roamed a leisurely path back.

"No."

She couldn't swear to it, but she thought he hadn't declined her offer of food so much as insulted her body. Frustrated, Melissa slammed the packs to the ground.

"What's wrong?"

"Wrong?" He lifted a dark brow. "What did you think? That I'd forget what you did? That I'm so taken with you it wouldn't matter? I was a fool for you once, but I've grown considerably wiser over the past few days."

"Forget I did what? *What* wouldn't matter?"

"Jageitci!" Clay thundered, his calm control lost.

Melissa felt the color drain from her face. "She's all right, isn't she? Last time I saw her she was lying down, and her head was bleeding."

"A crack to the skull usually results in blood. But then, you know that, don't you?"

"I-Is that what happened?" Melissa stammered. Clay was insinuating she knew more about the subject than he did. "You didn't tell me if—is she?"

"No, she's not dead."

"Thank God," she breathed, placing a hand to her heart.

"That won't save you, Melissa. It doesn't change what you did."

Clay stared at her in the oddest way. As if he didn't know her, hadn't lived with her during the past three months, hadn't made love to her.

"What is it you think I've done?"

He sighed, sounding exasperated. "The game is over. You don't have to lie anymore, or go behind my back and try to seduce my best friend. You don't have to look at me with just the right amount of confusion and hurt in your eyes. Your bottom lip doesn't have to tremble slightly. I know who you are now, Melissa Sheffield. You're a woman who'd trade your body like a common whore if it served a purpose. You're a woman who'd tell a man you love him if that's what you thought he needed to hear. And you're a woman who would kill a helpless mother-to-be. Jageitci trusted you. I trusted you. Now the Apaches want your life in exchange for the one you almost took."

Melissa gasped. She couldn't believe Clay was making these horrible accusations against her. More, she couldn't accept that he would consider them anything but false. "You think I'm capable of killing Jageitci? Do you honestly believe I'd bargain myself to a man—"

"Tell me you didn't offer to give yourself to Swift Buck in exchange for freedom? Look me square in the eye and say he lied."

She couldn't. Melissa lowered her lashes. Hot shame flooded her face. "You don't understand, Clay. I was still innocent then. I didn't know what really transpired during intimacy. My feelings for you were frightening. It was *me* I wanted to run from, the love I felt growing for you I needed to escape. It was wrong, horribly wrong, and I'm deeply ashamed of what I did that day. You believe me, don't you?"

"Almost," he admitted, but the coldness in his gaze didn't thaw. "Tell me why you couldn't wait for me to rescue you from the Apaches? Explain why you tried to kill Jageitci?"

"I didn't try to kill her!" she shouted. "You know I couldn't hurt anyone unless forced to defend myself!" Melissa attempted to cool her unruly emotions. She took a calming breath. "We were gathering wood. I told her to sit beneath a tree and rest, then went off for a moment of privacy. When I returned, Jageitci was slumped over, blood running down the side of her face. I bent to help her, but a pain exploded in the back of my head and the next thing I knew, I woke up in the company of the bandits."

Her story sounded incredible even to Melissa's ears. She rubbed her forehead, wishing the small knot at the base of her skull hadn't already disappeared.

"Clay, I know it doesn't make sense." She looked up into

his eyes. "But I swear it's true. You asked me to have faith in you, and I did. I knew you'd rescue me from those men. Now it's your turn to trust."

Their gazes held for what seemed an eternity. Melissa feared he might never touch her again, but he finally reached out and pulled her against his broad chest. She went willingly into his embrace, relieved no more accusations or false assumptions stood between them. Gently, she traced the line of his rugged jaw, then pressed her lips against his throat.

"Make love to me," she whispered. "I want you. I'll always want you."

"No. Not yet," he added when she pulled away in surprise. "You know we can't return to the Apaches now. We'll go to Santa Fe, but before we do, I want you to marry me."

"Marry you?"

He smiled. "It would cause you less embarrassment if we rode into Santa Fe as man and wife. You're to tell everyone I rescued you shortly after your capture, and it's taken us all this time to elude the savages. You can tell them we fell in love along the way."

Melissa's brow knit. "But Robert . . . I'd hoped to break off our engagement with a little more gentleness. In fact, I'd hoped to marry you someday wearing a white dress, standing before a priest."

"I can't get you a dress, but I can find you a priest. There's a small mission town not a day's ride from here." He tilted her chin upward. "You do love me, don't you?"

Lost in the depth of his blue eyes, she nodded. "When will you tell me the same?"

"I asked you to become my wife. In my opinion, that says enough." He pulled her close again, draped a blanket across them, and settled back. "By sunset tomorrow, we'll have a proper wedding night."

As she snuggled into his warmth, Clay stroked her hair. His hands encircled the slim column of her throat, and for an instant, he wondered what it would feel like to squeeze, to choke her until her lying tongue turned blue and swelled. He released her neck abruptly, afraid he'd be too tempted.

Clay had every intention of marrying her tomorrow. He wanted all she would have killed to give Robert. Clay Brodie might have rescued her, but Cougar would take his revenge.

Chapter Twenty-five

Melissa didn't know the person staring back at her from the cracked bureau mirror. The color of her skin reminded her of weak tea. Streaks so blond they appeared silver ran through her drying tresses, contrasting sharply with her complexion.

Her eyes looked greener than she remembered. Greener and wiser. She stared past her reflection to the spindle bed. A bed, her mind kept repeating, as if she'd never seen one before. Not only a bed, but a bath and a washbasin. A room, one with gas lamps and peeling wallpaper.

She couldn't believe she'd returned to civilization—or that she had married Clay Brodie an hour ago inside a crumbling mission. Her gaze snagged on an unwrapped package on the bed. Clay carried more than his mother's possessions and jerky in his saddlebags.

He'd withdrawn a small pouch of coins to pay the hotel owner downstairs. Once, Melissa would not have considered her accommodations fine lodgings—the mission town was in sad need of repair—but to her civilization-starved eyes, the place was grand indeed.

Unable to stand the suspense a moment longer, she clutched her towel tighter and approached the bed. Clay had sent the package. She had no idea where he'd gone, and despite his cool attitude since her rescue, the luxury of a private bath was thoughtful of him. The bath and the gift. After removing the lid, Melissa gasped with pleasure. A nightgown of fine Spanish lace lay inside.

Carefully, she lifted the delicate garment from the box and held it up against her. She suddenly understood the symbolism behind Clay's gift. The nightgown represented the proper wedding dress he would have liked her to have.

This was to make up for their hurried marriage, his unsettling silence throughout most of the day, for depositing her in this room and mysteriously disappearing. The gown, however, wasn't proper. Melissa flushed at the thought of Clay seeing her exposed flesh beneath the filmy white lace.

Her hands shook as she unbuttoned the seed pearls running from the low-cut neckline to the fitted waist. She gathered the material, slipping the gown over her head. The lace hugged every curve of her body. One glance downward set Melissa's cheeks to burning. Her nipples were visible through the gown, as was the darker shade of blond hair between her legs.

In truth, she felt more naked wearing the garment than she would have without it. She moved to the mirror to brush her hair. Earlier, she'd planned to pile the mass atop her head to create a more sophisticated appearance for Clay. Now, she hurriedly pulled a thick lock over each shoulder in an attempt to hide what the gown did not. Her gaze strayed to the bed again. Maybe she should be under the covers when Clay arrived.

He'd seen her body before, she reasoned, all of it, every single part. But they hadn't been together since the first time, and she felt suddenly shy. She replaced the brush, turning to approach the bed. The sound of a key jingling outside the door drew her up short.

A man stepped inside her room. Melissa opened her mouth to scream. When he turned to face her, the scream

257

died in her throat. Clay's hair was tied back, his face clean-shaven. He wore a black cutaway coat and a starched white shirt. His moccasins were gone, replaced by a pair of gleaming black boots. Snug black trousers hugged his slim hips and powerful thighs.

He wasn't in the least dandified, nor did he appear the gentleman. Clay reminded her of an outlaw. Dark and dangerous—and irresistible. A verse floated through Melissa's memory.

A more perfect man surely exists nowhere else on this earth. He is handsome and tall, and when he looks at me from across a room, I forget what is being said to me, or what I was about to say. I see no one but him, hear no words except his. I am totally, helplessly, irreversibly in love.

Where had she read those words? Melissa had trouble remembering, trouble breathing, trouble believing Clay could alter his appearance by simply changing his clothes. The lazy inspection he ran down the length of her reminded Melissa she stood gaping at him in next to nothing.

"Don't," he cautioned when her arms began to creep up across her breasts. "I told you once before, you have nothing to be ashamed of."

"I-I feel underdressed." She nodded toward his striking outfit. "You look different."

"More civilized?" he questioned, leaning against the door.

"I suppose so," she answered, not sure if it was entirely the truth.

The door lock clicked loudly after he reached behind him. "Then I've made my point." He untied the silk burgundy scarf around his neck, then unbuttoned the top button of his shirt. Shrugging away from the door, Clay approached her. "It doesn't matter how you dress a man, Melissa. He is what he is."

She unconsciously took a step backward. "What do you mean?"

"Tailored coats and leather boots won't make a savage civilized. I have the spirit of the cat inside me. You accepted Clay Brodie as your husband not more than an hour ago, and when you took him, you got Cougar, too."

258

Melissa moistened her dry lips. "And I can't love one without loving the other."

His gaze followed the movement of her tongue. Clay reached out and traced the full shape of her mouth. "But you haven't loved us both." Slowly, his finger moved down her neck and into the deep *V* of her nightgown. "Clay Brodie loves the sight of your body molded inside white lace, but Cougar prefers bare skin."

With a strong tug, the seed pearl buttons on her nightgown scattered in all directions. Melissa gasped, embarrassed and more than a little confused by her husband's actions. She wheeled away from him in order to hide her nakedness. The heat of his body engulfed her. He reached around and cupped her exposed breasts.

"Clay Brodie led you gently into pleasure. He was patient, controlled in his passion."

As he teased her nipples into taut buds of sensation, Melissa leaned forward and grasped the spindle footboard of the bed. Although Clay Brodie had loved her well the night she had sat before him with paint on her face, she'd sensed, even in her innocence, that he'd held the savage side of himself at bay. Now, when he pressed his hardened member intimately against her bottom, heat flooded her lower regions.

She moaned a protest when his fingers ceased their caressing strokes. He used his arms to hold her captive while reaching up behind her head. His hands reappeared in front of her, and in them, he held the burgundy scarf tied at his neck earlier.

Silk slithered down her arm and twined itself around first one wrist, and then the other. She closed her eyes while he nipped gently at her throat. When she opened them again, she noted her wrists were now bound to the footboard of the spindle bed.

"Clay?"

"He's not here," came his husky reply. "You're dealing with the other one, and he has no patience, no control. Cougar will take you like the animal he is."

Melissa fought the urge to struggle. Deep within, she

Ronda Thompson

knew neither man would hurt her. She also knew Clay needed her to accept the bad along with the good in him. What he didn't know was that Cougar appealed to her as much as Clay Brodie. His touch, not rough as he began gathering the gown up around her waist, but not particularly gentle, either, excited her—regardless of which man he chose to be.

She said nothing as his fingers brushed her bare bottom while unfastening his trousers. Nothing when he nudged her feet apart, positioning her so that her arms were stretched out full length, her back bent, her gaze focused on the floor. When he clutched a fistful of Melissa's thick hair, she felt him against her. He was bold, but not quite committed to surrendering to the savage within.

"You can't disgust me," Melissa said softly. "I want Cougar as much as I wanted Clay Brodie."

He forced her to look at him. His eyes blazed in the soft glow of gas lamps, then he bent over her, releasing the silk scarf tied around her wrists.

Freedom, in this instance, did not particularly appeal to her. Clay Brodie had won her heart, but Cougar appealed to her darkest desires. Melissa wanted to know why. She refused to move her hands from the footboard or straighten and pull the gaping edges of her gown together.

"Even Cougar can't take anything you're not willing to give," he said.

Melissa said nothing and waited. He didn't touch her for a moment, then her silence unleashed the beast struggling to escape Clay Brodie. The savage that lived in all men. With a thrust that made her gasp, he buried himself deep. Her grip tightened on the footboard while his mouth ravished the side of her neck. His hands strayed from her hips, one to her breast and the other to the soft curls between her legs.

He stroked her until she mindlessly matched the rhythm of his powerful thrusts. She moved with him and against him, conscious of only her body and his, the way they fit together, the overwhelming pressure she felt when he filled

260

her completely, the unbearable ache when he withdrew. Her hands jarred the footboard with each thrust, the steady creak merging with the sound of her soft moans and his labored breaths.

Over and over she heard that creak, until her concentration centered on nothing but need, nothing but the thick, throbbing length of him rendering her senseless, and the beginning tremors of release gathering within. His fingers took her the rest of the journey, skillfully plummeting her into a world of spinning shapes, muted voices, convulsing flesh, not only hers, but his as well.

She felt his spasms of release, the sharp ridges of his teeth when they sank into her neck, the warmth of his lips as he soothed the stinging. Slowly, her breathing returned to normal. Her gaze cleared. Or she thought it had, but the footboard seemed to be swaying. Melissa heard a creak. Clay swore. They'd barely managed to untangle themselves and scramble away when the bed collapsed.

The dust floating in the air attested to the hotel's uncleanliness. Melissa slid down the peeling wallpaper, staring at the heap of wood and quilts on the floor. Her gaze sought Clay. She found him leaning against the wall opposite her. He was still impressively dressed, although his trousers were around his knees.

Directly between them, the burgundy scarf made a bright slash of color against the dull carpet. With her foot, Melissa retrieved the object. She twisted it between her hands and smiled.

"There are two women living inside of me. One is giving, and the other takes. One likes to be controlled by you, and the other wants you helpless beneath her—at the mercy of her hands, her lips, her desires. I accepted Cougar. You must accept Huera."

Clay didn't return her smile.

Chapter Twenty-six

Clay watched Melissa stretch her back as he grazed Two Moons. Sunlight shimmered over the many colors of gold and silver woven through her hair. She wore a serene expression while she walked through the tall grass, running her palms across the feathery tips.

A vision flashed in his memory, her fingers running lightly over his chest, then ripping the buttons from his shirt. He'd been passive under her touch, still angry that he couldn't love her in truth, angrier that he'd allowed his thirst for vengeance to lead him down a path he'd promised long ago never to take.

Only an animal like his father would do what he'd intended to do to Melissa. It was no wonder he wasn't more eager to be with Sally the night Hiram had first taken him to Santa Fe. The only examples given him in early youth were his father's violent rape of his mother, and the disgusting grunts and groans he heard when Hiram's Apache woman sneaked out to lie with his father. But three nights past, he'd almost crossed the line of what even Cougar considered decent.

He'd wanted to humiliate her, the same way he'd felt after

realizing her words of love to him, her surrender, had all been for another man's sake. How well she played the game, and if she could look at him with her beautiful jade eyes and lie without batting a lash, the pleasure her body received from his couldn't be feigned.

He doubted Robert would understand why she'd gone so far beyond the call of duty in her quest for freedom. Why she felt compelled to strip a man, mount him, and take him to the edge of insanity and back. No, Clay didn't think Robert would understand at all, but then, he was certain she had no intention of confessing the damning details.

What would she say to the saint, provided she had an opportunity to see him again? Not that she would. Clay had made a promise to a people who had never lied to him. A pledge to bring her back to face punishment if he found her.

Well, he'd found her, and it wasn't as hard as he'd first imagined. He thought she might try to retrace their path to the meadow. There were berries there she could gather for food. Although she must have been wise enough to erase her tracks, the bandits weren't as smart.

He hated his first unguarded reaction to her dilemma, his fear the men would abuse her, harm her, kill her. Clay supposed he deserved the right more than they. She hadn't broken their hearts, made them look like fools, told them she loved them and blinded them to her scheming nature. He'd ridden hard to catch up with the group, and fought the impulse to rush headlong into disaster once he'd spotted them.

Instead, he'd watched, assured by Melissa's manner around the men that she hadn't been subjected to rape. But then the situation had changed. The leader had grown too bold, and luckily, Melissa had seen to it that Clay only had to deal with three of the men, instead of the whole gang.

Now they were two days into a marriage he'd kept mostly celibate by pushing them onward—to Santa Fe, Melissa believed—but by nightfall, she would understand Clay Brodie wasn't a man to be mocked or manipulated.

"Do we ride or camp tonight?" she called, standing a few feet away in waist-high grass.

263

"Ride. We're almost there."

Her face lit up. Clay wished she didn't look so damn beautiful in her Indian trappings, her hair the same color in places as the rain-starved grass. She seemed so innocent, so sweet, and he admitted part of him still wanted to believe loving didn't always bring pain. He wished she really was the woman who had stolen his heart, shown him a better side of himself—but she wasn't. His wife didn't deserve the love he fought against feeling for her.

"Do you think we'll actually get to sleep in a bed before morning?"

"Maybe." He couldn't bring himself to lie outright. "Why don't you climb up in front of me and rest for a while." Clay swung onto Two Moons's back as she approached.

"I'm suddenly too excited to be tired." Melissa smiled up at him. "Excited and a little scared at the same time. It's hard to believe I'm free, that I'm returning to civilization. Part of me is happy, and yet, part of me is sad, too. I-I'm going to miss them."

The tears gathering in her eyes were convincing. Clay glanced away and extended her a hand. "Maybe you'll see them again someday," he said dryly.

She settled in front of him and turned. "That isn't possible, is it? If even you thought for a brief time I tried to kill Jageitci, surely they couldn't be convinced of my innocence." Her gaze widened, as if just making a connection. "Clay, how will the Apaches view our marriage, and the fact that you helped me return to Santa Fe?"

"Not favorably."

"Then you've failed the test and are no longer welcome among them. Because of me, you won't be able to return to their camps."

"You knew the consequences," he reminded her, impressed by the sad expression in her eyes, and the slight tremble of her bottom lip.

"Yes, I did," she agreed, then sighed. "I'm sorry, Clay. I wish we could have the best of both worlds. Maybe in time they'll realize the test wasn't fair, understand that just because we're white, that doesn't make us their enemies. I want to see Jageitci's sons, who Mesa chooses for her husband, if Swift Buck falls in love again. Although I can't explain what happened, because I don't know, I'd like an opportunity to defend—"

"Rest," Clay demanded, pressing her head against his shoulder. "It's too late. Too late . . ." His voice trailed away. He couldn't stand her pretense that they would share a future together.

And now that he thought about it, they wouldn't have had much of one anyway. What could he offer her? He knew nothing except the fur trade, hadn't ventured past the territory, and wasn't educated. True, the money he'd stashed under the floorboards of his cabin and in a vault at Sally's was a sizable amount. A small fortune.

But could he purchase respectability with it? No. Most everyone in Santa Fe knew Clay Brodie could buy half the town if he wanted. The problem was, the town wasn't for sale to the likes of him. Not to the son of a crude trapper, one rumored to be an Injun lover, the same as his daddy.

A sardonic smile twisted Clay's lips. True justice would be to condemn her to a life of ridicule as his wife. A lifetime of grief and hardship. His mother's life. Glancing down, he noted that despite her claim, she'd fallen asleep in his arms. He committed to memory the way she looked just then. Trusting, innocent, beautiful. "Damn you," he whispered. "Damn you for backing me into a corner."

As he rode into the sunset, the world did appear smaller. Two Moons's strides quickly ate away the distance, bringing him closer to a final confrontation with his heart. He tried not to remember the sight of Melissa spinning in the meadow; the day she'd defied a fierce warrior and saved the lives of Gray Wolf's unborn children; and her bravery when she'd stopped the beating Clay had taken in her stead.

Those were memories of the woman who'd melted the ice around his heart, not the one lying contentedly in his arms now. This one had lied, deceived him, would have killed, and all for the love of another man.

Abruptly, Clay halted his horse. Not much farther and the sentries posted around the perimeters of camp would spot them. He glanced down at Melissa again. Twilight bathed her serene features in shadow. He'd lied for her, killed to protect her, deceived his brothers by planning to rescue her.

Reality struck him with force. Melissa wasn't guilty of anything he wouldn't have done himself. The difference was, she'd done those things for Robert. Could he sentence her to death for loving the wrong man?

Letting go of his anger proved difficult. Clay had lived most of his life feeling angry, vengeful, and mistrustful. Maybe it was because he thought his childhood had given him the right. After staring at Melissa for several minutes longer, both Clay and Cougar knew he had no right to judge Melissa Sheffield.

For the first time in his life, Clay understood the true meaning of love. It was loving someone even when they didn't deserve to be loved. Loving them despite their faults. Their weaknesses. Clay turned his horse around to flee with her. Behind him, ten Apache warriors blocked his retreat.

"Tell me you have suddenly lost your way, Cougar," Gray Wolf said. "I know it would be a lie, but because you have come this far, I will act as if I believe you."

The sound of voices roused the woman in Clay's arms. She moaned softly, opened her eyes, and smiled up at him.

"Say nothing," he warned softly. "Let me handle this."

"Handle what?" she mumbled drowsily.

He nodded toward Gray Wolf. She turned her head, gasped, then pressed closer against Clay.

"Give her to us, Cougar."

"That was my intention. But I cannot fulfill my pledge to you. I will not ride against my brothers in the days ahead, but I cannot let you have this woman. My heart no longer seeks vengeance."

The leader sighed. "Your forgiveness does not erase her crimes. I gave you a choice. A fair one. The council decided her guilt, Cougar. The crime demands a life."

Melissa's fear penetrated his senses. He knew she

266

couldn't comprehend the conversation, but the seriousness of their circumstances she understood. Deep down, he'd known from the beginning where loving her would lead.

"Then take mine," he said softly. "I trade my life for hers."

"No!" Swift Buck urged his horse beside Gray Wolf's. "She is not deserving, Cougar!"

He smiled sadly in the dim light left over from the day. "You and I are too much alike. When we mixed our blood, either I gave you my heart's stubbornness, or you gave me yours. You understand that it matters little to me if she is deserving or not. We walk the same foolish path, brother, and neither of us can turn back."

Swift Buck groaned in response. He glanced hopefully toward Gray Wolf. "As leader of our people, you can refuse."

"Yes," Gray Wolf agreed. "But I do not. If we take the woman from him and kill her, his heart will turn against us. It is better Cougar die with honor, than fighting those who have proudly called him brother for many years. I accept his trade and respect his courage."

It was an odd feeling, to be relieved you were going to die. Clay felt as if a heavy weight had been lifted from his shoulders. Almost. "I ask that you allow me to return Huera to her people. You have my word I will ride into your camp before the next full moon."

A dark shape joined Gray Wolf and Swift Buck. "Your word is not the word of an Apache!" Tall Blade growled. "You could not give the woman to us. Why should we trust you to return?"

"My blood brother is a man of honor!" Swift Buck glared at the brave. "To insult him is to insult me!"

"Then vow to give your life if he does not give his," Tall Blade goaded. "Declare before all present you will die in his place, as Cougar has promised his life for nothing more than a white slave."

Gray Wolf lifted a brow, waiting for Swift Buck's response. The brave straightened proudly.

"If Cougar does not return before the next full moon, I declare before all present to accept his punishment for the crime Huera committed against The People."

"You are a fool," Tall Blade spat.

"An Apache warrior does not fear death," Clay said. "But he fears for those closest to his heart." His tense features softened when he looked at Swift Buck. "Now I understand the battle you fought, but could not win. When I see the one—my sister, in the spirit world, I will speak well of you."

Swift Buck's dark gaze glittered brightly. "And I will envy your words with her."

"She is not in our sky," Tall Blade interrupted harshly. "The woman was white, and would not be allowed to enter. Usen has more sense than his people."

"Enough," Gray Wolf reprimanded. "She caused us no harm, why do you speak badly of her?"

Tall Blade nodded toward Clay and the woman in his arms. "Was it not her death that brought a witch among us? We should be wiser than those who allowed the red-haired man into our camps. His kind weaken us, they shame us! How can we call one brother, when each passing sun finds wagons of whites defiling our lands? We cannot call them anything but enemy!"

"I know this," Gray Wolf agreed. "Have I not told The People of my visions? Have I not warned them to hold their children close and cherish the day? Tomorrow is dark, but tonight, Cougar is still my friend. I will honor his word, and the word of Swift Buck. Go, Cougar. When I see you again, you will be our brother no more."

Clay swallowed the lump of emotion forming in his throat. He stared a moment longer at Gray Wolf and Swift Buck, remembering their faces before they'd become men. Gray Wolf had taught him to respect himself, and Swift Buck had taught him to laugh. The best days of his life had been spent in their company. Fitting, that he would pass his last moments with them.

Finally, he nudged Two Moons forward. The men parted to let them pass. Clay didn't look back. Melissa trembled in his arms, her fear betrayed by the uncontrollable clicking of her teeth. After countless hours without sleep, he didn't have the strength to let her suffer any longer.

"It's all right. They decided to let you go. I'm taking you to Santa Fe."

She sat stiff before him, shivering and silent.

"I said—"

"I heard you. Can we stop for a minute?"

Her request struck him as odd. Clay figured she'd want to ride from one sunup into the next to reach Santa Fe. He knew the Apaches would honor Gray Wolf's decision, but Melissa shouldn't be as trusting. She had no idea what had just transpired.

"Oh." He suddenly understood. After sliding off Two Moons and helping her dismount, Clay afforded her what privacy he could by turning his back. He wasn't prepared for the feel of her fists hitting him squarely between the shoulder blades. Surprised, he wheeled around to face her. The moonlight bathed her in white light. Moisture welled up in her eyes. Tears of accusation.

"You lied to me! We were never going to Santa Fe! You were returning a prisoner to your precious Apaches!"

He saw no point in denying it. "Yes."

Although Melissa didn't collapse, her features visibly crumpled. "Why?" she whispered.

The pain in her voice slashed into him. Clay steeled himself against the blow. She was good at pretending. "To get even with you for making me look the fool. The game is over, Melissa. I know that everything you've done, you did for another man."

A tear escaped the corner of her eye. "You never believed me. I asked for your trust, but you couldn't give it. I let you touch me, I stood before God and became your wife! Why did you insist we get married?"

Sparing her feelings wasn't uppermost in Clay's mind. Melissa's anger stirred his own. "Because I wanted all you would have lied, whored, and even killed to give *him*!"

She stumbled backward as if he'd slapped her. An expression of pure agony registered in her wide gaze. "You let

269

me believe you cared for me, wanted to share your life with me, out of revenge? Because you think I made you look foolish to the Apaches, you would have seen me killed for a crime I didn't commit?" Her cheeks were now streaked with tiny wet lines. "Why did I ever trust you? Why did I let myself fall in love with you? I'll hate you from this night forward, Clay Brodie! I swear I will!"

With a sob, she turned and buried her face against Two Moons's satiny coat. The anger churning Clay's blood cooled fast enough to make him shiver. A horrible revelation occurred to him. Melissa no longer had any reason to lie. He'd told her he would return her to civilization, told her the Apaches were letting her go. Why had she still professed to love him? Unless . . .

He couldn't complete the thought, couldn't let himself accept the truth. The pain he'd fought earlier enveloped him, squeezing his insides, cutting off his breath, almost buckling his knees. Why hadn't he listened to his heart when the evidence was brought against Melissa? He'd tried, wanted desperately to, but the hardened side of him couldn't trust in her, couldn't believe he was worth loving. And he'd proven he wasn't.

"I'll see that you're not bound to me for much longer. When we get to Santa Fe, tell Robert I made you marry me, tell him I forced myself on you. Tell him whatever is necessary. If he's the saint you say he is, he won't blame you. He'll take you away from this hellish territory so no one else will, either. You can still have the life you wanted. The life you deserve," he added under his breath.

Abruptly, she wheeled around. "And you'll just ride away like the coward you are! Maybe the Apaches will get you another white woman to torture!"

There was no point in defending himself. Clay had caused her enough pain. He wouldn't allow her to carry around any guilt over the sacrifice he'd made. Letting her hate him was the kindest thing he could do. "Maybe."

"I guess by taking me back you passed their test of loyalty," she fumed. "Why did they decide to let me go?"

Clay shrugged. "Since Jageitci didn't die from her injury, I convinced them to take a ransom for you and spare themselves further trouble."

"And I suppose you'll ask Robert to pay for my return?"

Her spirit remained intact. Clay almost smiled in relief. Melissa Sheffield was a survivor. He'd much rather deal with her anger during the ride to Santa Fe than her tears. To add kindling to the fire, he said, "I'll settle with them. It's the least I can do."

The narrowed slits of her eyes widened. Beneath the moon's silver light, Melissa's complexion darkened. "You'll pay for me the same as you would one of your women in Santa Fe! The *least* you can do is tell me if I was worth the price they demanded?"

His gaze roamed her face. The love he felt for her swelled inside of his chest. She'd made him realize many things about himself. That caring could scar, but it could also heal. He knew he wasn't the same as Hiram Brodie, and now he understood that loving his mother, despite her cruel treatment of him, didn't make him less of a man, but more of one.

Love began with accepting the strengths and weaknesses in yourself. He no longer felt trapped between two worlds, but only a small part of one. Too late, Clay Brodie had finally accepted that he was worthy of being loved, and could give his love in return, without shame.

"Yes," he answered honestly. "You were worth the price."

Chapter Twenty-seven

A short distance away, civilization twinkled like a bright star. Melissa stared through eyes blurry from lack of sleep. At her request, they'd ridden at a grueling pace to reach the outskirts of Santa Fe. She'd assured Clay Brodie the sooner the two parted company, the happier she would be. Yet now, close enough to see her dream of freedom becoming a reality, the numbness that settled over her bruised emotions began to wear thin.

Parting was inevitable. She memorized the feel of him pressed against her back. Clay had proven himself heartless. A liar. The wrong man. Then why did she feel panic crowding her? Why did the thought of living without him still seem impossible?

"Do you want to camp and ride in at daybreak, or go on and reach town after dark?"

Melissa didn't trust herself to spend another night in his company. How far would the desperation she felt push her? Into his arms? Could she rationalize as madness her desire for a man who'd betrayed her? Would she ask him to walk into the flame with her one last time? Her pulse leapt at the thought of his hands on her, his mouth, the husky words of passion he'd whisper.

"Ride on," she answered quickly. "I'd rather arrive under the cover of darkness."

"That might be best," he agreed. "I'm giving you my saddlebag. There's enough money inside to get yourself a room at the Exchange. I'll send someone over with more for clothes and necessities. My friend Martin Hanes is probably still in town. If you need anything, you'll find him at Sally's. It's a . . . place at the edge of town."

His instructions only increased her agitation. "You don't have to pay me off, Clay. I'm sure Robert will see to my needs."

She felt his arms stiffen on either side of her. "Well, in case he doesn't—"

"He will," Melissa insisted. Her broken heart demanded restitution. She could think of only one way to get even with Clay Brodie.

"I plan to do exactly what you suggested. Robert will believe whatever I tell him. Who knows, maybe once I see him again, the feelings you convinced me weren't genuine will reappear. I'll have the sort of life I once imagined. A nice house, an adoring husband, and blond-haired children. We won't live in Santa Fe. I want to return to St. Louis and the social circles Robert and I are accustomed to. Robert will indulge me. I'm positive—"

Melissa was babbling on one minute and found herself pulled off Two Moons's back the next. Clay pinned her against the horse's side.

"It makes me crazy when you ramble on like that!" His steely gaze cut into her. "Don't misunderstand, if he can give you all those nice things, measure up to what you think is important in this life, I wish you the best. I swear to God I do. But late at night, after he's asleep—when you're lying in the dark and you feel empty, as if something is missing inside, I want you to close your eyes and remember this." He took her lips gently, then deepened his claim on her mouth, forcing that little sound from her throat.

When he pulled away, Melissa opened her eyes. She felt dazed.

"Don't lose sight of Huera. She's your strength."

And you're my weakness, Melissa thought, cursing her trembling knees. "You can't swear to God if you don't believe in Him," she said flatly.

Clay smiled slightly. "Always pushing, aren't you? I don't envy that man." He turned Melissa around and hefted her upon Two Moons before hopping up behind.

They didn't speak further. Melissa watched the horizon darken and the lights grow brighter and closer. Her stomach was twisted in knots by the time the sounds of civilization reached them. The muted music of a badly tuned piano, voices, laughter—they were noises she doubted anyone but two people whose senses had been keened by the wilderness would have registered for another mile or so.

She tried to control the trembling of her body, partly due to the chill that accompanied sunset, and mostly the result of nervousness. It had been more than a year since she'd seen Robert. Should she try to locate him tonight, or wait until morning?

Tonight, she decided. Better to get the ordeal over and done with. Melissa had no intention of marrying Robert, even if he were still interested in such an arrangement. She wanted to go home, to live in that big empty house with her memories, her ghosts. In three months, she suspected she'd lived more than most people do in a lifetime. How could her mundane dreams of the past compete with all she'd been through?

Regardless of the fact that Clay had deceived her, there would be no man to take his place. Just because she'd given her heart foolishly didn't change the fact she'd given it. Before God, she'd pledged to love him forever, and with unjust certainty, Melissa knew she would.

"What is the saint's last name?"

"Towbridge," she answered irritably. "Why?"

"It might help if you were looking at the signs. I can't read, remember?"

Startled, Melissa straightened before him. She'd been too caught up with thoughts of Clay and the life she was leaving behind to realize they'd ridden into Santa Fe. The gas lamps burned her eyes as she squinted up at crude structures not nearly as lovely as an Apache village. Although the rutted road appeared virtually deserted, the loud laughter spilling from establishments farther down the street sounded abusive to her ears.

"There." She pointed. "The next one. Towbridge Trading Post." Melissa wished her voice held more excitement, but hoped Clay would mistake the nervous tremor as that very emotion, and not what it was: dread.

He rode up to the hitching post. "A lamp's burning in the back. Do you want to see if he's inside?"

"Yes." She answered the opposite of what she'd been thinking. "I'm anxious." *To get this over with*, she mentally completed the sentence.

After he helped her dismount, Melissa unconsciously smoothed the soft hide of her buckskin dress and fumbled with the braids hanging past her shoulders. She glanced nervously toward the shop, then back at Clay. Her heart slammed against her chest. This was goodbye.

"I'll wait to make sure you get to the hotel if he isn't there."

"That won't be necessary," she assured him in a raw tone. "He's surely there, and if he isn't, I notice the hotel is just down the street. I'll walk."

He seemed about to argue, then sighed, slipping his saddlebag off Two Moons's back. "Remember, find Martin Hanes if you run into any trouble."

His voice sounded as hoarse as hers had. Melissa tried to search his face, but the shadows hid his expression. Her fingers brushed his when she took the saddlebag. She shivered. They stood without moving until the moment grew awkward.

"You'd better go inside," he said finally. "The streets won't be safe much longer."

She giggled rather hysterically. "I've spent three months in an Apache camp in the middle of the wilderness and you're telling me the streets of Santa Fe aren't safe?"

"Didn't I teach you a lesson about judging people by the color of their skin?"

The question sobered her. "Yes. Should I thank you now for removing my blinders? For showing me how ugly a place the world can be? That you can't trust anyone and that all things can be bought, bartered, or sold when they're used up or become bothersome?"

He presented his back and Melissa had the strangest notion she'd managed to wound him. He's heartless, she reminded herself. She couldn't hurt him, although the fantasy was a pleasurable one. Her heart felt as if it were cracking, breaking in half, and he would walk away without looking back, just as he'd intended from the beginning.

The fact he hadn't walked away from her once without returning didn't occur to her. His recent betrayal pushed the countless acts of kindness and courage he'd performed on her behalf to the furthest recesses of Melissa's mind.

"Leave," she said with less emotion. "This time, you can ride away for good."

"I said I'd wait until you got inside," he reminded, turning around.

"And I told you I can take care of myself!" Melissa didn't want him staring through the glass of the shop window when she encountered Robert.

"Probably," he agreed. Clay bent and retrieved the knife he carried in his moccasin, extending it to her. "You might need this."

Her gaze went from his face to the knife, then back. "I won't have any use for that. You forget, I'm not dealing with a savage. Robert is a decent, God-fearing—"

"I didn't say he wasn't," Clay interrupted angrily. "I'd feel

276

better if you had something to protect yourself. This is all I have to offer you at the moment."

She shoved his hand away. "I don't want anything from you, and I don't want you to feel better. I just want you to leave me alone!"

"All right, I will," he ground through his teeth, replacing his knife, then pushing past her to mount Two Moons.

He'd reined his horse away from the railing and headed the direction they'd ridden in from before Melissa could react. Her heart began to pound loudly in her ears—her hands began to shake. *Stop*, she wanted to shout. She considered running down the rutted road after him, begging him to take her with him. Lest she make a fool of herself, Melissa hurried up the planked sidewalk and through the shop door. A bell tinkled overhead.

"Who's there?" a voice called from the back.

Melissa froze. She couldn't answer. A man appeared, the lamplight casting a halo around his blond head. He squinted in her direction, then removed the spectacles perched on the end of his nose. His eyes widened. He took another step.

"Melissa?"

"Robert," she said with a relieved whisper.

That was all she could manage as he approached. He stopped short, his gaze running the length of her before settling on her face.

"Good God, you've turned into a squaw."

They were not the words she imagined he'd say to her when they met again. Melissa straightened her spine. "I'm insulted by that word."

"Well, you have." He indicated her clothing and braids with a sweep of his hand.

"I don't mean I take offense at resembling an Indian, I mean the word *squaw*. It's a white man's term."

Robert glanced around nervously. "What are you doing here?"

Flustered, Melissa stammered, "I-I've been rescued."

"I assumed that much." He hurried past her and untied the

straps holding the window coverings in place. "I meant why did you come here dressed that way? This will be embarrassing enough."

Dazed, Melissa watched as he lowered the shades. "Embarrassing?" she repeated, stunned by his reaction. "If you thought my return would cause you embarrassment, why did you post a reward for me?"

A blush of guilt tinged his cheeks. "Because I knew that's what the decent folks of Santa Fe expected, although once the ladies were out of earshot, the gentlemen agreed it shouldn't be enough to entice anyone to actually go in search. Is some fool waiting out there to collect?"

"No," she answered, her voice shaky. "He isn't a fool. He knew you better than I did."

"He?" Robert approached her. "Has some filthy Injun brought you back?"

Melissa straightened her spine. "I expected better from you, Robert Towbridge. I guess I expected too much."

Again he blushed. "Be reasonable, Melissa. You should have thought before you came riding in here dressed like a . . . like that. What are people going to say? What are they going to think?"

She hadn't thought beyond wanting to part company with Clay. Now she had no choice but to confront the inevitable. "You don't want to marry me," she said, not a question but merely stating a fact.

Robert had trouble meeting her gaze. "People will talk. They'll say things . . . things about you being with the Indians. They'll wonder if . . ."

"If what?" she demanded, knowing full well what everyone would wonder.

He finally looked her straight in the eye. "If those dirty savages took you. They'll wonder how many had you. They'll wonder—"

"And what about you, Robert? Are you wondering?"

His gaze lowered to the floor. "Yes."

Melissa had to give him credit for at least being honest.

And she realized she hadn't been honest with herself. She thought about Mesa's return after being captured. The way the tribe had welcomed her home with open arms. She had a feeling that the question of which society was the more civilized would soon be answered.

"I wasn't molested," she said.

The slight sigh Robert issued spoke of his relief. He glanced up at her, really seemed to see her for the first time. "I doubt anyone will believe that. You're a beautiful woman, Melissa. Even dressed as you are." He rubbed his chin thoughtfully. "I suppose we could go away. Start over in a place where no one knows about your past."

Once, his suggestion would have suited her. Now, Melissa understood she couldn't keep running. The world must accept her as she was, whether she be Huera or Melissa Sheffield, formerly of St. Louis.

"I won't run, Robert. I'm no longer the girl you knew in St. Louis."

He turned away from her, obviously somewhat torn. "Then I can't marry you. My business would suffer if we stayed in Santa Fe. I'd be ridiculed for taking a woman to wife who had lived among the Apaches. I'm sorry, Melissa."

A tremendous amount of relief washed over her. True, she had misjudged Robert, but then, she'd misjudged herself. Without a doubt, she knew that she'd never loved him—realized she hadn't truly known the meaning of love until fate had tested her, until she'd fallen in love with Clay Brodie.

"I should be the one apologizing. I never loved you, Robert. Not the way a woman should love a man she agrees to share her life with. I'm sorry for misleading the both of us." She turned toward the door, closing a chapter in her past.

"What are you going to do?" Robert asked. "Where will you go?"

The thought of returning to St. Louis held little appeal to

Melissa. Still, it was her home. "I'm going home. Goodbye, Robert."

"Melissa," he called, and his voice held regret. "The sooner you leave, the better it will be for you. People can be cruel."

His warning brought a sarcastic smile to her lips. "I'll survive," she said, and for the first time in her life, knew she would.

Once outside, she breathed deeply of the night air, disgusted that it smelled of civilization. The streets were still deserted. A blessing. She would face society soon enough. Tonight she only wanted a place to sleep, a haven to weep for what had been lost. Sanctuary to gather what had been found. The strength to survive.

A figure stepped from the shadows when she reached the hotel. Clay thrust a key at her.

"I thought you might want to go up the side stairs. Avoid being seen."

Melissa silently cursed him for not riding away without a backward glance. Regardless of his sins, she wanted to rush into his arms. Beg him to stay, or demand that he go, but not without her. She understood the meaning of unconditional love. Damn Clay Brodie for teaching her this particular lesson. Without a word, she took the key and started up the side staircase.

"Did everything go as you expected?"

The temptation to lie surfaced. Let him believe she was right about Robert. But if she did, his conscience could rest.

"You were right. He isn't a saint. Does that make you happy?"

She didn't wait for an answer, just continued up the stairs. Her knees felt weak, her spirits low. She'd be damned if she'd let Clay Brodie know. She'd be damned if she'd tell him Robert couldn't break her heart, only the man who'd stolen it could.

"I'm sorry."

Melissa blinked back the tears his soft words brought. "You are that," she said, then hurried past the side door, afraid of what else he would be right about.

Chapter Twenty-eight

Everything, she answered herself the next morning. Clay knew human nature better than most people. After a restless night of tossing on a squeaky bed, Melissa awoke to a discreet knock on the door. She hated the way her heart leapt, hated that she hoped Clay stood on the other side. He didn't. A Mexican woman in a starched apron asked if they could bring in her bath.

Melissa gratefully agreed, and it seemed as if all of Santa Fe proceeded to march in and out of her room. The hotel servants gawked at her and regarded her fearfully from beneath lowered lashes. She wondered if they thought she'd pull a knife and come at them.

Once the tub had been filled with steamy water, the hotel clerk arrived, his face flushed. "These packages arrived for you downstairs," he informed her, thrusting the boxes into her arms. His nose wrinkled slightly while staring at her buckskin dress and moccasins. "Sally had one of her girls bring them over. She said they were clothes for you to wear." He lifted a brow.

Melissa supposed she was expected to react in some way. Suddenly, she recalled getting the impression that Sally owned a house of ill repute. Her blush of embarrassment seemed to satisfy him. The clerk left smiling slyly. After depositing the boxes on the squeaky bed, she stormed to the open door. A passing woman glanced in her direction and screamed. The scream ended abruptly when Melissa slammed the door in the startled woman's face.

She pressed her back against the sturdy wood, trembling. Had Clay sent the packages? Most likely, and she wasn't about to dress in clothes discarded by a floozy. Melissa could just imagine what sort of indecent apparel lay inside those packages. To prove herself right, she stomped to the bed and tore open the first box.

A loud gasp escaped her throat. She lifted a dress of white eyelet and held it against her. The collar was modestly high, the sleeves belled, and the skirt fashionably straight. The back had a large bow and a bustle. Melissa nearly squealed with delight.

Excitedly, she tore into the other boxes and almost wept when she fingered the delicate lace of a silk chemise and underdrawers. There were stockings, garters, and even a pair of dainty button-up shoes. Clay had surprised her yet again.

Why hadn't he gone when she had told him to last night? Why had he taken care of her hotel arrangements and provided her with these beautiful clothes? Because he did have a conscience after all, and she'd managed to prick it. Melissa hurriedly stripped from her buckskin dress and moccasins. Perhaps people wouldn't scream once she resembled a white woman again. Maybe Clay wouldn't be right this time.

A couple of hours later, bathed, perfumed, dressed to the nines, and with her hair piled on her head, Melissa sat in the hotel restaurant, choking on crow. No one had screamed, but they still whispered. They spoke behind their hands and nodded in her direction. The men eyed her lustfully, and Melissa knew what they were thinking.

She was soiled goods, Indian leavings, undeserving of respect. The few women present were no better. Judging from their disdainful glances, Melissa might as well have dressed like a floozy.

When she couldn't stand their ogling any longer, she rose, holding her head high as she marched from the restaurant. She continued her charade of haughtiness until reaching her room, then softly closed the door, ran to the bed, and burst into tears. She didn't cry for long.

Melissa wiped the tears from her cheeks. She needed Huera at this moment. The woman who didn't care what these people thought. The woman who loved Clay Brodie whether she was damned for it or not. He hadn't trusted her, hadn't believed in her. And if she'd given herself time to stop seething, Melissa thought she would have understood why. He'd been scarred deeply by his childhood, scarred more deeply than perhaps he even knew.

To him, love was a painful emotion. He expected the worst of people, and usually received it. Clay feared no man, but he was afraid to give his heart, to give his trust. Life had made him an outcast also. Why couldn't he see how alike they were? Why hadn't she?

Noticing his saddlebag on the floor, Melissa picked up the packs. She dumped the contents on the bed and stared dumbly down at them. The silver-backed brush gleamed brighter than the gold wedding band tied to a ribbon inside a Bible. Melissa touched the journal reverently. Why had Clay given her his mother's belongings? She knew he valued them. He surely must have forgotten they were in the saddlebag. As soon as he remembered, he'd ask her to return the items.

Her pulse leapt. To demand them back, he'd have to see her again. Melissa assumed, since he'd sent the packages, Clay was still in Santa Fe. After all they'd been through, she refused to accept that parting would be as simple as a goodbye. Distractedly, she flipped through the yellowed pages of Anna's diary.

Once, the journal had interested her, because fear had dictated a need to gain greater insight into Clay. Now she found

283

herself merely curious. The dainty button-up shoes, pretty as they were, hurt her feet. She slipped them off, then removed her dress. Her skin itched from the lace around the neck of her chemise, and the corset had cut off her breath.

Soon, Melissa had donned the soft buckskin dress, her leggings, and the comfortable moccasins. She removed the pins from her hair, rubbing her temples where her head ached from the tight pull of her hair.

Feeling more like herself, she settled on the squeaky bed and retrieved the journal. Melissa started at the beginning, planning to read the entire journal. She hadn't gotten far beyond Anna's girlhood when she came across an entry where Clay's mother dreamily described a young man whose name was Thomas Morgan.

Odd, Melissa thought, Anna seemed completely taken with him. When had she met Hiram Brodie? Her curiosity fueled, Melissa continued to read, discovering a mention of Hiram Brodie a few pages later. Her brow puckered with confusion. Anna didn't sound at all interested in the trapper. In fact, she wrote about her repulsion toward him.

Anna had asked her father to stop doing business with the man because of the way he stared at her. The man made her skin crawl, but her father refused to part with the fine furs Hiram Brodie brought every spring.

More curious than before, Melissa hurriedly scanned the entries, trying to discover when Anna's feelings for Hiram had begun to change. After reading several more pages, Melissa realized Anna couldn't have fallen in love with Hiram for at least another year. She wrote that the trapper had concluded his business with her father, and about how relieved she felt not having his eyes bore into her everywhere she went while shopping in town.

Anna's journal became cluttered with entries spewing adoration for Thomas Morgan. The entry Melissa read where Anna had professed to being helplessly in love wasn't about Hiram at all, but about Thomas. Intrigued, Melissa settled deeper into the stiff comforter stretched across the bed. She read until her eyes began to sting, until she became even more puzzled and at times embarrassed to read such intimate secrets, then she gasped in disbelief.

"Oh, Anna," she whispered, her eyes filling with tears. "He's gone. Killed when his ship went down at sea." Further she read, then gasped again. "What will you do? And what happened to the—"

Melissa's heart began to pound in her chest. She was beginning to suspect she knew what had happened, or at least had a strong suspicion. A few pages more and she began to weep in earnest. "No! He can't do this to you ! He's your father! Why should he care more what everyone will think than about his own flesh and blood?"

Cold dread settled over Melissa as she continued. "It's spring again. Run away, Anna," Melissa pleaded with the pages. "Run before—"

A groan left her throat. Melissa squeezed her eyes closed, wishing Anna hadn't confirmed that her worst fears were taking shape in the form of a crude mountain man named Hiram Brodie. A man obsessed with Anna Wingate. A girl whose father planned to do the unspeakable over a sin committed in love.

She wasn't certain she could force herself to read further. Anna Wingate had become Anna Brodie, therefore, her father had indeed carried through with his threat. With trembling hands, Melissa reopened the journal. She had to know the rest. For Clay's sake, she had to know why Anna had mistreated her son.

Had she held him to blame for the nightmare her life had become? He was innocent, and yet Clay had been forced to suffer, as she'd written in a later entry, for the sins of his mother, and of her father.

Morning had turned to afternoon when Melissa closed the journal. She stared with swollen eyes at the delicate rose pattern of the wallpaper. Anna's last entry seemed etched across her eyelids, chiseled into her heart.

The wind blows with bitter laughter against the frame of this crude cabin. Rachel is crying because I

*cannot get out of bed. My breath rattles in my chest,
and with each one, I fear it will be my last. Hiram will
not be back in time. I will be dead when he arrives.
With the last of my strength, I put food out for Rachel.
She is but three, and I worry for her more than for myself. My father is dead, also. Hiram told me he heard
news just last month. He left my child his fortune, and
parted this life having never seen me again. I know for
certain he died begging forgiveness for what he did.*

*At least I am not alone. I can see my beautiful Rachel,
and ask God to watch over her. Clay. Lord forgive me,
but I haven't told him. I planned to when he and Hiram
returned. He's a sturdy boy for thirteen, and Hiram
isn't nearly as free with his fists and insults around him
anymore. My husband fears him. He fears the cold
promise of vengeance in his eyes, and I do not blame
Hiram for being afraid, if I cannot feel pity for him.*

*My heart feels as if it might burst inside my chest.
Clay will never know the truth, for Hiram promised the
boy would go to his grave calling him father. All his
life, he will believe a lie. I can only leave this journal
hidden with my Bible and the ring Thomas gave me in
promise we would marry when he returned from England, and pray, although I know my prayers will be in
vain, that someone will find it while Clay still lives and
tell him the truth. Tell him I loved him.*

"I'll tell him, Anna," Melissa whispered brokenly. "He
won't go to his grave never knowing the truth. I swear to
you."

Scrambling up from the bed, Melissa smoothed her hair,
planning to go in search of Clay that very moment. She
didn't believe he would leave without seeing her again, but
she wasn't taking any chances. Her next problem was where
to find him. Perhaps his friend Martin Hanes would know.

Melissa glanced at the restrictive clothing she'd worn
earlier. What did she care if people saw her in the soft buckskin dress and knee-high moccasins? She'd dressed consid-

erably whiter this morning, and it had done nothing to staunch gossip.

So deciding, she snatched up the saddlebag, stuffed the diary inside, and crept from her room. The side stairs seemed the most sensible way to exit. Once outside, Melissa scanned the busy street in search of the establishment called Sally's. The place Clay told her she could find Martin Hanes sat at the end of the street, away from the more respectable shops.

She was halfway there when she realized she walked quickly, with her head bowed. Conversations dwindled into silence as she passed. Melissa took a deep breath and walked the remainder of the way with her head held high. She paused before Sally's, reluctant to enter.

"Looking for a job?" a male voice said from behind her.

A volley of male laughter followed the question. Melissa didn't turn around. She bravely pushed the door to Sally's open and entered. The place appeared deserted, but the air held the smell of liquor and stale cigar smoke. Her gaze traveled up the stairs. She understood what went on up there. For all she knew, Clay might be in one of those rooms. She wondered what he'd do if she kicked the door down and stormed inside.

"That's her."

Her head jerked to the right. In the dimness of drawn shades, she made out the shapes of two people. She squinted, almost certain the man was the very one she sought. The man she'd stumbled upon one night at the Apache camp. Martin Hanes.

"Mr. Hanes?" she asked.

He motioned her forward with one hand, holding the other to his forehead. "If I stand up, my dang head feels like it will fall off."

"Shouldn't've drank so much, you old fool," the woman sitting beside him said. "Come on over here, girl."

Even in the dimness, the bright blond shade of the woman's hair was unmistakable. Melissa approached the table.

"My name's Sally," the woman said. "I already know who you are. The whole town is buzzing about your return."

"Where's Clay?" both Melissa and Martin Hanes asked in unison.

"I was hopin' he was with you," Martin said. "I'd like to know what the heck is going on."

Melissa could only stare blankly at him.

A chair squeaked against the wooden floor when Sally stood. "Hanes is worried about Clay, and I must admit, when he came to my place last night, he did some strange things."

Melissa's cheeks started to burn. She'd assumed he'd gone there this morning to ask someone to deliver the packages to her.

"H-He was here last night?"

"Now don't go off half-cocked," Sally blustered. "He didn't stay but long enough to talk to Martin and give me some instructions." She turned her attention to Hanes. "What did he say to you?"

Martin rubbed his forehead. "It's all kind of fuzzy. Brodie came into the room I was sharing with a—a lovely lady, and talked to me. I'd had more whiskey than most men can tolerate, so I thought when I woke up this afternoon, that I'd dreamt he was at Sally's."

"He came downstairs holding his head and grumbling about Brodie intruding on his dreams," Sally explained. "I told him Clay did go into that room and talk to him, and I wanted to know what he said, because he told me to get you them clothes and to be sure they were fit for a lady. Then he told me to take all the money he had in my safe and give that to you, too!"

"Money?" Melissa repeated, confused.

The older woman waved her hand in the air. "I didn't argue with him. It was his stash, but then Martin said he told him he had a fortune buried under the floorboards of his cabin and he was to split it with Melissa Sheffield, only Hanes wasn't to tell you it was Clay's money. Martin was to act as if the money belonged to him and pretend he felt bad for what had happened and wanted to help you get home."

Her confusion growing by the minute, Melissa asked, "Why would he do that?"

288

"Conscience maybe," Martin said. "Although I was beginning to wonder if he had one. How exactly did Brodie get you out of that Apache camp?"

Melissa's knees had started to shake. She pulled out a chair and seated herself. "He said he made a trade for me. The Apaches wanted to kill me because they thought I tried to murder a woman in an attempt to escape. But I didn't, only I can't really explain what happened." Melissa began to rub her temples.

"Hmph," Hanes snorted. "Attempted murder is a serious crime—like you said, a killing offense. I can't figure what he'd trade to get you out of that. The Apaches usually demand an eye for an eye, and nothing else will do."

Thoughtfully, Melissa's gaze landed on the saddlebag she'd placed on the table. A horrible explanation for Clay's strange behavior occurred to her. His leaving her and Martin Hanes his money, the journal, and his mother's Bible? His prized possessions? It was almost as if he had no further use for material things. She jumped up from the table so abruptly her chair toppled over.

"Oh my God," she gasped. "I think he's done something horrible."

Martin and Sally both just stared.

"Don't you see?" she insisted. "He traded his life for mine! We have to stop him!"

"Hold on there a minute." Martin stood, wincing with the effort. "The Clay Brodie I know, and I'm not saying I don't like him, but he's not the type to worry about anyone's skin but his own. I think you're wrong."

For the briefest moment, Melissa reconsidered. He had taken her back to the Apaches. He'd married her, not for love, but for revenge. He'd . . . stood between her and danger countless times. He'd risked his life to save her. He'd entrusted her with the story of his mother's life, his story. Melissa took a deep breath and looked Martin Hanes square in the eye.

"I'm not wrong. I'm going to find him."

Martin argued with her all the way to the livery stable, but

Melissa wouldn't give in. "I have the money Clay told Sally to give me in the saddlebag. You'll have to help me pick out a good horse."

"I say you should stay here. If I'm going to ride into an Apache camp that's set on killing a man, I'll need a plan."

"I'll help you come up with one," Melissa offered.

The trapper sighed. "We don't know for sure Brodie's in trouble. He could be headed up to the cabin to settle in for the winter."

"How much time will it cost us to make certain?"

"A few hours' ride if I have my horse wide open all the way up the mountain and back down again. You couldn't stay with me at that pace."

"Then I'll wait at the bottom for you."

He grinned, his eyes almost disappearing within the fleshy folds at the corners. "I do believe I've met a body more stubborn than Clay Brodie."

Had Melissa not been eaten up with worry over Clay, she might have returned his smile. That fool! That insane, always-right-about-everything, mistrustful, deceiving . . . handsome, courageous fool.

"Hey, if it ain't the squaw woman who used to be white!"

Melissa stiffened. She'd been too busy fretting over Clay to notice that she and Martin were drawing a crowd as they walked toward the livery.

"She can beat my tom-toms any day of the week!" another voice shouted.

Crude laughter followed. Martin started to turn around, but Melissa grabbed his arm. "We have to get going. Clay has a good lead on us."

"They wouldn't be shooting their mouths off if he was standing beside us," Martin grumbled. "Folks around here walk a wide path around Brodie."

"Well, he's not half as mean as they think," Melissa said. "Not half as bad as *he* thinks."

"I know that, and I guess you know that, but they don't, and if it keeps 'em from having the nerve to ask him where them Apaches are camped, Brodie lets them believe whatever they choose."

"Where are you going, squaw?" one particularly daring man shouted. "Back to the Apaches? Are you hungry for more Injun loving?"

It was her turn to stop and turn. Robert stood on the sidewalk with several men, his face an embarrassed shade of red. He hadn't joined in with the men, but he hadn't stood up for her either. Melissa had become strong enough to stand up for herself.

"The Apaches treated me better than you have," she said, sending a cool glance over the citizens of Santa Fe. "They may be judgmental about us, but they aren't about their own kind. You've made me realize the Indians are more civilized than my own race. Ignorance breeds fear. And ignorance runs rampant on the streets of Santa Fe."

Further comment did not accompany Melissa down the street. Once they reached the livery, a small Mexican man greeted them. "The pretty señorita told them a thing or two, *sí*, Martin Hanes?"

"That she did, Armondo. I need my horse, and one for the lady."

Armondo frowned. "But your horse is not here. Señor Brodie said you gave him your broken-down nag because he lost his stallion to you in a card game."

"What?" Martin bellowed.

"He left Two Moons in the livery?" Melissa whispered.

"*Sí*. He said he was drunk or Hanes would not have cheated him out of his horse."

Nausea threatened Melissa. "Clay doted on that animal. He would never have given up Two Moons unless—"

"Might be that the horse was wore out is all, and Clay wanted to get on home," Martin said. "Brodie's sense of humor falls on the ornery side. He would do something like this, especially since he knows I'd have a hell of a time getting that stallion back up the mountain. He bucks with anyone but Brodie."

291

"He won't buck with me. Clay and I rode him over half the territory. I've been such a fool. I didn't trust in Clay and I should have. I'll take the stallion, you choose another horse."

Martin appeared as if he would argue, but Melissa walked into the livery in search of Two Moons. He whinnied when she approached his stall.

"That's right. You know me, know my scent." She held her hand out and let the stallion sniff.

"He'll take a bite out of you," Martin warned.

"No he won't," she assured him. "Look at him. He knows something is wrong."

The horse's ears were pricked. He snorted, shifting nervously in his stall.

"Knows he's about to send you flying and can't wait to get at it," Martin mumbled. "Get him some tack, Armondo."

"While we saddle Two Moons, hurry and choose a horse, Martin."

The mountain man left grumbling about bossy females. Armondo brought the bridle and slipped it over Two Moons's head, then saddled him. Once the stallion had been led from his stall, Melissa walked around and stared the horse in the eye. "Don't give me any trouble. We have to catch up with Clay."

Surprisingly, the stallion offered no resistance as Armondo helped Melissa mount. She took the reins and steered him outside, where Martin prepared a sturdy bay.

"Well, I'll be damned," he swore as she approached.

"Be damned some other time. Let's get going."

He nodded, and tightened the cinch on his saddle.

Chapter Twenty-nine

The breeze held the strong smell of pine, and tugged playfully at the long strands of Clay's hair. Bright sunshine beat down against his skin, and he'd never noticed that warmth had a scent. To his left, dark clouds hung over the mountains. It would rain up there. A light shower to cool the day and make the greenery sparkle when the sun appeared again. He'd been looking at this particular stretch of territory all his life, but today, it appeared more magnificent than before.

He guessed a person sometimes took beauty for granted, became so accustomed to it they forgot to appreciate what they'd been given. Four days' ride from Santa Fe, and one night away from the full moon, Clay saw the world through different eyes. The greens appeared greener. The blues, bluer. He heard sounds his ears had ceased to take note of: the gurgling rush of water over rock, the buzz of insects, the chirping of birds.

His senses were in a state of heightened awareness, and Clay wished he could be with Melissa while under this influence. He wanted to remember the way she moved, smelled, laughed, felt. Wanted to make slow love to her. Study every expression that crossed her face. Hear every moan, sigh, or gasp that escaped her lips. It ate at him to leave Santa Fe abruptly, abandoning Melissa to a fate still unsettled. But he couldn't take a chance on arriving back at the camp after the full moon. He'd given his word. Swift Buck's life depended on him.

Martin would take care of Melissa. The trapper and Clay's money, although he hoped she wouldn't figure that out. Damn his inability to write. He could have left instructions in a letter instead of depending on Hanes and Sally to see to Melissa's future. For a man who didn't have many responsibilities three months ago, one skinny white girl from St. Louis had managed to clutter up Clay's life but good.

Reining Martin's mule-headed horse to a halt so the sentries posted around camp could recognize him, Clay sardonically admitted that come day after tomorrow, he wouldn't have any problems, not in this world, anyway. Funny, he was just beginning to get used to chaos, didn't even mind it so much. Not if Melissa Sheffield happened to be attached to the other end of trouble. She got herself into one fix after another. Clay envied the man who'd spend his life trying to get her out of them.

He cursed Robert Towbridge for not being more of a man. Although the thought of another man touching Melissa, holding her, loving her, twisted Clay's gut, for her sake, he wished Towbridge would have honored his vow to marry her.

"She's young," Clay consoled himself. He refused to paint a picture in his head of her standing next to some dandified greenhorn, a couple of children clinging to her skirts, a big fine house in the background. He might have seen her living that life once, but she possessed more of a lust for adventure than she'd had time to realize. Sooner or later, Melissa would come to accept that about herself.

Silence blanketed the Apache village as Clay entered camp. The solemn faces of those he'd known for many years reminded him of that terrible day he'd ridden in and learned of Rachel's death. He'd made mistakes in his lifetime. She was one of the worst. His sister shouldn't have suffered his cold treatment because she'd been loved by their mother, and he hadn't. If Clay were given a chance to do anything in his life over again, he would change his relationship with Rachel.

Hanes had been right. Rachel had deserved to make a choice between her mother's world and the Apache life forced on her by their father. Clay should have stood up to him, even though he'd been only thirteen when their mother died. He should have taken the girl to Santa Fe himself and seen to it she was settled with a decent family.

A life with Hiram would have only brought her grief, but he knew their mother would have wanted Rachel to be educated, to live a softer life than she'd endured. Too late, Clay admitted to loving Rachel—admitted he should have taken care of her. Too late.

"I knew Cougar would keep his word, but my heart is not happy to see you."

"Gray Wolf." He nodded, then climbed down from Martin's horse. Clay retrieved the knife from his moccasin, dropped it to the ground, then held out his hands, understanding he was now considered an Apache prisoner.

The leader motioned a brave forward to bind his wrists. Clay wasn't surprised at who broke from the solemn group, seemingly anxious to perform the task.

"If Gray Wolf isn't happy to see me, you look very pleased, Tall Blade." He didn't wince when the brave pulled the rawhide strips tighter than necessary. A smile stole over Tall Blade's lips.

"Long ago, I knew a day would be born when no white man could walk among us. It took too long to get here."

To the brave's obvious disappointment, Clay merely returned his smile, then glanced at Gray Wolf. "What have you decided and when?"

"The morning after the full moon, as we agreed." Gray Wolf refused to meet his gaze. "Because we cannot bury you with honor among our own, you will burn, Cougar. It is the way I saw it in my vision."

Although Clay's indifferent expression remained set in stone, he felt his throat close and smelled the sickly odor of burning flesh. There were worse ways to die, but he couldn't think of one at the moment.

"And until then?"

"You are now our enemy, Cougar. The People must treat you the same as they would the woman you trade lives with."

"I understand."

And he did. As Tall Blade roughly shoved him toward a tree where he'd be bound and left without food or water for the remainder of his time, Clay displayed no resentment, only acceptance. A rock hit him as he passed. Not as hard as he suspected it should, but with enough force to graze his temple and draw blood. He felt a sharp pain in his shoulder as another bounced off his body. The thought of Melissa facing Apache justice made him feel sick.

Clay couldn't have stood to watch her suffer, guilty or not, and he chose to believe in her innocence. He would have interfered. Just as Gray Wolf's vision had predicted, Cougar would die for a white woman.

"Soon, Cougar will be gone," Tall Blade growled, binding Clay to a tree. "There will be no more reminders. No shame. No Brodies!"

"Why do you hate me?" Clay finally asked.

For a moment, he thought by the bright flare in Tall Blade's stare that the brave would answer. Instead, the Indian spat on him and walked away. Clay wiped his face with the sleeve of his buckskin shirt, staring at Tall Blade's broad back. The hair at the back of his neck prickled.

Something about the brave had triggered a memory. Something in his eyes Clay hadn't noticed until that moment. He'd almost put his finger on it when he caught sight of Swift Buck standing a short distance away.

His gaze locked with a dark brown one. They were no longer brothers, couldn't speak to one another as friends, but each relayed a message. When Clay felt his eyes begin to sting, he looked away. They'd said their goodbyes, now there was nothing left to do but wait.

Sometime during the night, he felt a light caress against his shoulder. He'd been dreaming of Melissa, rousing himself from restless sleep with the feel of her beneath him, the sound of his name on her lips. He blinked into the darkness, barely discerning a dark shape moving away. He smiled when the shadow disappeared into Laughing Stream's lodge.

She'd come to see him one last time, although any show of kindness was forbidden. Had he not been bound, Clay would have run his fingers over the spot she'd touched. Swift Buck's mother had loved his sister, and now he realized the old woman loved him as well.

A shiver wracked his tall frame. He shifted against the hard ground. His hands tingled due to Tall Blade's tight knots. Sleep would not find him again this night. He glanced up at the star-filled sky overhead—listened to a wolf's lonely cry from somewhere in the distance.

Melissa tried to creep into his thoughts. He locked her out. Soon he'd need her. Need to remember the fine bones in her face and the silky texture of her hair, need her to help him deal with the pain.

The time went faster than he thought it would. By morning, fog rose from the ground, wrapping to the waist in a hazy mist those who gathered. Clay stared at the strange phenomenon while mumbles ran rampant through The People. He felt weak from hunger and thirst, grateful he'd been lashed to a pole so he wasn't forced to support his own weight. All of yesterday, the women had gathered wood. Now, it lay stacked at his feet.

"Today we kill an enemy," Gray Wolf said loudly. "But after he is gone, we will remember Cougar as our brother. We cannot speak of him, cannot tell tales of his bravery and his skill with a bow. Cannot talk about his running gift. But to keep him in our minds, and in our hearts, is not forbidden."

With a nod, Gray Wolf ordered his wife to light the torch in her hand. Jageitci obeyed, her eyes lowered and the bandage gone from her head. Clay noticed the ugly cut on her forehead. She would wear a scar there for the rest of her life.

After she set the torch afire, using a flame kindled in a small grate for just this purpose, she approached him.

Once she stood before Clay, she looked up. The sincere regret in her eyes touched him. Since the crime had been committed against Gray Wolf's wife, setting the wood at his feet on fire became her duty.

"I know the burden is yours," Clay said softly. "But I leave this world defending Huera. She is not guilty of the crime against you."

Jageitci's face paled. "Have you found evidence of this, Cougar?"

"No," he was quick to assure her. "But my heart does not need proof. Life is precious to Huera. Killing is not in her nature."

"The council decided her guilt," Tall Blade reminded harshly. "It is too late to save yourself, Cougar."

"I ask nothing for myself. The trade is final. All I want is for Jageitci to believe in Huera and forgive her for a crime she did not commit. Huera would grieve if her friend carried this lie with her forever."

"You are our enemy and have no right to speak with my wife." Gray Wolf stepped forward. "Light the fire, Jageitci."

Clay remained silent as the trembling torch in Jageitci's hand stretched toward the wood at his feet. She glanced up again, her dark eyes shimmering with tears.

"I forgive her, Cougar. Can you forgive me?"

He nodded, then closed his eyes as the wood caught, the smell of smoke strong in his nostrils. For one day and one night he'd fought Melissa. Now Clay let her come to him. He opened his eyes and stared through the mist, imagining the perfect oval shape of her face. The highness of her cheekbones. Her small straight nose. The fullness of her lips. Her graceful neck. The splendor of her hair.

She appeared, a beautiful ghost floating above the mist. Clay saw her so clearly that he felt as if he could reach out and touch her. He blinked, his eyes stinging from the smoldering wood beneath him. A low curse sounded in the quiet, then a roar like a wounded puma.

"No!"

"Clay!"

Her shout blended with his as Melissa thundered into camp. The beating of her heart pounded louder than Two Moons's hooves. Oh God, what were they doing to him? She reined the stallion to an abrupt halt, slid off his back, and ran. Strong arms gripped her just before she reached him. Glancing up, Melissa confronted the fierce expression of Tall Blade.

"Let him go!" she screamed, struggling in the brave's arms.

"What the hell are you doing here?"

Melissa ceased her squirming. "I'm not an idiot! It only took me a day to figure out what you'd done!"

"You're smart all right. But obviously not smart enough to realize you risk your life by following me! How did you find the camp?"

"Martin brought me."

"Hanes?" Clay coughed, the dew-dampened wood beginning to catch in earnest. "Where is he?"

"He went to the cabin to make certain you weren't there. I waited at the bottom. When Two Moons became anxious to go, I thought the stallion probably knew the way to camp. I let him guide me."

Another curse left Clay's lips. He glanced at Gray Wolf. "The trade stands firm. She is not your enemy. Promise me you will let her leave?"

The leader looked confused. "I cannot promise, Cougar. Huera knows the way to our camp. She can bring others."

"But she will not!"

"If Huera is guilty, why did she return?" Jageitci broke in. "If she feels only hate for us, why is she here?"

"She came for Cougar," Tall Blade growled. "They planned her return as a trick to confuse The People."

"What are they saying, Clay?" Melissa demanded. A patch of kindling burst into flame at his feet. She screamed. A kick to Tall Blade's shin won her freedom. She raced to the fire and tried to stomp it out.

299

"Get back!" Clay coughed the words.

Melissa had no choice as Tall Blade wrestled her away from the fire, his fingers biting cruelly into her arms. She resorted to begging in Spanish so the Apaches could understand her.

"Please release him. I did not know he traded his life for mine. Take me instead!"

"They should both die." Tall Blade pulled his knife from the sheath at his waist and held it against her throat.

"No!" Clay choked out.

"It is not for you to decide, Tall Blade," the leader warned. "Take the knife away."

Tall Blade almost appeared as if he would refuse. He lowered the knife, but his expression bordered on hatred as he stared at the leader.

"Your heart is easily given to our enemies." His gaze settled on Jageitci with meaning. "The People should cut the half-breed child from your wife's belly."

A few gasps from the women followed his suggestion.

Gray Wolf's face darkened. "My wife has earned her place among us."

"As Cougar did," Tall Blade snarled. "Now he dies for his betrayal. Is his crime not the same as yours?"

Jageitci placed a restraining hand on her husband's arm. "He is right, husband. Your test was not one you could have passed yourself. It was unfair."

"Let her go, Tall Blade!" Clay's struggle made him cough all the harder. He'd begun to feel the heat, sweat running down his temples. He was helpless. Taunting him, Tall Blade flicked the knife around Melissa's face.

Clay tried to break free again, the ropes biting deep into the flesh around his wrists. Suddenly there was a ruckus. The thundering of hooves. A ghostly shape appeared among the mist and smoke.

The figure lifted a finger. "Murderer!"

Hair wild around her shoulders, Clay clearly saw the specter's face. The face of his sister. He wondered if he'd already died, but then, the rest of those gathered looked as shocked as he felt. He followed the direction of her finger. Tall Blade stood at the end of her accusation.

"Murderer!" she repeated, her blue eyes blazing.

"Return to the land of spirits, witch!" Tall Blade took the knife from Melissa's throat and pointed it menacingly at the woman. "You are gone!"

"The wolves are my friends, Tall Blade," she said. "You should not have depended on them to finish what you started. Watching you butcher the women who tried to stop you brought back the words that had died in me. *He* killed them," she told the Apaches. "He thought I walked alone and attacked me, but they saw him and ran to help."

"She lies!" Tall Blade dragged Melissa closer to the fire beginning to blaze at Clay's feet. "Will The People listen to a white woman? I am Apache!"

"My sister does not lie!" Clay thundered. "You had her bracelet because you were the one who attacked her!"

Tall Blade held the knife out, as if to ward off any who would approach him. "Who will you believe? These white enemies or one of your own?"

"Silent Wind has been raised among you!" Clay shouted. "You may now call me enemy, but she is of your tribe!"

"Cougar is right," Gray Wolf said. "We have no reason to mistrust Silent Wind."

"Is the color of her skin not reason enough?" Tall Blade shouted. "If I did try to end her life, is she worth more than an Apache in your eyes?"

"She *is* Apache in our eyes," said Laughing Stream, tears of joy streaming down her cheeks.

"And what of the other two women?" Jageitci asked. "They died by your hand, and they were not white."

Although sweat stung his eyes and the heat from the fire was almost more than he could stand, Clay saw Tall Blade's hatred turn to desperation. He pulled Melissa closer, the knife poised at her throat.

"They had to die. All the palefaces among us must die," he said, his voice cracking. "They are white! They are reminders!"

301

Dazed by the appearance of his sister, and frantic over the knife held at Melissa's throat, Clay scanned the stunned Apaches. He found his blood brother staring openmouthed.

"Swift Buck! Cut me loose!"

"Stay away," Tall Blade warned him. "Do The People not understand? They shame us, taint our blood! We must destroy them! Kill those who are called Brodie, and all of their kind!"

The bow had finally snapped. Clay knew he must act fast or Melissa would die. "Release the woman," he coaxed. "Let her go and cut me loose. It will be just us. We will see whose knife speaks the loudest."

The brave's eyes flared, a reflection of the flames growing higher around Clay. His clothes felt so hot he knew they'd catch any minute.

"Promise him no one will interfere, Gray Wolf," Clay instructed. "Give him your word."

"Cougar, I do not understand—"

"Give him your word!"

"No one will interfere," Gray Wolf agreed.

Tall Blade glanced mistrustfully at those gathered around him. He looked at Melissa, smiling at the roundness of her eyes, then ran his tongue down the side of her face.

"I wanted to make her suffer, but the chance was stolen from me. The Mexicans she also escaped. Now my knife hungers for her again." He shoved her away quickly and sliced through Cougar's bindings. "But it hungers for you more."

Leaping through the flames, Clay quickly gained his stance. Pinpricks of pain exploded throughout his body as blood raced to his hands and feet. He'd surrendered his knife, but Swift Buck, roused from his shock, tossed him his.

"I told no one that Huera had been captured by Mexicans." Clay narrowed his gaze on the Apache. "It was you who hit Jageitci over the head while she slept! When Huera ran to see what had happened, you hit her over the head as well. You took her to the meadow, and the Mexicans found her."

Tall Blade appeared to battle himself. As he glanced
around at the accusing faces, he apparently realized he could
hide his dark deeds no longer.

"She would not wake to feel the sting of my blade. This
one—" He held up the knife, then smiled. "—or the other
one. I went to get water, but when I returned, the Mexicans
had surrounded her."

"You heard by his own tongue, Huera is guilty of no
crime!" Clay shouted. If he died, he'd at least go knowing
Melissa wouldn't be punished. A quick slash opened the
sleeve of his shirt. Melissa's scream echoed off the bluffs.
He didn't trust her not to do something foolish.

"Hold her, Swift Buck," Clay instructed, never taking his
eyes off of Tall Blade's knife. "Explain what is happening
and promise that if I cannot, you will take her back to her
people. Huera and my sister."

Silence answered his request. Clay chanced a quick
glance at his blood brother. The brave had taken Melissa by
the arm, but his gaze was fixed longingly on Rachel.

"Give me your word!"

"You have my word," he promised.

Clay breathed a strangled sigh of relief, then quickly
sucked smoky air into his lungs. Tall Blade's knife connected with the skin of his exposed shoulder. He blocked out
the sound of Melissa's gasp, concentrating solely on survival, on killing the monster who'd tried to murder his sister, the man who'd stolen Melissa and shattered his feeble
belief in love.

They circled each other, thrusting and slashing as, behind
them, the flames meant to consume Clay grew higher. Sweat
trickled into his eyes and cost him a cut to the thigh. Clay
didn't feel the pain. He retaliated, opening a wound on Tall
Blade's neck.

"Your father bled more than you. He did not have much
courage either. He begged me to kill him before my knife
had finished cutting on him. The grizzly smelled his blood
from halfway up the mountain."

Poised to strike, Clay froze. "*You* killed him?"

303

Hesitation cost him a nick to the cheek.

"I was only fourteen the summer my knife found him, but already I had killed. My mother did not 'disappear' in my tenth summer. I sent her away so she would shame me no more."

Although Clay understood a child's rage, and had himself wished death on Hiram Brodie many times by his fourteenth year, he couldn't imagine actually killing the man.

Tall Blade used Clay's shock to his advantage. He leapt upon him, tumbling him to the ground and placing the knife against his throat. "Don't you want to know why I had to kill them? Look at me. Look close and you will see the reason."

The prickling sensation started at the back of Clay's scalp. Staring into a whiskey-colored gaze, he saw something he hadn't noticed once in all his years around Tall Blade.

"You have his eyes."

"And his white blood," the brave growled. "The man I believed was my father discovered a box of trinkets in our lodge one day. He went outside to ask my mother where she'd found them, and why they were hidden. She was not at her work, but away from camp, speaking to the red-haired man. My father glanced at me, then stared at Brodie, and the love and pride he'd felt for his son drained from his face. He said I was a half-breed, an embarrassment. Then he went into the mountains to end his suffering."

"Your mother was Hiram's Apache woman," Clay said.

"And I knew she must die for her unfaithfulness. She could not be trusted not to tell, then everyone would know my shame. I had to kill her, had to bide my time and kill the red-haired man, had to lie in wait for Silent Wind, have had to wait for you, Cougar. You are reminders of my shame!"

"Did Hiram know?"

"Yes," Tall Blade hissed, his spittle coating Clay's face. "He knew, but he would not acknowledge a half-breed son, either. I meant nothing to him, and to see him among us only brought me more shame. I could not find a woman of my own. What if my children had had red hair? What if they'd had white skin? Then all would know!"

"They all know now," Clay said quietly.

The Apache glanced up from him, his strange eyes scanning the silent tribe. "Yes, they know," he agreed. "And they will kill me for the crimes I committed to erase the reminders from my life, but I will take you before I go, Cougar. *Brother*." He spat out the last word and raised his knife.

Instinctively, Clay's wrist shot out and halted the weapon mere inches from his throat. In his weakened state, his arm shook. The blade nicked his neck before Clay managed to shove Tall Blade away. He rolled, gracefully regaining his feet, although he staggered slightly from hunger, thirst, and loss of blood.

Tall Blade was up in an instant. With an outraged war cry, he charged. The two men collided, falling to the ground again. The breath left Tall Blade's lungs in a loud *whoosh*. His eyes widened, grew dim, then closed. He collapsed.

"Tall Blade!" Clay quickly flipped him over, scrambling from beneath his weight. His hand still rested over the brave's, the hilt of the knife clutched in a death grip, buried deep in Tall Blade's chest. "What have I done?" he croaked.

"Clay!"

He felt Melissa's arms twist around his neck, and then she was clinging to him, sobbing his name over and over. "Tell me you're all right." Her hands clutched the sides of his face, forcing him to look at her. "Say something!"

Despite the dirt on her face, and the tangles in her hair, Melissa was the most beautiful woman he'd ever seen. His trembling fingers brushed her cheek, unable to believe he'd been given a second chance to touch her, to tell her what he once couldn't admit, and later was forced to hide from her.

The buzzing in his ears warned him the chance might still slip away. He couldn't assure her he was all right; he didn't know the extent of his injuries. Clay cupped her face between his hands and stared into her worried eyes.

"You've been nothing but trouble for me from the first

day you fell from Swift Buck's horse into my arms. You're hardheaded, and too courageous for your own good. You risked your life by charging in here to my rescue. I give you nice clothes, and you don't wear them. I give you money to return home, and instead you steal my horse and traipse over half the territory with a dried-up, self-righteous—"

"Watch who you call what," Martin interrupted.

Clay cast a dark look in his direction. "When did you get here?"

"Just now made it. I found Rachel up at the cabin, hiding. I could tell she was afraid of something. Didn't think I'd get her to budge, but when I started rambling on about you getting yourself killed by the Apaches, she ran out, jumped on my horse, and took off. I had to ride one of them stubborn pack mules we got grazing up there. Had to nearly beat the blue blazes out of him, but we made it."

After reassuring himself that Rachel wasn't a figment of his imagination—his sister stood wrapped in Laughing Stream's embrace—Clay turned his attention back to Melissa. She appeared to be on the verge of tears again.

"Where was I?"

"Berating me," she whispered.

"No, I was just about to say—"

"How come they didn't burn you?" Martin interrupted.

Clay sighed. "If you don't mind, Hanes, I'm trying to tell the lady something, and it's a damn hard thing for a man like me to confess."

"Oh." Martin blushed.

"Now, as I was saying—"

"You don't have to tell me. You've proven it in a hundred ways. I just couldn't see—"

He placed a finger against her lips. "I love you, Melissa. I didn't want to, but I couldn't stop my heart, and I couldn't help but love my mother, either. It seemed shameful to me, giving away something for nothing. Now I understand that it takes more courage to love than to hate. I forgive her for the hurt she caused me, and I hope Rachel will forgive me someday for what I've done to her."

"I know she will," Melissa said, tears streaming down her face. "And there's so much you don't know about Anna Brodie. She loved you, Clay, and I love you too."

Her words brought him pain. He winced, his expression turning solemn before glancing at Tall Blade's lifeless form. "I killed my own brother."

"No. I saw what happened. You were only defending yourself. Only holding the knife so he couldn't stab you. He fell. It was by his hand he died, not yours!"

"Why didn't I notice the resemblance? Hiram caused him as much grief as he caused me. If I'd known, maybe we could have been brothers in truth. Maybe Tall Blade wouldn't have had to suffer the shame, the insecurity of feeling—"

"Unworthy of love and acceptance?" Melissa finished. "You suffered, and it didn't make you a murderer. Besides, even if he hadn't died by his own hand, you wouldn't have killed your brother."

The buzzing in Clay's ears grew louder. He felt weak. "What are you saying?"

"Tall Blade wasn't related to you. Hiram Brodie wasn't your father."

Stunned, Clay continued to stare at Melissa, unable to comprehend what she'd just said to him. The day proved too trying. He promptly passed out.

Epilogue

"Thomas Morgan," Clay repeated. "The son of a shipping merchant?"

"A very well-to-do family, according to your mother's journal," Melissa said, straightening Swift Buck's lodge in preparation to leave. "Even though your father died before you were born, don't you think we should go to Boston and see if you have any living relatives left?"

Clay shrugged. "I'm not sure they would appreciate learning they have a bastard in their closet of family secrets."

Melissa stopped her straightening to regard him with a stern look. "Your mother wouldn't want to hear you refer to yourself in that manner. She loved your father desperately, and he loved her. The ring she kept tied to the Bible was one he'd given her as a pledge that they would marry once he returned from England."

"But he didn't return."

"His ship went down two weeks out to sea. There were no survivors. The news nearly killed your mother. Then she realized she was carrying Thomas Morgan's child."

308

"And my grandfather forced her to marry Hiram Brodie in his outrage that she would cause him such embarrassment."

"Grief-stricken as she was, your mother didn't have the spirit to defy him. Only when Hiram demanded his husbandly rights along the trail to Santa Fe did her numbness fade. Embittered and forsaken by her father, she told Hiram the truth about why she would stoop to marrying a crude, uneducated trapper.

"She swore she'd love Thomas Morgan until the day she died, and Hiram, obsessed with her, swore he would make the child she carried into a savage, into everything she detested about her husband. He threatened to kill you if she refused to deny her son the love she denied him. What she must have gone through . . . and seeing the very image of Thomas squalling in her arms, she complied with Hiram's demands. It hurt her to look at you, to remember the life and love that had been taken from her."

"I hated Hiram Brodie, but now I almost feel sorry for him."

Melissa hurried to where Clay lay resting. She'd stitched him up, and to her relief, his injuries were not serious. "Hiram didn't love your mother, not really. His obsession bordered on insanity, a desire to have something simply because it was denied him. Tall Blade inherited his madness."

"Rachel," Clay said quietly. "You don't think—"

"No," she assured him. "Your sister is strong-willed, afraid to love, as you once were, but she isn't evil. She has more of your mother in her than Hiram Brodie. Give her time. You'll see."

"She's furious about my decision to take her with us to Washington after winter's end."

"You're right." Melissa bent beside her husband and gently stroked the whiskered line of his strong jaw. "She should know her own heritage. Although I pity the finishing school instructor who takes on that wildcat, she'll thank you someday for giving her a choice."

"Swift Buck wants to burn me at the stake again."

"Deep down, he knows she must go. You've given your

sister a winter with The People. He at least has an opportunity to adjust to the inevitable."

"I shouldn't have agreed to Rachel's request," he grumbled. "One winter is longer than one summer, and we both know what can happen in that length of time."

She smiled. "Would it be so bad? If Swift Buck were to melt the ice around your sister's heart and tempt her into the flame?"

"Yes and no. I consider Swift Buck the same as I would a brother, but I would worry about their future together. Gray Wolf's visions are for the most part accurate. There are dark days ahead for the Apaches, for all tribes. Rachel would be caught in the middle."

"The same as we will be," she said softly.

"You're a smart woman, Melissa, convincing Gray Wolf I can fight harder for him with words than with weapons. Do you think you can educate me over the course of one long winter, hidden away on the side of a mountain, with only Hanes across the way as company?"

"Martin won't disturb our lessons too often, will he?" she whispered in his ear.

He pulled her closer, nuzzling her neck. "Probably," he grumbled. "Maybe I can convince him to spend the winter at Sally's. I don't imagine I'll get much trapping done."

"Careful," she warned. "You'll pull those nice straight stitches I've sewn into your shoulder loose again."

Her warning was ignored as Clay pulled her down into the soft buffalo hides. "That's all right. I married a medicine woman."

VIOLETS ARE BLUE

Ronda Thompson

Although Violet Mallory was raised by the wealthy, landowning Miles Traften, nothing can remove the stain of her birthright: She is the child of no-good outlaws, and one day St. Louis society will uncover that. No, she can never be a city gal, can never truly be happy—but she can exact revenge on the man who sired and sold her.

But being a criminal is hard. Like Gregory Kline—blackmailer, thief and the handsome rogue sent to recover her—Violet longs for something better. Gregory is intent upon reforming her, and then his kiss teaches her the difference between roguishness and villainy. She sees that beauty can grow from the muddiest soil, and Violets don't always have to be blue.

Madeline Baker

Chase the Lightning

Amanda can't believe her eyes when the beautiful white stallion appears in her yard with a wounded man on its back. Dark and ruggedly handsome, the stranger fascinates her. He has about him an aura of danger and desire that excites her in a way her law-abiding fiancé never had. But something doesn't add up: Trey seems bewildered by the amenities of modern life; he wants nothing to do with the police; and he has a stack of 1863 bank notes in his saddlebags. Then one soul-stirring kiss makes it all clear—Trey may have held up a bank and stolen through time, but when he takes her love it will be no robbery, but a gift of the heart.

__4917-1 $5.99 US/$6.99 CAN

Dorchester Publishing Co., Inc.
P.O. Box 6640
Wayne, PA 19087-8640

Please add $2.50 for shipping and handling for the first book and $.75 for each book thereafter. NY, NYC, and PA residents, please add appropriate sales tax. No cash, stamps, or C.O.D.s. All orders shipped within 6 weeks via postal service book rate. Canadian orders require $2.00 extra postage and must be paid in U.S. dollars through a U.S. banking facility.

Name_____
Address_____
City_____ State_____ Zip_____
I have enclosed $_____ in payment for the checked book(s).
Payment <u>must</u> accompany all orders.☐Please send a free catalog.
CHECK OUT OUR WEBSITE! www.dorchesterpub.com

RECKLESS LOVE

MADELINE BAKER

"Madeline Baker's Indian romances should not be missed!"
　　　　　　　　　　　　　　　　　　—*Romantic Times*

Joshua Berdeen is the cavalry soldier who has traveled the country in search of lovely Hannah Kincaid. Josh offers her a life of ease in New York City and all the finer things.

Two Hawks Flying is the Cheyenne warrior who has branded Hannah's body with his searing desire. Outlawed by the civilized world, he can offer her only the burning ecstasy of his love. But she wants no soft words of courtship when his hard lips take her to the edge of rapture...and beyond.

__3869-2　　　　　　　　　　　　　$5.99 US/$7.99 CAN

LOVE FOREVERMORE

MADELINE BAKER

The West–it has been Loralee's dream for as long as she could remember, and Indians are the most fascinating part of the wildly beautiful frontier she imagines. But when Loralee arrives at Fort Apache as the new schoolmarm, she has some hard realities to learn...and a harsh taskmaster to teach her. Shad Zuniga is fiercely proud, aloof, a renegade Apache who wants no part of the white man's world, not even its women. Yet Loralee is driven to seek him out, compelled to join him in a forbidden union, forced to become an outcast for one slim chance at love forevermore.

___4267-3 $5.99 US/$6.99 CAN

KENTUCKY BRIDE

NORAH HESS

Fleeing her abusive uncle, young D'lise Alexander trusts no man...until she is rescued by virile trapper Kane Devlin. His rugged strength and tender concern convinces D'lise she'll find a safe haven in his backwoods homestead. There, amid the simple pleasures of cornhuskings and barn raisings, she discovers that Kane kindles a blaze of desire that burns even hotter than the flames in his rugged stone hearth. Beneath his soul-stirring kisses she forgets her fears, forgets everything except her longing to become his sweet Kentucky bride.

___52270-5 $5.50 US/$6.50 CAN

DEVIL IN SPURS

NORAH HESS

Raised in a bawdy house, Jonty Rand posed as a boy all her life to escape the notice of the rowdy cowboys who frequented the place. And to Jonty's way of thinking, the most notorious womanizer of the bunch is Cord McBain. So when her granny's dying wish makes Cord Jonty's guardian, she despairs of ever revealing her true identity. In the rugged solitude of the Wyoming wilderness he assigns Jonty all the hardest tasks on his horse ranch, making her life a torment. Then one stormy night, Cord discovers that Jonty will never be a man, only the wildest, most willing woman he's ever taken in his arms, the one woman who can claim his heart.

___52294-2 $5.50 US/$6.50 CAN

Dorchester Publishing Co., Inc.
P.O. Box 6640
Wayne, PA 19087-8640

SNOW FIRE
NORAH HESS

She is lost. Blinded by the swirling storm, Flame knows that she cannot give up if she is to survive. Her memory gone, the lovely firebrand awakes to find that the strong arms encircling her belong to a devilishly handsome stranger. And one look at his blazing eyes tells her that the haven she has found promises a passion that will burn for a lifetime. She is the most lovely thing he has ever seen. From the moment he takes Flame in his arms and gazes into her sparkling eyes, Stone knows that the red-headed virgin has captured his heart. The very sight of her smile stokes fiery desires in him that only her touch can extinguish. To protect her he'll claim her as his wife, and pray that he can win her heart before she discovers the truth.

___4691-1 $5.99 US/$6.99 CAN

Fancy

NORAH HESS

After her father's accidental death, it is up to young Fancy Cranson to keep her small family together. But to survive in the pristine woodlands of the Pacific Northwest, she has to use her brains or her body. With no other choice, Fancy vows she'll work herself to the bone before selling herself to any timberman—even one as handsome, virile, and arrogant as Chance Dawson.

From the moment Chance Dawson lays eyes on Fancy, he wants to claim her for himself. But the mighty woodsman has felled forests less stubborn than the beautiful orphan. To win her hand he has to trade his roughhewn ways for tender caresses, and brazen curses for soft words of desire. Only then will he be able to share with her a love that unites them in passionate splendor.

_3783-1 $5.99 US/$6.99 CAN

TEXAS PROUD

CONSTANCE O'BANYON

Rachel Rutledge has her gun trained on Noble Vincente. With one shot, she will have her revenge on the man who killed her father. So what is stopping her from pulling the trigger? Perhaps it is the memory of Noble's teasing voice, his soft smile, or the way one glance from his dark Spanish eyes once stirred her foolish heart to longing. Yes, she loved him then . . . as much as she hates him now. One way or another, she will wound him to the heart—if not with bullets, then with her own feminine wiles. But as Rachel discovers, sometimes the line between love and hate is too thinly drawn.

___4492-7 $5.99 US/$6.99 CAN

Dorchester Publishing Co., Inc.
P.O. Box 6640
Wayne, PA 19087-8640

Please add $1.75 for shipping and handling for the first book and $.50 for each book thereafter. NY, NYC, and PA residents, please add appropriate sales tax. No cash, stamps, or C.O.D.s. All orders shipped within 6 weeks via postal service book rate. Canadian orders require $2.00 extra postage and must be paid in U.S. dollars through a U.S. banking facility.

Name_____
Address_____
City_____State_____Zip_____
I have enclosed $_____ in payment for the checked book(s).
Payment <u>must</u> accompany all orders. ❑ Please send a free catalog.
          CHECK OUT OUR WEBSITE! www.dorchesterpub.com